About the Author

Mark Hayden is the nom de guerre of Adrian Attwood. He lives in Westmorland with his wife, Anne.

He has had a varied career working for a brewery, teaching English and being the Town Clerk in Carnforth, Lancs. He is now a part-time writer and part-time assistant in Anne's craft projects.

He is also proud to be the Mad Unky to his Great Nieces & Great Nephew.

The Seventh Star

The Seventh Book of the King's Watch

MARK HAYDEN

www.pawpress.co.uk

First Published Worldwide in 2020 by Paw Press
Paperback Edition Published 2020
Reprinted with 6F Trailer, 05 October 2020.

Cover Design – Rachel Lawston
Design Copyright © 2020 Lawston Design
www.lawstondesign.com
Cover images © Shutterstock

Paw Press – Independent publishing in Westmorland, UK.
www.pawpress.co.uk

ISBN: 1-9998212-7-0
ISBN-13: 978-1-9998212-7-2

For the Awesome

Rachel Lawston

There's Only One Auntie Rah Rah

THE SEVENTH STAR

Dramatis Personae *(at end)*

After much nagging from Mr Hayden, I have put some notes here about the characters who appear in this book. I hope you find them useful.

Mr Hayden has put them right at the back of the BOOK.

I recommend that you glance at them and then refer back to them if you need to. As ever, there are full lists and a glossary of magickal terms on the Paw Press website:

www.pawpress.co.uk

I hope you enjoy the book,
Thanks,
Conrad.

1 — Elvenham Circus

I t was a beautiful day for a party.

We would have sunshine later, and more importantly, no rain. It was the last Saturday in September, and high pressure over the Atlantic had gifted us clear skies and light winds. It had also gifted us a near-frost last night and mist over the Severn Valley in the distance. All in all, it was such a perfect day that something was bound to go badly wrong. No one is ever that lucky.

'Scout! To me.' I called the manic mutt from the woods and headed back down to Elvenham. From here, I couldn't see much of the house because of the marquee on the lawns. The dew on the canvas glistened in the sunlight, and from behind it, a plume of steam showed that the poor boiler was working overtime to provide hot water for the girls. Being first up has its advantages.

Scout came to heel and looked up at me. 'Arff,' he said. I think that meant: *Why have you called me over? Have we got work to do?*

'Breakfast, chum. For both of us.'

Now that he's just a dog, and not a Bonded Familiar Spirit, I have to take a lot more responsibility for him. I don't mind most of the time, and Myfanwy loves him, too, so at least I'll be able to leave him here when we're off on a mission – or a holiday. I still wince when I remember smuggling him on to the cruise ship disguised as an assistance dog.

Second out of bed, and standing outside the back door in her dressing gown was my little sister, Sofía. '¡Hola! Conrad,' she said, somewhat sleepily. The cup of coffee in one hand was drooping dangerously as she fished for a cigarette. I took two out and lit one for her.

'How do you feel this morning?' I asked.

Last night had been fairly momentous for the Clarke family. Our sister Rachael and my friend Alain Dupont had become Entangled in the world of magick thanks to Rachael's meddling and Sofía's carelessness. Life for the Clarkes would never be quite the same again.

She pushed her long dark hair behind her ears. Her eyes were a little puffy, but otherwise she had the seam free skin that comes from being nineteen and staying out of the sun. 'I am feeling guilty,' she said. 'It was my fault and you got in trouble. I was showing off.'

'Not your fault. And I'm not in trouble. When you get to know the Boss better, you'll be able to tell the difference between railing and rollocking.'

'Eh? What are they?'

Sofía's English is so good, you forget sometimes that she's not fully bi-lingual. I cast around for a word that would make sense. 'Venting?' Sofía nodded. 'When the Boss uses Yiddish words, she's just venting. If you're in real trouble, it's 100% English.'

She tipped her head on one side. 'You know she is not my boss. Or Mina's, or Myfanwy's or Erin's or Rachael's...' She waited until I'd got the message. 'Mina says, and I think she is right, that sometimes your boss just wants to be *Hannah*.'

'Yes. You're right. She's here as a guest now.'

Sofía met the Boss for the first time yesterday, and she's wrong. The very hardest thing for the Peculier Constable to do is to be *Hannah*, because *Hannah* is a widow with enough trauma etched on her body to make looking in the mirror a major achievement.

I stubbed out my cigarette and headed in to get Scout's dogfood, and from the kitchen, I could hear the sounds of breakfast being prepared. Mina had appeared and was already poring over the list of jobs for today, fighting for space with Myfanwy, who was trying to lay the table for a Kosher spread. Vicky and Erin drifted in, and Myfanwy enlisted them to help nudge Mina out of the way. Yesterday had been Myfanwy's day; today was Mina's. Sofía and I kept our distance.

We'd had a houseful last night, and more were coming through the day as the party got nearer. First to arrive, bright and early, was my current work-partner, Saffron Hawkins. Everyone said *Hi*, but no one went to give her a hug. She's as welcome as anyone in my house, and I trust her with my life, but there's always a little bit of Saffron in reserve.

'Sorry I couldn't be here last night,' she said. 'Family obligations.'

'Talking of family, you missed a riot,' said Myfanwy with a grin.

'Not half,' added Vicky.

Mina lifted her nose in her *I-shall-rise-above-this* pose and looked at Saffron. 'Change of plan,' she said and handed over a sheet of paper.

Saffron scanned it. 'Who's taking the Boss to Synagogue, then?' she asked. 'Not that I mind missing the traffic in Cheltenham.'

Mina kept her face neutral. 'There were developments last night. Rachael – Conrad's sister – is now Entangled, and the Mowbrays are staying in the village. Hannah will be conveyed to synagogue in a stately fashion by Maggie Pierce.'

'No!' said Saffron. 'How did that happen?'

'Conrad, take her outside and tell her. And don't be long.'

'Here,' said Myfanwy, thrusting two mugs of tea at me. 'Poor girl's driven down from Oxford with no breakfast, least you can do is give her a drink.'

We backed out of the kitchen and I gave Saff her tea. She took a slurp and stared at the list of jobs. 'Help Mike set up the bar. With help from Ben.' She peered closer. 'What's the red "A" in the circle for?'

'*Artificer*. You may have noticed that Mina has gone into overdrive. She is encouraging you to use magick to ensure that the bar is running smoothly.'

'But…' she looked at me like a lost child.

'I know, Saff. I doubt your magickal gift will be of any use at all. Just humour her, OK?'

'Right. So, what the hell happened last night, and how come Rachael is Entangled?'

'And Alain. You'll meet him later.'

I told her what had happened. That story rightly belongs with my quest to bring a Druid to justice and is part of the French Leave adventure. I finished by giving her an apology in advance.

'I hate to say this, Saffron, but I'm afraid that my sister may be after you.'

She spat out her tea. 'You said she was straight!'

'She is. She wants to secure the Hawkins estate for the new company she's setting up: Occult Estate Management. She's got all the Mowbrays, including Ethan, to join her.'

'Seriously, sir, that's going to put me in a very awkward position.'

'I know it would, which is why I don't want you involved. If you could get Lady Hawkins to call me after the weekend, I'll handle it.'

'Thanks. Talking of the Mowbrays, I heard some very interesting gossip last night. You know it was my aunt's big birthday?'

I nodded.

'Cousin Bertie from Malvern came, and she's had guests.'

There was a truly malicious glint in Saffron's eye. Her cousin from the Malvern Hills is something of a shadowy figure. I've met her, but she gave nothing away.

'Go on,' I said. 'Do tell.'

'Bertie had the Earthmaster and Kenver Mowbray staying over while they did some work on the Ley lines. I was supposed to stay with them.'

I could see why my friend, Chris Kelly, would base himself with Bertie Hawkins: she may be shady, but she's part of the Salomon's House magickal aristocracy. She probably has a major junction of Ley lines on her land, and the youngest of the Mowbray siblings is working with the Earthmaster to sharpen his talents. He has the makings of a powerful Geomancer, like his late father, but we didn't see him at his best in Cornwall.

'Why did they want you there?' I asked.

'Mum thinks it's about time there was a marriage alliance between the Hawkins and the Mowbrays.'

'You!'

'Shh. This goes no further, right?'

'Erm, no.'

'There's no chance, of course. Kenver's only a baby, really, but I had to show willing and asked Bertie a few questions. It's not just Kenver Mowbray

11

and Chris Kelly who stayed. There was also Chris Kelly's kids. And a nanny, but no Mrs Kelly. And then I found out that you and Mina had been to the Kellys' house.'

We *had* been to Earth House. For dinner, and later Tamsin Kelly had helped Mina with the business of our engagement. 'Yes,' I said. 'So…?'

'What's she like? The bodysnatcher! And why isn't she with her children?'

I gave Saffron the deadeye stare I reserve for junior officers who've overstepped the mark. She has a huge mane of white blonde hair and she started to go red at the roots. She had the sense to keep her mouth shut. I do like her, but she can be more impulsive than Scout. Tamsin Kelly is … well, shall we just say that she wasn't born Tamsin.

'If you want to know what Tammy's like, ask Mina. She's her friend,' I said. 'The Kellys are spending some time apart while Tammy takes advanced studies. If tonight's party is a success, I'm sure they'll come to the next one.'

'Sorry. I didn't know.'

'Come on, it's time for breakfast.'

Mina had been exiled to the end of the table furthest from the Aga. She gave her ToDo lists one last glance and put them safely out of the way just as Hannah appeared.

The Boss is notoriously a city girl, and has been overheard saying that Hampstead Heath is way too rural for her. Now that she'd been forced deep into the countryside, and would be attending a strange Synagogue, she'd tried to blend in by donning a long sleeved, midi-length floral dress. With black boots. Well, it was definitely modest. She'd also added a Glamour – nothing extreme, just the illusion of shoulder length brown hair instead of her headscarf or her enormous explosive red wig (from which the gods preserve us).

'What do you think?' she said, pointing to the hair. 'It's not as if anyone's going to touch it.'

'It really suits you,' said Mina. 'Have a go with a fringe before you go out.'

Breakfast was a slightly more civilised affair than normal at Elvenham. Having the Boss there will do that. At the end, Mina handed out lists, starting with Erin.

'Now that Rachael and Alain are coming, we will have to re-do the place settings. Can you start with that?'

Hannah looked up. 'You wrote the invitations, didn't you, Erin?'

Erin is an Enscriber, part artist, part calligrapher and most definitely a Mage. 'Yes.' She looked worried.

Hannah smiled. 'And as I said last night, everyone praised your work on the Wessex documents. I'm not being picked up for an hour, and I'd really like to see your studio. If you can spare the time.'

Erin was definitely worried now. Vicky and Saffron both looked at me with their eyebrows raised. What on earth is the Boss up to?

'Of course. My pleasure,' said Erin. 'You know it's in the stables, right? For now anyway. If that horse doesn't move out soon, I'll have to.'

'Conrad showed me Evenstar yesterday. I can understand your point.'

Erin led the Boss out of the back door, and Vicky spoke first. 'She's up to summat. I have no idea what, but she's definitely up to something.'

Mina tapped her lists against the table. 'I don't care what the Constable is up to. Today is all about the party.'

'Yes, Rani,' said Vicky.

That's Mina's nickname: *Rani*. It means *Princess*. A lot of people think it's insulting and that it's used against her because she has ideas above her station. The truth is a lot more nuanced than that.

Mina is from a long line of the Indian version of the aristocracy. Her family are Anavil Brahmins, and while Mina has rejected most of what they stand for, she still likes being one. Most people can't understand that when she plays the lady of the manor, she is being both totally ironic and deadly serious at the same time. I am a long way from truly understanding Hindu culture, but I get that bit.

'Just so we know where everyone will be, here are the starting tasks...'

This wasn't just a party, this was going to be a charity Bollywood extravaganza. Tonight, the enormous marquee will be filled with 120 people, mostly from the village and all dressed in Indian clothing. You can supply your own, or you can rent/buy it from a pair of social entrepreneurs who call themselves *GoSareeGo* and who import the outfits direct from women's co-operatives in poor areas of India, ensuring they get paid a fair price for their work.

Catering is by a firm from Birmingham (mostly Bengalis, much to Mina's disappointment), who will be setting up in a tent annexe at the back of the marquee. The main event (Bollywood dancing) will be led by a lovely couple from Leeds, Rahul and Priya, who are doing it at cost on condition they can film the whole thing to promote their business.

As I told Saffron, the bar is being run by Mike from the Inkwell, our village pub, and there are a couple of other bits, but I'll come to them later. My first job was clean up after breakfast, by which time the van with the furniture should have arrived. That's my second job.

If you've ever looked into hiring a marquee, especially with a wooden floor, lighting and tables, you'll know the cost runs into thousands. I'm paying for that. Why? It's a good cause. But you know me, so you know that's only part of the truth.

The party is also a sort of engagement present to Mina, as well as being a useful strategic move in village and magickal politics.

Oh, and I do like a good party. Who doesn't?

More of the gang turned up during the afternoon, driven up from London by the Royal Occulter, Li Cheng. His passengers were Vicky's BFF Desirée Haynes, and the most junior member of the King's Watch, Xavier Metcalfe. Desi and Xavi, I was expecting, but Cheng wasn't on the original guest list.

His last visit had been rather traumatic for him, and had involved him summoning both my 11xGreat Grandfather *and* a snake woman from my well. He brought his own outfit, a beautiful silk … thing.

Because of Mina, I know my kurtis from my salwars, but traditional Chinese dress is an unknown territory. Cheng is both rich and talented: his social world is way above mine, so what was he doing here? I put the same question to Saffron as we watched the *Go Saree Go* partners bring their rails of vivid fabrics into the house and through to the dining room.

'As soon as Li Cheng heard who was coming, he jumped at it,' said Saffron. She gave me the sideways look she reserves for moments of insubordination. 'You don't realise just how A List this is, in magickal terms, do you? You've got the Constable, the Dean of the Invisible College, the Keeper of the Library *and* two Mowbrays.'

'Cador has no magick.'

'But his sister does, and so do his uncle and his little brother, all of whom respect him greatly.'

I gave her a satisfied smile. 'My plan worked, then.'

That stopped her. She looked around as if expecting to find a strategy board pinned to the wall. 'What plan?'

'To put Elvenham on the map. Magickally speaking.'

I might as well have told her I was planning to invade Russia. 'What on earth for?'

'Call it the lighthouse strategy.'

She waited for me to explain. When I didn't, she threw her arms in the air. 'You're worse than my mother some days. Sir.'

And if *you're* waiting for me to explain, then sorry. If it all goes wrong, I can deny it and pretend I meant something else.

After a light lunch, the first of the guests started arriving to visit *GoSareeGo*. Mina was there to assist and the rest of us started to mingle because, for the moment, everything was in hand. This was going far too well, so naturally my sister returned at that moment, along with the Mowbrays, the Boss and Alain.

Rachael checked to see who was listening and said, 'I hear that Eseld is going to do some magick on the house, and I want to watch. The illusions and stuff are all very well, but I want to see the real thing.'

Eseld heard her name mentioned and walked over. She was being very patient with Rachael, something I'm still trying to master after a lifetime's practice. 'Sorry, Raitch,' she said, 'but unless you've got the Sight, there's not a lot to see in Warding.'

'Even so,' said Rachael.

I really did feel sorry for her. There are ways for the mundane to experience magick directly, usually with the help of the gods, and without that help, today's Work wouldn't be much of a spectator sport. She'd find out soon enough.

Eseld was doing an upgrade to the Wards on Elvenham House. Saffron was right – there were going to be a lot of big Mages here tonight. We needed security to go with it. Unfortunately, it also needed a power supply, and to do the job properly, it needed a Ley line from the well. That was a job for another day. For now, it was going to run on the magickal equivalent of batteries. Big batteries, yes, but still finite.

I left them to it and went to seek out Erin. 'What on earth was the Boss up to this morning?'

Erin looked guilty. To be exact, she looked as if she were about to be guilty. Sort of premonition-guilt. 'Ooh. Yes. Well. She hasn't worked much with Enscribers before.' Erin is a terrible liar. It's one of the things about her I like.

'Hannah hasn't had much experience at dairy farming either, but she hasn't asked to milk any cows.'

Erin shuffled her feet and looked around to see if anyone was going to help her out. Was it worth pushing it? Probably not.

'If she asked to speak to you in confidence, Erin, that's fine.'

She breathed out in a *whoosh*. 'Yeah, she did, but I have no idea what she was on about. Have you got your outfit yet?'

'You should know Mina by now. What do you think?'

'I think she's chosen it for you and you just have to try it on.'

'Correct. What's up now?'

Scout had hared off round the front of the house, barking. It was Rahul and Priya's van. Right on time. I went to give them a hand, and then paused to check my phone. It was a message from the Keeper of the Queen's Esoteric Library, Francesca Somerton.

Running Late. Sorry. Will bring our own outfits and see you around seven thirty.

At least they were on their way.

Mina and I had a few minutes to ourselves at six o'clock. She came into our room and stood there, her eyes almost rotating in their sockets. I went over and took her in my arms and stroked the top of her back for a few seconds until she started to relax. A little.

'Only you can do that, Conrad,' she murmured into my chest. 'Mmmm. Don't stop.'

'Never.'

She sighed. 'I couldn't have done what I did today without you.'

'I didn't do very much. You did everything. You and the girls.'

'You were there. You were the great big lighthouse guiding everyone and keeping ships off the rocks.' She pushed back a little and grinned. 'Guess who said that?'

'I have absolutely no idea who would come up with a thing like that.'

'It's what Sofía thinks you said to Saffron. I think it lost something in translation, and I gather that there was a lot going on that I missed.'

'You were with Hannah for a long time. How did it go?'

Mina hesitated. To get Hannah to stay here and not run back to London, I'd promised a personal fitting by Mina. I'd also promised that the secrets of the dressing room were sacrosanct. 'Is she happy?'

'Happy enough. I think you may be in for a shock. Did Rachael behave herself?'

'She did. She followed Eseld round like she used to follow the plumber, asking questions. I think Eseld was both irritated and flattered in equal measure. And we now have better Wards on the house.'

'Good.'

'Oh, I hope you don't mind, but I paid for Alain's outfit. Poor bloke looked stricken when he saw the price list. And I've put him on our tab at the bar. He won't abuse it.'

She nodded thoughtfully. 'It's the least we can do for getting him Entangled. Right, out you go. You're in charge until seven. And remember: the front doors stay firmly locked until then. Got it?'

Between six and seven, there was going to be a shutdown while the girls were in the dining room getting ready. Nothing wrong with that – it's just that it left me, Cheng, Xavi and Scout in charge; Ben was coming later with Carole and their parents. We assembled in the hall and looked each other up and down.

'Daring,' said Cheng to Xavi.

Being young and as yet unscarred physically or mentally, Xavi had opted for loose cotton trousers, no shirt and just the half-waistcoat (i.e. it didn't fasten at the front). 'Go and supervise in the marquee,' I said. 'If you stand outside, you'll get hypothermia.'

'No problem,' he said. 'What do I do, sir?'

'Help Rahul and Priya set up the sound system and video link.'

'Sir.'

Cheng smiled. 'Is there anything I can help with, Conrad?'

I pulled my lip. 'Does that offer extend to magick?'

He looked surprised. 'If there's anything I can do?'

'Follow me.'

I ducked around to the cosier parts of the house and opened a cupboard that had been designed to be 'secret' in that it blended into the panelling. Inside was a five foot tall Victorian safe. This part of the house had been built around it. Scout had never seen it in his short life, and gave it an enthusiastic sniff. When the dust made him sneeze, he backed off and barked at it

Cheng smiled again. 'What's the problem? Have you lost the key? It does look rather old.'

'There were two keys made, and I have one. There's a small chance that the other one has fallen into the wrong hands. Could you hide it in some way? Just for tonight?'

He bowed. 'Of course. I take it there's something valuable in there?'

It was my turn to smile. 'Thanks, Cheng. We're going outside.'

'We?'

'Me and Scout. C'mon, boy.'

'Arff.'

I arrived outside at the same time as our paid helpers. Elvenham is less than five minutes' walk from the centre of Clerkswell, and most would arrive on foot, given the fine evening. We were also expecting some taxis and a few cars carrying those from distant lands (or "outside the village" as we say), and we needed marshals. We'd have offered a valet service if the helpers hadn't both been sixteen and too young to drive. Or serve at the bar.

Ross Miller and Emily Ventress are young fast bowlers who starred in Clerkswell's successes this summer. Myfanwy has been trying to match-make on the basis that they clearly have so much in common, and that's one of the reasons I love having her around: her blind faith in the face of reality.

If it weren't for the fact that Ross is very shy and reserved, and that Emily is way too serious (and goes to a private school), I'm sure they'd be perfect for each other. And if you think I'm being a snob about Emily's background, I'm not. Until they start driving and going to dodgy parties, they might as well live on different planets.

'You look smart, Mr Clarke,' said Emily. 'Mum and Dad are really looking forward to tonight.'

Ross's mother is a single parent. She won't be coming. He nodded to me and asked what their duties were.

I looked at Emily. 'Do you remember Dr Somerton, who came to the match in the summer?'

'The librarian? The one who got a warning for shouting abuse at the umpire?'

Ross smirked. Emily looked quite shocked at the memory. In her world, older ladies do not hurl four letter words at the cricket pitch. That's the trouble with Mages in the mundane world: they don't think the rules apply to them. Sometimes it's funny, and sometimes the King's Watch has to intervene.

'That's the one. She won't be driving, but her car can stay and everyone else's parks on Elvenham Lane. It's wide enough between here and the church, and we're not expecting that many. If you could offer a bit of firm guidance and direction, that would be great. Otherwise, just open people's doors, help out and smile. Your job should be done by eight o'clock. Oh, and when the caterers arrive, which is any minute now, they're allowed right up to the back of the marquee.'

'Right. Got it.'

'And you've both got my mobile number in case of emergency?'

They nodded, and I left them to it. I summoned Scout and walked the long way round to the marquee, taking the chance for a cigarette on the way. There were ten tables of twelve set out ready for guests, with minimal decoration so that they could be whisked out after the meal to clear the room for dancing. At the back of the marquee was an add-on tent for the caterers and a gazebo for the audio-visual system.

I stuck my head in the marquee as the big screen lit up with a classic dance number. After a few seconds, the speakers boomed into life. Xavi gave me a thumbs up and we retreated outside.

A van emblazoned with pictures of Indian food bumped over the grass and pulled up next to the tent. Two Bengalis jumped out of the front and sprang into action. A younger, European lad climbed stiffly from the middle seat and looked around him. The adults wore polo shirts with the company's logo, while the lad had one from a Birmingham FE college. An apprentice, presumably. In seconds, the doors of the van were open and catering equipment was being carried inside.

All is Good, as they say in Germany.

I patted Xavi on the shoulder. 'We'd better go and knock on the door. It's time.'

We gathered Cheng on the way and he modestly demonstrated why he's the Royal Occulter: all trace of the cupboard had disappeared from the panelling and there was a Discouragement Ward in place. The family secrets were safe.

At precisely 18:50 I hammered on the dining room doors. To none of our surprise, we were greeted with cries of, 'Just a minute!' and 'Won't be long!'

Xavi peered out of the window. 'There's a queue forming.'

'Is Miss Parkes there?'

'Not yet.'

'Then hold your fire, lieutenant.' I folded my arms and leaned against the mahogany newel post to take the weight off my bad leg.

Cheng tipped his head on one side. 'Will you open the doors at seven even if they haven't finished? Would you dare?'

'They'll be out before seven because they know I'll open the doors.'

He nodded, and we all jumped when the dining room doors were flung open. By magick. With added *whoosh* and *boom*. That would be Erin.

Mina led the parade, with Vicky, Myfanwy, Erin, Saffron, Sofía and Desi behind her. Right at the back, Hannah slipped into Desi's wake and lined up using the much taller woman as a shield. They looked beautiful. What? You're expecting a description? Not my forte, I'm afraid. Just think of seven attractive women, with bold colours, bare midriffs and bling. *Lots* of bling. And then add the subtlest of Glamours to push it to the max.

'What do you think?' said Mina.

'Wow,' I said. It seemed the safest thing. And it was true.

Mina was the only one who couldn't use magick. In my opinion, she didn't need a Glamour, but I may be biased. For a party like this, it's considered quite normal to add a little illusion to the mix – bouncier hair, smoother skin. One of the group had taken things a stage further: Hannah had turned herself into her twin, Ruth. At that moment I was *so* glad that I'm not the Boss's Rabbi.

I bowed. Cheng and Xavi bowed. Scout barked. There was no more to be said.

'Places, girls,' said Mina, and the group broke up. Myfanwy and Erin were in charge at the marquee end; Vicky, Desi and the Boss were heading straight for the bar, and they grabbed Cheng to help start the party; Sofía and Xavi were on cloakroom duty and went to get the clothes rails.

I took Mina's hands. I lifted them and kissed them. 'That pink suits you beautifully. You look stunning, Rani. Tonight, you really are the princess.'

She smiled and shook her hair. 'It is not pink, it's *cerise*. Now open the doors.'

Everyone had made an effort. With the tickets at that price, you'd have to, and we welcomed a stream of visitors in blues, reds and greens. I think Mina was right about colour getting people in the mood.

From outside, Scout gave a peculiar whine before barking rapidly. He may not be able to smell magick *per se*, but he could definitely smell non-humans, if that noise was a guide. I could just hear Ross saying, 'What's up, boy?' and I moved to meet the next guests, Lloyd Flint and his wife, Anna. Lloyd is a Gnome, and I found him standing on the doorstep, looking up at the carving of a dragon that sits over the main doors to Elvenham.

'Who did your Wards?' said Lloyd. 'They're good, whoever they are.'

'Eseld Mowbray. She's…'

He gave me a funny look. 'I know who Eseld Mowbray is. Having her do your Wards is a bit like having James Dyson to fix your washing machine. How do I get in without setting them off?'

'Salute the dragon and shake my hand.'

He saluted by waving at the block of limestone and shouting, 'Alright, mate?' in his thick Black Country accent. A shimmer of Lux passed over him, and his left arm, right hand, chest and shoes all shimmered. His shoes? Whatever. I stood back and they came into the house.

Lloyd and Anna look about the same age, early thirties, but they're not: Lloyd is a fair bit older. The first thing I looked at properly was the end of

Lloyd's long sleeved kurta: to save both our lives, he'd hacked off his own left arm. There was now a black glove instead of the oversized tuning fork I'd last seen him wearing as a prosthetic. He proudly lifted it up and flexed the fingers. Nice.

Mina was busy telling Anna that she looked good. Lloyd chimed in, *sotto voce* 'She's positively glowin', ay she?' (*ay she* is the Black Country for "is she not?" It takes a bit of getting used to.)

'I've decided,' said Anna. 'I'm going for the eight.'

'Congratulations,' said Mina. 'Oh. That's the Heaths coming. Catch you later.'

More mundane guests arrived, then Rachael and the Mowbrays, and I almost didn't recognise Eseld. The spiked hair had disappeared under a long black wig. An expensive one, by the look of things. Rachael looked good, because, well, she does look good.

They arrived shortly after Stephen and Juliet Bloxham, who were still in the hall talking to Myfanwy. The Bloxhams live in the Big House – Clerkswell Manor, and our families have traditionally not got on well. It's not a proper feud, because it only goes back two generations which is nothing in a village like ours.

'Hello Rachael,' said Juliet. 'I like your shoes.'

It was a nothing comment, but it meant that Rachael was forced to introduce the Mowbrays. Her exact words were, 'These are my friends, Eseld and Cador, and this is my colleague, Alain.' That's all she said.

They all shook hands, and Stephen Bloxham said, 'You're Cador Mowbray, the barrister, right? From the Cornwall Mowbrays?'

Cador took it in his stride and gave it back, 'That's me. Rachael's told me all about you.'

Eseld looked alarmed, but she got off lightly and managed to dodge the group exit to the bar.

'How did those people know about us?' she said. 'Has one of the Coven said something?'

By *Coven*, she meant the women who stay on-and-off at my house. She said it as if she couldn't believe it and felt slightly aggrieved. I shook my head.

'They wouldn't, Eseld. You're used to living in your own private estate, where all the staff pledge their loyalty. This is an English village. You made the AirBnB reservation, right?' She nodded. 'So the owners know your name. As soon as the neighbours saw that Rachael was staying with you, they told Nell Heath in the shop, and she looked you up. Then they told everyone, and Stephen Bloxham will want to be seen with your brother, the multi-millionaire. Simple.'

'Tell me you're joking.'

I gave her my best French shrug, inspired by the one I'd seen Alain give to Juliet Bloxham. 'Just be thankful you've been careful with social media. Oh, your Wards worked a treat on our first magickal guest. A Gnome of Clan Flint. He was very impressed.'

'And so he should be. Did he have any magick he shouldn't have?'

'Only his shoes. Never heard of magick shoes before. Outside fairy tales.'

'*The vanity of Gnomes*,' she said, gnomically. When I looked blank, she continued, 'The younger ones don't like being the shortest males in a mixed setting. They use Glamours, and the best height Glamours start with the shoes. I'd better try and rescue my brother.'

'How will you do that?' I asked with a smile.

'Chat up the wife. That usually does the trick.'

'I thought you were supposed to be a responsible adult now. My little sister is in your class at Salomon's House.'

'Sod that. Who says you can't have a bit of fun anymore? Now that I'm only doing fancy dress on special occasions, I get to really act out.' She wiggled her fingers. 'Bye, Conrad.'

When she'd gone, Mina folded her arms and said, 'Should we expect trouble?'

'I hope so.'

She glared at me and shook her head. We both turned round when a cough came from the door.

Ross and Emily had been nipping in and out with the odd query, and Emily popped her head through the doors to say, 'Dr Somerton's here. In a very nice Bentley. Ross is directing.'

Mina and I looked at each other. 'Cora drives a Range Rover, doesn't she?' I said. 'There was definitely no Bentley there the other week.'

'I'd better go and help them over the Wards.'

I went out with a smile, and it turned into a frown when I saw who was there. Instead of Cora Hardisty, Dean of the Invisible College, we had her best friend, Selena Bannister, with Francesca Somerton on her arm. Eh? What's that all about?

I've previously described Selena as *tall and aristocratic*. She's not only tall, I now know that she really *is* aristocratic. Her father is the mundane Earl of _____, though you're not allowed to call her *Lady Selena*. Not if you want to stay on her good side.

'Doctor Bannister,' I said. 'Welcome to Elvenham. This is an unexpected pleasure, and an honour.'

Selena bowed her head, 'Dragonslayer. The honour is mine.'

To the intense puzzlement of the helpers, our guests made peace with the dragon, and I led them inside.

Selena looked round the hall. 'What a charming house. I really do think that Victorian Gothic is underrated.' She returned Mina's Namaste and said, 'Miss Desai. Pleasure to see you again. You look stunning. Truly stunning.'

21

'As do you, Doctor Bannister.' (And she did, in a Woodstock hippy-goes-to-Mumbai chic sort of way.)

'Get on with it, Selena,' said Dr Somerton. 'The sooner we get on first names, the sooner we can get to the bar. And the food.'

'I hope you will call me Mina,' said Mina with a grin.

Selena gave Mina a kiss, and did the same to me. That way she could whisper, '*I'll tell you about Cora later.*'

I went outside to check if any more guests were coming. Emily and Ross were on their phones. Separately. 'Ross, look down the lane, will you?'

He jogged to the end of the drive and peered towards the church. 'No one's coming,' he shouted.

'Could you give it another half an hour, Emily? Just in case.'

'Yeah.'

I went back inside and took Mina's arm. 'I think everyone's here. Shall we?'

She took a deep breath. 'Are you sure you won't make the speech for me?'

'It needs to come from you, love, not me. Besides, you're a princess. Public speaking is part of the gig.'

'After all that meeting and greeting, I don't feel like a princess, I feel like the little Indian jailbird who shouldn't be living in the big house. Did you see how many of the women said, "Oh, you're *engaged* to Conrad?" Clearly I'm acceptable as a concubine, but not as Mr Clarke's wife.'

'They're just jealous. Did you notice how many of their husbands said that I was a lucky man?'

She gave the little sad smile. 'You are.' Then she stood up straight and said, 'Come on, Rani. You can do it. For Anika and the girls.'

2 — *Away with the Fairies*

'. . . And that is where your money will be going,' said Mina at the end of her short speech. 'To explain exactly what it means, I would like to introduce my cousin, Anika Desai, who has very nobly stayed up until three thirty in the morning for a live link.'

I had introduced Mina and then stood to the side, willing her on, and she had delivered. She wouldn't take my word for it, of course, but Erin had been filming her and I knew she'd be satisfied with the overall performance. I also knew that Mina would be hyper-critical of her hair / her top / the fact that she hadn't refreshed her makeup. That's Mina for you.

She stepped out of the direct line of the big screen that filled most of one end of the marquee and put her hands behind her back. Only I could see that she was crossing her fingers. The screen flickered into life, and I got my first proper look at Mina's older cousin, Anika. She looked as fresh as a daisy, in a modest yet elegant blue and cream saree. She made namaste and asked if Mina could hear her.

'Loud and clear, Anika Ben.'

Anika glanced at the monitor in front of her, then looked straight into her own camera. 'Sadly, none of you can vote in the Gujarat state elections next year.' She pretended to look to the side and leaned in to whisper confidentially to the marquee. 'Don't tell my father, but I'm standing as a candidate.'

She got a laugh for that, and it allowed her to segue into why she was standing and how the proceeds from tonight would help women whose lives lacked the opportunities her audience took for granted. She didn't lay it on too thick, just enough to loosen wallets, and she mixed in a few anecdotes and pictures. And jokes.

As I said, it's a very good cause.

The waiters started circulating with the food. The young white lad I'd seen before was lurking at the back of the catering tent, on his phone. Either he was suffering a genuine personal emergency or he was totally useless; the Bengalis totally ignored him until he'd finished on his phone and then he started filling trays.

If I didn't know better, I'd say he'd used magick to turn their attention away. I shifted so that I could keep an eye on him. I'd go and check him out shortly. Before I ate anything.

Hannah was the first to congratulate Mina when we sat down. 'At least now I know what the big screen was for. Your cousin is a brave woman, Mina.'

Mina adjusted some of her jewellery. 'She is, but that is not the main reason we have the big screen. That was a bonus.' She risked a smile. 'You will discover the real reason later.'

My thigh vibrated. 'Excuse me,' I said, digging in my pocket. Who could be ringing me? The screen said *Ross*.

I stood up and moved away from the table. 'What's up?'

'Sir! You're not going to believe who's just turned up!'

Over the phone, I could hear an ominous noise: Scout was giving distress signals and trying to tell the kids that something non-human had arrived. We'd tied him on a long lead at the front. 'Untie Scout. I'm on my way,' I said, disconnecting the call. 'Vicky, with me.'

She knew the tone in my voice and dropped her naan bread without argument, joining me as I strode towards the door. Mina was close behind. Before we got there, Scout shot into the tent, tail firmly between his legs. He skidded to a halt in front of me and dropped his front legs in a perfect Downward Dog yoga pose. He whined plaintively and little shivers ran up and down his body. What on earth?

'Oh my God, would you look at this. *Totally* amazing.'

A strong Scouse accent echoed round the tent, and everyone turned to look at the new arrival.

'Well, she wins the award for best outfit,' I murmured to myself.

A tall, beautifully proportioned woman with long, cascading auburn hair stood in the entrance. Her outfit (what little of it there was) shimmered in green silk, but mostly she was dressed in diamonds. Rubies, too, but mostly diamonds.

The reaction of the room split into three unequal parts: the under fifties, the Mages and the over fifties. The under fifties looked like they were witnessing the second coming, and many stood up, reaching for their phones. The Mages also stood up, but the look on their faces was a mixture of horror and awe. Hannah had already shed her Glamour and was moving her hands ready to make magick.

The third group, the over fifties, was looking blank, because they had no idea who she was. I was half-way between them and the Mages.

To my side, Vicky and Mina both spoke at once.

'Tara Doyle,' said Mina. Nope. That meant nothing to me.

'Princess Birkdale,' said Vicky. As soon as I'd processed that, just as phones started to flash, I jumped forward to intercept our visitor.

I bowed low. 'Welcome to Elvenham. Your presence is an honour. Please, accept our hospitality.'

The visitor gave me an ironic smile and a small bow of the head. 'I am the one honoured, and would be more so to accept your hospitality, Guardian.' The Fae won't use the words *King's Watch*, so we're *Guardians* to them. She spoke at a normal volume, with just a flat edge to the tone that told me she'd blocked it from travelling into the rest of the room. I relaxed a little. We were safe for now.

'May I present my fiancée, Mina Desai,' I said, 'and this is Watch Captain Robson.'

'Namaste,' said Mina. 'Please join our table.'

Vicky was scared to shake hands, and also made namaste.

'A pleasure,' said our visitor.

She turned to face the crowd and gave a radiant smile. Phones flashed and the room buzzed. Our visitor took a step forwards and raised her voice, the Scouse accent undiminished. 'You all look brilliant, and I can't wait to get dancing. I'll see you all later, but right now I'm starvin' hungry, okay, and I wanna talk to our amazin' hostess. Thanks.'

Vicky had grabbed a spare chair and was making room at our table. Eseld was whispering something to Rachael, and Rachael's mouth was literally hanging open. Unlike me, she clearly knew exactly who Tara Doyle was, and no doubt Eseld was explaining that the new arrival was not, in fact, a beautiful young woman but was actually a two hundred year old member of the Fae nobility with the title *Princess Birkdale*. That takes a bit of getting used to.

Mina didn't need to snap her fingers at the waiters. They'd seen Doyle's arrival and were already on their way with an extra plate and fresh food. The food was brought by the apprentice, who bowed low and called her *My Lady*. A spy in the camp. No wonder her timing had been impeccable – he'd been texting her the moment when the charity appeal finished. One mystery solved.

'Hannah! Your Glamour!' hissed Selena.

Our new guest approached the table and bowed to the company. 'Dame Guardian, Keeper, Doctor Bannister. Well met. And well met to you all.'

Hannah (now restored to the image of Ruth) spoke for the table, rising marginally out of her seat. 'Well met, my lady. I had not looked to see you here this day.'

(When Mages encounter Fae nobles, one of the side effects is a tendency to speak like an extra from *A Midsummer Night's Dream*. No one is immune. The notable thing was that Hannah showed no surprise at the Princess being around, only that she was here tonight.)

The Princess sat and it was my job to go round the table with introductions. She clearly knew who everyone was already, but that's the Fae for you: when in the world of magick, they're sticklers for protocol. Absolute sticklers, which is why I'd asked her to accept our hospitality. Once accepted, she had to come and go in peace. That went for us, too.

This was the first time I'd met a Fae long enough to talk. I'll refer to her as Tara for convenience, because tonight there is only one Princess, and I'm engaged to her.

All Fae project an Aura, and no human is immune. You can ignore it or overcome it, but you can't stop yourself feeling it. When Mina met the Duke of Ashford, he projected a combination of violent menace and powerful, rugged masculinity. Those weren't her words, but I could tell from the glint in her eye that he'd made an impression.

Tara Doyle was attractive. Stunning, even, but that's not what she projected in person. In person, she projected glamour (small "g") and fun. And there was me thinking that Rachael's Entanglement was going to be the biggest talking point of the weekend.

'This calls for a drink,' I said. 'Vicky, could you give me a hand?'

'Erm, aye.'

The Fae often have two identities: a rank and name in the world of magick and a position in mundane society. I leaned in to Vicky. 'Princess Birkdale is the most senior noble in the court of the Queen of Alderley, yes, and based in Birkdale, Lancashire?'

'Aye. That's her.'

'Who's Tara Doyle, then?'

She stopped and stared at me. 'Eh?'

I waved my hand. 'Never heard of her.'

'You're jokin', aren't ya?'

I stared at her.

She shrugged her shoulders as if consigning me to an early middle age and shook her head. 'Six million Instagram followers? Winner of Strictly? Most Vogue covers of anyone under thirty?' She raised her eyebrows. 'Married to Robert Doyle? Even you must have heard of him.'

It clicked. 'Aah. You mean "Conan" Doyle.'

'That's the one.'

We found Ross and Emily outside the tent, both staring into their phones. Emily looked up, starry eyed. 'We both got selfies with her,' she said. 'I've already got seventy Shares and over two hundred Likes.'

Ross was (slightly) less star-struck. 'She said we could have selfies if we let her car stay on the drive.'

'And get a sandwich for her driver,' added Emily.

We were in the middle of the countryside. Quiet. Hidden down a lane and behind trees. None of that would stop people getting in their cars and driving here, if the Princess truly had that level of mundane celebrity.

'Great,' I said. 'Emily, you organise refreshments. Ross? Can you go and watch the drive? Call me if anyone turns up.'

'She said not to bother,' he replied. 'Something about Mr Ward looking after things.'

So, Tara had created Wards to give us some privacy. Thoughtful of her. 'Better safe than sorry,' I said. 'Extra thirty quid to both of you for another hour. And food.'

'Yeah. Great.'

As you know, I'm not a lover of football. I don't dislike it, but it doesn't do much for me. However, when you pull out the sports section of the newspaper (yes, I read newspapers), there's often a picture of Mr Robert Doyle on the front, celebrating some victory. He left Ireland as a youngster and joined the academy at Merseyside United. He's huge. A man mountain of a midfielder, and with typical Liverpool humour, his new teammates nicknamed him "Conan", an ironic double tribute to the creator of Sherlock Holmes and Conan the Barbarian. I'm surprised that Tara had chosen a footballer over a member of the royal family. Perhaps another Fae beat her to it.

Once I'd convinced Mike on the bar to put his phone down, I collected more champagne and glasses. 'What's she doing here?' I said to Vicky.

'How the heck should I know?'

'She obviously knew about the Bollywood party, hence the outfit. From the looks on their faces, none of the Mages knew she was coming.'

'No doubt we'll find out.'

No doubt. I was now very uneasy, on all sorts of levels.

Back in the marquee, almost everyone was looking at her, some openly and some sideways. Whenever she spoke, she turned her head, just enough to stop the cameras recording her lips. I felt the heat of Lux around our table, and that meant she was also running a screen of some sort.

I passed her a glass, and she proposed a toast, 'To Anika Desai.' No one could argue with that, and it reinforced the message that she hadn't come to cause trouble.

She turned to me, suddenly businesslike. 'Mina says you're having a charity auction next. How much do you expect to raise?'

We'd thought five hundred would be good. The lots weren't up to much, and it was more of a filler than anything. 'Two thousand,' I said.

'I'll give you ten thousand for all the lots. More dancing time that way.'

'That's very generous. Thank you. And thank you for Warding the property.'

She waved her hand. 'Her Highness the Queen of Alderley told me about the well. I didn't believe it was still so powerful, so a little Displacement was no problem. Any Ghoulies who turn up will find themselves standing outside a field.'

'Ghoulies?'

'It's footballer's wives' slang for people who have nothing better to do than drive miles to look at you. Unlike your guests, who forked out good money for a good cause.' She turned to Mina and gestured at her plate. 'That was gorgeous. Thank you. Please accept this. It's made of Fae silver, which is sterling grade but doesn't tarnish.'

She pulled a bracelet off her wrist, with difficulty. It was at least three inches wide, more of a sleeve than a bracelet, made of fretwork silver and studded with diamonds. She offered it to Mina, who looked wildly round the table. It was Selena who responded, with a tiny gesture of her hands: *take it.*

Mina bowed and slipped it over her own, much thinner wrist. It had clearly been made specially.

Tara looked around the table. 'Business later, eh? Pleasure first.' She glanced at the room. 'Not much space, is there?'

'The auction was a cover while we moved the tables outside,' I said.

'Oh, right. Well, get up there and tell them I'll do photos with a fifty pound voluntary donation instead.' She grinned, and I got just a hint that her teeth were longer and sharper than showed up in the photographs. 'I'll do Mages and family for free. Can't say fairer than that, eh?'

I lasted until the third number before limping off the dance floor. Everyone in the marquee knows how badly injured my leg is, and of those who'd started, none of them wanted to quit before the Wounded Host. When I turned round and sat down, nearly half the men had joined me. Bollywood dancing is not a couples' pastime. I use the word *Bollywood* loosely, of course.

Rahul and Priya introduced us to a few different traditions in loosening up exercises, and when they'd sorted the wheat from the chaff, they started working on a big number. Mina had given me a strict instruction: 'No talking to Mages until after the party. Focus on the real guests.'

The two hundred pounds that Selena had dropped into the bucket for a picture of her and Francesca with Tara Doyle looked real enough to me, but who am I to argue?

I went for a comfort break, and then started to work the edge of the marquee, which was now lined with chairs. As the topics of conversation were usually my parents, my engagement, the weather or the cricket team, I'll spare you the details.

I kept one eye on the dancefloor, of course, and had to smile as guests manoeuvred to get closer to or further away from Tara Doyle. Almost everyone was in the first category, leaving only the Boss and Lloyd Flint to avoid her. Hannah's reluctance I could have bet on, but seeing Lloyd act out the historical animosity between Gnomes and the Fae was quite amusing, especially as it was mutual: Tara went to as much trouble to avoid him as he did her.

It was Anna I felt sorry for at first, until she shoved her finger in Lloyd's face and told him that she didn't give a flying fuck what he thought. At least, that's what I think she said. Shortly after, she elbowed the secretary of the WI to one side and had her moment in the spotlight. When that was done, she spun off and plonked herself next to me.

'They should put them dances on the National Health,' she said, blowing heavily. 'They're magic for your pelvic floor.'

'I'll take your word for it. How's it going?'

'Good. Looks like this one's a go-er.'

Anna has three daughters already, and she is Lloyd's first wife. Gnomes are cursed when it comes to children. Literally cursed: all their female children are human, and it's only when they get to the eighth that a Gnome is born. Somehow, this curse spreads across different partners, and Anna could have stopped having children knowing that Lloyd would finish the job with someone else. It takes a special woman to marry a Gnome, though I am told it's worth it in other ways.

'I had two who passed,' she added, 'so that makes this one number six.'

Poor woman. She was referring to the fact the children she'd lost through miscarriage counted on the tally as much as they counted to her as children. No, that's one area of magick that I have no clue about. I blame the gods.

Lloyd joined us and invited me to shake his left hand. It was bloody strong, and I congratulated him on his work with the prosthetic.

He looked at the dance floor. 'You're gonna be busy, Conrad. We'll have another drink then head off. I'll try and catch up soon. Thanks for a lovely evening. I mean that.'

'And so do I,' said Anna. 'We won't interrupt Mina, so thank her, too.' She gave me a kiss and they left the marquee.

Shortly after, Hannah found out what the big screen was *really* for. Rahul switched on the top-mounted camera and got the crowd to turn round. That way, they could see themselves projected live on the screen. Several more left the dancing at that point.

At eleven o'clock, Rahul and Priya dragged the survivors, including me, back to the floor for one last blowout. I took my place next to Mina and did my best. After that, I shut the bar and asked Sofía and Xavi to bring the rest of the coats out. Ten minutes later, Mina made an announcement.

'Let's all go to the kitchen after we've got changed. I don't know about you, but I am very hungry. All of this can wait until tomorrow.'

'Not the kitchen,' said Tara. 'Or anywhere in the house.' She turned to Eseld. 'The way you've worked them Wards, you'd almost think you knew I was coming.'

Eseld kept her voice neutral. 'I knew a Fae noble would come along at some point. You'll note that I didn't try to hide them. No surprises on either side.'

Hannah looked around, and the only guests left were all Mages or Entangled. She shook her head, shed her Glamour and peeled off the cheap wig that she'd used as the foundation of the magick. Underneath was her favourite headscarf. 'It's good to get some air,' she said. 'I know why Princess Birkdale is here,' she said. 'I was going to have this conversation tomorrow, but now's as good a time. Could I trouble Doctor Bannister to join us, as well as Conrad and Mina. And you'd better come, too, Vicky.'

29

'Then we'll be going,' said Eseld. She made a big point of thanking Mina for the party and gave the barest of nods to Tara. Rachael had the sense to follow suit.

'Are you going to the swing?' said Myfanwy. I nodded. 'Then I'll bring tea out.'

'And I'll help,' said Mina. 'See you shortly.'

Tara looked at Eseld's back as she turned the corner of the drive. 'And thanks to Ms Mowbray's Wards, I'm gonna have to find a bush to pee behind. Unless…?'

'There's one by the stables,' I added. 'Erin will show you the way.'

The group broke up and we headed for the swing seat and picnic table next to the well. I stacked some logs into the fire pit and Vicky lit them for me. I really must practise my Pyromancy; it comes in very handy sometimes.

Hannah took the comfiest seat and groaned when she sat back. There was a look of pleasure on her face mixed with physical exhaustion. 'You did a good thing tonight, Conrad. You and Mina and all the others. Tomorrow, I will ache, but tonight I will give thanks.'

'I couldn't agree more,' said Selena.

Vicky looked at me and raised her eyebrows. I nodded in return. I didn't need telepathy to know that we were thinking exactly the same thing: *This is all lovely, but we're not having a midnight meeting to critique each others' dancing.*

As soon as Myfanwy had retreated, Hannah sat up and addressed Tara. 'Princess, I'm surprised that you decided to raise this issue in person. Your Queen was quite happy for me to brief the Dragonslayer.'

Me? I should have known that this would end with me getting a job. If so, then why was Vicky here and not Saffron?

Tara grinned, and again I got a flash of those extra, sharper teeth. In the firelight, they looked even more menacing. She was the only one of us who hadn't put an outdoor coat over our party clothes. The diamonds in her necklace and bracelets glinted and sparkled way more than they should. More magick.

'I was passing,' she said, 'so I thought I'd drop in.'

It was a challenge. Hannah said nothing, but Mina picked it up. We hadn't had a chance to talk properly tonight, and I couldn't work out whether Mina was grateful for the extra cash for Anika's charity and the publicity or whether she was annoyed at having her thunder stolen.

'You live in Liverpool, yet you were passing a village in Gloucestershire and happened to have something to wear?'

'Birkdale is not Liverpool,' said Tara. She paused long enough for us to get the message. 'Robert is in Southampton for tomorrow's game, and I always go to watch him play. When I found out about the party, it was too good a chance to miss.'

Mina nodded and held up her arm. The sheath bracelet was a beautiful thing, the fretwork so delicate you wondered how it didn't get crushed. 'I will treasure this forever, and the girls in India you have helped will offer prayers of thanks. Ganesh knows that the prayers are for you. Thank you.'

It was a clear enough statement. When dealing with the Fae, clarity is a commodity in short supply.

Tara inclined her head in acknowledgement, every inch the Fae aristocrat. 'Thank you, Rani,' she said. 'I can call you that, can't I?' She added a twinkle to her eyes, once again just one of the girls.

'Cut the crap and get on with it,' said Hannah.

Both Mina and Tara pretended to ignore her, and Mina said, 'You have a problem, Tara?'

Tara put down her mug of tea. 'I do. One of my people, a noble, was assassinated last weekend.'

'Ooh,' said Vicky. She and I looked at each other. This was big news on its own. For it to be raised here was unprecedented.

Tara continued, 'I only have – had – two Counts who owe fealty. One of them was the Count of Canal Street.'

'As in the gay village in Manchester?' said Mina.

'Precisely,' said Tara. 'Entertainment and property. He was big in both. He left one venue at midnight to go to another and never arrived.' She looked around the group. 'When one of the People is bound, we know when they die. He is gone, and his passing was painful. Naturally, we have tried to find out who did it. To no avail.'

The last three words were delivered in the same Scouse accent as the rest of her statement. It didn't sound *wrong*, it just set up a big disconnect in my head between the language and her voice. That was my problem, not hers. I'm guessing that her actual problem was going to become my problem very soon. Oh, and *The People* is the Fae's name for themselves. It's a direct translation from their own language.

Hannah broke the silence. 'Princess Birkdale went to her Queen. This wasn't a mundane mugging. The killers must have used magick, and no one has claimed responsibility. The Queen of Alderley has her suspicions, of course, and this would once have been settled in an orgy of retaliation. The Queen does not want that, and she came to me.'

Everyone looked at me. *The buck stops here*. Well, my job title is Watch Captain at Large. I looked at Tara. 'You're not entirely happy, are you?'

'I wasn't. That's the real reason I came here – to see you for myself. I will have my revenge.'

A shiver passed down my spine, like an advance payment from winter. The fire flickered, and both the Fae Princess and the Constable seemed to glow. Ever so slightly.

31

'The King's Watch does not offer revenge,' said Hannah. 'Only justice. Take it or leave it.'

Tara lowered her head. 'As my Queen wishes.'

'Good. Conrad will be in touch next week, if you're not following Merseyside United to Spain or somewhere.'

Tara stood up. 'Thank you, Dame Guardian. We're playing at home on Tuesday.' She looked at me. 'There is no debt in justice, Dragonslayer. Remember that.' She went round the group, 'Doctor Bannister, Guardian Robson, go well. Rani, thank you again for your hospitality, and for a great night.'

I offered to escort her back to her car, and she accepted. We walked in silence for a while, and then she said, 'The People have a reputation for being devious and planning for the long term. If I didn't know that it was biologically impossible, I'd swear that your boss has some of our blood in her.'

'The Children of Israel know a thing or two about the long term.'

'I suppose they do.'

We crunched on to the gravel and came to the front of the house. I don't think Elvenham has ever had *two* Bentleys parked outside it. Selena Bannister's was an older, more sedate Mulsanne. Tara Doyle had of course opted for the full Bentayga. A huge man, a Fae Knight in her service, got out, and he was all shadows and muscles. He held the back door open for her and stood guard.

She offered me a hand to shake. 'Until we meet again, Dragonslayer.'

'Go well, Princess.'

When the whisper-quiet engine started, I heard a patter across the gravel, like rain. Scout. 'Where've you been hiding, boy? Feel better now she's gone?'

'Arff.'

'I couldn't agree more. Let's see what long game the Boss is playing, and why on earth Selena is here and not Cora.'

Yes, I do talk to my dog. When he was a Bonded Familiar, he used to understand a lot of what I said. I reckon he still does.

I met Mina at the back of the marquee. She'd nipped inside to grab a bottle of brandy and some glasses. 'I remember Vicky telling me that the Fae metabolise alcohol almost instantly when they want to. I didn't want Tara Doyle metabolising your father's best brandy.'

'How are you feeling, love?'

'Exhausted. Like one of those runners who crosses the finishing line and can't stand up on the podium.'

'Worth it?'

She nodded. 'Absolutely.'

There was more to that than simple pride. It had validated something inside her, or answered a question, and I'm not sure what it was.

The group round the fire toasted Mina's health, then Hannah said, 'Your turn, Selena.'

'I won't be long,' she said, and looked at me. 'I have a personal message from Cora. She wants to thank you for everything you've done to help her election campaign, Conrad, and hopes that you and Mina will accept her hospitality in the future.'

Cora Hardisty is standing for Warden of Salomon's House, the leading Mage in England and Wales, and had said she'd appoint me as her Security Attaché if she were elected.

Selena looked down. 'Cora is pulling out of the election on Monday. For personal reasons. Someone has spiked her campaign.'

'Spiked?' said Mina. 'How?'

'Cora is my dearest friend in magick. She was my first doctoral student when I was the rising star at Salomon's House, and she's still the best I've ever had. Whatever has happened is still too painful for her to talk about outside her family.'

'It's good of you to deliver the message personally,' I said, 'but you didn't need to come down here just to do that. A phone call would have been enough.'

Hannah interrupted. 'There's much more to it, Conrad. I asked Selena to come.'

'Not that I didn't jump at the chance,' added Selena graciously. 'I've had a marvellous time, thank you.' There's no disconnect with her: the accent and the aristocratic bearing are in perfect harmony. She became more businesslike. 'There are two things you need to know, Conrad. First, that I will not tolerate Heidi Marston becoming Warden. It would be a disaster for Salomon's House.' She took a breath. 'Hannah can tell you the second thing.'

'The Occult Council are going to meet on Tuesday,' said the Boss. 'They're going to vote on a motion mandating that there are at least two ballots for Warden, one in London and one in the North.'

'Can the Occult Council do that?' said Mina. 'I thought the election was purely a matter for the Invisible College.'

'It is,' answered Selena. 'However, we have to acknowledge the natural justice of the argument, and it's in my interests. I shall be standing for election.'

'Why?'

'To split the London vote. The Manchester Alchemical Society are organising a northern hustings. Whoever does best at the hustings will stand for Warden, and if I split the London vote, I reckon they'll win.'

'ABH – Anyone But Heidi.'

'Precisely.'

'Is there anything I can do to help?' I asked. I don't know Selena at all, but if Cora trusted her, I was willing to make the offer.

She stood up. 'That's most kind of you, Conrad, and in other circumstances I would be honoured. I'm afraid that in this instance, Hannah has put her foot down. I'll leave her to explain why. I'll see you in the morning.'

And then there were four. Mina, Vicky and I turned to the Boss and stared at her. 'What?' she said with a grin. 'Put another couple of logs on the fire, Conrad, and I'll tell you.'

3 — *Home and Away*

'As you can imagine,' said Hannah, 'holding a secret ballot of Mages isn't easy.'

'Mmm,' said Vicky.

I can't say I'd given it any thought whatsoever, but I suppose when you have an electorate who can pretend to be someone else or use magick to change the votes in the ballot box, it must be a challenge.

'Who conducts the election?' I said as a starter.

'The Peculier Constable, a nominee of the Cloister Court and the Royal Enscriber do it together. Unfortunately, none of us can be in two places at once.'

I could see where this was heading, and so could Mina. Now that I was no longer officially tied to one of the candidates, I could be impartial. Mina is already an officer of the Court, and no doubt Hannah was sounding out Erin when she asked for a tour of her Scriptorium this morning.

Hannah waited for us to work this out before she dropped her bombshell. 'Unfortunately, there's a problem. The Returning Officer has to be at least my Deputy.'

'I can work with Iain Drummond,' said Mina. 'Anyone who can put up with Annelise van Kampen can't be a bad man.'

'Don't go there,' said Hannah.

'Aye, but she's right,' added Vicky in sisterly solidarity.

'Be that as it may, Iain won't wash. The Occult Council will want it to be a proper Deputy, based in the North. You, Conrad.'

Vicky shrank back. She knew what was coming next.

'No, thank you, ma'am,' I said.

I could have dressed it up and said I was flattered and that I didn't deserve it. Hannah and I know each other better than that.

She nodded slowly, and for a fraction of a second she reminded me of my mother, or Mina, when they're playing bridge and an opponent has played exactly the card they were expecting.

'That's another reason I came here tonight,' she said. 'To see just how attached you are to this place. I thought that if you were happy to go off and leave it to join the RAF, I'd be able to talk you round. Now I know better. I'm sure if Vicky analysed the bricks of Elvenham, she'd find Clarke DNA baked into them.'

There was silence for a second. Mina broke it. 'Yet you still made the offer.'

The unspoken *why* hung in the air. Hannah picked up her brandy glass. 'A year,' she said. 'One year as Deputy in residence, and then I'll ask for a new post to be created: Assistant Constable. You can do that from here.'

Mina stirred uneasily and glanced at me. She took my hand and squeezed it. The gesture wasn't lost on Hannah.

She rolled her brandy glass and sniffed it. 'You're going to be in London a hell of a lot over the winter, Mina. The hearings in the Flint Hoard will last months. At least. Most of that time, Conrad will have duties outside London whether he accepts the job or not.'

'I know that, Hannah-ji.'

Hannah nodded. 'Here's my sweetener, then. Two weeks' extra leave either side of your wedding, and I'll make the promotion to wing commander permanent.'

Wing Commander Clarke. That was a sound I could get very used to. Mina was still holding my hand, still squeezing it. 'There's one more thing,' I said. 'Flexi-time during the cricket season. No weekend duties when there's a match on.' Mina gave my hand an extra squeeze.

Hannah narrowed her eyes. 'Oy vey, Conrad, it means that much to you?'

'To both of us,' said Mina. She shook her hair away from her face and smiled, first at me, then at Hannah.

'You're asking a lot,' said Hannah. 'As it happens, I trust you not to run off and play cricket if there are lives at stake, Conrad, so that's not a problem. Even so…'

Mina looked at me for a second, then back at the Boss. 'Hannah-ji, I have made a decision. We will get married on Bank Holiday Monday, the second of May. Not a Saturday. You would be a guest of honour.'

Hannah leaned back and laughed. 'Is there a Hindi word for *Chutzpah*? Because you have it, Mina. I have to give you extra time off just so that I can go to your wedding?'

Vicky had been sitting very still. She coughed very quietly and almost whispered, 'Don't forget Myfanwy. She's still got a lot of her sentence to serve. It would be cruel to make her leave Elvenham and go to Cheshire. Conrad and Mina need to be here for her.'

The softness of Vicky's voice faded into the sound of burning logs. Deep in the woods, the resident tawny owls set up a terrible screeching competition. Hannah and Vicky jumped and looked around them.

'Does that happen often?' said Hannah, rubbing the skin under her neck.

'It's just beginning,' I said. 'It'll carry on through the autumn, until they've got their territories sorted out. They'd be doing it near here if we didn't have a fire going.'

There was something in Hannah's reaction to the owl that was more than just a shock. Whatever it was, she tried to mask it with a joke. 'You can have your time off for cricket if I get a seat at the top table for the wedding.'

Mina put on her most transparently innocent face. 'Hannah-ji, you can be mother of the bride if you wish.'

Hannah jerked back for a second, then chuckled. She leaned forward and said, 'You don't want a Jewish mother, do you? But I'm sure you could find room for a Matron of Honour.'

Mina opened her mouth and then closed it. My own 100% authentic Mother of the Groom has already made several comments about who could fill the role of chief bridesmaid, and it's a topic I'm forbidden from raising until I've chosen a Best Man. Mina put her head on one side and reflected.

'Done,' said Mina.

'Then I give you a toast. To Deputy Constable Wing Commander Clarke.'

'To Conrad,' said, Mina.

'Uncle C,' said Vicky.

We drank, and I enjoyed the moment, letting a smile drift over my face until a shiver reminded me that it was well after midnight. My bad leg was getting distinctly chilly from a cold breeze. I stood up and moved downwind of the fire to light a cigarette.

Vicky moved her chair to get closer to the fire and said, 'I get why Saffron's not here. You wouldn't want her to hear what Selena has to say about her cousin Heidi. But why am I here?'

'I was getting to that,' said Hannah. 'I didn't just talk about enchanted ballot papers when I was with Erin this morning. I was getting the latest news from the Arden Foresters.'

'You what?'

The Arden Foresters is the name of a mixed coven of Witches and Warlocks, just up the road in Warwickshire. Vicky and I were involved in the case of the Phantom Stag there, and Erin has sought refuge here in Clerkswell since she fell out with one of the factions. She still attends some of the meetings and services, though.

'Do you remember Karina Kent?' said Hannah.

Vicky snorted. 'I tend to remember people who've aimed a hunting arrow at me. It makes an impression, that. Conrad had the mad idea that she could join the Watch. Please don't tell me she has.'

'She has, and I have accepted her.'

Vicky looked from Hannah to me. I shrugged.

'Howay, ma'am, you don't expect me to tutor her, do you? Is that why I'm here?'

'No, Vicky, that wouldn't be the best use of resources, and I don't think the two of you would be a good match. For all sorts of reasons.'

'Aye, mainly because I think she's a psycho.'

'Which is why I want Conrad to tutor her. But not here. She can't have responsibility over the Foresters.'

'Another reason for me to go to Cheshire,' I said.

'Precisely. Vicky, you still have work to do with Xavi, but Saffron is nearly ready to stand on her own feet. Nearly. I want you to go to Cheshire with

Conrad until Karina has done some work with me at Merlyn's Tower. This business with Princess Birkdale needs my number one team, and you two are still that.'

It was nice to be flattered; it was less nice to realise that Hannah really thought the Birkdale case would be so difficult.

'What about France?' I said.

'As soon as you get word from Keira Faulkner, you're off. Both of you, and I'm off to bed.'

'Me too,' said Vicky.

Mina and I moved to the swing seat and I put my arm round her.

We had a lot to talk about. We'd made a lot of decisions on the spur of the moment, something we don't usually do. Mina snuggled in a little closer and we ignored them all. Ten minutes later, when she was fast asleep, I scooped her up and carried her back to the house. I think she was half-awake when I took her sandals off and pulled the quilt over her.

As quietly as I could, I slipped on more warm clothes and went back outside. 'Scout!'

He wandered up and wagged his tail. 'I know it's late, but we're going for a walk,' I said. I slipped a harness over his shoulders and clipped on the lead. A few seconds later, we were on Elven Lane and heading into the village.

It was as quiet as the grave, a point I made to Scout when we walked past the churchyard. He was happy to be out and be with me, because that's what dogs love, day or night. He didn't need a walk, but I did.

Tara Doyle, aka Princess Birkdale, was right about one thing: Hannah was definitely playing a long game. And so was Tara's Queen. The King's Watch is on the trail of a book, the *Codex Defanatus*, a book of powerful old magick that's been wreaking havoc. The Codex was released into the world by a Fae noble, and Vicky has managed to rule some of them out as suspects. I've seen her list, and I know that the Queen of Alderley Edge is still on it.

This could be a trap of the most subtle design connected to the Codex. Or the Queen of Alderley could know for a fact one of the other Fae families – Howarth, Keswick, even Grosmont – were responsible for the assassination and wanted us to do her dirty work.

And then there was the Warden election. The Boss desperately wanted *me* up there as Deputy, not Iain Drummond. Why? Iain is a trusted colleague, but he's not Hannah's ally or partner.

I would have to do what I've always done: go with my instincts, and my instincts were telling me that I could trust Hannah and Vicky completely and Erin mostly. The rest, not at all.

Mina had woken up by the time we got back and was making the effort to remove her makeup and get undressed before going back to bed.

'Do you mind me setting the date for the wedding and asking Hannah to be Maid of Honour without asking you?'

I went up to the dressing table and started massaging her shoulders. 'There's all sorts of glitter in your hair. Where did that come from?'

'I have no idea. Nor do I care.'

'What happened between you and Hannah this afternoon? That offer didn't come out of nowhere.'

'You said it, oh Great Lighthouse: the secrets of the changing room are sacrosanct.'

I stopped massaging. '*Great Lighthouse*? That nickname had better not stick.'

She chucked her last cleansing pad in the washing bag and stood up. 'I'm sure it will be forgotten in the morning. Unlike the sudden appearance of Tara Doyle. I've just had a message from two of my former cell-mates congratulating me.'

'How the hell did they know?'

'They follow Tara, and I was clearly visible in the background. Can we go to sleep now? There's a lot of clearing up to do in the morning.'

Everyone did their bit in clearing up, including a lot of folk from the village. Even Selena had rolled up the sleeves of her peasant dress. The one person who had other orders was Li Cheng: the Boss wanted all the pictures of Tara Doyle checked to make sure that she was scrubbed out of them. Tara had used magick to hide most of the Mages at the time the pictures were taken – the Fae were early masters of photographic manipulation – but Hannah wanted to make sure.

It was warmer and slightly muggy this afternoon, sure sign that it was going to be wet later in the week, an observation that interested no one except Ben, who was currently advising Gloucestershire's farmers on the best time to sow their winter wheat.

The last job of the day was to load the boxes of empty Prosecco bottles into the Inkwell's van. 'Did we really drink so many last night?' said Erin. 'No wonder my head hurt this morning.'

'Is Italian,' said Sofía. 'Italian wine always gives the worst hangovers. You should tell Mike to stock Cava. Spanish wine is much better for your health.'

I looked around to see if there were any Italians to be offended. Nope. So long as she didn't try telling Alain that French wines were the worst, we should be okay.

The van clinked and rattled off and we were done. Vicky and Francesca were laying out afternoon tea in the kitchen, after which the party was going to disperse back to London. It had been good to have so much life in the house again, and I'd be sorry to leave it behind.

Myfanwy looked at the margin between the house and the marquee, now denuded of its dancefloor; the event company would be coming to take down the tentage tomorrow. 'Look at that mess! I've seen horses create less damage than all those high heels. Why didn't people use the matting?'

Erin pointed to the door of the morning room. 'People desperate for a drink will take the shortest route. Especially after the second bottle. I told you to lay it that way.'

'Talking of horses,' said Hannah, 'what are you going to do about Evenstar? Keep her here or stable her at Middlebarrow?'

'What's Middlebarrow?' I said.

'The Deputy's house,' said Hannah. 'I thought you knew.'

'You didn't tell me there was a house!' said Mina.

'Oh yes, there' a house. With a servant.' She took a sideways look at Myfanwy. 'You'll be right at home, Conrad.'

'Oi! Who are you calling a servant,' said Myfanwy. 'Garden and Domestic Manager I am. So there.'

Vicky and Francesca came out to say that the tea was ready, and Mina grabbed Vicky's hand. 'I have just heard about this house. That changes everything. I shall go on Wednesday. I'll pick you up from Preston station or somewhere.'

'That'd be champion. Saves a trip with the sheep.'

'Talking of Middlebarrow,' said Hannah, 'I need to give you the deputy's Badge, Conrad. Amongst other things, it disables the boundary Wards. And because we've got Mina here, you can take the new oath now, while we're outside.'

'Why me?' said Mina.

'You're an officer of the Cloister Court, to witness it. Francesca, would you mind being the Salomon's House witness?'

'An honour, dear.'

Hannah had made the announcement about my appointment and promotion at the extended brunch after having a private word with Myfanwy first so that she didn't panic. The most gratifying thing about everyone's response was that no one was surprised, and the only one who showed any disappointment was Saffron: she quite fancied a posting away from Mercia with me.

Hannah passed me her phone. I have sworn a lot of oaths over the years, but reading the words off a phone was definitely a first. She had even gone to the trouble of customising it for me.

'I, Conrad Clarke, call upon the Allfather to witness my oath to be faithful and bear true allegiance to Her Majesty Queen Elizabeth II, Her Heirs and Successors, and that I will, as in duty bound, preserve the Peace of His Majesty King James and serve the Peculier Constable in the Office of Deputy.'

I got a round of applause, and Hannah took back her phone after we'd shaken hands. She passed me a velvet lined box, as used to hand out MBEs and such like. It contained a medallion, mostly bronze, with the image of Caledfwlch on the surface in silver.

'When you get to Middlebarrow,' she said, 'you'll find a spring in the gardens. Make it your first job to take the Badge to the spring and then drink the water. After that, the magick will be inside you and the Badge will be a souvenir.'

'That sounds rather alarming, ma'am.'

She grinned. 'You'll cope. Now where's this tea?'

My phone chose that moment to interrupt proceedings. It was Hannah's sister, Ruth. 'Hi, Ruth.'

'Hi Conrad. My nephew, Moshe's oldest brother's son, has just sent me a video.'

I could hear barely suppressed rage in her voice, like a steam boiler about to burst. 'Oh yes?'

'It's a video of a party, with everyone in Indian dress. My nephew was more interested in Tara Doyle doing a solo at the front, but he couldn't help noticing me in the background. Please tell me that one of your friends did this.'

Most people had gone inside. The Boss was towards the rear, and I shouted, 'Hannah!' She turned round. 'Are we friends?'

She laughed. 'On a day-by-day basis. Today, yes. What's going on?'

I put the phone back to my ear. 'A friend. Yes.'

'I heard that, as you no doubt intended, Conrad. Put her on.'

Hannah was lingering to see what was going on. I walked through the back door and passed her the phone. 'For you.'

'What...?'

I moved quickly to get out of range and dodged into the house.

The back door of Elvenham leads to a passage with the scullery, the old kitchen (now a utility room) and the old servants' staircase, as well as the new kitchen and the original green baize door to the Upstairs part of the house. Li Cheng was waiting there and intercepted me.

'You missed a video, Cheng, and it ended up with Ruth Kaplan. I wouldn't want to be you on the drive home.'

'Aah. It's good that Hannah is going with Vicky, then. Conrad, could I show you something before we eat?'

'Of course.'

He led me through the upstairs door to the passage where he'd used Occulting, now discharged, to hide the safe cupboard. 'I took the liberty of integrating an Image Capture into the Work I made. See?'

Cheng is the leading human expert on the integration of magick with technology. He created the sPad (Sorcerer's iPad), among other things. I'm reliably informed that it's the future of magick. He opened his sPad and

41

showed me a picture. 'I do not know these people, but I did see you talking to them at the party.'

It was a still image of Stephen Bloxham, running his hands over the panelling, while Juliet stood in the background, keeping a look out.

'Well bugger me,' I said. 'I didn't think they'd have the nerve. Thank you, Cheng. Could you copy that to me? I owe you one.'

He closed the sPad. 'A pleasure. They say it is good discipline to suppress your curiosity. I've always found the opposite to be true.'

'They're looking for something that doesn't exist. I'd tell you more, but it's a Clarke family secret. Even Mina doesn't know.'

'Does Rachael?'

I'd noticed Cheng dancing with Rachael last night. 'No. There are only ever two of us who know it. Me and Dad.'

He bowed, 'Then I shall respect your secret.'

We entered the kitchen, and I said, 'Rachael is very high maintenance, you know. And she works very hard.'

'She plays hard, too.'

I took my place at the kitchen table, and noticed an empty seat. 'Where's the Boss?'

Myfanwy went to get the tea pot and looked out of the window. 'Still on the phone. Who was it?'

I grinned. 'Vicky will be able to tell you all about it later.'

'Eh? You what?' said a suspicious Vicky.

'When you get in the car, just ask what Ruth wanted.'

Vicky put her head in her hands. 'Why me? What have I ever done to upset anyone?'

4 — *On the Case*

Scout jumped out of the car and looked around, sniffing and not knowing which way to turn. He took two wary steps backwards, towards me, and gave his *worried* bark. Poor lad, coming back to your birthplace must be unsettling. There were answering barks from inside the cowshed, and a brace of border collies scampered out to see who'd invaded their territory. From inside the trailer at the back of my car, a sheep bleated nervously.

We were en route to Lunar Hall in the Ribble Valley with a very special mission, one that necessitated moving fourteen sheep from one end of the country to the other. I wouldn't mention the sheep at all if I hadn't turned up with them at Ribblegate Farm. As well as being Scout's birthplace, the farm is also the home of the Kirkhams, the first members of the Merlyn's Tower Irregulars.

The two resident collies were Scout's mother and brother, and they weren't exactly pleased to see the prodigal son. I wonder if he smelt differently to them since he'd been a Familiar. Did he have the lingering odour of Lucas on him? The dogs stopped at a distance and barked loudly. Joseph Kirkham, tall man in overalls and a flat cap, followed the dogs out of the cowshed to see what the fuss was all about.

'Give over,' he said to the collies. 'Lie down!'

The mother obeyed him immediately, her son reluctantly.

Joseph walked steadily across the yard and shook my hand. 'Conrad. How's things?'

'Good. Thanks for this. I'll see you right afterwards.'

'You always do. That dog of yours has grown up. He was the runt when you took him away.' Joseph lowered his hand and let Scout smell him. I moved over to the farm dogs and did the same, after which a canine truce broke out.

'He's a good dog,' I said. 'Works well to the whistle. I'll show you when the transporter gets here.'

'It's in the blood,' said Joseph, which is pretty much the livestock farmer's answer to everything. 'Your namesake's doing well.'

The Kirkhams had used some of the money I'd given them to keep a bull calf for breeding, and on my last visit, they'd named him Nostromo. They were investing a lot of time and money in that bull, and wouldn't have an idea of its worth for at least a year. What with the English weather and Brexit, I sometimes wonder how farmers sleep at night.

A small hatchback drove into the yard and stopped by the farmhouse, away from the yard. Joseph's daughter-in-law, Kelly got out of the driver's seat and gave me a cheerful wave. The passenger got out and nodded briefly.

Kelly is in her early thirties, a mother of two and played a small but significant role in getting Mina and I together. Her passenger is ten years younger and played a crucial role in getting Mina out of jail.

Stacey looked better than the last time I'd seen her. Her prison-black hair had been dyed brown, and she'd put on a little weight. She now looked thin rather than emaciated.

'I'll put the kettle on,' shouted Kelly. 'Where's Mina?'

'Picking up Vicky from Preston station. Won't be long.'

'Good.'

'We've got the pen sorted,' said Joseph, 'and somewhere for that ram. Shame we can't run them in the field.'

'I doubt we'll be more than an hour. Too much of a risk.'

'Reckon you're right. You never know what they've got. Welsh, you say?'

'Black faced badgers.'

A deep rumble up the lane signalled the arrival of the livestock transporter. The driver did a three-point turn and killed the engine. He got out and moved round the back to put the ramp in place. This wasn't the final destination for the sheep, but they deserved a rest after their trip from Gloucestershire and before heading on to Lunar Hall.

I don't want to go into detail about the sheep here because they have nothing whatsoever to do with Tara Doyle, so can you just take my word that they'll be important one day?

Joseph moved to the end of the yard and opened the gate of a holding pen, already stocked with feed and water. The thirteen ewes bounded out of the transporter and milled happily around the yard like tourists released from a coach at the motorway services. 'Come by, Scout,' I said.

He shot off round the lorry and intercepted the sheep before they could make a break for the sweet smelling grass beyond the yard. Together, we had them in the pen before the driver had raised the ramp.

'Always was a strange dog,' said Joseph. 'He's not bad. You could win trials with him.' He paused, conscious of his habitual understatement. 'It's not natural, Conrad. No pup should be able to work sheep like that.'

'You're right, Joseph. It's not natural. As Vicky keeps saying, I'm a lucky bastard.'

I unloaded the solitary ram from my trailer and penned him as the lorry negotiated the exit, giving way to Mina's car on the way in. Mina and Vicky got out and went to the back to pick up suit hangars.

'Hello, Joseph, said Mina. 'You've met Vicky, haven't you?'

'Aye. Kelly's back with Stacey, and she's got the kettle on.'

Mina turned to me. 'I may never forgive you for this, Conrad. Why you had to meet in a farm is beyond me.'

'Where else could I leave the sheep,' I replied. 'And we're guaranteed privacy here.'

'I just hope we have time to get changed before she turns up. In fact, you can stand out here and delay her until we're ready.'

Mina turned on her heel and went into the farmhouse.

'Who on God's earth are you expecting?' said Joseph. 'The Queen?'

'She has more Instagram followers than the Queen.'

'Oh. One of them. Roll-up?'

'Thank you.'

We stood outside the farmhouse and smoked and talked about his family, sheep and sheepdogs. When Kelly opened the door and said that they were ready, we went inside. I waited while Joseph took off his boots, and with perfect timing, Tara Doyle's Bentley cruised into the farmyard. I hung back to welcome her and, yes, I did give a moment's thought to what a multi-millionaire footballer's wife and model would wear to a secret rendezvous at a farm.

The answer is ripped jeans, trainers and a leather jacket. Just so you know. And Mina and Vicky had opted for something you'd wear to a boardroom presentation (if you were a young woman). Even Joseph was impressed by his visitor. You could tell that because he took his cap off.

Once the introductions were finished, Tara led the discussion, starting with further thank-yous for the party last Saturday. She is a class act, is Princess Birkdale. She induced Stacey to speak (the poor girl was dumbstruck), she praised Kelly's refurbished farmhouse and in five minutes, everyone without a Y chromosome was hanging off her every word.

When Joseph had finished his tea, he put his cap back on and said, 'Best be off and check on that heifer.'

I nodded to Kelly, and she took Stacey's arm. 'We need to check on the bungalow. We've got a booking for the weekend. We'll be back before Tara goes.'

When the door closed behind Kelly, everyone changed slightly: sitting straighter, crossing their legs or folding their arms. Tara checked her phone and gave a Fae smile.

'I can see why you wanted to meet here,' she said, 'but why have you dragged that poor kid Stacey along, Mina?'

'To check on her. To try to help her believe that the future can be different from the past. You have no vacancies in your entourage, do you?'

'For a convicted thief? No, not in the sídhe. It would be all over the tabloids in no time. I can put her in the Gardens and give her a bedsit.'

'Gardens?'

Tara gave a fixed smile. 'The late Count of Canal Street liked to be unconventional. Liked sticking two fingers up at the People. His People. The jewel in his crown is a club called The Fairy Gardens, and that's the only time I want to hear it referred to by its full name in my presence. It's *The Gardens*. OK?'

'Ooh.'

'Ouch.'

The Fae do not like the word *Fairy*. Humans have been slit open for using it to their faces. For the Count to have done this was a monstrous, grotesque insult to every Fae in the North West. If he was like that about a nightclub, what else had he got up to?

'Is Stacey Entangled?' said Tara.

Mina shook her head. 'No. She is not stupid and she has very sharp instincts when it comes to people. The first time she saw Conrad, she immediately stood behind me. She smelt the danger on him.'

Tara nodded thoughtfully. 'Fine. I'll take a proper look when we're done here. What do you wanna know?'

'Start with background,' I said.

'The Count was young. Only sixty-four. When he was made Knight, he saw an opportunity in the Gay Village and went in as he was. No changeling. He's built up some property, a couple of restaurants and the Gardens. He also had a private members club. He really knew how to give people a good time. It was a gift. I wouldn't have become Tara without his inspiration.'

'What happened on the night he died?'

'Assassinated. He was taken out deliberately for who he was, alright?' She paused to make sure we'd understood. 'He left the Gardens at midnight to walk to the private club. He took his latest pet with him.'

'Pet?' said Mina innocently. Then she looked at me and Vicky and saw the frowns on our faces. If *Fairy* is insulting to the Fae, referring to their human associates as *pets* is equally insulting to you and me. Assuming that you're human, of course.

'I didn't say that word,' said Tara, as bold as brass. 'Sorry, it must be me accent.' She looked at me and blinked her exquisite eyelashes. That was the closest we were going to get to an acknowledgement or an apology.

'Carry on,' I said. 'We got the message.'

'Right. Well, he was with one of his entertainers. Fake Lass.'

Vicky frowned. 'A fake lass?'

Tara laughed. 'Not half. She's a drag queen. *Fae Klass*. Another of the Count's little jokes.'

'And they left together?'

'They did. Five minutes later, he was dead. I felt it all the way over in Liverpool. I was at a charity gala and I had to run out to be sick. He was a part of me, and I can still feel the hole inside.' She took a deep breath. 'As well as losing the Count, the next morning I had to deal with Twitter telling me I was an evil bitch for drinking while pregnant. Celebs are not supposed to be ill in public. Oh, and I'm not pregnant.'

'What do you know about what happened?'

'As soon as I could stand upright, I rang his Knight. Wayne. He was in bits, too. He still is. He messaged me Fae Klass's number, and you know what, she answered. She was still alive.'

'What did she say?'

'Nothing. She cut me off and disappeared. Vanished in a puff of smoke. I think she's up to her neck in this, but we can't find her. Wayne got one of his tame bizzies to look for her, but without a real name it was difficult.'

Mina spoke this time. 'You don't even know her name? His name?'

'No. The Count found her somewhere and took her in. She lived with him. She hasn't been back to his place. Disappeared off the face of the earth leaving all her possessions behind. I think she set him up and whoever killed the Count killed her later.'

I didn't think that at all. If this person had been guilty, they'd never have answered the phone. That didn't mean they were still alive, though.

I took out my notebook and jotted down a couple of facts, then asked, 'Who do you suspect?'

She threw up her arms. 'You tell me. Could be anyone.'

'With respect, my lady, we do not know your world. None of us even know the area, not even the mundane version. It would be useful to have your thoughts.'

One of those extended canine teeth emerged and stroked her lip. 'I'm under a geas not to say.'

Mina frowned. A geas is a magickal imposition or compulsion, and it's a Fae speciality. Only the Queen of Alderley could have done it, and it was humiliating for Tara to have to admit she'd been disciplined like that.

'Who's running the show now?'

'Wayne is doing his best, but he's not the sharpest pencil in the box. Head of security is about his limit. I want to know what's happened before I consider who's going to take over. I've already had two Knights kill each other over this.'

The People, to use their own name, have many junior members with ambition. A lot of their internal pecking order at the lower levels is decided with violence. Whoever took over from the Count of Canal Street would have a big leg-up.

'Thank you, my lady. Vicky? Mina? Any questions?'

'Have you located where it happened?' said Mina.

'No. Wayne went looking, but couldn't find anything. He could have taken any number of routes to the Well ... I mean, to the club.'

Vicky leaned forward. 'The Well, my lady?'

Tara gritted her teeth. I think she may be under another geas: to answer our questions. This was one she'd been trying to avoid. 'The Well of Desire. Private members club. Very private. Catered to the more extreme tastes of

47

very rich people. I've had to shut it down. All the contacts were in the Count's phone, and that's disappeared.'

You hear about these places, but you don't really believe that they exist. Not really. Or if they do, you like to think that they're not as bad as the stories tell you. I had a feeling that this one might be worse.

Vicky shook her head. She had no questions.

I sent a quick text to the driver of the livestock transport, then said, 'If you'll excuse me, I have some sheep to move.'

Tara laughed. 'I've never heard it called that before.'

'If only it were a euphemism,' said Mina with a shake of her head. 'He really does have some sheep to move. I'll call and get Kelly to bring Stacey back.'

Mina made the call while I got my boots back on. She stood on the threshold of the farmhouse and we kissed. 'I'll see you at the café in Cairndale,' I said.

'Our first date was there,' she replied. 'Take care at Lunar Hall. Love you.'

We kissed again and I whistled Scout over. 'Back to work, lad.'

5 — *The Dogged Detective*

MINA

'Doesn't this place bring back painful memories?' said Vicky. 'I mean, you were in prison just up the road.'

'Some. A lot of happy ones, too. This way – there's a shortcut to the old town.'

We had just arrived in Cairndale, a small railway/market town right on the border between Lancashire and Westmorland, with the railway being on the northern, Westmorland side. Why am I telling you this? Why do I even *know* this? Because of Conrad, of course. This is the sort of thing he thinks is important.

It was nice to travel with Vicky, and that way avoid spending another day in the tatty old Volvo to which he is so attached and which now smells of cigarette smoke *and* dog. We also got to discuss our second encounter with the amazing Tara Doyle. We didn't discuss the murder of this Count of Canal Street person because it was not nearly as interesting as getting a glimpse into the gilded world of a footballer's wife, even a non-human one. I used to think that my mother spent a lot of money in a month on trying to look good. Hah. Tara Doyle had already spent that before she left the house this morning.

At least it wasn't raining, or the middle of winter, like it had been on most of my previous trips to Cairndale. We had parked up by the railway station, and from there the road dips down a hill to a very old bridge, now pedestrianised, then up again to the Market Square. I stopped to admire the new marina just down from the bridge, on the river Cowan (again, who cares about the name of a river in a little place like this?).

'Do you think life on a yacht would be good?' I mused. Vicky gave me a strange look. 'Never mind.' I checked my phone. 'Conrad and his furry friends have arrived safely at Lunar Hall.'

'Good.'

We strolled up the slope, past some really quaint looking shops and into the Market Square, which today was quiet and empty, there being no market. I led us to a coffee shop in a stone building to the right, tucked into a corner. It was an independent business, and they had gone for a Victorian look in the decor.

'I shall get the coffee. Do you mind if we sit outside? Conrad will only move out here when he arrives anyway.'

'Fine. It's almost sunny.'

I got the coffees and joined Vicky outside.

'Do you see the dental surgery over there?'

'Aye.' She gave me the sympathetic look and said nothing else. She thought she knew what was coming. She was partly right.

'Yes, I was a patient. When I first went, my great-grandmother had more teeth than I did, and she's been dead for a long time. I spent a lot of time in there. In the company of Luke the hot dentist.'

She smiled. 'Oh aye?'

'Oh yes. When I walked in, he took one look at me and got very excited. About my bone grafts. He said he'd never seen a jaw rebuilt quite so much.'

'It was that bad, was it?'

'No. It was worse. Thankfully, the only surviving photographs are in my medical files and the police archive.' I grinned. 'The only time Luke treated me like a person and not a potential case-study was when he advised me not to eat rare steak ever again.'

She winced. 'Ouch. Did you tell him?'

It has been over year since I finished my treatments, and only now can I start to smile about it. With my lips closed, of course. 'Vicky, it is hard to stand on your dignity when you are high on dental anaesthetic and have a mouth full of blood and cotton wool. When he finally realised I was saying *I'm a Hindu* and not *I'm into you*, he was mortified.'

'I bet the other girls inside were jealous.'

'They would have been if they knew. Morrisons is a private dentist. They had to make do with an NHS dentist who fitted them in on his way to play golf. That's not the only reason I remember Luke's surgery. It's where Conrad and I did a lot of our courting, as my grandmother would say.'

'Courting? Like you went on dates to the dentist?'

'I was in there all day sometimes, and it was too expensive to have an officer with me one-to-one. Conrad used to sneak in when he could, while he was based at Fylde Racecourse. I was sitting in Luke's actual chair when he got down on one knee and promised never to lie to me.'

'You're joking. As in he actually made a Clarke-grade promise?'

'He did. I released him when we got engaged.'

'Mmm,' said Vicky. She wasn't quite sure what to say about that.

'Two doors down from the dentist is an Indian restaurant, but don't look at it. There is a woman standing in the doorway. She has been watching us since we sat down, and has taken pictures. Can you tell if she is a Mage?'

Vicky shifted in her seat to face the restaurant. Without looking directly over the road, she moved her hands apart and then glanced at the doorway. 'She's not using magick actively.'

I pushed my chair back and stood up. Vicky did the same. I put my hands on my hips and stared back at the woman. She was a little taller than me (so not very big by most standards), and wearing a short denim jacket with a big woolly scarf. A cloud of brown ringlets emerged from the scarf. From under the jacket, I could see a short purple skirt and black tights. As soon as she realised I was staring, her hand flew to her mouth and her eyes widened.

She dashed across the cobbles as fast as she could and stopped at a safe distance. 'I'm really sorry, I wasn't looking at you. Honestly.'

I kept up the poker face. 'Then what were you looking at, and why were you taking pictures?'

She pointed behind us. 'The coffee shop.'

'It's not that interesting,' said Vicky.

'Can I sit down and explain? I can prove it.'

We sat down and she pulled up a third chair. 'I run a coffee shop in Southport. *Caffè Milano*, and we're expanding. We already have a place in Garstang, and this is on my shortlist. Here's my card.'

Vicky was nearer, and she took the card. She stared at the name, and then at the woman. Closer up, she was nearer to my age than Vicky's. About twenty-eight, then. Without comment, Vicky passed me the card and got out her phone.

I scanned the card.

Caffè Milano Enterprises
Lucia Berardi
Chief Executive Officer

I flipped it over, and there was a picture of an espresso cup nestling in a mound of roasted beans. It was a good cover story. The name of the company – and her name – was Italian, but her accent was a soft English one, with just a trace of Northern in it. And then I made the same connection that Vicky had.

'Lucia White?' I said.

She went bright red. 'Yeah. You must have good memories. Most of the stories in the papers didn't mention me.'

'Aye, no, but *Celebrity Enquirer* did,' said Vicky.

She tried a smile. 'I didn't have you two down as readers.'

'We've given up now. Vicky has yet to recover from Prince Harry not marrying her, and me, well I had a lot of time on my hands when you were in the news. Now I know who you are, I can see that you could afford to buy this place. Perhaps you could improve the coffee.'

Vicky passed me her phone. It was a TripAdvisor review of the coffee shop in Southport, and it mentioned how much the new management had changed it for the better. There was even a picture. I passed Vicky's phone back.

'Sorry for doubting you.' I smiled to myself. 'You're not going to use those pictures with us in, are you Lucia?'

'Call me Lucy, please. No. Of course not. Shall I delete them?'

I looked at Vicky, and she shook her head.

'Can I make it up to you?' said Lucy. 'I'll buy you more coffee, and cakes. Whatever.'

Given that we had just intimidated her and acted like gangsters, it seemed like the least we could do.

'Won't be long,' said Lucy.

'I'll give you a hand,' I said. 'I could use the bathroom. Two Americanos for us, and Vicky will have an allegedly home-made muffin.'

After washing my hands, I checked my phone again: Conrad was on his way, sheep safely grazing in their new home. Good.

Lucy needed help. As well as our order, she had a slice of cake, two double espressos, a cappuccino and a sandwich. Oh, and a glass of water. I took the second tray and said, 'You lost your step-brother, didn't you?'

'Half-brother. Same mum. He was the full Italian, though.'

'My brother was the full Indian. I lost him, too. I'm sorry, Lucy.'

'Thanks. All we need now is someone to open the door. Is there a reason you were sitting outside?'

A young mother with a buggy backed into the door and we somehow got her in and us out with no accidents involving hot coffee and babies.

'We're outside because my fiancé smokes and will have his dog with him. He'll be here shortly.'

'So will my boyfriend and his partner. I'll leave you in peace when they get here.'

When we sat down, Lucy remained standing. 'Feel free to move away if you want,' she said. She picked up one of the espressos and gave it a good sniff. Then took a big sip and *gargled* with it. She looked around to see if anyone was watching and spat it back into the cup.

'That was gross,' said Vicky. 'I hope it was worth it.'

Lucy tilted her head to one side. 'Nice bitterness but no real depth of flavour and poor crema. That's down to the machine, I think.'

'Are you gonna do that with all of them?'

Lucy ignored her and peeled back the froth on the cappuccino like a surgeon. She grunted and poured in the second espresso before finally taking a sip and grimacing. When she took a drink of water, I thought it was over, but no. She prodded the sandwich like my mother used to prod mangoes and she smashed the cake to mush with a fork.

'I can see why your boyfriend isn't with you if this is how you behave at cafés,' I observed.

She waved vaguely towards the other end of the Market Square, beyond the giant Celtic Cross that stood in the middle. 'He's used to it. It's Scarywoman who objects.'

'Scarywho?' said Vicky.

'His partner. His work partner.' She looked at us again. Now that Vicky and I had changed back into our travelling clothes, I supposed we looked like a couple of young mothers having a coffee. Neither of us looked like we were at work. 'Do you live here?' she asked.

Vicky started to explain our situation, but I wasn't listening. A couple were walking towards us, heading for our table. I held up my hand and interrupted.

'Lucy, is your Scarywoman tall and thin and does she wear bright red Doc Martens?'

Lucy twisted round and waved at the couple. The man waved back and said something to Scarywoman. She did look scary, all lean and full of aggression.

'How did you know?' said Lucy.

'Because I recognised your boyfriend. He's bought a new coat since I last saw him.'

Vicky sat up. 'Ooh, he's not an ex you've failed to mention is he, Mina?'

A bell clanged in the back of Lucy's head when she heard my name.

'Tom is not an ex,' I said to Vicky. 'Detective Chief Inspector Morton was the one who arrested me. He was only a Sergeant at the time.'

'Mina Finch!' blurted out Lucy.

'Aye aye,' said Vicky. 'Here's Conrad as well. Will you look at them two! Like gunslingers they are.'

Conrad and Scout had appeared from over the old bridge. Conrad and Tom Morton had seen each other and stopped about twenty yards apart. They stared first at each other, then at us, then back at each other. Scout picked up on the atmosphere and switched to guard-dog mode. Scarywoman was utterly mystified, until Tom said something and pointed at Conrad.

Tom moved first, heading for our table. He had definitely spotted me now. Conrad limped along to join him. He ordered Scout to *stay*, and the two men shook hands, very formally, greeting each other by surname.

'Morton,' said Conrad.

'Clarke,' said Tom.

I stood up and made namaste.

Tom was keeping his face utterly bland. 'Mrs Finch. You are looking ... very healthy.'

'It's Ms Desai, or preferably Mina.'

'And this is DC Fraser. With an "s".'

'Elaine,' said Scarywoman. Unlike Tom, she was having great difficulty keeping a straight face.

'And I'm Vicky,' said Vicky. She hadn't picked up on the undertone of awkwardness and saw the scene as a confrontation between two alpha males. In a commendable show of loyalty to Conrad, she added, 'Captain Vicky Robson, Military Police.'

Conrad smiled. 'I saw you coming from the main road. Have you been to Cairndale Division? How's Commander Ross? He still hasn't properly forgiven me for landing a chopper on the golf course.'

Tom Morton does not get flustered easily. He's younger than Conrad, but he totally embraces the Fogey look – three piece suit in impeccable pinstripe, Crombie overcoat and highly polished shoes. He sensed a wind-up in Conrad's reference to this Ross person. 'The Commander is as always. Should I give him your regards?'

Conrad relaxed his grip on Scout and the dog went to investigate the newcomers while Conrad fished in the pocket of his old Barbour. I am definitely buying him a new one for his birthday: that coat smells of smoke *and* dog *and* horse. Ugh. He passed a plastic card to Tom, who looked at it without a word and passed it to Scarywoman.

Tom shook his head. 'I should have known. You're the one responsible for the Driscoll Case, aren't you?'

Conrad took the card back from Scarywoman. I must stop calling her that. I have no reason to be afraid. He took the card back from *Elaine*. It was his ID card as a Special Constable in the Lancashire & Westmorland Constabulary.

He pocketed the card and said, 'I think you'll find that Sexton was responsible for the Driscoll case, and yes I arrested him. Are you still with Professional Standards?'

'For my sins. As is DS Fraser. No point in asking what you're up to, I suppose?'

'This morning? Just delivering some sheep. Generally, I'm with one of the special units now. Could I trouble you for a new business card? Here's mine.'

Tom looked very suspicious, but couldn't really argue. He handed one over and glanced at Conrad's. 'Congratulations. I take it the promotion to wing commander is recent since you've written it in.'

'Two days,' replied Conrad. He looked at our table. 'Have I missed a kids' party or has the food got even worse?'

'Ohmygod sorry,' said Lucy. 'I'll clear this away.'

'I think we're ready to go,' I said. 'Vicky and I have already had too much caffeine. Conrad can get himself a takeout.'

Conrad, Tom and Elaine piled up the trays and took them inside, and I started to pick up my things. Lucy went to give me a hug and whispered in my ear, 'Now I know who you are, you lost a lot more than your brother didn't you? I'm sorry.'

'It is for the best,' I said. 'Ganesh always opens a door to the faithful, if you can see it. Tell me, do you know Tara Doyle, or have you left all that behind you?'

'Well behind me. Mostly. Why?'

I gave her one of *my* cards. 'Have a look at what Tara was up to last Saturday. I might need your advice. It was lovely to meet you, Lucy.'

'And you Mina.'

She said the same to Vicky and followed the others inside.

Vicky turned back to me. 'You've talked about your marriage to Miles, but not really how you got to be arrested. Every time I've talked to Conrad, he just shrugs and says, "It's Mina's story, not mine." Either that or he cracks a joke. He's told me about landing a chopper on the golf course, but not *why* or anything.'

'He's being protective. Of me and the memory of another woman.' I saw the look on her face. 'They barely knew each other. It was nothing like that. It was an army thing. He pays for it every time he walks on that bad leg of his or puts his life on the line.' I shook my head. 'And that really is his story. Here he comes. Next stop Middlebarrow.'

Hannah talks blithely about Middlebarrow being *in the North*. It's not really: it's in Cheshire, a distinction that will be lost on most non-English readers of this story. The house is located just east of the ancient city of Chester, and is a lot closer to the Welsh border than it is to the authentically Northern city of Manchester. And having got to Manchester, you'd still have to drive a good three hours to get to Vicky's home city of Newcastle upon Tyne.

The Volvo convoy turned off the Motorway and wound through narrow lanes hiding big houses until we came to the hamlet of Little Barrow. As you might expect, there is also a Great Barrow further along; I shall take Scout there later and check out the pub. Middlebarrow is in the middle.

Unlike many magickal properties, the house isn't Occluded at all. It even has a public footpath running next to it. Having said that, there are many Wards round the house itself. From the road, there is the usual screen of trees behind a stone wall, and then the wall is interrupted by a deep semi-circular driveway and your eye is drawn to the chocolate-box thatched cottage bearing the sign *Middlebarrow Lodge*. We'd been told to stop here first.

The turn-in was big enough for both cars to pull up, and Vicky had messaged ahead to say we were nearby. A curtain twitched in the lodge and a woman came out to meet me. She was in her mid to late forties, with shoulder length blonde hair and a thoroughly *Cheshire* combination of red checked shirt and jeans with a green gilet. She took a look at me and then her attention was diverted by a curious Scout. From inside the cottage, I heard another dog protesting that its territory was being invaded. Scout bared his fangs and took a step back.

'He and Benji can smell each other,' said the woman. 'Don't worry, the door's locked. Welcome to Middlebarrow, Deputy Constable. I'm the warden, Saskia Mason.'

'How'd you do. It's Conrad, please.'

She had an open face and an earthy voice. So far, so good.

While Mina and Vicky got out of the car, she said, 'You're the biggest news up here in years, Conrad. We thought Constable Rothman was trying to abolish the residency requirement so she could have a deputy down south.'

'It's a pleasure to be here,' I said with a smile.

She smiled back, rather grimly. 'But not such a pleasure that you're going to be here full time.'

'I'll just have to work twice as hard, then, won't I?'

I introduced the girls, and after handshakes, Saskia said, 'Piers has come up to welcome you all. He's waiting at the grove with Evie, who's doing a light lunch for everyone.'

'Evie?' said Mina.

'Evie Mason. Housekeeper and my older daughter. My younger daughter is at Salomon's House. I told her not to say anything to Sofía until after I'd met you, Conrad.' She smiled. 'The world of magick is truly a small one.'

'Indeed.'

'Just follow the road until it forks and leave your cars there because you can't get through the Wards yet. Follow the left fork and the signposts to the SSSI.'

Vicky said, 'Is that a scientific thingy?'

'Site of Special Scientific Interest. Also known as Nimue's Grove, but not in public.'

I thanked the warden and got back in the Volvo.

The drive was a short one, round a couple of bends and then a grassy parking area with room for about six cars. To the right was a high hedge with a gate. No warnings or signs saying Private Property, just a post box with the label *Middlebarrow Haven*. We parked up and sorted ourselves out.

The path to the SSSI rose over the crest of a slight hill then descended gradually to a copse surrounded by a wire fence, and this time there was a warning:

Middlebarrow SSSI.
No Public Access.
For Research Access,
Please Contact the Lodge

There was also the second welcome party, in the shape of Piers Wetherill, oldest and longest serving Watch Captain, and Evie Mason.

Officially, Piers's patch is the Marches, the counties that border Wales, but in the absence of a Deputy Constable, he's also had to cover the Palatinate, the area from Cheshire up to Lakeland. Hannah said he'd sent her roses when she told him I was taking up the job. Actual roses, not virtual ones. They had been waiting for her at home after work, delivered by a local florist.

Evie Mason was a younger, larger and less polished version of her mother, with wellingtons instead of loafers and a hoodie instead of a gilet. She was frowning at something, hard to say what because her eyes were on the horizon. She looked like she frowns a lot.

As well as being the oldest, Piers is also the shortest of the male Watch Captains. He's got a sharp, foxy face and lots of wisps of white hair. He was wearing an old red fleece, jeans and walking boots. It was only when you tried to see his deep-set eyes that you realised how alert he was. We've met before, but only briefly, and he smiled with warmth when we all shook hands. Evie's face changed at that point, and she looked genuinely pleased to meet us, especially Scout. As he got an extra scratch behind the ears, the feeling was mutual.

'Well, you're here at last,' said Piers. He flicked a metal disk in Vicky's direction, like he was tossing a coin. She caught it and nearly dropped it when the magick hit her. 'If you could leave that behind when you go back to London, I'd be grateful.'

'Nice to meet you all,' said Evie. 'If you'll excuse me, I'll go and get the food ready.'

When she'd gone, Piers opened a gate into the wood and held out his hand. 'All yours, Conrad. You'll find her in there.'

Her. The Nymph, Nimue, the closest thing that Albion has to a guardian spirit. And I had to find her without making a fool of myself. I pulled my lip and thought about the lie of the land, the slope and the behaviour of groundwater and Ley lines. Sod that.

I took out my gun, the Hammer, and contemplated the image of Caledfwlch (aka Excalibur) stamped into the butt which serves as my Badge of office. I rubbed my hand on the grass and picked up some moisture on my fingers from last night's dew. Nymphs are creatures of water, and you don't get fresher than dew. I worked the droplets down to my fingers and touched them to the Badge, closing my eyes and thinking hot thoughts. Literally, thoughts of warmth. It's my way of concentrating Lux. Magick flared in the badge and I got a whiff of spring meadows.

'Scout! Here boy.' I held my fingers down to his nose. 'Find the Nymph! Find Nimue!'

It was a high risk strategy. If he couldn't smell anything distinctive, he'd just sit there wagging his tail and wondering what the fuss was all about. And I'd look a right numpty. He gave my fingers a good sniff, and a lick.

'Arff!'

And he was off, into the wood.

'Novel,' said Piers.

'I use what I can,' I replied. 'Saves getting out my dowsing rod.' A distressed whine was followed by barking. 'This way, I think.'

'You could just have followed the path,' said Mina. 'Piers was showing you the way.'

Vicky chortled. 'Where's the fun in that? Wait till I tell Myfanwy what he did.'

Oops. Mina was right. I'd been so focused on the magickal/geological challenge, I hadn't noticed a fairly clear path through the trees. I set off with as much dignity as I could muster, which wasn't a lot. Behind me, I could hear Piers talking to Vicky.

'No wonder Hannah made you his minder.'

'You don't know the half of it,' replied Vicky with some feeling. At least her response was ambiguous. I lengthened my stride.

Scout was at the edge of a small clearing, keeping a safe doggy distance from the damp patch in the middle. Perhaps Hannah had first come here in the winter when she did a short stint as Deputy. Very short, and I don't think she spent more than one night at Middlebarrow before heading back to London.

It had been a dry summer. Mostly. The water table hasn't risen enough yet, so that damp patch was Nimue's spring.

I took out the case with the Deputy's Badge in it and clipped Scout on to the lead. I handed him to Mina, took off my coat and said, 'You'd better keep your distance. She can be unpredictable.'

I'd last met Nimue deep underground at Draxholt in Yorkshire, and you don't go looking for her if you can help it. I knelt down and touched the Badge with my left hand before placing my right hand on the sodden grass.

There was a flash of Lux across my chest as something went up one arm and down the other. I jerked both hands away and fell backwards on to the ground. Water trickled out of the spring, then burbled into a proper flow before turning into a vertical jet, like a hidden fountain. When the jet subsided, it took the familiar form of a naked woman, made wholly of water. Think of an animated ice sculpture – you can really only see her at the edges, where the light gets bent. You can definitely feel her presence, though. Behind me, I heard Scout whimper and Mina say something in Gujarati.

'Well met, Captain,' said Nimue. 'How fares the realm?'

Her voice changes all the time. Today, it was as clear as the sound of a girl singing on a frosty night. Clear and sharp.

58

I rose to one knee. 'Troubled, my lady. As ever.'

Nimue pointed to the Badge, and water dripped from her fingers as they formed and re-formed. 'I have been waiting a long time for this to be brought here. I am in need of a new priest.'

That did not sound good. Nimue is not always the full shilling, and it's hard to tell whether she knows what she's talking about sometimes. 'Priest, my lady?'

'Priest of the Dyfrdwy Altar and Lord Guardian of the North. You, I presume.'

'My lady.'

'Then give me your left arm.'

'My lady?'

'Well, we both must drink this time,' she said, as if I should know what she's talking about.

With nervous fingers and a mounting sense of unease, I unfastened the button on my left cuff and slid up my shirt. I held out my arm, and Nimue lowered herself to an approximation of kneeling, but without the knees or the lower legs. She just sort of sprouted from the ground in mid-thigh. This close, I could see that she was anatomically correct in all details.

She touched my arm, caressing it with her hands. Water immediately ran down and dripped off my elbow. She lowered her face and two points of white formed in her mouth: teeth of ice. Before I could register that properly, she plunged her face into my arm and bit me.

My arm went cold, and I barely felt the puncture. I could see it, though, and blood flowed into her watery face and then all through her. In seconds, she was turning a palest pink as my blood gave definition to her shape. I started to sway, and still she drank.

I heard a distant whining behind me and some shouting. I wasn't that bothered, because I was going very cold, and all I wanted to do was lie down. A good sleep would sort me out. That was what I needed. A good sleep.

I closed my eyes, and an icy drench hit me in the chest. I gasped, and cold water flooded into my mouth and up my nose. I opened my eyes, but all I could see was red mist. Reflexively, the shock made me try to breathe, and a sharp pain flooded my lungs, like I'd taken a breath of fire and lava was spreading through my veins. My eyes bulged and I strained to scream, and then the red mist went black.

6 — A Vision of Loveliness

We walked by a happy stream, in dappled sunlight beneath the spring boughs. She was still naked, but now with silver skin that glinted when the sun hit her. For the first time, she had feet, with shapely toes that skimmed the ground.

'It was once all like this,' said Nimue.

I knew her name as soon as I heard her voice, and I knew that we were sharing something intimate. A shared vision of some sort.

It became more real, and I could feel twigs and grass under my feet. Naked feet. I looked down. Yes, all of me was naked. Fair's fair, I suppose. I wasn't going to get a vision of a naked Nymph without having to play by the same rules, was I?

I leaned back slightly so that I could see my left leg. Aah. Oh dear.

Instead of a great puckered scar, the whole of my lower leg had gone silver. Like a statue. But I'd been walking normally. Eh? I tried to wiggle my toes, and they wiggled back.

I looked up, and Nimue was giving me an amused smile. 'I wonder where you got that from?' she said. 'No wonder your blood tasted strange. No matter. You're here now. Thank you for the gift of life.'

'I'd like to say that it was a pleasure.'

She touched my arm and ran her fingers up it, brushing back the hairs with a feathery caress. 'Such a shame you are bound to the princess.'

A horrible thought struck me. She didn't mean Princess Birkdale, did she?

'Mina,' I said.

She ran her fingers back down my arm. 'Who did you think I meant? Most priests of the Dyfrdwy Altar are single, and we celebrate by coupling. We still could, if you wish.'

'I'm sure you didn't celebrate like that with Hannah.'

She took her hand off my arm. 'Wouldn't you like to know. Come on, we haven't got long. Well, you haven't anyway.'

She walked off through the trees, and I followed. Without limping. Definitely a vision.

'Haven't got long before I wake up?' I said.

'Oh, no. Before you die,' she said over her shoulder. 'Here we are.'

The trees gave way to a lake, a perfect mirror of water, disturbed only by a few ripples where the stream joined it. It was big, as big as Grasmere at least, with trees all the way down to the waterline and no great hills beyond. We were cut off from the world here, a little slice of sylvan heaven. I walked up to the shore and out into the sun. It warmed my bones, and even the muddy bank was soothing. I stared around and my jaw dropped when I saw something pad out of the woods opposite.

I've seen plenty of deer. I've flown a helicopter over a herd of Elk in Norway and stroked the nose of a moose in Canada, but never have I seen anything like that. It was huge, much bigger than a horse and had antlers the size of coat racks.

'Drink,' said Nimue. 'It will bind you to me and me to you.'

I got down on my knees by the water and scooped it up in two hands. Just before I drank, I got that hint of flowers. It was cool and clear and fresh and ran down my throat like the finest single malt Scotch whisky, warming on the way.

I felt her hand on my shoulder. 'Go well, Conrad. I hope that they can save you. I would be sorry if our acquaintance were so brief.'

'Not half as sorry as me, my lady.'

She gave me a squeeze as the water of Dyfrdwy spread its magick through my body, relaxing and tickling at the same time. When it reached my head, I pitched forward and landed in the water.

I woke up in the ambulance, struggling to get a breath. No matter how hard I tried, I couldn't stop the ache in my chest and the struggle to get air inside me.

There were voices, screaming. I shook from side to side and tried to sit up. There were hands pressing me down. And pain. Lots more pain. Would you like some? I've got pain to spare, shooting all over me. Everywhere. Then the cold, biting deep inside me. I didn't know my liver could get cold, or that I could even feel my own liver. Why am I burning when I'm so cold? And why can't I scream?

And darkness. That's nice. I'll have some more of that.

Shiver. Shiver, shiver, shiver. And shake. Shake, roll and rattle my teeth. Shiver, shiver.

'Conrad?'

'Mnnhhh grrrrrr.'

'Conrad. I'm here. Don't try to speak.'

'Mnnh.'

Shiver, shiver. Why can't I move?

'Shh. I've got you. Don't fight it. You've been restrained.'

I couldn't stop jerking my wrists. I was cold. So bloody damned cold. And itchy. Cold and itchy. No matter how much willpower I put into it, I couldn't stop my hands, my arms, my legs all twitching and jerking, and why did my insides ache? And somewhere down there, my arse was very sore. All I could see was a dim light overhead. Dim, but bright enough to hurt my eyes. I closed them.

'Conrad! If you can hear me, give me a thumbs-up.'

I could just about manage that. I squeezed my fingers into a fist and stuck out my thumb. My whole hand was still shaking, but at least Mina knew I was still in here somewhere.

'Good. I'm going to get someone.'

I let go of the thumbs-up and carried on twitching and freezing. It didn't take long for a male south Asian voice to start speaking. I twisted my head, opened my eyes, and a youngish doctor was standing by my bed, too close for me to see more than the dangling end of his stethoscope.

'Mnnh,' I said.

'Mr Clarke, I'm going to hold your head so that I can take your temperature.' He didn't wait, he just grabbed my head in one hand and shoved a thermometer in my ear with another. He held me still for a minute, then grunted. 'Good. You're not going to die just yet, Mr Clarke. I think it's safe to give you a little sedative now.'

He let go of my head and I heard him say something to Mina in Hindi. It had something of a challenge in it, because Mina's reply was very curt. And then it went quiet again. And dark.

I hurt a lot the next time I surfaced, and I took this as a positive development. When I woke up after having my leg rebuilt, I felt on top of the world, and that's a sure sign that you're so doped up the pain would be immense otherwise, and that you're going to have to come off the meds sooner or later.

Once I'd had that comforting thought, the actual pain took over and I was tempted to ask for the hard stuff, only I couldn't speak. Not with a mouth full of wombat droppings. I risked turning my head. Ow. That hurt, but it worked, and I could see a drip going into my left arm. I turned right and tried to lift my arm. That worked, too, so the restraints had gone. I looked away from the bed, and there was Mina.

She was fast asleep, curled up in a patient's chair with her trainers on the floor and my Barbour covering her. I couldn't do that: it's those bloody chairs. Only someone as small as her could be comfortable in one.

I rolled slightly to the right to check for water on the nightstand. No such luck. There was, however, a call button, which I pressed after some fumbling. I looked round the room and realised first that it was still night-time, and then that I was in a room of four high-dependency beds, so not the ICU. Even more encouraging.

It didn't take the nurse long to appear, a hollow-eyed African woman who looked like she'd done too many night shifts. She came over and I mimed a drinking action.

'In a minute,' she said. She shook Mina's shoulder gently and whispered, 'He's awake. I'm going to check his temperature, then I'm going to get him a drink.'

She worked quickly and in silence, leaving Mina to stretch and then look into my eyes. It was when I saw her smile that I knew everything was going to be alright. As soon as the pain went away, that is. When the nurse came back with a beaker and straw, she handed it to Mina.

Mina came over and kissed my forehead. 'Ganesh has answered my prayers again. Here you are. No more than a quarter of the cup to start with.'

The water tasted beautiful. It was Chester tap water, but it had the floral tinge of Nimue in it. That was nice, but alarming. I don't want *everything* to taste of spring flowers for the rest of my life.

Mina took the cup away before I'd got properly started. 'Spoilsport,' I croaked.

'It's for your own good, Conrad. You can have some more in ten minutes.'

She put the beaker down and held my hand. Hers was cold, and I realised that I was no longer freezing. The pain didn't subside, but it came more into focus. It seemed to be muscles that were hurting. And my backside. What was that all about? I didn't make the ten minutes and fell asleep again before I got to have another drink.

'Wakey wakey, Uncle Conrad,' said a familiar Geordie voice when I emerged again.

'Go away, Vicky. You are not Mina.'

'Tough. You'll have to make do with me for now.'

'Drink?'

'Here you go.'

It was daylight and the other three patients were already awake and two were out of bed. Vicky raised the bed and gave me the beaker to take as much water as I wanted. After that, I felt a lot better. 'Has Mina gone to get some sleep?' I asked.

'Why nah. She's gone outside to scream at the Boss. She's not entirely happy with what happened yesterday.'

'Neither am I. What did happen? Medically speaking.'

She breathed out a long sigh. 'It was close, Conrad. Are you sure you're up to hearing the gruesome details?'

'I'd prefer breakfast, to be honest.'

'You'll have to wait for that. Well, in the absence of cornflakes, I can tell you that I still hold the record for being deadest the longest. Your heart didn't stop once.'

'So why did I black out and why do I feel like shit?'

'Terminal exsanguination. I had to look that up.'

'You mean I nearly bled to death.'

'Aye. And hypothermia. With almost no blood, there's nothing to pump heat round. And you spent twenty minutes submerged in freezing water.'

'Submerged?'

'Totally. Nimue flowed around you and we couldn't get close. Piers said that Nimue must have put something other than water in your lungs so you could get oxygen. He used the time to save your life.'

'How?'

'He rang 999 and pretended to be a doctor. He was dead convincing and he had the paramedic ambulance on the way before he'd finished the call. Then he said they had to put a rapid transfusion system on standby. He told them to activate the hypothermia protocol and prepare the blood as well.'

Something wasn't quite right here. 'How did he know my blood group?'

'He didn't. He told them to look up your trauma records from when they operated on your leg. They're all on the national system. The ambulance was already at the gates when Nimue let you go.'

'Then what happened?'

'Piers showed me how to keep you alive using Lux instead of oxygen while he got the ambulance up to the woods. After that it was a matter of luck and your constitution. And Mina says Ganesh had a hand. I couldn't possibly comment.'

'So why do I feel like this? And why does... never mind.'

She laughed. With relief, I hope. 'Why does your arse hurt? They had to flush your intestines with warm water to stop your internal organs shutting down from the cold. The doctor was none too gentle, I don't think. And your muscles hurt because of acidosis. Side effect. I know Mina wanted to tell you herself, but you deserve to know. There should be no lasting damage.'

I nodded to myself, focusing on the memories of water and pain. Then I held out my hand to Vicky. She reached over and took it. 'You've saved my life again, Vic.' We've done that to each other so often now that we've gone beyond thanks. I gave her hand a squeeze. 'I owe Piers big time.'

She carried on holding my hand for a second, then let go. 'Aye, well, there's a problem there. I was focused on scanning you while Nimue had you in her clutches, so I didn't really listen to what Piers said. He didn't just tell the operator about your medical history, he gave them your date of birth. And he'd brought a compression bandage in his pocket. Mina spotted both of those.'

'Wetherill knew what would happen. Surely Hannah knew that, too.'

'Which is why Mina got on to Hannah as soon as you came out of the treatment room, and why Mina's downstairs giving Hannah grief in the car park.'

'If Hannah doesn't hang up on her.'

'Hang up? She's here. Arrived overnight.'

Whoa. Hannah was here? Actually in the North? 'What prompted that?'

'It was when Mina said that she'd taken your firearms. She said that if Hannah didn't explain herself and suspend Piers, she was going to hunt him down and shoot him in both kneecaps before she went to London and did the same to Hannah.'

We both knew that wasn't an idle threat. And so did Hannah. No wonder she'd come up. 'Has Mina got the guns now?'

'No. She's left them in a safe place. Hannah said on the phone that when she performed the rite, she was only immersed for a few seconds and only lost a syringeful of blood. Clearly Piers was expecting the worst this time. He's gone to ground and isn't answering his phone.'

I took some more water and rinsed it round my mouth. This was serious. I was glad to be alive, of course, and clearly Piers hadn't wanted me dead at all costs. He still had a lot of questions to answer, though.

A new nurse appeared, much brighter eyed than her night-shift colleague. 'I'll bet you're hungry, Conrad. Let me take your readings, then I'll put you on the breakfast list before they come up from the kitchens.'

Vicky stood up and bent down to give me a kiss. 'I've saved the bad news till last. You have to do it again every year at the Vernal Equinox. The good news is that you can have help. I've already put it in me calendar.'

'I can't wait. Thanks, Vic.'

'Aye. You get some rest, Uncle C.'

The nurse finished her readings and told me that I was doing well. 'Don't quote me, but I reckon they'll kick you out in the afternoon unless you're showing signs of an infection.'

Mina appeared shortly afterwards. For obvious reasons, she doesn't clench her jaw when she's angry. Instead, she purses her lips and pushes her head forward. Under the LED lights, her nose looked a lot pointier than normal.

'Vicky says you're doing well.' She stopped a foot from the bed and closed her eyes. She breathed out slowly and forced her shoulders to relax. When she sat on the bed and put her arms round me, she was crying.

My left arm still had the drip, and a big bandage over the puncture wounds, so I hugged her as best I could with my right arm and kissed the top of her head. When the sobs had calmed down, I said, 'Is Hannah still Matron of Honour?'

'Don't. It's not funny. Not this time. If I catch up with Piers Wetherill before she does, the wedding may be postponed while I serve another jail sentence.'

'Vicky told me. We'll do a knee each, shall we?'

She gave me an extra squeeze. 'Still not funny, Conrad.'

'Where's the gun?'

'In Scout's basket, of course.'

'Of course it is.'

She drew back and grabbed a tissue to wipe her eyes. 'Hannah is consumed by guilt. She wanted the bonding to be a surprise. Her way of getting you back for all the problems you've caused her. She is genuinely mortified.'

'Good. And so she should be. All I need now is some breakfast.'

Mina didn't let Hannah come to see me until the official visiting hour at three o'clock. I don't know what the Hebrew for *mea culpa, mea maxima culpa* might be, but I'm sure she said it ten times before I convinced her that hers was a sin of omission.

'Piers has retired,' she said. 'He sent his Badge of office to Middlebarrow Lodge by courier this morning. And before you ask, I haven't been able to get in touch with him.'

'What did Mina say?'

'"Good." She also cursed him a long and painful illness. I think she's moved on.' She paused. 'What do you feel about him, Conrad?'

She was politely asking if I were plotting my own revenge. 'Don't tell Mina, but it's not over for me. He made a calculated move in letting me perform the rite, and until I know why, I won't know what's going on.'

'Tell me about it. I'll put the word out.'

'Let me sort it out. Please.'

'As you wish. You realise what this means, don't you?'

'That you've lost another experienced Watch Captain. What are you going to do?'

'I've called up that lad who came third at your assessment session. Andy. He was still dead keen for some reason. Bloody fool.' She shifted in the seat. 'I'm going to put him with Dominic Richmond.'

'Eh? The man whose pelvis and femur are in more pieces than a jigsaw?'

'Dom is a good healer. The bones are knitted. He just needs the pins out and physio. Andy can drive him round and run errands.' She saw the look on my face. 'I know you didn't get on with Dom, but he's not a bad Watch Captain. You put his nose out of joint when you turned up, and then he got in out of his depth. He's learnt his lesson. He actually suggested you should run a training weekend.'

'Flattery will get you nowhere. A fresh jug of water might sway me. There's a chilled water dispenser by the nurses' station.'

She came back with the drink and a nurse, who said, 'That's your third jug this afternoon, Conrad. I'm just going to take your temperature in case you're running a fever.'

'I thought it was just hot in here,' I said while she stuck the thermometer my ear. Then she frowned and did it again.

'I think the doctor had better see you. It's up one and a half degrees. Are you feeling alright in yourself?'

'Fine.'

'I'll be back shortly.'

Hannah grimaced and leaned towards me. 'I keep forgetting that you weren't born a Mage. You may be experiencing some Imprint stress while your body adjusts to being part Nymph.'

'Part Nymph? As in female?'

'And what's wrong with that?' She grinned. 'Has water started tasting funny?'

'Yes. Sometimes.'

'It took me a bit of getting used to at first. When you focus, you can smell fresh water systems. Another reason I don't like going into the countryside. And before you say anything, I can't smell the Thames until I get to your friend's house at Richmond. Not that I go very often.'

'Is the adjustment dangerous?'

'No. A bit uncomfortable. They might keep you in for an extra day or two.'

I nodded. 'Boss, I need you to think about something.'

'What?'

'The Count of Canal Street. We'll never solve it on our own. We need a proper detective.'

'What do you mean?'

'Either Tom Morton comes on board, or Ruth is sent up here.'

'Tom Morton! You're hallucinating already, Conrad.'

'Hear me out. Please.'

'You've got until the doctor turns up, then I'm going.'

'Did Vicky tell you what Tara Doyle said at Ribblegate Farm?'

'She did.' She looked at the machines bleeping quietly over my shoulder. 'I must admit that I haven't had much head-space to think about it.'

'There is no crime scene to investigate. No body. None of the Fae dependent on Tara did it. I can only see two options: find that witness or start running around accusing people and shaking the tree, and that's what the Queen of Alderley hired us to avoid.'

She did give it some thought. As expected, there was no hurry for the doctor to appear.

'You're right,' she finally said. 'You do need help from the police. Why Tom Morton? After what you went through, I thought he'd be the last policeman you wanted to see.'

'He's good. He can keep his mouth shut. He's got no loyalties.'

She nodded her head. 'I can see that. I also know you, Conrad, and I know about your little band of warriors.' She gave me a dark look. 'If I ever find that you've given a Merlyn's Tower Irregulars badge to one of the Watch, I'll lock you in the cellar with Nimue. Are we clear?' I nodded. 'So, under no circumstances are you to Entangle DCI Morton. And I need your word on that.'

I was starting to sweat and took another drink. 'I give you my word that I will not seek to Entangle Tom Morton or DC Fraser and do my utmost to keep them away from magick.'

'Good. Now, how do we get him? What on earth are we going to say?'

'I've been thinking about that. We use the Security Liaison guy, John Lake. And we need a proper cover story for the King's Watch.'

'Go on.'

I'd just got started when the doctor appeared, and I noticed that sweat was starting to drip off my nose.

'I'll go and get Mina,' said Hannah, and that was the last thing I remember about Thursday.

7 — *No Complaints*

VICKY

They sent me to Garstang because they think that I don't have a history with either Tom Morton or Lucia Berardi. Conrad knows differently, but he's locked in an isolation ward and complaining about the smell of flowers. He'll get over it.

We've all made mistakes. Sometimes I think that the Merlyn's Tower Irregulars should be renamed The Second Chance Club. We're all members of that group, and I got my ticket stamped over a handbag.

A handbag?

Yes, but in my defence, it wasn't just any handbag, it was a di Sanuto Exclusive.

For any blokes who might be reading this, a di Sanuto Exclusive is one of the most expensive bags in the world, and the most exclusive of Exclusives are the ones designed by Lucy's mam, Paola Berardi. You could say that I pawned my soul for one; Conrad helped me get it back.

The latest addition to Lucy's coffee empire was down one of the alleys off the High Street in Garstang, which happens to be the nearest town to Ribblegate Farm, and goodness knows what the Kirkhams did to get their membership of the Irregulars. I dread to think what sort of mischief farmers could get up to.

Caffè Milano at Garstang had scaffolding round it and it looked like Lucy was spending a lot of money on refurbishment. A big sign pinned to the scaffolding said *We are still Open!* and had several smiley face emojis on it. The interior still needed a lot of TLC, judging by the chipped tables and rickety chairs. The only new feature was a huge, bright red coffee machine that was so Italian you could almost hear it singing opera while it foamed the milk. Lucy was standing on a small plinth and polishing it until it gleamed.

'Hi,' she said, stepping down and coming to shake my hand. 'I've cleared some space in the back room. What would you like? On the house, of course.'

'You know what, I'd really love a hot chocolate if it's not too much trouble.'

She smiled. 'Whipped cream?'

'Hell aye. It is Friday afternoon.'

'Coming up. Katya! Can you open the back room?'

A smiling barista showed me through to a staff room cum office with lockers, boxes of supplies and barely enough room for a table and chairs so battered they'd been exiled from the café. I took my coat off and sat down, then got out my phone to check my cover story.

Poor Conrad went delirious yesterday evening, and I'm not sure he wasn't seeing things when he convinced the Boss to come up with this scheme. Mine is not to reason why and all that.

From today, the King's Watch has a new cover identity: say hello to MI7. Even I could have come up with something more convincing than that. As far as the mundane government is concerned, we are a new unit dedicated to rooting out biotech companies and oligarchs who threaten national security. Would you believe that? Would the Dogged Detective, Tom Morton believe that?

I'd asked Mina about him, and she'd said that he was posher than Conrad, and when I said that wasn't possible, she told me his dad had just inherited a title, and one day Tom would be Baron Throckton. 'The thing to remember about Tom Morton is this, Vicky. He comes from a rich family. He could walk away from the police any day.'

'So?'

'That makes him want to be the best policeman he possibly can be. Otherwise, why stay?'

The best policeman's girlfriend backed through the door and put a tray down. She passed me a monumental hot chocolate with a tower of chocolate-sprinkled whipped cream that had my arteries groaning in anticipation. She took an espresso for herself.

'How many of those do you drink a day?' I asked.

'I try to stop at six o'clock in the evening.' She smiled. Now that she wasn't wrapped up against the cold, I could see she had an open face with lovely round brown eyes. Her hair was tied back in a bun that kept trying to explode.

When she closed the door behind her, I saw a gorgeous purple bag with one corner of bright yellow piping. 'One of your mother's?' I said, pointing to it.

'You are well informed.'

'No. I just like bags.' Something made me blurt out, 'I had one of the 2014 Exclusives.'

Lucy clearly didn't believe me. 'Oh yes?'

I flicked back on my phone and found one of the few pictures I've saved of me and Desi out on the town. She looked at it carefully. 'Good choice.'

Her face was full of questions she was too polite to ask. Questions like *Did you have the certificate?* And *How did you afford it?*

'It wasn't a choice,' I said, looking down at the table. 'It was a gift. A gift I shouldn't have accepted.' I left a pause and she said nothing. 'I'd better start on this before the cream melts.'

When I dug in, she said, 'Did you know Mina before Conrad or vice versa?'

'Mmmm. This is delicious, Lucy. I suppose you know all about them.'

'And you know all about me. I was just being curious, that's all.'

'Which leaves me as the enigma. I've always wanted to be an enigma.' I gave her a smile, to show I didn't take it personally. 'I met Conrad first and Mina shortly after. She was still in prison then. She's a friend now.'

'She seems very strong willed.'

'Not half. We don't call her Rani for nothing.'

'So what's her connection to Tara Doyle? Tara doesn't turn up at random places for no reason. And you had some great moves, by the way.'

'Thanks. She came to see our boss. Mine and Conrad's.'

'That's what I thought.' She put her empty cup down. I don't think she drinks espressos, she just inhales them. 'Is this case going to be dangerous?'

'If it is, it won't be for Tom. I didn't know Conrad when Tom first met him, but I can tell you that he never breaks his word and that he prides himself on never having lost anyone in his command.'

She looked uncertain. 'Are you going to be involved?'

I shook my head. 'I'm back to London on the train tonight. Conrad's getting a new apprentice, or subaltern as he calls them. And Mina's due in court as an expert witness.'

There was a knock at the door and Katya said, 'Is here,' in a Polish accent. I'm guessing it was Polish. I never did find out.

Lucy excused herself and a few seconds later I was joined by the one Lucy calls *Scarywoman*, also known as Elaine Fraser.

'Now then,' she said. 'It's Victoria, isn't it?' She had a strong Lancashire accent. Or Yorkshire. I never could tell the difference.

'Vicky. Aye. Thanks for coming.'

'Like you. Orders. I go where Sheriff Morton goes.'

'Sheriff?'

'Long story. At least we're done for the week, and Rob's at home tonight, so I get a proper weekend.'

She had quite long hair for a police officer, tied back in a brutal ponytail, and she was dressed at the sporty end of *plainclothed*. She reminded me a bit of Keira Faulkner, the rogue Mage we sent into exile, and who might be about to come back to haunt us. Metaphorically speaking. She's not dead, yet. Worse luck.

'Oh?' I said in my polite voice. 'Does Rob work away?'

'Sorry. I thought you knew. I meant that he's playing at home tonight. He's a centre for Irwell Mancunia.' I gave her a blank look. 'Rugby Union. You're not a fan?'

'I prefer football, and whatever you do, don't get Conrad started on cricket. You'll never shut him up. Nor Mina.'

She smiled. 'Good to know.'

'And don't let him near the car radio. All he listens to is Classic FM.'

'Tell me about it. Tom has a thing for choral music. If only he could bloody sing, I wouldn't mind. I know Conrad smokes. Anything else I should be aware of?'

'If he puts on his RAF voice and gives you an order, don't even think about it. Just do it.'

'Oh. Right.' She went to the door and opened it. 'Come on, Tom. You can snog Lucy later.'

There was an edge to her voice that went beyond banter, as if she didn't quite approve. Tom Morton appeared with a pot of tea and a coffee for Elaine. I must say, he is without question the best dressed copper I've ever seen. That pin-striped suit must have cost him a fortune. He hung his equally rich woollen coat on a hanger and sat down.

He stirred his pot of tea and said, dead casual like, 'So how long has this farrago of nonsense existed? As far as I can tell, MI7 was created last night, despite what the Angel of Death would have me believe.'

'Who?'

'John Lake. I call him the Angel of Death because he rarely has good news.'

'Oh, that security liaison guy. I've only seen him on a video link.'

'Lucky you. Unfortunately for me, he has a big budget, which means that he can offer some of it to my section if they'll send me off on this mission. So who am I really dealing with?'

'MI7 is a multi-disciplinary agency from the police, military and technical backgrounds,' I replied.

'Bullshit,' said Elaine in a friendly voice. 'You can do better than that, Vicky. Are you really a captain in the Army?'

'Do you know the real reason they sent me? Apart from Conrad being ill? It's 'cos they reckon I'm a terrible liar.'

'What's up with Clarke? He seemed fine on Wednesday.'

'Injured in the line of duty. Sort of. He should be back by Monday. And I am a captain, but it's a technical role. I'm not a real soldier. And the Boss was a detective in London. Inspector, no less.'

'Really?' He looked very sceptical.

'Really. Conrad said you should ring Ruth Kaplan if you want a reference.'

'I'll do that. Assuming I agree to get involved, what's the nature of the job?'

'A missing person. There's more to it than that, but basically that's what it is. A missing person.'

'So, they want to put a wing commander, a captain, a DCI, and a DS on to a missing person's case full time with no deadline? Do you know how much that costs?'

I shrugged and grinned. 'It'll be a second lieutenant, not a captain. Haven't a clue about the costs. Why should I?'

'Follow the money,' said Elaine. She pointed at her partner. 'That's his motto. He loves a good spreadsheet, does DCI Morton.'

He pretended to ignore her. Their double act is very good. Almost as good as me and Conrad's.

Before he spoke again, he rubbed a spot at the top of his left arm. I wouldn't mention it except that Elaine half-raised her hand to stop him, then realised I was watching. He stopped rubbing and said, 'The amount of resources tells me that this case either involves a Very VIP or it stinks. I don't like stinky cases.'

'My boss said to tell you that MI7 upholds the law. All of it.'

'We'll think about it. We're busy on Monday, so where do we start?'

I looked at Elaine. 'Do you know a place called Sackville Park in Manchester?'

'I do indeed. It means I get a lie-in for a change. Unless he wants to meet at the crack of dawn.'

'Nah. Eleven o'clock at the Alan Turing memorial.'

'Why there?' said Tom.

'Because Conrad likes to meet outdoors. That way he can smoke. Right pain sometimes.'

'Fine.' He took out his phone. 'That's in South Lancashire Constabulary's jurisdiction. What's the case number?'

'What do you mean?'

He put his phone down. 'You say you uphold the law. In that case, there will be a missing person's report. If you can't remember the reference number, you can text it to me.'

'Erm. Fine. I'll tell the Boss.'

'Not Conrad himself?'

'Last time I saw him, he was complaining that the Countess of Chester Hospital smelled of gardenias and jasmine. See? No stinky cases. Anything else you want to know?'

'Nothing you're likely to tell me. If this is above board, then I'm a leprechaun.'

It was too tempting. I used my Sight to investigate his Imprint, on the off-chance. Was that a tiny hint of a latent Gift? Well, what do you know.

'You're not a leprechaun,' I told him as I put on my coat. 'Can't be too careful. Genetic engineering is more advanced than people realise. That's part of our remit, by the way. In MI7. Have a great weekend, and I hope Rob scores lots of tries or whatever it is he does. Thanks for coming.'

'Thanks,' said Elaine. 'Safe journey.'

I said goodbye to Lucy on the way out, and she waved, then smiled. 'You don't use TripAdvisor, do you?'

''Fraid not. Uncle Conrad won't let us use social media.'

She burst out laughing. 'Uncle Conrad? Tom will love that when I tell him.'

'Aye, well, Elaine gave me Sheriff Morton, so it's a fair exchange. Have a nice weekend.'

For Elaine's sake, I hoped the stands at Irwell Mancunia had a roof. It looked like rain again. I could never live over this side of the Pennines. Far too wet and miserable. Give me cold and miserable any day.

8 — *Safe Haven*

The second time I arrived at Middlebarrow, the reception committee was down to two: Saskia and Evie, and they met us at the car park before the gate to Middlebarrow Haven. Saskia looked troubled, and Evie just looked happy that I'd come back.

The fever hadn't broken until yesterday evening, and then they'd called a crash team because my temperature plummeted instead of slowly returning to normal. I felt like shit, yes, but also *different* in some way, the same way that I'd felt different after the Allfather had first brought me into the world of magick. I just had to figure out how.

The women of Middlebarrow stepped up and opened the passenger door for me, and Evie offered me a hand to get out. As you know, I'm never too proud to accept help, even if she did nearly fall over.

'How are you feeling?' said Saskia.

'In need of a proper meal and a good night's sleep,' I replied. 'Basically, I'm fine.'

'Let's get you inside.'

I shook my head. 'Not until I've made my peace with Scout.'

The first time he'd seen me, he'd gone ballistic and freaked out, running away. A quick phone call to Hannah (squeezed in before Shabbos) suggested that I now smelled of Nymph, and that he'd need to get used to it. I had an idea about that.

'Could you bring him and give him to Mina? I'm going down to the grove.'

They disappeared through the gap in the hedge, and I realised that it wasn't just a gap: it was a tunnel of trees and I could now see a building beyond it. So the bond had worked.

'Are you sure about this?' said Mina, who'd been trying to stop me since I walked out of the hospital after lunch.

'I'm sure. And thanks for getting new clothes. I feel much better.'

All the ones I'd been wearing on Wednesday had been cut off me in A&E or were too water-damaged. There was one thing missing, though, and to my delight, Saskia brought it out, while Evie hung back with a very agitated Scout.

'Thank you,' I said to Saskia, accepting my Barbour and harvesting a filthy look from Mina. For some reason, she doesn't like my coat. I took a deep breath through my nose. I got a faint tingle of something different, but that could just be the fresh air after the hospital. I decided to wait before trying to combine my sense of smell with my magickal Sight.

'Better get it over with,' I said to Mina. 'You stay back and walk with him.'

I started walking the 250m to the grove. When I had a good distance, I shouted, 'With me, Scout!'

My voice was clearly the same, and he started to follow me, with Mina trailing behind. He still didn't look happy, and didn't come any closer. My sense of smell told me that I was getting close to something, and that something was in the woods. The odd thing was that I'd passed a stream on the way and detected nothing. I reckon Hannah was a bit off in her diagnosis.

As soon as I entered the wood, the hairs on the back of my neck told me that I was near magick, even without the strong smell of flowers. I followed the path, water from last night's rain coating my new boots. And there, at the centre of the clearing, I realised that I wasn't smelling fresh water at all. I was smelling *Nymph*. It was the creature, not her environment that I could sense.

Proper Mages can sense Gnomes, the Fae and other non-human creatures. I can't, or I couldn't. It looked like this was part of the bargain: in return for a near-death experience, some of Nimue's magick had rubbed off on me.

There was water trickling out of the spring. I whistled Scout and rubbed the water all over my hands. He came reluctantly to the edge of the clearing, Mina hanging back to watch.

'Here, boy. Come on, Scout.'

He walked slowly towards me, constantly ready to jump back, until he could sniff my hands. I sat still. No sudden movements. Finally, he gave my hand a lick and wagged his tail. I gave him a scratch behind the ears and reached into my pocket. The dog-treats were still there, and he lapped a couple off my fingers happily.

'Shall we go?' I said to him. He looked happier when I stood up and walked away. By the time we got to the edge of the woods, he was off exploring his new territory. 'Is there a bench we can sit on before we go back?'

Mina gave me a dark look. 'I thought you might give up smoking after what you've been through.'

I patted the other pocket of my coat. 'Not yet. Maybe when I'm forty.'

'If you live that long.'

She filled me in on a few more details while we sat admiring the view over rich, rural Cheshire, starting with the headlines from Vicky's meeting with Tom Morton and Elaine Fraser. I wasn't entirely happy about his insistence on a missing person's report for "Fae Klass", but if that was his price…

'Hannah has been on to Tara Doyle,' said Mina. 'The report is filed. She also said that Karina will drive up on Sunday. Do you think you'll be well enough to start working with her?'

'I'm not planning on any combat exercises. I was thinking a few walks round the grounds and a chat. How have you got on with the Masons?'

76

'Saskia has been professional and helpful. If that sounds like I'm writing a review, that's how she comes over: she has a responsibility and a duty, but she didn't warm to me as a person, but then again we didn't get off to a good start. She asked me if I wanted one of the rooms in the house set aside for Friday prayers.'

'Ouch.'

She looked peeved. I've learnt that when one of my fellow countrymen is guilty of casual (or deliberate) racism, the best thing to do is to acknowledge what she felt and then keep quiet.

She went from peeved to a proper frown. 'Middle class racism is bad, but not as bad as that doctor.'

A dim memory surfaced of the treatment room in A&E. 'Did I hear you speaking Hindi to him?'

'You did. He asked if my family knew what I was doing. He made it sound like I was prostituting myself with the rich Englishman.'

I tried some humour. 'He got that bit wrong, then. I'm not rich.'

'He saw Vicky lifting half a ton of gold bling off your neck so they could give you a scan. I told him that I hoped his medical education was more up to date than his values. It was all I could think of.' She shrugged and changed the subject. 'I can't work Evie out. She is very nice most of the time. She was very worried about you on a personal level, unlike her mother. She loved watching the videos of the party and wants us to invite Tara Doyle for tea.'

'I can hear a "but" coming.'

'She has a tendency to bang around like a teenager. When she had to make up an extra bed for Hannah, she slammed doors and didn't speak to anyone for an hour.'

I stood up and stretched. 'What's the house like?'

'See for yourself, and you won't be getting any surprise visits from me. Only Mages with a token can get through the Wards.' She smiled and frowned at the same time. 'Even getting out is near impossible for me, and the one time I managed it, I couldn't even find the gap in the hedge, never mind go down it. I had to get Saskia up from the Lodge to get back in.'

I whistled Scout over and he came at once, and didn't object when I clipped his lead on. We strolled back to the house and I felt the magick building as I approached the drive of Middlebarrow Haven. As soon as I felt the first tingle, it pushed against me, then receded when it sensed who I was.

I took Mina's hand and walked down a short avenue of ancient trees, and when I say *ancient*, I'm referring to species and not individual specimens: ash, beech and willow all led to a short hedge of yew. I'd seen the same species in my shared vision with Nimue.

At the end of the drive, my new lodgings did their best to develop the theme of continuity by offering a Victorian take on our mediæval past. Middlebarrow Haven is a Tudor revival house of brick on the ground floor with half-timbering above, with the upper storeys being all angled dormers and projecting windows. I studied it for a moment and said, 'I still prefer Gothic.'

'Gothic what?'

'Architecture.'

'Oh. I thought you were looking for the stables. They're round the back, and they were converted to garages. I don't think that Evenstar would be comfortable. Scout seems happy enough in the old coal bunker.' She waved at the house. 'Evie said that the architect is famous, but she couldn't remember his name. It's not as old as it looks.'

'I'd have said about 1880.'

Mina shook her head and headed around the side, away from the formal front door. 'Why can't you be an expert on useful things.'

Scout and I trailed after her. 'We're experts on getting in trouble, aren't we, lad?'

'Arff.'

The inside of the Haven (as it's known) was what you'd expect. Mina went to get changed while Saskia showed me round and Evie got the tea ready. Saskia told me the name of the architect (John Douglas, a very talented man), and showed me the Deputy's study. There was a large formal dining room and connected drawing room, both of which I was subtly discouraged from using, and then we ended up back where we started, in the expensively refurbished family kitchen-diner.

Evie took great pride in bringing over the most delicate three-tiered cake stand, loaded with home-made sandwiches and cakes from a patisserie in Chester. 'I'm not really a baker,' she said.

'Or a cook,' added her mother. 'I should know, I'm the one who failed to train you.'

'Yeah, well, it's not in the job description, is it?' said Evie.

'I'm sure we'll sort something out,' I said diplomatically. Mina was smirking. Actually smirking.

Evie sat down and said, 'How are you feeling now?'

'Much better, thanks. When your life's in the balance, the good part is that you're too ill to notice.'

She shook her head. 'I still can't believe that Piers set you up like that.' She addressed the remark to her mother, with a glare.

'We don't know what Piers was thinking,' said Saskia, who looked at Mina. 'I can't believe that it was deliberate. Or negligent. I don't think we've had the full story yet.'

'What's the food like in the pub?' I said before Mina could respond. The women took the hint and we reached the end of the meal in peace and harmony.

'I'm going out tonight,' said Saskia. 'If you're recovered, Conrad, can I take you and show you the Wards? You need to know what they mean.'

I looked at Mina, who nodded. I grabbed my coat and followed Saskia outside. I turned right, towards the drive, but Saskia said, 'This way. It's a shortcut to the Lodge. Much quicker.'

On the way to the edge of the Haven property, I asked her about Evie. 'Did she go to the Invisible College?'

Saskia shook her head. 'You guessed, didn't you? She has very little magick, barely enough to get in and out and sense the Wards. She took the housekeeper job as a fill-in while she worked out what to do. Five years later, she's still trying. She's starting a part-time MA in creative writing at the end of next week, subject to your approval. If you think she resents your presence, that'll be why. She thought she'd never have a real Deputy to look after.'

I filed that away for later, because we'd arrived at a wrought iron gate set into a wall. This wasn't just a barrier, it was the hinge to the entire system of perimeter Wards, or so Saskia told me. 'How does it work?' I said. 'I'm sure that the Boss has told you how incompetent I am when it comes to complex magick. Or even basic magick.'

'You've survived Nimue, Conrad. I doubt the gates will be a problem.'

'I survived Nimue because I'm a survivor. This is different. I'm closer in magickal talent to Evie than I am to you, let alone Vicky or the Boss.'

'That's refreshingly honest of you. For a man.' When I didn't rise to the bait, she turned into the professional that Mina had described so well. 'All the Wards run in a circle round the edge of the property. There are eight altogether, two Distraction, two Discouragement and one Disorientation, plus the Alarms.'

These are pretty standard on Mage properties. Or so I've been told. They are the Wards that stop mundane people knocking on your door or getting suspicious. They didn't require any input from me, unlike the Alarm Wards.

'I'll approach without my token,' said Saskia. 'Despite twenty years, I'm no more bonded to Middlebarrow Haven than your dog is. I'll go out, go away and then come back in a few minutes without it. You should try doing something requiring a lot of concentration, then you'll find out what the first and second Alarms are like.'

'Fine. I'll go back to the stables.'

We parted and I went to seek out Scout's bolthole in the coal shed. Mina was right, he'd found himself a lovely little niche on the other side of the wall to the boiler. I could feel the heat radiating from the aluminium flue, and someone had given him a pile of tatty old blankets to shred. I felt around under the rags and found my weapons: the two guns and the Gnomish sword. Both the hiding place and the sheer cunning behind it is one of the many reasons I love Mina so much.

To any Mage looking for them, the enchanted gun and sword are easy to find when they've been "hidden" by a mundane person. Of course, no one but me can use either item without killing themselves, but that's not the point. Mina *can* use my mundane SIG pistol, and her threat to kneecap Piers Wetherill was a real one. By hiding them in Scout's den, she was throwing down a gauntlet and ensuring that any thief would leave a trail. Simply putting them in a cupboard would not have had the same effect.

DING!

What the fuck? A great bell sounded in my head. From the depths of my childhood, a TV voice said, *'There's someone at the door.'*

'I know that,' I announced to the shed, then turned and walked back towards the Lodge gate.

CLANG CLANG CLANG

I staggered for a second as my eyes started to water from the pressure of the Lux being discharged. These Alarms were designed for someone with a more robust magickal constitution than me. Saskia found me leaning against an oak tree and smoking.

'Are you okay, Conrad?'

'You said that they were the first and second alarms. In Odin's name, please tell me the third is quieter.'

'I'm afraid not. The good news is that it's never gone off.'

I gave her a look. 'What do they mean?'

'The first alarm is a serious attempt to breach the Wards using mundane means. It would have told Evie that Mina was trying to get in if Evie hadn't been out shopping. We get about two or three of those a year, mostly from scientists who've come to look at the SSSI. They go away in the end.'

'And the second alarm?'

'An attempted breach with magick. As you'll know, there are more than enough Mages with criminal intent to make Middlebarrow Haven a target. Luckily most of the Mages and Creatures of Light in the North know better. I didn't try very hard, but if you really push it, the house pushes back. The effects can be life-changing.'

I stubbed out my cigarette. 'You know what I love most about the world of magick? The almost total lack of regard for health and safety. What does the third alarm mean?'

'That the Wards have been breached. If that were to happen, I think you'd feel it wherever you were in Britain.'

'Right. Can you turn them down?'

'Me? Goodness, no. Sir Roland Quinn made those Wards, decades ago.'

I rubbed my chin. 'If Eseld Mowbray is in the area, I might get her to have a look at them. She likes a challenge.'

Saskia gave me a strange look. 'If that's all?'

'Thank you. I'm going for a lie down.'

The upstairs of Middlebarrow Haven included the Deputy's Suite. It was in need of a makeover, but with an emperor sized four poster bed, a sitting room, a bathroom and a dressing room, the excess chintz was worth putting up with. Mina was waiting for me, and the first thing we did was lock Scout in the sitting room before testing out the bed.

I don't know what Evie did with her evening. When we went down to get something to eat, she'd left a note saying *Lots of meals in the freezer. Enjoy. See you tomorrow. E. X.*

'Evie and I agreed to cook together tomorrow,' said Mina while I rummaged in the ancient chest freezer. 'Karina's coming, so we'll do a late Sunday Lunch.'

Karina. I'd been trying not to think about having a new partner. I found a small stash of Mina's favourite supermarket curry and decided that Karina could wait until tomorrow. 'Is there a Deputy's wine cellar?' I said.

'Yes. It was empty, but Saskia left a mixed crate as a welcome present.' She gave me a grin. 'There is a hospitality budget, would you believe.'

I looked around the kitchen. 'I could get attached to this place. So long as you were here.'

9 — Fresh Starts

After breakfast, I pottered around the Deputy's study. It was clear that Piers had been using it as his office and that Evie had designs on it as well: one section of the shelves held bright new paperback textbooks with titles like *Creativity: Theory, History, Practice.* I silently wished her luck and made a note to offer her a room-share.

Evie (or Piers) had also equipped the room with a shiny new printer and the Haven was well served by Wi-Fi. When I'd been given the tour yesterday, Saskia had pointed to a secure metal cupboard and said, 'The incoming Deputy usually re-sets the binary locks. Hannah implied that might be a challenge for you.'

Before I could reply, she'd moved on, and until I could get someone I trusted to adapt them, I might as well use Scout's dog basket as secure storage.

'You'd look after my secrets, wouldn't you?'

He'd sniffed the room and curled up on the rug in front of the cold fireplace. He opened one eye when he heard me talking to him, then went back to sleep. I was still trying to decide what to do when Mina wandered in and looked hungrily at the leather-topped desk. She was carrying her laptop and three lever arch files.

'Are you working in here today?' she said in that tone which expects the answer "no".

'Your need is greater than mine. I'll use the park as an office and give Scout some exercise.'

'Don't overdo it, Conrad. You only came out of hospital yesterday.'

I grabbed a 1:25000 OS map and loaded up with hat, gloves and a flask of coffee. The day was overcast and gloomy, with a thin wind blowing; the sort of bleurgh day that can easily put you off the English countryside. Not me and Scout. We are hardy creatures. Up to a point.

We set off along the public footpath that passes Nimue's altar, and Scout gave the woods a wide berth. After that, we wandered across fields and along roads in a sort of expanding spiral away from the Haven. If this was going to be my home base for a year, I wanted to know everything about it.

I'd reached as far as the Chester-Manchester railway line when Hannah called me. We have to respect her Shabbos; the respect is not mutual when it comes to Sundays. She asked me how I was doing and what had happened magickally since I'd been discharged from hospital.

When I'd finished telling her, she said, 'Can you handle DCI Morton on your own.'

'I wasn't aware he needed handling. What's up with Karina?'

'Two things. First of all, her Sorcery isn't what it needs to be. She's got the potential, but shall we say that the educational philosophy of the Foresters is rather more laissez faire than the Invisible College.'

You can't become a Fellow of Salomon's House without passing certain modules at the College; the curriculum at the Circles is more relaxed.

'That's … concerning, ma'am.'

'What you're trying to say is that she's no use, and you're right. I had to call in a favour from Cora.'

'Aah. How is the Dean?'

'Grim. She's been at work all week, and my spies tell me that she's not said a word about why she's withdrawn from the election. When we spoke on Thursday, I avoided the subject. And then she jumped at the chance to give Karina some one-to-one tuition. I think she wanted to get out of the house. They're closeted together in one of Cora's holiday places in Norfolk over the weekend.'

'You spoke to Cora on Thursday?'

'Yes. I didn't want to bother you with it while you were in hospital. The other reason Karina's delayed is that she thought she was going to go round with her Badge of Office on a set of bows and arrows. And I thought you were an awkward sod, Conrad.'

'I do my best, ma'am. I've seen her bow, and it's pretty fearsome, but you're right: not practical in downtown Manchester. Or anywhere really. What's she doing instead?'

'The usual. A dagger. Hledjolf will finish it tomorrow, so I'll swear her in on Tuesday. Expect her with you on Wednesday.'

'What are you not telling me?

She sighed. 'I don't want to pre-judge her, but I do wonder why you suggested that she join the Watch.'

'Because she's brave, resourceful and has a strong sense of right and wrong. Pretty much nailed it, really.'

'You'd think. We also need good communication skills, and the clams I ate on Friday were easier to open.'

'Oma Bridget did say that she was very shy.'

'And the rest. I'll email the basics from her file to you.'

'Thanks. How was Friday night dinner?'

'Ha ha. I'm sure that one of you lot sent that video to Moshe's nephew. Awkward doesn't even come close, and I have to babysit my nieces every night this week as a punishment.'

'I give you my word it wasn't me, and you love it really. Ma'am.'

'And that's the only reason you're not on a Unicorn hunt in the Outer Hebrides.'

'You know who my money's on? Francesca. Who else knows your family well enough?'

'You think the Keeper of the Queen's Esoteric Library would do that?'

'The more I get to know her, the more I think that having her brother as Warden was a great inhibitor. Now Roly's gone, the real Francesca is coming out.'

'Another thing to worry about that I don't need. Keep me posted and have a nice day.'

Scout and I worked our way back to Great Barrow and went to check out the White Horse. In response to the inevitable question ('Are you just visiting?'), I gave the reply that Saskia had told me was acceptable.

'We're staying at Evie's place.'

'Oh. Nice.'

Evie and her mother are both very much part of the village, and Saskia is perfectly visible in Middlebarrow Lodge. The village think that Evie's place is a modern house on the main road, and they do indeed own it. They also let it out as an AirBnB. How Evie will find time to run that, and the Haven *and* study creative writing is a mystery. Mina said, 'That is because you are a man. Women have to get on with these things.'

So that's me told.

The beer was excellent, the food looked good, and the welcome was more than friendly. I finished my pint outside, checked my watch and unhooked Scout from the fixed ring set into the pub wall. 'It's time for us men to go home and see whether the womenfolk have got our dinners ready.'

Scout wagged his tail, and I took that as a sign of agreement. You could call it a male/tail bonding exercise.

We returned along the main road and ducked into the Lodge grounds so that I could take the shortcut to the Haven. When we got to the path at the side, Saskia was emerging from her back door. And so was Benji. Before his mistress could stop him, a springer spaniel shot out of the cottage and through the gate. He bounced up and barked at Scout. Big mistake.

Scout hasn't met many other dogs since he stopped being a Familiar; ever since then he's been submissive when the newcomer asserted dominance. Not this time. He jumped at Benji and snapped at him, barely missing the spaniel's shoulder. Benji ran back and hid behind Saskia.

'Heel, Scout.'

He barked at Benji and came back to me. I reached down and gave him a scratch, and Saskia frowned at me. She shooed Benji back into the Lodge and locked the door, then zipped up her anorak and smiled. Professionally.

'How are you feeling today?'

'Much better for a long walk, thank you.'

We set off for the Haven, and I remembered something. 'Karina's not coming today. Perhaps Thursday.'

'Fine. Excuse me, I'm going to check on something before I join you inside.'

She went round to the side of the Haven, and I grabbed a towel to give Scout's paws a good wipe. I let him off the lead and ruffled his neck fur. 'How does it feel to be top dog in Middlebarrow, eh?'

'Arff.'

'Thought so.'

Sunday dinner was a very civilised affair. We all got to know each other a bit better, and I include Evie and her mother in that equation. Saskia didn't appreciate quite how keen her daughter was to do this MA, and was taken aback by her gratitude when I told her that the Deputy's Study was hers at any time I wasn't actually in the building.

'It's only a room,' said Saskia. 'You've got a spare bedroom in your flat, Evie.'

'But it's a Room of One's Own,' I said. 'Up to a point, of course. My mother insisted on having one, even though she wasn't allowed to take work home.'

'Thank you, Conrad,' said Evie. 'Piers said I couldn't use it at all if there was a Deputy in residence.'

'And we've sorted out a rota for cooking,' added Mina smoothly. 'Conrad will be cooking tomorrow, and he'll do the shopping, too, because he has to go to Dale Barracks.'

'What for?'

'Kit,' I said. 'You'll notice that Mina has scheduled my turn on the rota for the day she leaves. She's tasted my cooking.'

And so the day wound down, and the evening, and in the morning I kissed her goodbye at dawn. She was driving back to Clerkswell, then taking the train to London. I didn't know when I'd see her again, a state of affairs that we'd both have to get used to.

'Are you sure about this?' said Saskia when we reached the railway station on Tuesday morning. 'I don't mind taking you into town if you're not well enough to drive. A day's shopping in Manchester would be wonderful.'

'That's very generous. I might end up anywhere, so you needn't bother. I'll save it for another time, thanks.'

'On your own head be it,' she said with a smile. I should have realised she was being serious.

The name of the station was Mouldsworth. Not the most promising of beginnings. Who calls a village that? There are a lot of minimalist stations around, with nothing but a strip of concrete platform and a bus shelter. This one at least had all the original buildings, and I settled down to worry about my upcoming meeting with Tom Morton and Elaine Fraser while walking around to allow Scout to have a good sniff. He doesn't like sitting still on cold stone. Who would?

After a few seconds, I gave up and focused on Mina and tried sending her my love telepathically. In the near future she will have to be cross-examined in the Cloister Court by the magickal world's finest and most expensive lawyers. As if that weren't enough, her snooping around in Cambridge had started to turn up a whole treasure trove of Artefacts which will have to be included in the pot. She is going to be eating, sleeping and breathing the Flint Hoard for weeks and probably months.

The tinny Tannoy announced the 09:14 to Manchester Piccadilly, and my jaw dropped when I saw the state of the boneshaker that rattled into the station. 'What's that?' I said to Scout.

'It's a Pacer Train,' said a woman who'd come up behind me. 'Should have been phased out years ago, but that's what we have to put up with here. Not like down South.' She stared at me, as if I were personally responsible for the North/South divide, then she looked down and saw Scout staring back. 'He's gorgeous. Those different coloured eyes are amazing. He's not wearing lenses, is he?'

Contact lenses? On a dog? Maybe it's a northern thing.

'No. He was born like that.'

We went to opposite ends of the almost empty carriage, and I got out my phone to message Sofía. *Are you going to be in tonight?*

Si.

Can you get a bottle of red in for Mina? She's going to be having a bad day. I'll transfer some money.

Si.

Because I'd been concentrating on texting while the train bounced over the tracks, I missed the first part of the announcement, but I heard the end. '...arriving in Manchester Piccadilly at 10:30.'

10:30? An hour and a quarter for forty miles? Surely not.

Wrong. By the time I staggered off at the terminus, I understood why Saskia had been worried about me. My back was killing me from the terrible seats, my head ached and even Scout looked ill. I made it to the concourse and headed for the coffee shop.

I'd chosen the Turing Memorial as a meeting place because it was close to Canal Street and open to the air, a decision I was beginning to regret when it started to rain. The bronze statue of the father of British computing was oblivious, holding his apple and seated on a bench. I wondered if the apple was a reference to Sir Isaac Newton or was it because Turing just liked fruit. Scout gave me an accusing look. I think he was trying to say that if we had to be in the rain, at least we should have some sheep to chase.

'Do you always bring your dog to work?'

By Odin's eye, how does he do that? Tom Morton had appeared behind me like a ghost, and only years of training stopped me dropping the tray of drinks. I didn't even get a prickle of warning. Nothing. I looked down at Scout. 'You're supposed to bark,' I told him. He lay down and said nothing.

We shook hands, and I pointed to the drinks. 'It won't be up to Caffè Milano standards, but I got you tea. There's coffee for DC Fraser. Is she on her way?'

'I told her to give us ten minutes to have a chat.'

I didn't smile. 'That's nice. Shall we at least shelter under the tree?'

'As long as you don't smoke anywhere near me. Ever.'

I nodded and chose a well canopied ash tree. The leaves were starting to turn pale yellow and were barely up to keeping off the rain. 'What else?' I said.

Morton kept his distance to minimise my height advantage and he tested the temperature of his tea before getting down to business. 'I was going to say no to this caper,' he stated, 'until I spoke to Ruth Kaplan. She gave you a glowing reference without revealing any details whatsoever about what it is you've been up to. Except for one thing.'

'Oh yes?'

'She let slip that her twin is your senior officer. I knew that Hannah Rothman had left the Met. I didn't know she'd vanished in a puff of smoke down the security service rabbit hole.'

I had to suppress a smile at the image. 'She didn't mention that she knew you.'

'She didn't know me. We all heard about what happened to her, though. And about Mikhail. When did you come across her?'

'When I was recruited for MI7. And before you ask, she's seen the redacted Operation Jigsaw file. I was on strict probation.'

'As far as I'm concerned, you still are, Clarke. And that goes for Ms Desai as well. She's been messaging Lucy.'

That was news to me. What on earth for? I sipped my cappuccino. 'Do you tell Lucy who to associate with? Because I don't tell Mina.'

He looked away, across the park towards the University buildings. I think I must have touched a nerve.

He turned back and said, bluntly, 'What's your connection to Tara Doyle? And don't lie to me.'

'She turned up at our party and made several very generous donations. I'd literally never heard of Tara Doyle before that night.'

He shook his head. 'And that's why I'm so reluctant. You've told me a truth. Now tell me the whole truth. I'm giving you a chance.'

'No. Can't do that, Tom. I can tell you that this case involves an associate of hers.'

He nodded slowly and looked over my shoulder. This time Scout showed an interest and went to meet Elaine. 'Morning all,' she said. She looked down at Scout. 'I thought your name was Scout, not Lieutenant Kent.'

'Ah. She's been delayed. Should be with me on Thursday.'

Elaine bent down to give Scout a friendly scratch, then wiped her hand on her jeans. 'Is this case going to smell of wet dog? I can think of better signature odours.'

'Yes,' said Morton. 'You didn't answer my question about whether he's going to be a permanent fixture.'

'No. Not when there's someone at the house to keep an eye on him. There isn't today, so I thought I'd get him a bit more used to cities.'

She came to shake hands with me. 'How are you feeling, sir? Vicky said you'd not been well. Nothing serious, I hope.'

I looked at Morton, who clearly didn't care a monkey's about my health. 'Much better, thanks,' I said. 'I got you a coffee, but it may be cold.'

'Thanks. All good, are we?'

She tried her coffee and didn't wince. We both looked at Morton, who said, 'Tell Conrad what we found out yesterday about our missing person.'

She gave me a combined frown-and-smile. 'You mean Kenneth Williams, also known as the Count of Canal Street.'

It took me a second to figure it out. Then I burst out laughing, so hard I had to double over.

Morton waited until I was upright, then he pointed his cup at Elaine. 'I had to tell her who Kenneth Williams was. She'd never heard of him. Now would be a good time to share the joke.'

'I'm sorry. This is what happens when you delegate to the boss. The Count of Canal Street isn't missing as such. It's the witness to his alleged murder who's missing.'

Morton visibly bristled, and I held up my hands. 'I couldn't tell you until you'd agreed to come on board. It was why I wanted to meet here, so I could put you in the picture properly. I think the Boss and I are even now.' I shook my head. 'What else did you find out?'

He wasn't happy. 'I have never seen such a cat's cradle of red herrings in my entire career.'

Elaine sighed. 'Forgive him. He can't see a metaphor without mangling it.' He glared at her. 'What? Do you think Conrad didn't notice? And why are we still standing here getting wet and scaring the natives? Have you noticed that no one has used that path since I arrived? Can we not go somewhere dry?'

I looked down at Scout, who looked cold, wet and bored. Unless I pretended to be blind, no one was going to allow him across the threshold. I clearly hadn't thought this through properly. That's not his fault, though. 'The Fairy Gardens are expecting us. What did you find out?'

'So you can work out what not to tell us?' said Morton. He looked like he could stand here having this debate all day.

Patience, Conrad. Patience. 'No. I have no idea what the legal footprint of the Count is. Nor do I care, because it won't tell us what happened to him, and that's pretty much my remit: find out what happened. I'll be straight with you, Tom. Like you, my main aim is to keep the peace and stop a turf war breaking out. I doubt this case will come to trial.'

I could now feel water seeping down my back, having soaked the fleece underneath my Barbour. I was sorely tempted to leave Scout to roam free for half an hour. I trusted him.

With careful deliberation, Morton got out his phone and scrolled through the screen. 'Kenneth Williams was listed as a director of Lancashire Birkdale Holdings Ltd, and he had a driving licence which listed his address as a demolished block of flats. Apart from that, nothing. One of the other directors is registered as living at a property which belongs to Robert and Tara Doyle. Hence my interest.' He locked his phone, wiped the screen on his sleeve and returned it to his coat. 'Who was this man?'

I shrugged. 'Call him the Count. No one will have heard of his other name. He's distantly related to Tara Doyle and liked to live close to the edge. He's definitely missing, and Tara's convinced he's dead. I believe her.'

'He ran at least two night clubs,' said Elaine. 'That says drugs to me.'

'I can understand that. His family probably did get their money illegally, but if they're into drugs now, they'll face the full force of the law. I'm sure you've been on to the South Lancs drug squad since the weekend. I would have.'

Morton looked around for a bin to dispose of his cup and started walking north. We fell into step beside him. 'Clean,' he said. 'According to the local officers, drugs are taken at the Fairy Gardens but not sold. None of the door staff are on their radar. Why you? What is MI7's interest?'

'I told you. Keeping the peace. Tara's relatives can be volatile.'

He'd picked up his pace and we left the rainbow flags of Sackville Street behind and crossed the Rochdale Canal. The famous (or infamous) Canal Street ran off to the right, bedecked with even more rainbow plaques, signs, banners and Pride advertisements.

'That'll do for now,' said Morton. 'I'll reserve judgement on the big picture.' He stopped outside the narrow street that had the Fairy Gardens on its corner. 'Before we go in, why do you think that this Fae Klass is alive when the Count is dead?'

'Tara spoke to her. Briefly. Just after she got a distress call from the Count. It is literally all we've got to go on.'

We were now out of the rain, sheltering under an art deco awning. Morton unbuttoned his coat and ran his fingers through his wet hair to rub some life into it. Lucky dog. I'd love to be able to do that. He stared at the tiny alley

89

leading to the back door of the Gardens (where we were expected), and something Vicky mentioned came back to me. As he stared, his right hand went inside his coat and he rubbed his left arm. Elaine's fingers lifted to stop him, then fell back when she saw me watching her, and she turned her head away.

Morton turned round and said, 'How are we going to handle this?'

'I am going to follow you like Scout follows me. Unless someone draws a gun. You should see this.' I handed him my Lancashire & Westmorland warrant card with the authorisation to carry firearms.

He glanced at it. 'Why am I not surprised? Have you done a threat assessment?'

'Yes. It's low. At the moment. I'll let you know if it changes.'

He strode down the alley and Elaine walked with me. She lowered her voice and said, 'If you're going to follow him like your dog, does that mean he has to give you treats?'

'I'm not going to hold my breath for one, and why did Vicky call him Sheriff Morton.'

'Shh! Don't you dare repeat that.' She checked to see if Morton had heard. 'I'll tell you later, alright?'

Morton put his finger on the bellpush next to the back door and held it for a good ten seconds. When the door was opened, I got a waft of earth and sawdust, nothing like the smell of water and flowers from Nimue. I don't know if Scout experienced it the same way, but we both knew that a Fae had answered the door. Naturally, he went mad.

I backed away from the door, tugging gently on his lead. 'I'll join you in a while,' I said. 'When Scout's calmed down.'

Elaine nodded. Morton didn't turn round; he just lifted a hand and went into the Gardens.

10 — *Assisting with Enquiries*

TOM MORTON

When the back door to the Fairy Gardens opened, Tom thought at first that there was another door behind it, and then he realised that it was a man. A huge man who filled the doorway and blocked out all the light. By the time he'd registered this, Clarke's dog had gone mad, and Clarke was backing down the alley. Had he ever taken a dog up in one of his bloody helicopters, or was he only unprofessional when it came to proper, lawful police work?

'DCI Morton and DC Fraser' said Tom. 'I believe we're expected.'

The man mountain stepped aside from the door and held it open for them to enter. Tom had been inside countless licensed premises in his time, and he had an unconscious checklist that he went through as a way of taking the venue's measure and possibly stockpiling ammunition for later.

He did it now, looking back to see if this was a fire door. *Yes.* Proper bars to open? *Yes.* Proper signage and no signs of chains to lock it from the inside. *Yes and No.* So far, so legit.

The man who'd opened the door was wearing a black bomber jacket, black jeans and bright white trainers that gleamed in the soulless glare of the LED lights. When the door closed behind them, Tom felt like he'd been shut in a world of permanent darkness with no trace of healthy daylight or fresh air. At least no one was flouting the smoking ban in here.

'This way,' said the man in a strong local accent. He led them down the corridor, and he filled it like a cork in a bottle. *No,* thought Tom, *There's a gap at the sides of him, it just feels like he's filling it.*

Elaine was keeping a neutral face next to Tom, and he looked nervously over his shoulder at the now closed fire doors, and he got the fleeting impression that they wouldn't need a chain to lock them in. Was there something more to Clarke's sudden disappearance? Was he sending them into a trap? *Pull yourself together, Morton,* he thought. Their visit here was logged on the police computer. They had radios. What possible motive could Clarke have for setting them up? *Several* said his subconscious. Tom forced himself to reflect on how happy Clarke had seemed with the newly released Mina Desai and the fact that he'd said the threat risk was low. According to all the evidence, that Geordie lass was right: Clarke never broke his word.

Tom took a deep breath and caught up with their host. Just as he'd convinced himself that they would be okay, he noticed that Elaine had loosened her baton in its holster. *Why bother,* he thought. *That guy would just use it as a toothpick.*

The man opened a door marked Staff Rest Room and offered them chairs at a battered kitchen table. Tom took off his coat and looked around at the lockers, sink and kitchen cupboard with microwave and kettle on top. It was in need of a makeover, yes, but it was clean. If he were offered food in here, he'd accept it. When they sat down, the man did, too, and no offer of refreshment was forthcoming.

Tom realised that he hadn't looked at the man's face properly, so intent was he on working out if that mass were fat or muscle. There was plenty of muscle where the man's neck should have been, and a massive head to match the body. Tom looked for signs of steroid abuse – acne or disproportionate breasts being the visible ones – and there were none. He forced himself to take a breath and took out his notebook. To his side, at ninety degrees to their host, Elaine had taken a police issue tablet computer from her rucksack.

'Are you Mr Wayne Moss?' said Tom.

The man's eyes weren't just brown, they were almost black against the pale skin, and they didn't give much away. For some reason, he found Tom's question almost amusing.

'Moss. Yeah. I'm Wayne Moss.'

'What's your position here?'

Real steroid abusers get paranoid and short-tempered. They would consider Tom's second question intrusive and a waste of time. Moss didn't seem bothered, and he said, 'Head of security.'

'You filed a missing person's report last weekend and made a statement to PC Inverdale?'

Moss nodded.

'How long have you known Kenneth?'

'The Count,' said Moss with an abruptness that made Tom flinch. Moss said nothing, clearly waiting for Tom to correct himself.

'The Count of Canal Street. Was that his stage name?'

Nothing. The table between them might as well be a yawning chasm and Tom might as well be using semaphore. He had a decision to make: did he push the question of the Count's identity and his life, or did he stick to the disappearance. He knew what Elaine would do: she'd go at the witness like a terrier until she got an answer or until he swatted her aside. Tom was a firm believer in avoiding confrontation unless there was a purpose. As yet, there was no purpose.

'As you say. How long have you known him?'

'Pretty much forever. We're distantly related. On our mothers' side. I was his head of security since before he opened the Gardens.'

Elaine shifted in her seat. She'd noticed it, too: the use of the past tense. Moss was utterly convinced that the Count was no longer in the land of the living.

'Could you go through again what happened on the night he disappeared?'

'From what time?'

'From when you arrived or when he arrived, whichever was later.'

'I was here first. Six o'clock, if you're interested. Staff and performers turned up between six and seven. At seven my team for the door arrived and I briefed them. I did a tour of the building and opened the front doors at seven thirty. The Count and Ms Klass arrived while I was doing the tour, and he came to see me just after the doors opened.'

Moss had given them a lot of extra detail. Was that a blind, or was he trying to be helpful in his own way? 'They arrived together. Was that normal?'

'Yes. They lived together and he came every night she was working. She came in her first costume and went straight to the dressing room carrying her costume changes. I didn't see her again until I went for a break after her first set. About ten o'clock. The Count spent the night around the bar, checking the performers, talking to the punters, generally keeping an eye on things.'

'Was that all as normal?'

'Totally. Nothing unusual at all.'

'Did you have to refuse anyone admission or throw anyone out that night?'

'No one. I ...'

He was cut short when the rest room door opened and a woman came in. Moss was about to tell her to go away until he recognised her. He frowned and said, 'What are you doing here?'

'I heard you were having the coppers in,' she said, and without waiting for further invitation, she sat down on the fourth side of the table, between Tom and Moss and opposite Elaine. *Having the coppers in.* The woman made it sound like the club was having the decorators in.

When Moss said nothing, Tom turned to her. 'And you are...?'

'Jaycee the MC. That's spelt "JC".'

She was in her forties, with a lined face and rough skin. She was heavy in the shoulders and thick in the thighs. The loose trousers and sweatshirt were made of heavy fabric and did nothing for her, neither did the short, gelled hair.

Moss didn't move. He didn't confront JC, nor did he turn away. It was as if he were totally indifferent to her presence. In the hierarchy of the Fairy Gardens, they looked as if they ranked equally.

'Go on,' said Tom to Moss. 'You had a quiet night?'

Moss shifted some of his weight in the chair, and the chair complained loudly. 'It wasn't quiet. It was very busy. No one misbehaved, though.'

'And what time did the Count leave?'

'Ms Klass finished her last set at midnight. I knew the Count was going out, so I went down to see him. He likes to take some cash to the Well, so I gave him some and checked everything was okay.'

'How much?'

'Four grand.'

Elaine looked up from her tablet, and Tom let her ask the question. 'Four thousand pounds cash? That wasn't in your statement.'

Moss glanced at her, then looked back at Tom. 'I was in a hurry. I stuck to the basics.'

'Was that usual?' said Tom.

'I said. Yes.'

Suddenly they had a big motive for something to go very wrong. Something that had nothing to do with turf wars or power struggles. Tom moved on. 'What were the Count and Fae Klass wearing?'

'The Count was wearing his dinner suit. He always wore it to work. I can't remember what Ms Klass was wearing. Oh yes I can. It was cold, so the Count put his cloak on her.'

'I can show you,' said JC. She pulled a phone out of her pocket and stood up, peering down at Elaine's tablet. 'Have you got your Bluetooth on? I'll Airdrop the pictures.'

Elaine tapped for a few seconds. JC tapped twice and there was a *tang* noise. Tom leaned over and looked at the pictures.

There were three of them. As soon as the first picture loaded, Elaine let out an involuntary *Mmm*, so quiet only Tom heard it. The Count was heart-stoppingly handsome in his snugly fitting dinner jacket and immaculate white shirt. He was tall, muscular and (unlike Wayne Moss) perfectly in proportion, with a brilliant smile that caught the lights outside the Fairy Gardens. He was posing next to a billboard that advertised the special guest for their Christmas extravaganza.

'What on earth is this man doing running a nightclub and not starring as the next James Bond?' said Tom.

He looked to JC for an answer, but it was Moss who spoke up. 'The world isn't ready for a promiscuously gay James Bond. And he couldn't act. He was born to play one part, so he played it.'

'He was good,' added JC a little wistfully. 'I put the second one in because he's wearing the cloak.'

Elaine swiped the screen. 'Less James Bond, more Count Dracula,' she said.

She was right. It was the same dinner suit (or its twin), coupled with a jet black cape lined with red silk. She flicked on and Tom did a double-take. Two people stood next to each other, and you had to look hard to see that the one on the right was JC the MC.

She, too, was in a man's dinner suit, and with makeup and slicked back hair you couldn't work out whether she was a man pretending to be a woman or vice versa. The same could not be said of the figure next to her. If you looked at the jawline, and only the jawline, you were looking at a man; every other inch said *woman*. 'This was taken on the night they disappeared?'

'Yes,' said JC. 'Just before her last set. She always wore red for the last set.'

Tom looked at his notepad. 'What can you tell me about Fae Klass?'

He looked up and caught Moss and JC sharing a look, and it was the woman who looked down first.

Moss cleared his throat. 'The Count found her about six months ago. Picked her up at some low rent bar in Blackpool. Brought her here and polished her up. Changed her name and moved her in with him.'

'And after a few weeks, she was top of the bill,' added JC. 'The punters loved her. She sang, she danced, she worked the room.' This was delivered with professional respect, and then her tone changed to one of disdain. 'The only thing she couldn't do was patter. He scripted that for her.'

'And before?' said Tom. 'Her given name, for example? Her friends and family?'

'When you moved in with the Count, you left everything else at the door,' said Moss.

Tom looked at JC, who gave a slight nod to confirm it. 'Talking of left behind, we'll need access to the Count's flat. Who has the key?'

'It's been emptied,' said Moss.

'Just like that?'

'He's gone.' Moss frowned. 'There was nothing in there for you. You can have a root through Ms Klass's things if you want. I've put them in storage. And you can have this.'

He took a brand new iPhone out of his pocket and slid it over the table. 'The Count didn't have a phone. Ms Klass had one, but it's disappeared. I got a replacement with her number, but all the data is backed up and we couldn't hack her account. I did get a printout of the calls and called them all. They were all businesses. Nothing personal.'

'The Count didn't have a phone? Really?' That was Elaine. 'So how did he make a distress call?'

JC grinned. It was the predatory grin of the shark. 'Yes, Wayne, how *did* he call you and the Management? I'd love to know.'

For the first time, Moss was at a loss for words. He blinked twice and said, 'I don't know. It came up on my phone as an Unknown Number.' He spoke with the robotic cadence of a man who doesn't normally need to lie, not even to the police: the only record of Wayne Moss on the system was a registration and licence with the Security Industry Authority. He had never been arrested, questioned or even given a witness statement. Unheard of.

Tom took the phone and checked that there was no lock on it before passing it to Elaine. There was a polite knock on the door, and Moss shouted, 'Yes? We're busy.'

The door opened and Tom caught a glimpse of a scared young woman before Conrad Clarke moved in front of her and came in. He turned and said over his shoulder, 'Thanks, Stacey. I don't know how long we'll be. And don't give in to temptation and feed him.'

JC the MC looked up with curiosity at the newcomer; the impact on Moss was altogether different. He stood up and bowed to Clarke before saying, 'Welcome in peace, Lord Guardian.'

Lord Guardian? What's that all about, thought Tom.

Clarke bowed in return. 'In peace, thank you, Saerdam, and it's Wing Commander Clarke.' He looked at the room and saw a chair in the corner. He moved towards it and said to Tom, 'Forgive me, DCI Morton. Scout took a while to settle.'

Moss waited until Clarke was seated before sitting down himself and turning back to the table. JC was still twisted round, observing Clarke through narrowed eyes. Clarke flashed her a smile and sat back, trying and failing to make himself less visible.

'Going back to the Friday night,' said Tom. 'Where were they going?'

Moss looked over Tom's shoulder. Even Clarke's dog could have told that he was about to be lied to. Big time.

'The Well of Desire was a private member's club started by the Count as a separate business. It met in the upstairs rooms at the Earl of Moir pub after normal licensing hours. Because all of the details were kept in the Count's notebook, the club has been closed. I had no part of that operation.'

Elaine snorted her disbelief and looked at Tom with raised eyebrows. JC had the biggest smirk on her face, and Clarke gave a shrug that said he had nothing to add to the mystery of the Well. Another thing they could leave until later.

'Two more things from me,' said Tom. 'First, do you have any idea of the route they would have taken?'

Moss shook his head. 'There's about ten different ways to get there from here. I followed them all, but I couldn't see any evidence.'

Elaine looked up from her tablet and spoke to JC. 'Did Fae change her shoes, do you know?'

'What? No, she didn't.'

Elaine grinned. 'Then which way has the fewest cobbles? You'd break an ankle if you fell over in those.'

JC laughed. 'Good point. It's longer if you go by the canal, but every other route has to go over a cobbled street and down some dark alleys.'

Moss jerked a small nod to confirm what she'd said. 'Yeah.'

Tom picked up his pen for the first time and said, 'Who would want to hurt the Count?'

Moss flicked his eyes to the left. 'We've provided a list to Wing Commander Clarke. He has all the details.'

Tom couldn't resist it. 'I'm sure he does. It wouldn't be the first time.' He made a show of closing his notebook and said, 'Do you have anything to add?'

To Tom's surprise, they did: a flashdrive appeared from Moss's pocket. 'CCTV for the night in question,' he said. 'We have two cameras covering the outside front and another one on the lobby. Then there's two on the bar, but they're more for staff protection than anything else. We also have a camera in the bar cellar, but that's on a motion sensor. I haven't included it.'

'Thank you.' He looked right round the room. 'Anyone else?'

Elaine, Moss and JC shook their heads. Clarke stood up and rubbed the leg that had been shattered in Afghanistan. It looked to be giving him as much pain as it had the last time they'd met. Clarke grimaced, straightened up and said, 'Perhaps JC could show us out through the club, and I can collect Scout. It'll save him going off the deep end again.'

Moss gave Clarke a frown. 'Where did you get a dog like that? Don't tell me you trained him.'

Clarke gave a grim smile. 'You could say it's a familiar story.'

Moss's eyebrows showed something approaching emotion by shooting up. 'Is that so? Then I'm sorry for your loss.'

Tom's mouth opened and closed. He had the feeling that the men had just switched to a parallel universe where words sounded the same but had entirely different meanings.

The corridor ran along the back of the building, with staff toilets, a closed door marked *Dressing Room* and then steps up to a stage. They passed those and went through a door that led behind the bar.

The club's lighting was switched off, with only the bar's spotlights showing the way. Beyond the stainless steel counter, the club disappeared into darkness. A dim glow from the backstage exit showed a decent sized thrust stage and a few of the tables. The whole place smelled of rotten fruit, presumably from cocktail adornments dropped and ground into the carpet. Before Tom could look any further, they were through the club and into the foyer.

The smell of rotten fruit was replaced by bleach from the open doors to the customer toilets and just a hint of wet dog. It looked like Elaine was right.

'Arff,' said Clarke's dog with a wag of its tail. The collie's owner bent down and gave it a rub.

The girl who'd shown Clarke into the rest room appeared from the ladies, a giant pair of yellow Marigolds on her hands that only emphasised how slight and how pale she was. Her shape said late teens; the lines around her eyes told a different story.

'Thanks again, Stacey,' said Clarke with a nod.

The young woman flashed a nervous smile and said, 'I'll get the doors.' She bent down and stroked the dog. 'Bye, Scout.' Then she unlocked the heavy security doors and pushed them open to a flood of grey daylight and rain. It felt very good to be outside.

Clarke checked the wind and lit a cigarette. He was far enough away that any objection would be seen as point-scoring, so Tom just said, 'I don't know about you, but I'm starving. Any recommendations, Elaine?'

She looked at Scout the dog and said, 'There's a place along Canal Street that has outdoor seating with patio heaters. We could go there.'

'If you wouldn't mind,' said Clarke.

Tom pointed at his hand. 'No smoking.'

Clarke made a surrender gesture. 'Lead the way.'

Tom went first on the narrow pavement, and heard Elaine say, 'You're a fast worker, Conrad. You had that cleaner dog-sitting for you in less than five minutes.'

'She's a ... friend of Mina's. She only started on Monday. A favour from Tara Doyle.'

'Friend, eh? What was she inside for?'

'Was it that obvious? She was very good to Mina, and she's not just a cleaner. Junior housekeeping.'

Tom stopped and turned round. 'What are you playing at? Are you putting her in there as a spy for Tara? For you? Are you mad?'

'None of the above,' said Clarke. 'She's there because she needs a job with an employer who knows what she did but doesn't care. She's safer there than anywhere else.'

Tom hadn't planned to have this conversation on the pavement. Now he'd started, he might as well get it out of the way before they sat down for lunch. 'And what's with this *Lord Guardian* business?'

'Aah. Yes. There's a group of ex-servicemen with connections to Special Forces. Because I flew them in and out, they gave me the honorary title of Guardian.'

'What did you call him? Surdam?'

'*Saerdam*. It's a Pashtun word.'

Elaine touched his shoulder. He was doing it again: rubbing the scar tissue on his left arm, and this time Clarke had definitely clocked him doing it. Damn. That man just got under his skin. Literally, it seemed.

'It's just here,' said Elaine, drawing his attention to the bar café. 'I'll nip in and see if they're serving food outside.'

'Put it on a tab for me,' said Clarke, handing over a credit card. 'I'll text you the PIN. Are we on duty this afternoon, or shall we split a bottle of something?'

Tom's hackles rose. 'Yes, I am on duty, and sharing a bottle of wine in the rain is not something I planned on when I got out of bed at the crack of dawn.'

Elaine almost snatched the card out of Clarke's hand and bounded up the steps. Like the rain, Tom's aggression ran down Clarke's waterproof coat without leaving a trace. Clarke chose a table with a big umbrella and took the seat with least protection from the elements. When he'd tied up the dog, he said, 'Where are you living now, Tom? I got the impression from Ruth Kaplan that you've had cases all over the north of England.'

It was wet, none too warm, and today had been a very frustrating day for many reasons. Tom tried to summon the energy to take it out on Clarke. Because he was there. Because it was his bloody genial obfuscation that was making this "case" such a murky pit of tangled snakes. And then Clarke's dog lay down and rested his head on his master's boot, and Tom knew that the real reason he was frustrated was not Clarke, or MI7, or Mina Desai worming her way into Lucy's good books: it was being beholden to Leonie, the Deputy Director of Tom's branch of professional standards.

He let out a huge sigh. 'I'm living out of a suitcase, mostly. Lucy has a flat over Caffè Milano Number One, but it's tiny. Sometimes I stay at the Cloister in York – that's home, by the way. And there are a lot of hotels.'

Clarke nodded. 'That bad, is it?'

Tom laughed. 'And the rest.' He leaned forward. 'Can you give me some clue, any clue about what's going on here?'

Clarke leaned down to stroke the dog and move its head off his boot. He crossed his legs and looked up at the sky. 'Birds of a feather, Tom. There are a number of connected groups around here. Not gangs, groups of related individuals. Related by blood, drawn together by ethnic ties, or joined by money. You could call them families if you want. The Count was a player in one family, and he was probably assassinated by one of the other families. I'm under strict orders not to name names, and yes I do have a partial list.'

Elaine had reappeared with menus and heard the last part of Clarke's answer. 'Or he was killed for the four grand in cash he was carrying and Fae Klass is living it up on the Costa Blanca.'

Clarke took his menu and said, 'If she moves up the coast, I'll ask my father and little sister to track them down. Steak and kidney pie and chips, for me. Are you sure about a bottle of Rioja?'

Elaine dug Tom in the ribs. 'Go on, sir. Come round to my place after this, because you know what we'll both be doing tonight, don't you?'

She was right, even if he wished she weren't. 'Go on then.'

'Oh?' said Clarke. 'What are you doing tonight?'

'Taking pictures of Fae Klass to every low rent bar in Blackpool, because that's the only bloody lead we've got. And talking of the missing witness, why did Moss call her "Ms Klass" all the time?'

'Mmm. To avoid confusing her with any other Faes who might be lurking. There are a couple of them in the briefing notes.'

Tom gave his order to Elaine, and she went back inside. Something that had tickled the back of his mind came to the surface. 'I know your parents live in Spain. I thought Rachael lived in London and worked for billionaires. If I hadn't left the City Police, she might be on my radar by now.'

Clarke shifted in his seat and stretched out his bad leg. 'I shall ignore the slur on my sister for your sake. You wouldn't want her on your case, believe me.' Elaine came down the steps with a bottle and three glasses. 'It's my other sister, Sofía, and that is a story I *can* tell you.'

11 — New Blood

I did offer to assist the police with their enquiries. Honestly I did. Elaine Fraser looked at my bad leg, took pity on me and said, 'I don't think that would be the best use of resources.'

Morton was more brutal: 'You are not coming in my car with that dog, no matter how well behaved he is normally.'

'He is cute, though,' said Elaine. 'Those funny eyes look right through you.'

'He's a proper working dog, isn't he?' said Morton. 'I grew up with them at Rooksnest Farm, and they have a leaner look to them than most border collies.'

I gave the manic mutt a scratch. 'He is. Keeping him exercised is almost a full time job.'

We left the restaurant shortly after that, and I was tempted to blow a week's allowance on a taxi back to Middlebarrow. It was only the thought of arguing about Scout that made me limp back to Piccadilly Station and submit myself to one of those "Pacer" trains. If this was the standard of public transport in Lancashire, no wonder Manchester has so much vehicle traffic and pollution.

It was Evie who collected us from Mouldsworth, and she told me that she would be out for the evening. I Skyped Mina and brought her up to date.

'How were things between you and Tom?' she asked.

'I can tell he thinks there's unfinished business. I think he can live with it, but I'm not expecting a Christmas card. Scout might get one, but not us. It helps that Elaine wasn't directly involved in the Jigsaw affair.'

I didn't mention Morton's warning about keeping clear of Lucy. As I said, I don't tell Mina who to associate with.

She had worn a saree to work for some reason, and kept fiddling with the pin that holds it all together. 'How do you feel about the case?' she said.

'I'm not happy about it, that's for certain. Tara Doyle was adamant that the Count had not Entangled Fae Klass, or not yet. I think it's possible she'd worked it out for herself. That and the cash, plus things she might have stolen. I don't know. I really don't.'

We moved on, and she told me that the date for the Flint Hoard case had been put back, so she wouldn't have any problem getting away on Friday morning.

'That's why I wore the saree,' she said. 'Practice for meeting the Northern Mages.'

Mina's clothing choices follow a code that is sometimes beyond me. I know that she doesn't often wear sarees, and usually does so to project a more Indian vibe. I also know that she changes the spelling of saree / sari at will.

'I'm glad you're going to be there. Let me know the train.'

When we'd finished, it really hit home to me that I was on my own. For the first time in months, I had nothing to do and no one to do it with. That left me with no option but to light the fire, stretch out on the couch and turn on the television. Sometimes, doing nothing is exactly what you need, a point I made to Scout.

He stood on the rug, turned round a few times and then curled up with his head on his paws. I think he was agreeing with me.

Next morning, Karina Kent messaged me with an arrival time in Middlebarrow, and I caught up on some paperwork until my leg hurt and Scout had started sniffing an armchair with a gleam in his eye that said he fancied some canine woodworking. 'Come on, let's go for a long walk.'

'Arff.'

This time I went further south, towards yet another Stamford Bridge (that's four I know of in England), and the village of Tarvin. On a whim, I called Karina and told her to meet me at the pub in Great Barrow instead of at the Haven.

Scout and I got to the White Horse, and I took a pint outside to the bench. I reckoned that Karina would be here in about ten minutes, so it was time to refresh my memory. I took out the printed sheets from her file and cast my mind back to the Foresters Hall near Henley in Arden where I'd met her for the first and only time.

Karina Kent had belonged to the same Circle of Mages as Erin, and had followed Erin in being Handmaiden to the Circle's leader, Oma Bridget. Karina had been with the Arden Foresters since the age of thirteen, and she was now twenty-one, even younger than Saffron. The file from Hannah told me nothing I didn't know already, with one exception: Karina had listed her strengths as *offensive magick, tracking and concealment*. And that's it. No wonder she wanted to join the Watch.

I was slowly sharing a packet of pork scratchings with Scout (after washing off the salt from his share), when a black Mini Countryman came uncertainly round the corner and looked for a parking space. I brushed my hands and stood up.

Karina had dressed down for the drive and was sporting what the experts call *athletic lounge wear*. I would have called it a tracksuit if I'd been allowed an opinion, which when it comes to fashion, I'm not. She looked both ways before crossing the country lane and sprang over to join me.

I use the verb *sprang* with care. The most noticeable thing about Karina is not her long mousy hair (tied into a Goddess braid), nor her thin face, nor her slight frame. All of those make her pretty anonymous when she's sitting down. What really makes Karina into Karina is her innate grace and poise. I haven't been to the ballet often (twice – an ex made me), and even the prima ballerina was no lighter on her feet or faster than Karina. When she'd reached my station, she stopped and saluted.

I returned the salute, and she said, 'Did I get that right, sir?'

I shook her hand. 'You salute better than Vicky ever does. Have you been practising?'

'The Constable said I had to salute you once and then never again unless you're in uniform. I wanted to get it right.'

'We call her *the Boss* or *Hannah* amongst ourselves. What can I get you to drink?'

She looked at the pub and at the table. She was going to say no, I think, but something made her change her mind. 'I'll have a coffee, please.'

'I'll leave you to get to know Scout. Here.' I passed her a dog treat and went back to the bar. There was an ache inside Karina that was so strong I could smell it: an ache to fit in and do the right thing. Not a problem in itself, but something to note.

I put the coffee down and tipped another half of beer into my pint glass. 'Cheers.'

'Thanks.'

She carefully lifted the sugar packet and milk carton off her saucer and placed them in the middle of the table. I decided to push her buttons a little.

'How does it feel to be a Witchfinder?'

She flinched back. Amongst the Circles, the King's Watch does not have a good reputation, and I've been called a *Witchfinder* more often than I can remember, even in my short career.

She shrugged, a tiny movement with minimal effort and no grace. ''Salright,' she said with a mumble before taking a sip of coffee.

Oh dear. I felt a rush of sympathy for Hannah.

'Did you have a good journey? Warwick, wasn't it?'

'Yes.'

This time I said nothing to see how she reacted. Instead of fidgeting, she went still. Totally motionless, with her eyes on a point to my left. Then she started to blink rapidly. With an audible rush, she took a breath and said, 'Quite bad. The traffic was quite bad. Took me a lot longer than I thought. I really like your dog, sir. He's got loads of personality.'

He's got a load more personality than you was my first and cruellest thought. I forced myself to give her the benefit of the doubt and remember that I can be a bit intimidating. 'Karina, I've got a question for you. I want you to think about it while I have a smoke. Why do you think the Boss put you with me as your training officer?'

I stood up and moved away from her. She frowned for a second and answered me before I'd got my lighter to work.

'I was a bit disappointed, to be honest. I thought she'd put me with one of the female officers. I was hoping for Vicky. Sorry, I meant *Captain Robson*.'

'There is only one female Watch Captain at the moment, and Vicky's got her hands full with Xavi and Saffron.'

She blinked again and spoke rapidly. 'I'm really sorry, sir, that must have sounded like I was disappointed. I'm not. I'm really looking forward to working with you because you have the most interesting cases.'

'That's one way of putting it, Karina.' I looked away and frowned. 'It's not just about you. What about me?'

She chewed it over. 'I'm sorry. I don't understand.'

'Why have I had a trainee throughout my whole time as a Watch Captain and now Deputy Constable?'

She blushed and looked at her cold coffee. 'Because your magickal talents are differently developed. Is that what I'm supposed to say?'

'No. It's too politically correct to say they're *different*. I simply don't have them. You have to be my magickal eyes and ears, especially the ears. Helicopters are very noisy. Got that?'

'Yes, sir.'

'And I'm relying on you to speak up on all matters magickal. I need you to do that, Karina. Both our lives could be at risk if you don't. OK?'

She nodded and tried to smile. 'OK.'

'Good.' I drained my pint and put the glass down. 'Scout and I are going to walk back to Middlebarrow and I'll see you at the Lodge. Saskia is expecting you and has a token to get you through the Wards. If you could take the empties back inside, I'll see you shortly. And from now on, it's Conrad, okay?'

'Right.'

It was a five minute walk back to Middlebarrow. As soon as we'd left the pub, I said to Scout, 'What do you make of her then, eh?'

It was a good question (for me, not for him. He knew he liked her). I had a few alarm bells ringing in my head. They weren't as loud as the Alarms that Warded the Haven, thank the gods, but they were definitely there. Was it just shyness, or was there something else? Genuine dislike of men? Genuine dislike of me, for some reason? But who could dislike me? Don't answer that question.

Karina had overtaken me and was actually talking to Saskia. There was also pointing and directions being given. Benji the spaniel saw Scout coming and retreated behind the Lodge gate.

Karina turned to me. 'Conrad, I didn't know you had an altar here. Saskia's been telling me all about it. Is it okay if I use it?'

'I've warned her about ramblers,' said Saskia.

'Of course,' I said. 'Whenever you want if you're not on duty.'

'Thanks.'

'I'll leave you to it, then,' said Saskia. 'See you at dinner, Karina, Conrad.'

When Saskia (and Benji) had returned to the Lodge, Karina's nervousness/shyness/awkwardness returned. 'What do we do about food here?'

'That's subject to negotiation. Evie will get you a bite when we get to the Haven, and we're eating together tonight. Saskia has generously agreed to join us. It's in your honour, not mine.'

She chewed her lip. 'About that. I only eat naturally.'

'I guessed. You're not the first natural eater to visit here. Just don't mention beef when Mina's in residence and you'll be fine.'

'Mina. That's your fiancée, right?'

'She. Mina is a *she* not a *that*. Come on, let's get you settled in. You should be able to drive through the Wards now, and if you park round the back, I'll give you a hand with the luggage. Scout and I are going to take a shortcut through the gardens.'

She nodded and got into her car. When I'd pulled her up about the use of pronouns, you'd think I'd slapped her. I looked up at the clearing sky and decided that Karina would probably feel more at home outside than in.

After they'd eaten, while Karina was upstairs putting her things away, I helped Evie tidy the kitchen. 'She's very quiet,' said Evie. 'I had to work really hard to get her to talk at all.'

'Oh?' I said. 'What floats her boat?'

'Hunting. And the Foresters, which is weird, because from what I can tell, they weren't very nice to her all the time. And even weirder was that she spent ten minutes asking questions about the food before I figured out what was really bugging her. I don't think she's ever eaten a meal in company when she wasn't wearing her robes as a Forrester and she wanted to know what our dress code was.'

'I hope you told her that we always dress for dinner and that tiaras should be worn.'

'No, because that would be cruel. Is she really twenty-one, not seventeen?'

'You went to a mundane school, didn't you?'

'No need to rub it in.'

'Don't knock it, Evie. Sometimes lifelong Mages are at a real handicap. While we've got a minute, can I ask you about Piers Wetherill?'

Evie stopped putting things away and turned to face me. 'What do you want to know? I didn't see much of him. It's Mum you should ask.'

'What were his interests, and did he leave anything personal behind?'

She may not be much of a Mage, but Evie is anything but slow. 'You're trying to find him. How do you know he's not at home in Shrewsbury?'

'Because it's listed with a lettings agency. No Mage does that unless they've taken all the magick off their house.'

'What will you do if you find him?'

105

'Ask him some questions. If I'm not happy with the answers, I'll lock him in a small room with Mina, and she'll ask him again.'

'Ha ha.' She saw my face. 'Oh. Right.' She thought for a moment. 'You're not going to hurt him? Promise?'

'If he's done something wrong, he'll answer to the Cloister Court.'

She shrugged. If I had to guess, I'd say that Piers wasn't the most obliging lodger. 'He left nothing behind except the stuff from the last election. Mundane election. He campaigned for the Liberal Democrats. A load of leaflets. I put them in the recycling.'

It wasn't much, but it was a start. I heard a door close in the hall, and Karina appeared in her new combat uniform, complete with second lieutenant tab. She didn't look happy.

'Is this the right size? It's baggy in all the wrong places. Do I have to wear it?'

'Not today. I can get Saffron to give you the number of her seamstress if you like, but when we're on an op, it's uniform orders, I'm afraid.'

She looked disappointed. 'What are we doing now?'

'Going for a long walk. Get changed and I'll meet you by the kennel. I'll fill the flasks.'

She found me ten minutes later, putting my phone away. 'I've just heard from Sheriff Morton. They've struck gold. We're on for tomorrow.'

She brightened up considerably. 'Great. What are we doing?'

'Let's go to Nimue's spring, and I'll tell you all about it.'

Karina was disappointed when I told her we were on the hunt for a drag queen and not a Dragon, and she was even more disappointed when Nimue didn't make an appearance at the spring. After that, we walked and talked. I went through my magickal cases with her, pausing at the places where I'd had to make decisions to see what she thought. Short of organising the Watch to run combat simulations, it was the best I could do.

We trespassed on to the thirteenth green of a golf club and I told her that we were stopping for tea and a test.

'What test?'

'We'll get in serious trouble if the golfers see us. I want you to use magick to stop them. I'll pour the tea.'

There was a mound at one side of the green, and Karina pointed to it. 'We'll sit there. Give me a minute.'

Scout and I settled on the mound, and in the distance I could see a foursome gathering on the tee. Tom Morton is a rugby fan, which was disappointing, but we do share a mutual loathing for golf. Another plus point for the Sheriff. I must find out where he got that nickname.

Karina jogged back from the woods carrying a tree branch. I could spend all day watching her move – her feet barely seemed to touch the ground. When she got closer, I could see that she'd cut the branch from a living tree.

If that sounds like vandalism, most Mages and all Witches are careful to harvest from Mother Nature only what can be spared. If that wood had been coppiced and well maintained, she'd have come back empty handed.

She cut the branch to a point and drove it into the mound. Scout lifted his head to take an interest, then dropped it when she started performing magick. He may have kept his ability to detect non-humans from when he was a Familiar, but he can't sense magick anymore.

'Look away,' she said. 'Much easier if I don't have an audience to amaze.'

That's the old sense of a-maze: to put someone in a maze, or befuddle them. I turned away and felt the tingle of Lux being applied. Then I heard a curse. More Lux. More cursing. I had to fight the urge to turn round.

She was breathing heavily when Scout barked and she announced that she was done. 'Just your peripheral vision, if you can.'

I focused on a tree in the distance, and instead of the branch and dog, I saw a state-of-the-art bag of golf clubs on a motorised trolley, and a pile of discarded waterproofs. 'You'd better stay still for a bit, boy,' I said to Scout, then, 'Well done, Karina.' I had more to say, but I wanted to hear her self-appraisal first.

'Sorry it took so long. I wanted to include Scout, and I had to work around him. If we're in the field and he's with us, he's pretty distinctive. I can do it much faster without him.'

'Good. I'll bear that in mind. What about us?'

'From a distance, we look the part. There's a golf course on the Forest of Arden, so I've seen plenty of golfers from a distance.'

'Good work, though if you take pictures of me in a Pringle sweater, even a magickal Pringle sweater, I may have to kill you.'

That was the cue for a joke. She passed.

The Forest of Arden is a Fae realm that exists in the same physical space as a piece of the Warwickshire countryside, but on a different plane of energy. The sacred grove of the Arden Foresters is at the northern end of the invisible wood, and Karina spent a lot of time there. She made some bad choices recently, and her mention of the Forest allowed me to bring them up.

I passed her a mug of tea and said, 'You deserve that. Do you know how Colwyn is getting on?'

Colwyn is her half-brother by the same father. Unusually for a Witch, Karina was brought up by her father; her file said that her mother died when she was very small. Colwyn and Karina had been drawn into a plot by the Foresters' Mother (that's a title, not a biological descriptor), and Erin's close friend, Ioan, had been killed. Another reason to keep Karina away from Clerkswell.

Karina hadn't hurt anyone, nor would she have let Colwyn go ahead if she'd known what he'd planned. Her punishment had been pilgrimage from Glastonbury to Ireland. By foot and ferry. It was the one thing she was willing to talk about at dinner last night. Colwyn's punishment was much more severe.

'I've been dreading this moment,' she said, and then lapsed into silence.

'Oh yes?'

'I don't want to talk about it, but I know I've got to.'

'Only to me or the Boss.'

'That doesn't make it any easier.' She looked away, further to the right. A flash of movement to my left signalled the arrival of a golf ball on the green. It bounced beyond the pin and rolled away into the rough, followed by a distant swear word.

'I saw him yesterday morning, first thing, just as the mist was rising. He has to start at dawn and work all day. Tending the Forest. Every day except the full of the moon and the equinoxes. For thirty-two years. He's beginning to wish he'd surrendered to you.'

Before I could arrest Colwyn, he'd confessed and begged judgement from the Fae Prince of Arden, an ancient right. He wouldn't age as quickly in the Forest. Even so, thirty-two years is a long time.

'Have you ever been in a Limbo Chamber?' I said. 'I have.'

She shook her head. 'I can't imagine having no magick.' She took a small breath, then blurted out, 'We argued. He thinks it's wrong, that it was an accident.'

'What did you say?'

'I told him that just because he shot the wrong person, it was still murder. When I went to the celebration of autumn, everyone stared at me and no one spoke to me except Oma Bridget and Alex.'

'I'm sorry. It must be tough.'

Three more golf balls had arrived, all much better placed on the green, followed by the golfers. 'Won't be long,' said one of them cheerfully, waving at me.

'Take your time,' I replied. 'We're in no rush.'

We fell silent until they'd all potted their balls, or whatever the term is. There was a lot of banter as they filled in their score cards, and they left us with another wave.

'Shall we go?' I said. 'One of us needs to start cooking, and that would be me. Oww!'

'Are you all right?'

'Bloody leg. After a long walk, it can seize up. Give me a hand will you?'

She heaved me upright and stared at my bad leg. 'Did you have that wound before you joined the world of magick?'

'It's a bit more than a wound, Karina. It's a constant reminder of what can happen when your moral compass gets pulled off true north. I'll tell you about it one day.'

I shook out the kinks in my leg, and she uprooted the branch she'd used as a focus of her magick before tossing it into the wood. That was a throw of at least seventy metres, and I felt the ripple of magick as she accelerated the branch. While it was still in the air, I shouted, 'FORE!'

When no one screamed from the woods, I said, 'Impressive. Dangerous, but impressive. Did you scan for life first?'

She went bright red and shook her head. I left it there.

'What are your plans now?' I asked when we started walking away from the mound.

'To make an offering at the spring, if that's okay.'

'Of course. Mess at seven thirty. Is beef bourguignon acceptable?'

Was that the ghost of a smile? 'Yes. Great. My dad makes it a lot. I think it's a good excuse for him to finish the bottle of wine.'

We parted in the yard behind the Haven. When she'd gone inside, I settled down on the chair I'd set up inside the kennel to have a cigarette. Scout yawned and flopped on to his bed. 'Don't get too comfy,' I told him. 'We're going inside when I've finished this.' I bent down to scratch his head. 'Do you think if I prayed to the Goddess, she might send Karina a sense of humour? She hasn't cracked a joke or so much as smiled at one of mine since she got here.' Scout lifted his head. 'And before you say anything, even Saskia laughed at the one about Mina and the umpire from Bishop's Cleeve.'

Scout rested his head down. Even though he couldn't understand me any more, I didn't have the heart to tell him that he was staying with Evie tomorrow.

12 — Sheriff to PR1
Sheriff x Queen

I'd like to tell you that I warmed to Karina on the drive up from Middlebarrow. I'd like to tell you, but I can't. We'd talked about dealing with mundane colleagues, and her first remark had been, 'Do we have to?'

There aren't many positive places you can go after that.

I had opened my mouth to tell her off, and something struck me: she was being honest. She simply didn't/couldn't face initiating a relationship with someone who wasn't from the world of magick and wondered why we were doing it.

'Yes,' I'd said. 'We don't have the skills or resources to do this on our own. Unless your idea of a good time is traipsing round pubs in Blackpool.'

'No. I wouldn't like that.'

After sorting out the ground rules for dealing with Morton and Fraser, I'd encouraged her to talk – it was that or put the radio on. All she really seemed interested in was further details about how I'd tackled some of my cases, and when I asked her about things, her first response was to deflect me or go quiet. It was a long drive.

The Charnock Richard service area on the M6 is not my favourite place for a meeting. It's not my favourite place for anything except getting a coffee and sneaking a quick smoke, both of which I did while we waited for Sheriff Morton and Deputy Fraser to arrive. I may have lied about the time we were supposed to meet, just in case they were early and wanted to get straight on with it.

Charnock Richard is only a short drive from Preston, and that's all I knew about our plans for the day: a visit to the City of Preston. It turned out that I was even wrong about that.

Our police colleagues arrived in a black 3 Series BMW, and did I see Elaine's lip curling slightly when she looked at my Volvo XC70? I think I did. She also cast her eye over Karina's outfit: black leggings with *adidas* written up them, black trainers and a black top to match the leggings. Elaine's lip didn't curl, but her eyebrows did go up.

I made the introductions and said that there was a quiet corner in the depths of the café. Karina surprised me by offering to join the queue. 'It's Yorkshire tea for everyone, isn't it?'

When had I said that Morton and Fraser were Yorkshire tea addicts? Had I even said it? No matter. We settled down in a booth with no one on either side, and Elaine started by saying, 'If this was a secret test to join your lot, I think we passed. It was quite a challenge.'

'We are not joining MI7,' said Morton. 'You just want to take the credit for having an idea.'

Elaine kept a straight face. 'Me and Lucy. It was Lucy who spotted that Fae Klass could have had surgery. After you showed her the picture, Tom.'

It was there again. Vicky had told me that Elaine seemed to disapprove of Lucy in some way. No wonder Lucy called her Scarywoman.

'Go on, then, you're dying to tell him,' said Morton.

'We spent hours getting nowhere on Tuesday night, so yesterday I thought, "If Klass has had surgery, why not show them pictures of the Count?" We got on the trail almost straight away.'

Karina appeared with a tray laden with teapots, cups and three cupcakes. 'I didn't know if anyone would be hungry.'

We looked at the desiccated baked goods. You would have to be very hungry to eat those. 'Thanks, Karina. I hope you remembered to get a receipt.'

She nodded and started unloading the tray. Elaine took a closer look at Karina's bent head and said, 'That's a lovely braid. Must have taken you ages to learn that.'

The Goddess braid has three strands and is physically impossible without three hands – or magick. So I'm told, because there may be a Goddess braid, but there is no Goddess combover.

Karina kept her head down. 'There's a knack to it.'

Elaine swirled the teapot round and put on a casual air. 'How are your digs, Karina? Where is it you're staying?'

'Middlebarrow Haven. It's…'

She stopped speaking because I'd given her knee a hard squeeze. It was the only part of her anatomy I could reach without getting an immediate slap. I focused on Elaine. 'Well done, constable. I wouldn't bother looking for it, though. Middlebarrow Haven is an MI7 code name.'

Elaine grinned, totally unabashed. 'It was worth a try. Nice, is it?'

'I'm so sorry, sir,' said Karina. 'I won't let that happen again.'

Elaine and Morton exchanged a glance. 'Doesn't matter, Karina,' I said. 'At least you didn't tell them about the heated swimming pool and the torture chamber for witnesses.'

Elaine gave a polite smile. It wasn't the funniest thing I've ever said, but at least it should have defused the tension a little. I hadn't counted on Karina, though.

'But, sir, we don't have a torture chamber, do we?'

This time Elaine snorted with suppressed laughter, and Karina went even redder. Oh dear. There was no way out of that one.

'Nor do we have a swimming pool. Tell me what you found,' I said to Morton.

He'd got the message and was already reaching for his briefcase. He pulled out the inevitable plastic wallet. Wallets, plural. He actually handed one to me. I was impressed.

'Meet Kirk Liddington,' he said. 'Also known as Fae Klass, also known as Acie Decie. Have a look at the top sheet.'

I slid out an A4 sheet with three pictures on it. The first was the image of Fae Klass that we'd picked up from the Gardens, and the second was a DVLA picture of a young man with sandy hair and no distinguishing features. In the third picture, a much rougher version of Fae Klass stared back at me, almost defiant. I moved my index fingers around the outlines of the two drag faces.

'Nose, and lips, I reckon,' said Elaine. 'But not the jaw.'

'No,' said Morton. He looked me in the eye and spoke quietly. 'Jaw surgery is not for the faint-hearted. It takes a special person to go through that.'

It was his way of acknowledging what had happened to Mina. The women just thought he was labouring the point. I turned to the second sheet, which was mostly negative: no current address, no activity on his bank accounts (which were registered to the Count's flat), no father, mother untraceable in Glasgow (?). Clearly, the big reveal was on sheet three. I turned to it and was met with a picture of a real woman. Or genetic woman. Whatever you want to call her, Amy Lofthouse (née Liddington) was definitely Kirk Liddington's sister, and she definitely lived in Preston.

'So we're off to Preston,' I said. 'Excellent. Thank you.'

'Penwortham,' said Elaine. 'They won't like it if you say Preston, even if it is just across the Ribble.'

'Noted. What's the plan?'

'Turn up and knock on the door. I reckon she'll have heard from him.'

'Sounds good to me. Shall we?'

We stood up, and Karina said, 'I'll see you at the car.'

She loped off across the café, and Elaine said, 'You'll have your hands full with her, Conrad. Is she old enough to join the Army?'

Morton shook his head. 'Did your HR lot do any tests?'

I was starting to get worried about Karina. Morton had offered an olive branch, and I accepted. 'No. She was recruited based on her technical experience.'

'Then I think she may be on the autism spectrum.'

All three of us looked towards the atrium of the service station where Karina had disappeared.

'Possibly,' I said. 'And she grew up in an alternative religious community. She's still a member.'

'Poor kid,' said Elaine. 'There's two postcodes on that sheet. The second one is for Middleforth Green car park. If we meet there, we can go on foot to Amy Lofthouse's place. It's not far.'

'Fine. See you shortly. I'll be a good boy and clear the mess away.'

The cupcakes were untouched, and so was Karina's tea. She'd poured it carefully, added milk and moved it to her side of the table, and then not touched it again. Was it the milk? Did she just not like tea? This was something I'd have to look into later.

I visited the Gents and lit a cigarette on the way out, thinking about work partnerships. Morton and Fraser are a good team, almost the mirror image of Vicky and me. With them, it's Morton who gives her a long leash and lets her be the attack dog; with us, when we're dealing with Mages, it's Vicky who gives the impression that she's barely containing my innate tendency to violence.

I was just getting used to Saffron and her gung-ho approach to most things when she was taken off me, and now I had Karina. I watched her skip down the steps and jog towards the car. 'Sorry, Conrad. I'm not late, am I? And I'm really sorry about before. Will it cause a problem that they know about Middlebarrow?'

'Elaine is just trying to wind you up, Karina. It goes with the territory, I'm afraid. If you're not sure what to say, just smile. And don't worry about giving away our location – if they want to follow us, they will.' I finished my cigarette and unlocked the car. 'Where are we most vulnerable, do you think?' I opened the door. 'You don't have to answer straight away. Hop in.'

Middleforth Green was just that: very green. It was also pleasant. 'Scout would have loved this,' I said when we got out and walked over to Morton's BMW. 'I doubt we'll come back, but it's good to know that it's here.'

Elaine looked at the four of us – Morton's Crombie overcoat, my Barbour, her fleece and Karina's technical black fabrics, now with added utility belt. She had a baton on one side, as a distraction, and her Badge of Office on the other, disguised with a Glamour as an LED torch. 'It's a good job we're not undercover,' said Elaine. 'We'd never pass as Mormons or Jehovah's witnesses, that's for certain.'

'Good point,' said Morton. 'Conrad and I will go round first and have a look. It's a circular road.'

We crossed the main road and went into a 1990s development of private housing, a mixture of executive and family houses, with a road of starter homes tucked away inside. On the way, Morton told me that Amy Lofthouse had been married for three years and had kept the house when she divorced her husband two years ago. She was thirty-two, five years older than her brother.

'If she's paying the mortgage, she must have a job,' I said. 'Won't she be at work?'

'Her shift starts at two. Look, there's her car in the drive.'

We passed Number 9 on the opposite side of the road. There were too many closed curtains to say whether anyone was around. We both noticed that it was a corner plot, and when we rendezvoused with the girls, Morton said, 'Conrad and I will take the front. You two cover the back and side. Do you have Airwave radios, Conrad?'

'No. Too complicated. We're working on an alternative.'

'If we do anything bigger than a door-knock, I'll get two more and bill you. Ready?'

'Ready.'

There was no doorbell at Number 9, so Morton rapped firmly and rapidly on the door before standing well back. After ten seconds, he stepped forward and knocked again, louder and longer. After a short interval, the door opened a crack and a woman's face was just visible through the gap.

'DCI Morton and PC Clarke. Are you Amy Lofthouse, formerly Liddington?' said Morton, holding up his warrant card. I didn't follow suit, because I wanted to keep my hands free. Just in case.

'What do you want?'

'We're trying to contact your brother, Kirk Liddington. He may be a witness in a serious crime. We just need to take a statement from him.'

'I haven't heard from Kirk in months. Sorry. If you'll excuse...'

Morton's radio burst into life. 'We've got him, sir. We're bringing him in through the back.'

Amy heard the message loud and clear. She went to close the door, but my boot said otherwise. She let go of the door and moved away. I pushed it open and saw the retreating figure of a nurse in a dark blue dress but no belt or shoes.

'We don't do that,' said Morton, pointing to my boot. 'Too dangerous. Come on.'

Beyond the door was a tiny hallway with a staircase on the right and an open door at the end. From out of sight, Amy said, 'Leave him alone! He's done nothing.'

Tom was ahead of me. Alarmingly, I heard Elaine say, 'Let him go, Karina. I don't think he's a risk.'

The kitchen/dining room was only a dining room if you never had more than two guests. It was made to feel bigger by the conservatory beyond it, which took up eighty percent of the tiny garden. The action was taking place where the dining room carpet gave way to the conservatory's tiles.

Of the four actors, Elaine was the tallest, a good three inches above Kirk Liddington. Karina was the shortest, and she was holding Kirk in place with a fierce grip on his shoulder. Elaine was trying to stop Amy from rescuing her brother. From the look in Karina's eyes, that wouldn't have ended well.

Morton took charge, and I took a good look at Kirk. No wonder his sister wanted to rescue him. He looked close to emotional and physical collapse: drawn and haggard around the face, bags under the eyes and rounded shoulders. His cheap denim shirt and jeans hung off him, and the only trace of Fae Klass was the red varnish on the toes of his bare feet. On nine of his toes. One of the nails was missing on his left foot. The whole nail.

'Don't worry, Ms Lofthouse,' said Morton. 'Your brother's quite safe. We're only here to ask questions.'

'How do I know you're who you say you are?' said Amy, with a distressed Lancashire accent.

'Call 101 and ask them to confirm my identity,' said Morton with a reassuring, professional tone. 'I'd rather you did that than worry.'

'Who sent you?' said one of the girls. No they didn't. It was Kirk. Clearly some surgery isn't visible.

I'd been leaning on the door jamb, trying to look non-threatening. I stood up straight and coughed. Morton looked at me and then gave a small nod.

'No one's sent us,' I said. 'I've spoken to the Management and whatever happened to the Count, I'll make sure they leave you alone.' I looked at Karina and nudged my head up. She let go of Kirk and stood back to block the conservatory exit.

Kirk's rounded shoulders slumped further. 'I'll be fine, Amy. You get off to work. I knew this would happen one day. I'd rather get it over with.'

If I'd closed my eyes, I'd have thought a teenage girl was speaking. Weird isn't in it. Morton and Fraser were equally shocked, and only Karina didn't seem surprised. Either that or she should take up poker for a living.

'Are you sure?' said Amy. Kirk nodded, and she moved to the little round dining table. She picked up a red nurses belt and clipped it round her waist, then started tying and fastening her hair.

'Can I have a cigarette before we start?' said Kirk, pointing to the garden.

Morton nodded. 'Of course. PC Clarke will keep an eye on you, and no doubt join you in ruining your health. Shall we wait here?'

Kirk pointed to a door that led to the living room. 'We'll go in there.' He moved to Amy and gave her a hug. 'Thanks. I'm sorry.'

'Take care,' she said. 'And text me the minute they've gone.'

'I will.' An impish grin flashed across his face. 'Show them where the kettle is, yeah?'

She pushed her brother away, and I followed him outside. He picked up a pair of supermarket trainers from the square of grass and shoved his feet into them. 'I dropped these when your pet ninja jumped me. I haven't got that close to a woman in a long time.' There was a bigger smile this time, enough to show that he was hanging in there. Just.

In the corner where the conservatory joined the house, there was a small patio set, with an overflowing ashtray on the table. He patted his pockets, and I offered him one of mine.

'You don't look like a regular policeman,' he said. She said. That voice was playing tricks with my head.

'I'm not. This is a joint operation, and DCI Morton is in charge today. I have just one question for you: did the Count say why he gave you that name? Fae Klass?'

'Who's a clever boy, then? You must know something.' He crossed his legs in a totally feminine way and opened his big eyes in my direction.

I kept my face straight. 'Did he?'

Kirk shrugged. 'Something to do with winding up his family. *The People*, he called them. Big Wayne and Auntie Iris always called me *Miss Klass*. It didn't make any difference to me. I quite liked being Fae Klass. Shame she's gone. How did you find me?'

'Ask DCI Morton. Better still, ask DC Fraser. She'll enjoy telling you.'

'Is she the tall one?' I nodded. 'Does the ninja even have a name?'

He clearly loved romance, in all its forms. 'Lieutenant Kent. She's part of a new all-female special forces unit. It's a good job you didn't put up a fight.'

He shivered. Not a scared shiver. A shiver of anticipation. 'Ooh. I'll remember that.'

I stood up. 'Where did you have the surgery? They did a good job.'

'The voice, sweetie? That wasn't surgery. If you go under the knife, they shorten the vocal chords with scar tissue. Not good for a singer. The Count sent me to a woman he knows. Therapy and drugs. It's already starting to wear off.' A shiver of pain, real pain this time, passed over his face. 'The withdrawal was terrible.' Kirk stood up and followed me back inside. 'I don't even know what it was they gave me, so I couldn't try to score some of my own.'

'Oh? What did they call it?'

'Fairy dust, he called it. Said it was our secret.'

Elaine was in the kitchen zone and didn't hear us. Karina had been keeping an eye on me and heard every word. She'd certainly heard the last part and looked visibly distressed. The only problem was that she didn't look at Kirk with sympathy, she looked at me. Either she had real difficulty with empathy or she was re-living a trauma all of her own.

Tom emerged from the living room and said, 'It's a bit cosy in there, Conrad. Would you mind if Karina sat this one out?'

'We'll leave the door ajar.'

Morton wasn't wrong. The living room had a big TV on a stand, a comfy couch and a mismatched old armchair. And that was it, seating-wise. I grabbed a dining chair and plonked it in front of the TV. Elaine and Morton took the couch, and Kirk settled in the armchair. Karina deposited matching mugs of tea and slipped out.

'I was asking Kirk about his surgery when we were outside,' I said, just to clear the air. 'The Count paid for it all.'

'Thanks, Conrad. I'll make a note,' said Morton. He didn't; he looked at his notebook and smiled at Kirk. 'Just to be clear, Mr Liddington, this is a completely informal interview. You are a witness. That doesn't mean it's not official, just that nothing you say will be used against you, because I'm not going to give you the Caution. You know the one, *You have the right to remain silent*. None of that. Just tell us what you know and we'll produce a statement for you to sign later. Is that clear.'

'Yeah.'

'Then I'll cut to the chase. Is Kenneth Williams, also known as the Count of Canal Street dead?'

Tears were already forming. 'Yes, he's gone, and yes, I saw it happen.'

'Then you tell us, in your own words, what happened that night.'

Kirk shook his head. 'It feels like it happened to someone else. To Fae, not to me.'

'So tell it like that.'

13 — Mayfly

'Thank you. Thank you all. I've felt so much love from you tonight. I'm blessed. Goodnight.'

Fae Bowed one last time and retreated off the stage, waving and not turning her back on the audience until the lights had dimmed. She grabbed the handrail and hitched up her dress to get down the steep concrete steps that marked the boundary between the intimate spotlights of the club and the bland wash of LEDs backstage. She paused at the bottom and closed her eyes, taking a moment to let the tingles subside and the adrenaline to stop pumping.

On the stage, JC took the mic and whipped up the audience again, ready for the next act: *Girls Alewd*. Fae kept her eyes closed as five sets of heels clattered up the stairs. They weren't a real tribute act, just a handful of the house troupe who would mime a couple of songs with the lights up while the audience went to the bar and the toilets. It was midnight, and the Count never put the best acts on after midnight. Fae opened her eyes and headed down the corridor before the music started.

The smell of discount perfume and chemical punch from the club faded and was replaced by sweat and hairspray when she opened the door to the dressing room. Lamé, sequins and nylon hung from every hanger and boy clothes were piled on top of boxes and bags. Fae checked that her own outfits were still where they should be, and then she felt the tingle down her spine that told her *he* was there, behind her. She stood up and composed herself before turning round.

'You were brilliant,' said the Count. 'As always. I'm not paying you enough, clearly.'

She glided across the dressing room and put her satin gloved hands on his shoulders. 'You're not paying me at all. Was I that good?'

He gathered her in, and the aroma of earth and musk filled her nostrils. He smelled so good she could drink him in all night. He ran his hands down her back and his mouth dropped to her neck. She felt his teeth rub along her skin, teasing her. 'Oh yes,' he whispered. 'You were very good. And you're going to be even better at the Well. I've heard that the judge is coming. She asked for you especially.'

Better and better, Fae couldn't wait to get to the Well of Desire and change into something less comfortable. It was going to be a night to remember.

The Count pulled back and turned to the corridor. The black shape of Big Wayne loomed behind him. Wayne's coarser jacket fitted his enormous shoulders as closely as the Count's silk one did. They even had the same tailor. Fae had been sharing the Count's bed, his bathroom and his many adventures for six months, and yet the people the Count was closest to in the world were Big Wayne and his live-in PA / housekeeper, "Auntie Iris". He was even close to the mysterious Scouse bitch he called *The Management*. He'd once joked that the voice belonged to Tara Doyle. No way.

Big Wayne cleared his throat before speaking. 'Sorry, my lord. We've got a bit of a problem with the Rolls – it's been clamped. Someone must have forgotten to put the protection on it.'

The Count laughed. 'Someone? You mean me, don't you. I must have been in a rush. What's the weather like? I fancy a walk.'

'It's not raining. Still cold, though.'

'Here,' said the Count. He hooked his silk-lined cape off the coat rack and wrapped it round Fae's shoulders.

'Expenses,' said Wayne, offering the Count a brown envelope. 'Four thousand.'

The Count took it and weighed it. 'I've still got five in the safe.' He handed the envelope to Fae. 'Yours. Whatever you do, don't spend it wisely.'

Fae took the money and rooted through the pile of clothes for her knock-off Chanel bag; she had the real thing in her dressing room at the Count's flat, along with a Di Sanuto. He'd promised her a Di Sanuto Exclusive for Christmas, but only if she was a bad girl. She checked that her phone and lipstick were in there and shoved the envelope to the bottom. 'Shall we?'

The Count swept her out into the cold and held her arm until they got to the canal path. It was a thin, sharp wind tonight, giving them a real Lancashire welcome after the overheated stage. Fae wrapped the cloak more tightly around her, loving the feel of the silk on her arms above the gloves.

The path next to the canal was pretty wide normally. Just ahead, yet another old building was being dragged into the twenty-first century as part of Manchester's never-ending property boom, and the scaffolding encroached well over half way to the railings that protected drunks from a late night dip in the freezing waters. In the narrow gap, Fae saw two of tonight's audience.

The Gardens hosted a lot of hen parties, especially on a Friday, and these two were part of a group of eight, seven dressed in bright red fancy-dress cabin crew costumes and one in a fancy-dress bridal gown. All of them had white sashes across their shoulders, emblazoned with the words *Trolley Dollies on Tour: Leah's Hen*. Fae had spoken to them after her first set and the chief bridesmaid, a tall woman with a German accent, said that they really were cabin crew. The costumes were supposed to be ironic. They certainly got a lot of attention.

As they got closer to the hens by the canal railings, Fae could see shadows under the scaffolding, behind the builder's barrier. The bride-to-be was on her knees, throwing up in the gutter while the chief bridesmaid held back her hair. Par for the course on a hen night.

The two in the open air were struggling to light cigarettes. They were struggling because they had false nails and they simply weren't used to them in the everyday world of boarding passes, safety demos and drinks carts. When one of them saw Fae and the Count, she looked up and said, "Ere, you haven't got a light, have you?' And then she nudged her companion. 'Suze, look who it is! Fae Klass and the Count.'

'Ladies,' said the Count. 'Allow me.' He produced a lighter from nowhere, like a magician, and lit their cigarettes.

Another two hens drifted out from the darkness when they heard the voices. 'Wow, you were great tonight! Can I have a selfie with you?' she said, reaching into her bag for a phone.

'I want one with the Count,' said one of the smokers.

'And me,' said another.

There was a bit of jostling as they got into position, and Fae nearly stuck her stiletto through one of the hen's flip-flops.

Flip-flops?

She looked down at their feet. Not one of them was wearing the heels they'd had on in the club. They'd all got changed into flip-flops, ripping the ends of their tights to get the rubber thongs between their toes. But where were the shoes?

'Now!' screamed the German bridesmaid, and the hens under the scaffolding parted. Behind them, black shapes appeared, charging forwards. Fae froze.

The two hens who'd been taking a selfie with her didn't freeze: they dragged her away from the Count, just as the two women with him pinned his arms to his side.

Four shapes shot out of the darkness in two pairs. Each pair was carrying a long pole like a caber. Instead of tossing them, they brought them down with a vicious swipe, deliberately missing the Count and the hens and smashing the poles into the top railing with a ringing crash of steel on steel. It was all happening so quickly that Fae's brain couldn't catch up with what she was seeing.

The two hens on the Count let go of his arms and dropped to the floor, mud splashing their outfits and crawling between the legs of the men. They'd rehearsed this. They knew what they were doing.

Freed from the trolley dollies, The Count raised his arms, but the bride and her chief bridesmaid were approaching, *and they were carrying fucking flares. Fucking lit flares.* The Count backed into the railings, and two more men appeared with a third pole. They put it on the ends of the other two, making a square with the railings, and trapping the Count inside.

Why doesn't he fight? thought Fae. She knew exactly how strong the Count was, and she'd seen him in the gym, punching and hitting the bag like a pro, so why wasn't he fighting? The men holding the poles weren't even men, really, probably boys: they were all short, well shorter than most of the hens, and had ski-masks over their features. And their hands were full of metal pole. Surely a jab to the throat and the Count would be away?

Instead of fighting, the Count screamed and clutched his hands to his head. Nothing was touching him, but the pain in his voice made Fae feel like his face was being peeled off. Two more men emerged from the shadows, and when Fae saw the javelins they were carrying, she knew it was time to get out.

She pushed one of the hens holding her and this time she really did bring her stiletto down on the woman's foot. When the hen let go, Fae swivelled and jabbed the second woman in the eye. Then she ran.

She got round the corner before the other hens reacted. Hide or run for safety? The thought of waiting behind a dumpster for them to find her was unbearable. Fae ran.

She had one chance, and high-stepped it away from the main streets and into an alley. She couldn't take her heels off without stopping and stripping her gloves: the shoes were strapped to her feet and going nowhere on their own. Down the alley and turn left.

'There she is!'

As well as slowing her to a parody of running, the heels clattered out her location to the pack behind her. Right into the next back street.

The slap of flip-flops followed her. A glance over her shoulder. At least those fancy dresses were slowing them down. Not enough. Fae kept running and one of them dived at her in a rugby tackle.

And landed flat on her face with an armful of the Count's cloak. Fae staggered from the impact and bounced into the wall. She looked back, and the other one was too close. The hen grabbed Fae and tried to pinion her arms while her friend got up. Fae wrestled her left arm free and tried to grab the woman, but her gloves slipped off the nylon. She bent forward and tried to bite her arm as the other hen closed in.

The first one moved her arm out of the way and did what came naturally to her: she grabbed a big handful of Fae's hair and pulled it down. Hard.

When the wig ripped off her head, putting the hen off balance, Fae pulled her right arm back and smashed the heel of her hand into the woman's nose. She felt it crunch and heard the scream.

There were more on the way, and Fae had to get out. The second hen was a bit warier, just enough to give Fae the courage to move towards her. She ran, but she'd be back. Fae pivoted and got out of the alley with a prayer bubbling on her lips: *Please, let him be on duty.*

She turned right and saw the ugly face she'd been dreaming of standing outside the district's seediest nightclub. It was a face from Blackpool, a face she'd reconnected with last month, a face that knew who she really was.

'Fae? What's wrong?' said the doorman.

'Let me through, for pity's sake, and don't let in any trolley dollies, OK?'

He pulled the door open and said, 'Go through the cloakroom and keep going. Back entrance is straight ahead on your right.'

Keep going. That was all she could do. Keep going past the cloakroom boy, through the Staff Only door, down the corridor and, *smash*, through the exit into an alley with no access from the warren of streets where she'd left the hens. Keep going.

Out of the alley, round the corner, round another and into a tiny square. There. Third on the right.

It was a four storey, grimy Victorian boarding house with no questions asked for those with cash. Even if Jana-from-Estonia wasn't there, she could hide in the stairwell. No lift, of course, so hitch up the dress and wake everyone as she clumped up the stairs. Second floor, Room 203.

'Who is it?'

'It's me. Fae Klass. Acie Decie. Kirk. Please, Jana.'

The woman opened the door and let her in. She looked at the blood, the smeared makeup and the bare head, and fear blossomed in her eyes. Jana knew violence intimately from the receiving end thanks to her father and a lot of men since.

'Two minutes and I'll be gone,' said Fae. 'Just call me a taxi and give me some trainers. Please. They don't know where I am, but I can't be seen on the streets.'

Jana stepped on to the landing and listened. When she heard nothing, she nodded to Fae and closed the door behind her. 'Take what you want.'

It was one room originally, made into a studio room by a tiny toilet/shower space built into one of the corners. Fae sat on the edge of the bed, near a neat stack of shoes, and peeled off her gloves. She looked at her feet, and there was red running up from inside the left shoe. When she'd managed to get the straps off and loosened the shoe, only her tights were holding her little toenail in place. Ugh. She grabbed the comfiest looking pair of trainers and gritted her teeth before shoving her feet in.

She took her phone out of her bag just as it started to ring: Big Wayne.

'Hello, Wayne, something terrible…'

The screen showed Wayne's name, and another: PBirk. The Management.

'What have you done?' said the woman, her voice a mixture of pain and fury. 'What have you done to him, you little bitch?'

Fae was stunned. How did they know? 'Nothing. We were attacked. Ambushed.'

'Where are you? Wayne? Go and get her.'

122

Fae had already disconnected before Wayne could answer. She dropped the phone on the floor and grabbed her shoe. She gripped the toe and smashed the heel into the screen time and time again, until it got stuck inside. She yanked it free and ran to the micro-bathroom where she threw the phone in the toilet. There. Take that, you bastards.

'Taxi will be here in one minute,' said Jana. 'You can wait downstairs.'

'Thanks. Thanks so much. I won't forget this,' said Fae, flinging her arms round the woman's shoulders for a second. She reached into her bag and took sixty pounds out of the wad of cash.

'This is for the trainers. You can keep the shoes and sell them on eBay for a couple of hundred, easy. Stop panicking, Jana, I'm off.'

Fae saw something else she needed sitting on the desk that doubled as kitchen counter and dining table. She grabbed the packet of cigarettes and lighter and shoved them in her bag.

When she got to the bottom of the stairs, she could hear the taxi's diesel engine rumbling outside. With a quick check down the street, she dived into the back and passed forty pounds to the driver. 'Head for Bolton Station.'

14 — Cherchez le Gnome

It took us two hours to get Kirk/Fae's story into order. We had breaks for tea, tears and cigarettes, not to mention several calls from Amy, worried about her little brother. One thing that was both really obvious and inexplicable (at first) was that Kirk's voice dropped a good octave during the interview. Inexplicable until Karina told me that being around human magick hastens the metabolisation of Fae dust, the "drug" that Kirk had been fed to change his voice and enhance his aura on stage. It had also saved his life: giving him the power to smash women in the nose and shatter their metatarsals with high heels.

Morton handled the interview much better than I could have. He rarely interrupted and asked few questions when Kirk was in full flow, saving them for breaks and the beginning of a session. Here are some of the questions and answers that came out of further probing:

Morton: What did you do when you got to Bolton Station?
Kirk: Got a coffee and waited until the first train to Preston at half past five in the morning. I spent an hour in a homeless shelter until the real psychos came in and started hassling me.

Morton: Why didn't Wayne mention the PA, Auntie Iris?
Kirk: How should I know? She used to keep the drugs. Goodness knows where she got them, because she never left the flat.
Morton: What drugs?
Kirk: Poppers, G, weed, coke and the special stuff for my vocal chords.

Morton: When you said "The Judge", did you mean a real judge?
Kirk: Not going there. Never going there. Not saying a word about the Well of Desire.
Morton: We'll leave it there. For now.
Kirk: Now and forever more.

Elaine: Why do you call him Big Wayne?
Kirk (with a smirk): Why do you think?

Me: Are you sure there were eight men?
Kirk: I think so.
Me: Think carefully. Very carefully.

Kirk (after some thought): I definitely saw eight. 100%. There might have been eight thousand in the shadows, though.

Me: And eight women?

Kirk: Same. I'm sure there were eight.

Morton (giving me a strange look): Where were the women from? Any clues? Did they use names?

Kirk: Like I said, the bride was Leah. She said she was from Essex. The chief bridesmaid was German. I heard her speak in German to one of the others. Just one. The rest were all English. English and Irish. The German lass said they all flew out of Manchester.

Morton: Can you describe the men?

Kirk: No. They were all short and wearing black. Oh, yeah, they all had bits of white skin showing, and when I'd calmed down, I reckoned I was wrong. They were too broad to be kids, really.

We had to leave it somewhere, and Morton called a halt when it looked like Kirk might faint from hunger. I was feeling the same way.

At the end, Morton passed over the top grade iPhone that Wayne had given him. 'I've checked it,' said Morton. 'There are no tracking apps or anything, and you can do a full reset on it. I think they wanted you to have it.'

Kirk took the phone and held it like a contaminated specimen. He turned to me. 'Is it safe to get in touch with them?'

'Not yet,' I said. 'I don't think they mean you any harm, but they're desperate to know what you know. It may not be safe for you to tell anyone yet. We'll talk to them and let you know what happens. Don't worry, Kirk, we won't leave you hanging, and believe me, you are ten times safer now you've spoken to us.'

He frowned. 'How come?'

'Because you are an innocent victim, which protects you from the People, and you can't identify the attackers directly, so that protects you from the assassins.'

He didn't look convinced. I don't blame him.

By unspoken agreement, we walked in silence to the car park, and Karina surprised me by being the one to break it.

'While you were talking, I looked up places to eat. There is a place called the _____ _____ nearby that scores very highly on Trip Advisor. It has cask conditioned beer and steak pie.'

Elaine looked in her handbag. Morton looked at his car keys. 'What about you?' I said.

Karina blinked. Twice. 'I can eat vegetarian. They have options.'

'Sounds good. See you there, Tom.'

'Right.'

As soon as I'd turned on the engine and Karina had entered the postcode into the Satnav, I said, 'Well. What do you think?'

'I think the attack was carried out under a Glamour. I don't think we can trust what he said.'

I pulled slowly out of the car park behind Morton's BMW. 'Why not?'

'Because it sounds like Gnomes did it. I can't believe that. It must be other Fae who are trying to set up the Gnomes.'

'Take a leaf out of Tom Morton's book, Karina. Consider the evidence.'

She waved her hands in a complicated pattern of magick, and a small garden gnome appeared on the dashboard. Or the illusion of one did.

'What value can we put on mundane evidence?' she said. The gnome vanished.

'A good point, and you have to weigh that in the balance. What evidence do we have that definitely isn't Glamoured?'

She struggled for a moment, and I had to remind myself that she was greener than the grass at Middleforth Green. The Socratic method might not be appropriate here.

'The women,' I said. 'They were definitely human, or Fae Klass wouldn't have escaped. The People wouldn't use humans like that. At least one of the trolley dollies pursuing Fae would have been Fae. If you see what I mean. Shall we just call him Kirk for the avoidance of doubt?'

She nodded.

'And there's the method. That's exactly how a gang of Gnomes would have acted. I'll bet that method has never been used before. It's ingenious and it solves several problems at once, both very Gnomish characteristics.'

She looked upset. 'I wouldn't know. I've never met a Gnome.'

'What? Never? Not even when you were Handmaiden to Oma Bridget?'

'They're not welcome in the Forest. For obvious reasons. And she never took me with her when she went to see them. The Foresters didn't have much to do with them.'

Of course. The Arden Foresters were very close to the Fae Prince of Arden, and he wouldn't be happy with Gnomes sniffing round his domain.

A flash of excitement crossed her face. 'I remember now. Boss Hannah said you had a Gnome at your party. She even showed me a picture.'

'She did? How did that come up in conversation?'

Karina looked puzzled, as if she hadn't wondered why a senior officer was going around showing pictures of a Bollywood party. 'I don't know.' She shook her head as if the question were irrelevant. 'Do you carry the Clan Sword with you?'

'It's in the back, in the weapons cabinet. It's too big to take anywhere unless the threat level is high, as Tom Morton would say. I'll show you when we're back at the Haven.'

'He's creepy.'

126

'Who? Tom? What makes you say that?'

'It's the way he knows what people are thinking.'

'It's a bloody good job he doesn't really know, or we'd be up shit creek without a paddle. He's a very good detective, that's all.' We followed the man himself into a car park. 'Right, Karina, it's show time.'

'Sorry?'

'I've got to lie my way out of a very sticky corner. Feel free to back me up at any point.'

'I'm not very good at lying. Sorry.'

'Don't be sorry. I'm very good at lying, and who's the one with a smashed leg? Are you going to have a drink?'

She brightened up a little when I said that. 'If I say no, will I have to drive back?'

'Yes.'

'I'll have mineral water, thanks.'

Her first answer was the mildest bit of banter you could imagine, and I wouldn't have reported it normally. What made me tell you is that I'd swear she was repeating a line from some TV show that she'd learnt by heart, and her smile had come from finding a chance to use it. I knew she wouldn't be drinking, because she'd eaten the beef bourguignon but refused the burgundy that went with it.

We got out of the car, and I would have gone for a cigarette if I hadn't seen the predatory look in Elaine Fraser's eye. She would love to get Karina on her own and give her the third degree. Poor kid wouldn't know what had hit her.

We had to hunt around for a table with some privacy and spent a minute ordering. I sent Karina to the bar and settled back. 'While we wait, I was wondering, Tom, how do you access the electoral roll without going through the police?'

I half expected him to scowl and think this was a wind-up. That he didn't, I took as a good sign. 'Do you have a tame hacker?'

'I'd rather not use his services on this one.'

'Then you just walk into the nearest public library to your target and ask to look at it. And prepare to get a funny look from the librarian. They're a suspicious bunch.'

'Thanks.'

'Mmm,' said Elaine, sucking diet Pepsi through a straw. 'That reminds me. Who the hell is Myfanwy Lewis and why is she living in your house?'

'And why is there no trace of her on the system until this year?' added Morton, with just enough menace to let me know the long arm of the law could stretch down to Gloucestershire if it wanted to.

'You tell them, Karina.'

She nearly choked on her mineral water and she blinked furiously before saying, without punctuation, 'She's Conrad's best friend's fiancée and his housekeeper and his gardener and she does the cricket team with Mina and she grows cannabis and she's under house arrest for conspiracy to release a Dragon.'

She paused, drew breath and went red. 'InthenameoftheGoddess no she isn't.'

Elaine's mouth had dropped slightly open; Morton retained more decorum. 'No she isn't what?' he asked with the mildest of airs. Karina's jaws clamped shut.

'The cannabis belongs to my little sister,' I said. 'Myfanwy is only guilty of not digging it up. She didn't plant it.'

'Mmm,' said Morton. 'The quiche is going to be a while, so you've got plenty of time to tell us what the hell is going on. I take it that you believe our witness, that the Count really was murdered by javelin wielding assassins?'

I moved my pint glass further away from me. 'Yes I do. Every word, pretty much.'

'So do I. He left a few things out, of course, but I believe him. So, in that case, who are the People?' He sat back and smiled. He was looking forward to this.

'The People are just that: people. It's the translation of a word in their own language. Imagine you were in New York, Tom,' I said. 'Imagine you were some sort of law enforcement supremo. Sheriff, perhaps.'

He managed to keep a straight face. 'In New York it would be captain or Chief of Detectives, but go on. I'm intrigued.'

'Some Russians come to you. Russians who are just this side of the line when it comes to criminality.'

'Russians who call themselves *The People*. I can go with that.'

'They've come to you because one of their number has been assassinated. There's been pressure internally for them to settle it themselves, but the patriarch says no, we can't be legit and undertake vendettas.'

Morton leaned forwards again. 'Are you saying that's what happened? You were called in because there might be a chain of reprisals?'

'Yes. This is not about a cover-up, Tom. This is about avoiding violence, which is why the People mustn't know what Fae Klass saw that night. Not until we're ready to tell them.'

'I see.'

'Let me take it further. Imagine you came across a tape recording of the assassination, and on the tape recording, the killers speak nothing but Calabrese. What would you think?'

'I'd think *What's Calabrese?*' said Elaine. 'Unless they're talking broccoli, which I doubt. You fed me Calabrese once, didn't you, Tom? He's a bit of a foodie, is our DCI.'

'It's a dialect of Calabria, southern Italy. South of Naples,' said Morton. His hand was already under his jacket, rubbing the top of his left arm. His eyes met mine, and I looked down. He flinched and drew his hand out. 'I'd think 'Ndrangheta, that's what I'd think. I'd also think that the recording could be a plant or a bluff. And that there are many 'Ndrangheta families.'

'So you can see my position. I need to proceed with extreme caution and pass this one up to the Boss before I even plan an approach.'

Elaine frowned. 'Just to be 100% clear, you're not talking actual Italians and Russians here, are you, Conrad? You two are doing my head in with this code.'

'Sorry. I wish we were dealing with real Calabrese,' I said. 'Here comes the food.'

When we'd started on our food, Morton went back to some of the loose ends.

'They may not have been dealing drugs at the Fairy Gardens, but what about the other place? The Well of Desire? Talking of which, who are you trying to protect there?'

Elaine had her two pennyworth as well. 'And what's this business with Kirk's voice. I've never heard anyone's voice go that high. It was bloody creepy at first.'

I had a particularly juicy bit of steak on my fork at the time, and I waved it round in a circle. 'It's all connected,' I said. I popped the beefy chunk in my mouth and chewed thoroughly. 'And this is the real reason MI7 are involved.' I pointed my empty fork between Morton and Elaine. 'Which of you gets the short straw this weekend? Who's going to be searching the CCTV for Trolley Dollies on Tour?'

Elaine blushed and held her hand up. 'That would be me.'

'Then watch carefully. I'd be very surprised if you see them. Try and watch for the gaps.'

Her face creased into incomprehension. 'You what?'

'This was an assassination. They knew exactly what they were doing, didn't they?'

Morton nodded. 'They certainly clamped the Count's Rolls. They knew he'd have to walk. I bet there was a plan B in case he didn't walk along the canal.'

'Precisely. They would have visited the Gardens in advance and known where all the CCTV was, and that's why they wore the sashes.' I gave them a steady look. 'The Calabrese are specialists in technology; the People are at the cutting edge in genetics and pharmaceuticals.'

'You're joking,' said Elaine. 'A trashy hen party sash isn't going to fool CCTV cameras.'

I looked at Morton. 'You've talked to Commander Ross, haven't you?'

He nodded, and it was his turn to use his fork to point at me. 'Conrad's associates caused a coffin, complete with corpse, to appear in a locked police compound with no forensic evidence whatsoever, never mind CCTV.' He put the fork down before turning to Karina. 'And that's your brief, isn't it, Karina?'

She nodded. I crossed my fingers under the table for her. When she spoke, I could almost hear a North London accent. 'Conrad isn't safe to be let out on his own. He's a total liability and I'm his minder.'

I sighed inwardly. Another item to put on the list for discussion with Hannah.

'What my comrade is trying to say,' I said, 'is that the Calabrese used technology to jam the Count's mobile signal. Hence the poles. There was just enough time for a distress call to get away, which is what Saerdam Wayne was trying not to tell you.'

Elaine nodded thoughtfully. 'Makes sense. Doesn't explain the javelins, though.'

'No, it doesn't. That's down to ethnic traditions. I think. Along with the way they disposed of the body. You don't want to know about that. Any more questions?'

Morton looked at Elaine. She shook her head. 'Not for now,' he said.

'Then I'll follow up what I can,' I said. 'Shall we agree to meet on Monday unless I message you otherwise? I'll decide on the venue when I know more.'

'Busy weekend?' said Elaine. 'Mina coming up?'

'She is. I can't believe it's only three days since she left. Seems a lot longer.'

Morton couldn't resist it. 'Aren't you used to separation and limited physical contact?'

Elaine gave him a dark look. 'Don't go there, sir.' She turned to Karina. 'Are you in a relationship?'

Karina shook her head and stared at her empty glass. It was time to go.

Karina and I left via the beer garden, where I nipped into the smoking shelter and Karina stood well clear. It was time to put the Fae, Gnomes, Russians and Calabrese behind us and focus on important things. 'Have you decided what to wear for Saturday's trip to Manchester?'

She frowned. 'What do you mean?'

'What do you think I mean? We're meeting the Malchs. You, me and Mina. I know I only mentioned it in passing, but you can't have forgotten.'

'No, of course I haven't forgotten. You said it wasn't an occasion for uniform so I'm going to wear my Forester robes.'

'Not on public transport, you're not. I told you: we're doing a park-and-ride from Stockport.'

'So? I'll put a Glamour on.' She shrugged. 'What are you going to do about the Gnomes?'

'It's up to the Boss. I'll ask her when we report in tonight.'

'Won't she want to know before then?'

It was my turn to shrug. Expansively. 'No one's life is at risk. She trusts me, even if she does think I'm a total liability.'

Karina frowned. 'She said that, but I don't think she meant it. Not really.'

There was nothing I could say to that without wading into a swamp of irony, empathy and motivational psychology. One thing I was certain of was that Hannah would not be my first phone call tonight.

'Let's go, Karina. No shop talk on the way back.'

'So what are we going to talk about?'

I gritted my teeth. 'Whatever you want.' Under my breath, I repeated the mantra: *Anything but the bloody Dragon. Anything but the bloody Dragon. Anything but...*

'Can you tell me again about the Dragon?'

'Of course I can. What do you want to know?'

Tom Morton watched carefully as Clarke and Karina left the pub by the side door and turned towards the beer garden. When they were out of sight, he hurried Elaine along and went not to his car but Clarke's. He walked round it, taking a good look inside and stopping by the number plate.

'Look,' he said. He squatted down and tickled his fingernail under the edge. A tiny corner of clear plastic film came loose. 'Clarke has form when it comes to false number plates. I'm sure this is the real one because he knows I'll check, but I'll bet he's got a stash of false indices inside the car, ready to use when he wants to stay off our radar.'

He stood up and looked inside again. 'I'll bet they're in that locked steel box. You can just see it under the dog blanket.'

Elaine followed his gaze. 'Looks like a secure gun cupboard to me. All in order.'

'I know, but look at the size of it. You don't need that for a handgun. Let's go before he appears.'

'I think Conrad Clarke is a bad influence on you,' said Elaine when they got back to their car. 'That's twice this week you've had chips for lunch, and it's only Thursday. If he rattles you that much, why did you agree to take the case?'

Tom started the engine and tried to suppress his irritation. The trouble with giving people the right to speak their mind is that they sometimes use it. A bit like democracy, really.

131

When he didn't answer straight away, Elaine went even further. 'And you've rubbed your scar more since he reappeared in your life than you have for months.'

'You're right. He literally gets under my skin. I thought about that all the way back to Southport after the trip to the Fairy Gardens. I think I know the real answer now.'

'And are you going to share? Just so I know why I've ended up on the wrong side of the looking glass.'

'It's not going to sound good, I'm afraid. I may need your forgiveness on this one. I think I took the case for two reasons. First, to save some other poor sod from having to work with him. He did need a crack team of detectives to find Fae Klass, and his lot seem to have the sort of budget we can only dream about. They're paying Leonie a fortune for our time, and I couldn't inflict Conrad Clarke on some unsuspecting colleague.'

'Don't I count?'

'No.' He grinned at her. 'You knew what you were letting yourself in for when you didn't ask for a transfer after the Sevenbridge case. And didn't you spot that I called us a crack team of detectives?'

'I know we are. What's the other reason you took the case?'

He concentrated on the road for a while until they came to rest at some lights before the M6 junction. 'I wanted to see if he'd really turned gamekeeper or if he was still a loose cannon.'

'Tom, that metaphor was bad. Even by your standards. And what's the verdict?'

'I think he's a bit like that dog of his: useful if kept on a tight leash. From what I've heard of Hannah Rothman, she'll do exactly that. A bit like what I imagine went on at the Well of Desire. I should think that there were a lot of collars and leashes there.'

She groaned. 'I so wish you hadn't said that. I do not want that image in my head. Do you reckon we'll ever hear from Clarke again now that we've found his witness?'

'If we don't, there's always the nuclear option.'

'Now you're scaring me.'

'Did you notice Clarke's phone? It didn't have GPS. He won't have it because he thinks people will track him. I don't think he's plucked up the courage to tell Karina that, because she used it to find the pub. We can always track her. I get the impression that Clarke's going to keep her very close while they're on duty.'

'You're not joking. I still can't get over the way she tackled Kirk Liddington. You'd have been proud to put in a tackle like that. Even Rob would have given her full marks, to say nothing of the way she vaulted over that fence. I'd swear she had springs in her trainers. I went through the gate.'

'I'll bear that in mind. And then there's the Dragon. Did you notice that Clarke denied that Ms Lewis was guilty of growing cannabis and ignored the Dragon. It was the thing that Karina was most guilty about mentioning.'

'I think you're imagining things, sir. Should we ask for a report from the Cheltenham CID?'

He sighed. Clarke really had got under his skin, and yet the man seemed genuinely concerned about this case. Clarke was handling the investigation as if it were an unstable explosive, and Tom didn't want to knock him off balance. 'We'll leave it for now. At least we can have the weekend off. I'll help you with the CCTV tomorrow, then I'm taking Lucy to the Cloister for the weekend.' He glanced at Elaine, whose face had gone neutral as soon as Lucy was mentioned. 'I'll have a word with Dad about the judges on the Lancashire circuit.'

Elaine grinned. 'Oh yes? To see who might have a membership card for the Well of Desire tucked in their purse?'

'Without spelling it out, of course.'

'Of course.'

15 — Duty of Care

Scout bounced up to the car windows like he was on a trampoline as soon as we got back to Middlebarrow Haven. Evie heard the barking and came out to say hello.

'How's he been?' I asked.

'He spent half an hour sniffing around looking for you then came to pester me. It's a good job I needed to clear my head at lunchtime, so we went for a walk. He calmed down a bit after that.' She dropped her voice to a whisper. 'I am not doing that again in a hurry unless it's an emergency. There's a doggy day-care place just up the road. I looked.'

'Point taken. Thanks Evie.'

I turned to Karina, 'I'll get myself a flask and take him out for a long walk, or we won't have any peace tonight. You can start writing the report.'

She looked appalled. 'Me? What if I make a mess of it?'

Evie snorted and said, 'I'll put the kettle on.'

'Yes, Karina, you are going to write the report, and when you've gone to bed tonight, I shall read it through carefully.'

'But what do I put in? What do I leave out?'

Oh dear. This could be more of a hurdle than I thought. 'Try to imagine that we disappear in a puff of smoke and Vicky has to take over. What does she need to know? And Iain Drummond, what does he need to know if there's going to be a case in the Cloister Court?'

She put on a brave face. 'Right. Is it okay if I go to the altar first?'

'Of course.'

She left to get changed and I went to make some tea. When Scout and I left the Haven, I went in the opposite direction to the grove. I had some phone calls to make and I didn't want Karina sneaking up on us for hunting practice. I gave Scout a good long walk, then found a tree to sit under while I poured my tea and got out my phone. As I said, the first call was not to the Boss, it was to Oma Bridget.

The leader of the Arden Foresters is Oma ("Grandmother") Bridget, who really is a grandmother. Her son is my friend, Chris Kelly, the Earthmaster of Salomon's House; they have a difficult relationship.

'Conrad,' she said. 'I'm surprised it's taken this long for you to call me. Karina's been with you for over a week.'

'She's been with me for two days. Did Hannah call you?'

'The Constable? No. How is Karina doing? If I didn't know that you have her interests at heart, and that your job can be very dangerous, we wouldn't be having this conversation.'

'Thank you, Oma. She's doing her best, I'll say that. What can you tell me about her? We were working with a mundane but very astute detective today, and he thinks she might be autistic.'

'And what does that mean? We're not in favour of labels like that in the Foresters.'

There aren't many in the RAF on the autism spectrum, partly because the medical form specifically says you can't join if you have it, and I know that because I had a class 1 medical in the summer and read all the exclusions. Even so, the few people I've met who are on the spectrum all said that their lives became a lot easier after they were diagnosed. However, that was not a conversation for today.

'How did she get on while she was your handmaiden? Why did you choose her?'

I could almost hear her shifting in her comfy chair by the fireplace in Foresters' Hall. 'This really is between us, Conrad? You won't put it in a report and fire her?'

'I want her to succeed. I also want both of us to stay alive.'

'I understand.' She took a breath. 'I chose her because she was struggling to fit in to the advanced classes. She wasn't being bullied, as such, she just wasn't fitting in. Perhaps you should think about PTSD instead of autism, if you want a diagnosis. Losing her mother like that is bound to have a lasting effect. I thought that if she had the authority of being handmaiden she might have a chance to find her feet.

'I got her brother, Colwyn, to mentor her, and she did make progress. She's better than she was, it's just that she has a chronic need to fit in at the same time as finding social situations very difficult. Instead of hanging out with her peers, she preferred to wander in the Forest.'

I pulled my lip. There was no easy way to approach this. 'About the Forest. Just how much of a taste for Fae dust did she develop?'

'Why do you think I sent her on that pilgrimage? She had to complete it without forest manna, which is what we call it. I made sure she had stopped before I let her join you. As you've no doubt discovered, she takes her commitment to the Goddess very seriously, and I told her that forest manna is *not* a gift from Mother Nature.'

'That's good to know, Oma. Perhaps it's common knowledge in the Foresters, but I only have her file to go on, and it's pretty sparse. What happened to her mother?'

'She was killed when Karina was barely a few days old. That was in Kent, of course, hence her surname, and I know nothing of the details.'

Poor kid. No mother and an older father who hadn't planned to be in her life and who palmed her off to the Foresters when she hit puberty. Perhaps Oma Bridget had a point about PTSD vs autism.

I had one last question. 'Tell me, if you would, what did you find worked best with her?'

'Have you put her on the spot yet?'

'Yes.'

'Then you'll know it's not always the most successful approach. I wish I could help more, but I really believe that practice and patience are the keys.'

'And I am grateful for your honesty, Oma. If you don't mind me asking, how did it go with Chris and your granddaughters?'

'I do mind you asking, but you have the right. What did you say to his wife that allowed him to bring them here?'

'Me? Nothing. Mina may have said something.'

'Then I am grateful to her. It was horribly painful, Conrad. Only now do I truly realise what I've been missing. It makes the whole mess even more painful. I cannot, I will not have anything to do with that creature, yet she is the mother of three beautiful children. I have been praying for guidance. None has been forthcoming as yet.'

'How was Chris?'

'As torn apart as me. He only got through the visit by pretending to himself that they were orphans. I think that's what he does at work. I'm only telling you all this because you and Mina are the first to get inside their bubble. I'm sure the Goddess smiles on you both for that. And now I must go. May She walk by your side, Conrad.'

'Thank you, Oma.'

I looked down at Scout, who was taking a power-nap. 'What do you make of that, eh? Anything we can do?' He opened his eyes. 'Don't bother waking up, lad, I've got to talk to the Boss first.'

'What's up?' said Hannah. 'I was expecting you to Facetime me.'

'Later, if that's okay. This is a clear-the-air call with just you, me and Scout.'

She groaned. 'What misery are you going to heap on my head now?'

'We'll start with the pictures of the Bollywood party, the cannabis plants in Myfanwy's herb garden and, I quote, "Conrad isn't safe to be let out on his own. He's a total liability and I'm his minder." She actually said that to Tom Morton.'

There was a long silence. 'You know what, Conrad, I'm trying to feel guilty and failing. You recruited her, not me. I was just doing my best. I'm sorry that she spouted it to DCI Morton. That was out of order of her, and a lesson for both of us.'

'If she had said it to the Queen of Alderley, I might be bothered, but Tom knows me too well.'

'Apart from that, how was she?'

'She hasn't had to do much, yet. I won't say any more than that.'

'Fine. I know you'll take care. So what happened?'

'We have a lead, but I don't know what to make of it. I don't want to spoil the surprise, so I'll call you at six, if that's okay.'

'Make it six thirty. I'll make sure I'm at home.'

'Until then, ma'am.'

Later that evening, I was very glad I didn't tell her about the alleged Gnomish participation in advance. She couldn't have faked her reaction, which was to say, 'Karina, tell me he's joking.'

And do you know what Karina said?

'Not this time, ma'am.'

Hannah shook her head mournfully. 'This I do not need. Are you going to talk to your friend, Conrad?'

'I don't see any other option. If I go charging into the local clan with no more evidence than this, they might not let me out alive.'

'You're right. Tread very, very carefully. And have fun at the Institute.'

'We'll do our best.'

My final call that night was made from Scout's kennel, and it was to Mina. 'I can't wait to see you tomorrow. How's it going?'

'It's like deja vue, Conrad. Like being back at the accountancy practice when I had my own family, my own teeth and no knowledge of magick. At one point today I found myself talking about the mummified head of a Forest Elf. A mummified head with enhanced properties. I was treating it like a piece of art in a divorce case. I'm afraid I found it very funny.'

'Did you do many divorce cases?'

'A few. I was very good at finding the things that husbands don't want their wives to know about. Let that be a warning to you.'

'Consider me warned.'

'And then Marcia thought I was eating Myfanwy's hash cake when I started giggling. You know, Judge Bracewell has levels of scary that we can't even begin to imagine. If I thought I might have to face cross-examination from her, I'd quit my job now. I mean it. Having her as a boss is bad enough, never mind having her as an avenging angel. Tell me something about your day.'

'I need you to get in touch with Anna. I can't see anyone tapping her phone.'

'Of course. Why?'

'Tell her I need to have a totally untraceable, off-the-record conversation with Lloyd about a very serious matter.'

'This does not sound good, Conrad. What happened?'

When I'd finished telling her, she went quiet. 'I shall text Anna and tell her to meet me on my way up to see you tomorrow. I shall pretend it's to talk about our wedding.'

'Thanks. Talking of our wedding...'

You don't want to know the rest of the conversation. It would spoil the surprise. I did have one last thing to say before we said goodnight. 'I'm on a mission to the library tomorrow.'

'The Esoteric Library? Do they have a branch in the North?'

'No. The regular library. I need to consult the electoral roll.'

'Aah. Project Piers. Good luck.'

Thick grey clouds had settled over Stockport when we got on the train, and by the time we'd arrived at Manchester Piccadilly, it was chucking it down. Mina handed the oversized umbrella to Karina and said, 'He is too tall to keep me dry properly. You can hold it.'

'Yes, of course,' said Karina, jumping to it. Maybe when Mina is in full Rani mode, she sounds like Oma Bridget. I just stood in the open getting wet. One of the few good things about a receding hairline is that you don't mind the rain so much. At least we didn't have to wait long for the tram to Victoria station.

We were met by the current president of the Manchester Alchemical Society (Malchs). He stood just back from the queue waiting to get on and stepped forwards as soon as Karina had got the umbrella up again.

'Welcome to Manchester. We've even laid on some of our special weather for you.' He wasn't joking. Even on the short tram ride, it seemed to have got heavier.

Our host for the day was Seth Holgate. When Hannah had briefed me, she'd said, 'With Seth, what you see is pretty much what you get.' And what we saw was a tall, thick set man in his early sixties with a big, bushy beard, still mostly black and matching his collar length hair.

I shook hands and Mina made namaste. Karina looked too scared to let go of the umbrella and was going to settle for a nod until Seth reached out and pumped her hand vigorously.

He stood back and looked at us. 'What an assorted bunch you are. One god-favoured Mage, one from the Circles and an officer of the Cloister Court with no magick.' He laughed and smiled. 'You'll fit right in at Malchs. Come on, let's get out of this rain.' He turned and set off through the buildings, pointing to an open piece of ground. 'That's Cheetham School of Music. We've got part of their site, or they've got our old gardens, to be accurate. One of my predecessors made some unwise investments.'

The Malchs building was hidden in plain sight. It was set back slightly from the road and protected by tall iron railings with large gates set into them.

A notice on the railings said *Private Entrance. All enquiries to Cheetham's Library on Long Millgate.* Simple and effective. With a few additional Wards, of course. Seth pushed back the gates and held them open so we could enter without triggering them.

The home of the Manchester Alchemical Society was clearly modelled on the baroque excess of Salomon's House in London, toned down a little and slightly more regular in its proportions. It was also more decorated, with a golden statue of Athena standing watchfully over the pediment. For added security, she was joined by her owl, perched uncomfortably on her right shoulder. Seth saw me admiring it.

'Classic bloody compromise,' he said. 'The first President wanted the owl, the Council wanted Athena, so they ended up with both. I always wince when I see those claws digging into the poor lass's shoulder. Allow me.'

He closed his umbrella and used a powerful arm to pull open the doors. Mina dashed in, and through the whole journey I don't think a single drop of rain had got on to her hair. Karina followed, and the peasant dress Glamour vanished to reveal her Foresters robes. Unlike the Daughters of the Goddess, the Foresters' woollen habits are edged and embroidered, in Karina's case she had a small oak tree with buds and yellow Sprites flying around it to show that she had served as a handmaiden.

The entrance looked as if someone had planned something much bigger and been told to cut it in half. It had height and ran the full width of the building, but wasn't more than twenty feet deep. Half way up the far wall, a gallery landing had a lot of doors leading off it, accessed by matching marble staircases at either end. Underneath the gallery was a single pair of ornate, gilded doors in the original white. Again, unlike Salomon's House, the decoration was mostly white-painted wood and plaster and not dark oak. It certainly felt more civilised. The same sculptor who had inflicted the owl on Athena had produced bronzes of Hermes and Apollo to stand guard either side of the gilded doors.

'Excuse me one second,' said Seth. 'Put your brolly here, lass.' He tossed his umbrella in a bucket by the entrance doors. A bucket in the shape of a Dragon's foot. He moved down the windowed outside wall to a marble-topped console table with a gong next to it. 'Put a Silence on or cover your ears. I mean it – this thing's amplified.'

I held up my hand to forestall him while I took off my dripping wet Barbour. Then I did something I love doing: gathering Mina into my arms and holding her close while I made one of the few Works of magick I can manage, a Silence. Seth gave the gong three big blows and then stuck his thumb up.

I cancelled the Silence and Karina edged into our personal space to whisper, 'He called me a *lass*. Is he allowed to do that?'

'Have you never seen Coronation Street?' said Mina.

Karina shrugged. 'I've heard of it. I don't watch television.'

'Give it a try. They have quaint customs up here, and one of them is that older people are allowed to call all women *lass*. It's up to you whether to correct him.'

Mina and I had eaten out last night, so Mina hadn't spent much time with Karina yet, and Karina didn't look happy. Then again, she rarely does.

The interior doors opened with a flourish and a large group of Mages came out, all smartly dressed in normal clothes with not a cloak, cape or gown to be seen. I got a tang of something, something non-human, but there were too many to narrow it down.

Around two-thirds of the company were female and the average age was well over thirty. Two women led the group, one about ten years older than Seth and one around ten years younger. The younger woman went and took the place nearest to Seth, not so close as to be standing next to him, but close enough to detach herself from the rest of the Malchs.

Seth waved us over and dumped his waterproof under the console table. On top of the table was an ornate book, open about two thirds through, and with an old-fashioned ink stand next to it. With suitable ceremony, Seth cleared his throat.

'As President of the Alchemical Society, it gives me great pleasure to welcome the new Deputy Constable, and to extend that welcome to the Peculier Auditor and Watch Officer Kent. On behalf of the Society, can I say how pleased we are that the Constable has finally seen fit to fill the vacancy, and more than that, she has done the Palatinate the honour of appointing Albion's first Dragonslayer in hundreds of years. You are most welcome here.'

He bowed, and started a round of applause that was supported enthusiastically by all the Mages. If they had any reservations about me, or my insistence on a short term of office, they hid it well. I bowed to the crowd and shook Seth's hand again.

'Thank you, Mr President. I look forward to getting to know as many of you as possible and I shall do my best to live up to your welcome.'

'You can call me Seth, now,' he said. 'And there's one more thing. The Deputy Constable is always made an honorary member of the Society, and the Council have decided to extend the offer to the Peculier Auditor. And before you say anything, Watch Officer Kent can enrol as a Visiting Member, subject to the President's approval, and I do approve. Please, sign the book. You only need to do it once. From then on, it will know when you're in the building. Clever book, that.'

The book had already been filled in with our names, titles and status within the Society. I picked up one of the three pens in the tray and dipped it into the ink. A tingle of Lux flowed up my arm, and the wooden body of the pen got very hot. I quickly signed my name, and the pen flashed white with magick.

'Will that work for me?' whispered Mina.

Seth overheard her, and said, "Course it will.' And it did.

140

Seth reached into his pocket. 'And finally, your membership badges and Key to the Wards. The Deputy President will take a picture, if that's okay?' One by one, Seth handed the enamel badges to us, posing for a handshake while the older of the leading women used Seth's iPhone to capture the moment. 'Right,' said Seth when it was done. 'A bit of business first, then lunch. I'm starving.'

I'd noticed that the younger leading lady wasn't entirely happy with Seth's posing for the pictures and I wondered whether she was one of the Mages thinking about standing as Warden of Salomon's House.

Seth led us through the group of Mages and down a corridor with portraits and ornate doorways. At the end was another pair of doors, and beyond them grey daylight. 'Welcome to the Agora. As you may have noticed, our founders had a thing for ancient Greece. They designed this space to be bigger than anywhere in Salomon's House, which is why they have their public meetings on the staircase or off site.'

Why had he immediately compared the Society building to Salomon's House? Was it politeness, given that it was a point of reference for me? Or was it an inferiority complex?

'This is a lovely room,' I said. I meant it, too.

'It's a lovely room if you have a thing for naked men,' said Mina. 'Personally, I can take them or leave them.'

'There were naked women, too,' said Seth. 'They got taken down by the Victorians and put in a secret room. Now we're in the absurd position of having no majority to put the women back and no majority to take the men down.'

We were well into the room by now, a circular space with windows above and alternating doors and pedestals below it. Half of the pedestals had vases of flowers on them and the other half had the naked men. I looked up to the domed ceiling expecting more extravagant art. No. Plain white. Seth saw me looking.

'They couldn't agree on a subject for the ceiling and the moment passed. Probably for the best. I've saved you seats at the front. Now, if you'll excuse me.'

The floor of the Agora had a plain table at one end, with three plain chairs behind it. Very democratic. A few dozen more chairs had been placed in a fan before the table, and three of them had white notices on them. They would be ours. In the empty space behind the chairs, a group of Mages were putting the finishing touches to a buffet. Suddenly, I was hungry, too. Just before we sat down, I breathed a sigh of relief when I saw that one food table had a sign saying Natural Eating. Good.

Seth took the central chair, with his deputy to his right and a much younger woman holding a minute book to his left. The other leading lady from the reception committee chose a seat towards the back. When everyone was seated, Seth opened a box on the table and took out a chain of office made up of interlocking shields and badges. He stood up and placed it around his neck.

I felt the magick straight away, and Mina flinched when her arm started to throb; Karina remained impassive. I suddenly felt more private, that the walls were thicker and that the roof lower. Before I could try to work it out, Seth started speaking.

'I declare this extraordinary meeting of the Society open. We have three short items on the agenda today...'

I won't bore you with the details, though Seth did indeed keep it very brief. In short order, the Society voted to:

1. Acknowledge the Occult Council's ruling on joint polling for the Warden election and give the President powers to host the poll and to organise a preliminary hustings.

2. Accept Seth's resignation as President.

3. Elect his Deputy, Meredith Telford as President.

Seth removed the chain from his shoulders and stood back. The new President moved to her left and Seth lifted the chain over her head. 'It still fits, Merry,' he said.

'But it's no lighter, Seth,' she replied.

He bowed to her and left the top table, striding to the nearest empty seat and sitting down. The new President turned to face the Society.

'Just so you know, I'm doing this for six months only. When I stepped down three years ago, I was ready to put my feet up. I still am.' She lifted a finger and pointed first to Seth and then to the other leading lady. 'I wish both of you the best, and I hope one of you becomes the new Warden. Before then, I expect you to behave in a manner becoming of the Society. Both of you, alright? Good. I declare the meeting closed and the bar open.'

The Mages stood up, and two of them bore down on us like heat-seeking missiles: the new President and the other leading lady; the President won by a short head and shook my hand.

'Meredith Telford. Pleased to meet you, and can I introduce Doctor Lois Reynolds.'

When Meredith shook my hand, she could barely open her fingers, so bad was her arthritis; it's sometimes known as the Mage's Curse and is one of the few conditions more common in the world of magick than in the mundane population.

She looked in otherwise good health and had that unflappable spirit that can control mutinous committees with humour. I bet she'd been a good President in her day and would keep a steady ship during the coming ructions.

The other candidate for Warden was in her early fifties, shorter than average and wore black trousers under a cream blouse. She had pale blue eyes, a small mouth and the most noticeable feature about her was her long auburn hair in a meticulous Goddess braid. There was a round of handshakes, namastes and greetings, and when Lois met Karina, she added, 'In Her name, welcome,' to the standard, 'Pleased to meet you.'

'Let's get a drink,' said Meredith. She started walking towards a drinks table and continued, 'How are you settling into Middlebarrow Haven? Are the Masons looking after you? I hope we'll see Saskia here again soon.'

We joined the queue for drinks, and I heard Meredith talking to Mina about the embroidery on her saree, and where she got her fabrics from, and had she ever been to Manchester before? Karina was giving Lois monosyllabic answers about the Arden Foresters, and I wondered how long it would be before Lois gave up on her and turned to me. Across the room, Seth was waiting for us to get to the front of the queue, and when I picked up a glass of Merlot, he plotted a course for the empty space where he'd guessed that Meredith would lead us. He was spot on.

'There's someone else you should meet, Conrad,' he said.

I'd guessed that his companion was a Gnome before a new smell hit my enhanced nostrils. Not all short, dark haired, broad shouldered men in magickal circles are Gnomes, but I haven't met one who isn't. Even so, it was good to know that the tang of a Gnome is distinctly metallic, with a hint of game. You should know that my sense of smell is otherwise no different from what it was, and I still can't tell Merlot from Pinot Noir by smell alone.

I shook hands with the Gnome, and Seth said, 'This is Lachlan Mace of the fifth house, Clan Blackrod. Unlike Salomon's House, we allow anyone with magick to apply for full membership here.' He laughed. 'But I think we'd draw the line at Dragons. You must tell me about that sometime soon. Preferably over a pint.'

'How d'you do?' said Lachlan with the sort of patience that any friend of Seth's would need – the human Mage really does like the sound of his own voice; in other words, a natural politician. Lachlan continued, 'I must confess that I'm more interested in how you became Swordbearer to Clan Flint.'

Lloyd had told me that being their Swordbearer shouldn't be a problem so long as I didn't actually take the sword to another clan's First Mine, and that reminded me: I hadn't heard from Lloyd since Mina saw his wife yesterday. Anna had promised to get straight on to it, but so far nothing.

Lachlan took out a card and I followed suit. We'd just exchanged them when my phone went off with the spectacular *Yee Hah!* of an electric cowboy. Or sheriff, in this case. Seth and Lachlan gave me a strange look (as you'd expect), and I said, 'Excuse me. This may be important,' before stepping aside and beckoning Karina over.

I could hear outside noises when Morton spoke to me. 'Conrad, I've got something you should take a look at. Where are you?'

'Central Manchester. What is it?'

'Good. You're not far away then. I'm in some woods between Kearsley and Farnworth, looking at the body of an unusually short, stocky man wearing a ski mask.'

'Murdered?'

'Don't know, yet, but it's certainly a suspicious death. Are you interested?'

'Very interested. It could be important for us to see the body in situ and run a few tests. Could you help me out, Tom, and ask them not to move it.'

'I don't need to ask. At the moment, I'm the ranking officer.'

'Thanks. I've heard of Farnworth, but…'

'If you're anywhere near Victoria Station, the quickest way to get here is one of the many trains. It's only fifteen minutes. Text me your arrival time at Kearsley and I'll have uniforms pick you up.'

'Thanks, Tom. This really is one of those situations where I hope that it has nothing to do with me.'

'So do I, believe me.'

I disconnected and looked up. Shit. I keep forgetting that most Mages have much better hearing than I do (but worse eyesight). Half the room had probably heard me asking someone not to move a body. Karina's hearing is so good that when she came over, she caught most of Morton's side of the conversation as well. Mina was standing back with her eyebrows gracefully arched in query and her head tilted to show off the ruby necklace. She's so gorgeous I could stand and watch her all day sometimes. Aah well, you can't have all you want all of the time.

I went over and kissed her, whispering that there might be a dead Gnome in the woods, and would she be all right on her own?'

She opened her mouth to say *of course*, and then closed it when she realised that she would have to cross a strange city in her finery. 'Yes. I'll be fine.'

I made my apologies to Meredith and grabbed my coat on the way out. Karina was hot on my heels and nearly bumped into me when I stopped to check the weather: it had actually stopped raining. Small mercies and all that.

'What is it, sir?' she asked.

I opened the iron gates and felt a pulse of magick from the key they'd given me to the Wards. When we stepped into the mundane world, Karina put her Glamour back in place. I closed the gates but didn't move.

'There's been a suspicious death,' I said. 'Tom thinks it might be one of the Calabrese, as it were. A Gnome in our language. We're heading to Victoria Station, but you'll have to lose the disguise.'

She flinched. 'What for? Why? I can't walk around Manchester dressed like their idea of a Druid.'

'Sorry, but as soon as we leave this side-street, we'll be on CCTV. Do not think that Morton won't track our journey back at some point. If he sees you in disguise, it'll cause problems. You can borrow my coat if you want.'

She wrinkled her nose. 'No thanks.'

No joke, no sarcastic comment, just *No thanks.* Oh well.

I got out my cigarettes and said, 'Which way?'

'Left at the end, then right, then left for the railway station or right for the trams.'

'Excellent. You have no idea what it's like to work with people who have no sense of direction.'

16 — *Fall Guy*

Conrad had wondered why I had bought a new saree for this trip to the Alchemical Society, but as usual he was too polite to ask. He thinks that I would look good in a bin liner, and has said as much on several occasions, which just goes to show that he is either very much in love with me or that he just wants a quiet life. Or both, I suppose.

I hope that some of you are already saying, 'Why shouldn't Mina have new sarees? It's her money!' and you would be right, but that is not the whole story. The whole story is that I wanted to set myself apart and be something more exotic than an accountant from London with no magick. It worked, too.

When Conrad and Karina swept out of the Agora, I suddenly found myself the centre of attention in a most unwelcome way. Meredith Telford at least had the decency to ask straight out. 'I didn't know Conrad was on an active case,' she said.

'For such a tall man, he can normally move about quiet stealthily,' I replied. 'He doesn't normally rush out of social occasions quite so dramatically, or leave me on my own in a strange place, miles from home.'

'If he hasn't come back when we're finished, my daughter can give you a lift home,' said Meredith. 'She almost passes the gates of Middlebarrow, so it's not an imposition.' She noticed that both Seth and Lois were coming over and raised her voice, 'Now you two, don't forget that Mina doesn't have a vote and that she will be impartial at all times.'

Seth and Lois stood about six feet apart, which seemed like a good idea to them. To me, it meant that I had to keep turning my head. Seth spoke first. 'But you and Conrad have friends in high places. A little bird tells me that you even had royalty at your party recently, Princess Birkdale, no less, along with the Keeper, the Constable and the Mistress of Masques and Revels.'

I smiled, but before I could think of something to say, Lois picked up on his little list. 'And how is my old pupil? Or should I say, how is my potential rival?'

I tried to remember who that might be. Aah. Conrad told me that Lois Reynolds is an expert with all forms of illusion. 'You mean Selena? She enjoyed letting her hair down and afterwards she helped with the washing up. She is more than welcome to come back next time.'

'Mina's got our measure, Lois,' said Seth. 'I don't think we're going to get any gossip out of her. It is intriguing, though. Princess Birkdale and Lady Selena go to your house on Saturday, then on Monday morning, not only does

Cora Hardisty pull out of the race, the Constable announces that we have a new Deputy. Makes you think.'

It was time to fight back. 'This is so not fair, Mr Holgate. You have pictures of my party, yet all that Conrad could find out about you and Ms Reynolds was that you live here.'

Seth kept a straight face. 'One of us does.'

'What he's trying to say,' said Lois, 'is that I live over the Pennines in Yorkshire. Between Haworth and Hebden Bridge. It seems to matter to him.'

Seth's comeback was cut short by Meredith. 'At last, the buffet is ready. I'm going to take poor Mina away and make sure that she gets something to eat. You two can save your speeches for the hustings.'

'And when are they going to be?' I asked Meredith. When I'd discussed the elections with Judge Bracewell last week, she'd said that she wanted Conrad, Erin and me to run the hustings ballot as a dry run for the real thing.

'Salomon's House aren't happy about us having a hustings at all, not with them fielding two candidates. It's their own fault.'

'How come?'

We arrived at the buffet, and I felt a pang of sympathy for Conrad and Karina. It looked very good.

'Some of the bright sparks on the Board at Salomon's House insisted on transferable votes for Warden elections. That was before they realised that Northern Mages would be able to vote here. When the real election comes, either Selena Bannister or Heidi Marston will come third and their second choice votes will probably go to Seth or Lois and hand them the election. Now let's forget all about those two and I'll introduce you to some normal people. They do exist round here, I promise you, and you may even enjoy yourself.'

The marked police car was waiting for us on the double yellow lines outside Kearsley Station. We walked to the car with as much space between us as the footbridge would allow: Karina was not in a good mood. Her only verbalised comment had been when we got off the train: 'It's like coming back from a festival with my dad.' She was not a happy Watch Officer, though to be fair we had been getting a number of very odd looks from the good people of South Lancashire.

'Constable Clarke?' said the nice policeman when I flashed my ID.

'That's me. Where are we heading?'

He drove off quickly and took us into a residential estate. 'Through here, over the River Irwell and into the woods, and before you ask anything, I was pulled off preparation for the Bolton Wanderers match to pick you up. All I know is that there's been a suspicious death.'

'Thank you for collecting us. Sorry you got diverted.'

'I don't mind. It's not as if we're expecting hordes and hordes of Trotters fans. There's usually more people in the retail park than in the ground these days. Here we are. Follow the track and look for the ghouls.'

'Ghouls?' said Karina.

'Concerned members of the public with nothing better to do than gawp,' I told her. It's not her fault that when she hears *Ghouls* she thinks of corporeal ghosts. She really does need to get out more.

'And bloggers and so-called internet journalists,' added our driver.

I thanked him and we set off up the farm track that led away from the river. A group of half a dozen citizens had seen that we'd got out of a police car and were getting ready to intercept us. Karina saw them and stood still.

'Surely we shouldn't be all over the internet, sir.'

'I doubt we'll be *all over* the internet, Karina, but you're right. How about a light Glamour to change our appearance?'

She looked even more uncomfortable. 'For both of us? I don't think I could do that without physical contact.'

'Then I'll hold your hand. You can make me really look like your dad. Or your boyfriend. Whatever works best.'

'That's gross.' She shuddered and took a deep breath. 'Take my hand and look straight ahead at all times. Please.'

I held my hand out and fingers gripped mine. I felt the magick and kept my eyes riveted on the trees ahead of us. 'Okay,' she said. We set off, and I let her dictate the pace.

'Are you with the police?'

'Can you tell us what's happened?'

'Is it true he was killed by a pack of wild dogs?'

I almost stumbled at the last question. That was not what I'd expected, and Karina almost dragged me through a field gate where a female constable was keeping the onlookers at bay. 'Straight ahead,' she said.

Once past the dry stone wall, I could make out white shapes flitting through the trees. I kept hold of Karina's hand until we were into the wood, then let go. 'Well done,' I said.

'We'll see,' was her less than enthusiastic reply. 'What now?'

'We'll talk to that man with the clipboard. He's a crime scene technician and he'll take our names. After that, I have no idea.'

Once logged at the outer perimeter, we moved through more trees and I could see the blue and white tape of the inner perimeter. There must have been half a dozen more white-suited technicians inside it, and outside it were Morton and Elaine.

Elaine did a double-take when she saw us. 'Where have you two been? Or shouldn't I ask?'

Karina looked down at the trainers poking out from her robe (she'd hitched it up when we left the Alchemical Society). I tried to keep it light. 'I was literally sitting down to lunch with Mina when Tom rang, and I should warn you that I am now hungry. Karina was meeting fellow practitioners. In private, but she's too polite to make pointed remarks.'

Morton poured some oil. 'There's little enough private life in our jobs. With luck this will turn out to be someone else's problem. You didn't bring your dog, then?'

'Scout is on probation at Doggy Day Care. I had to sit with him for half an hour before we left to make sure he didn't get into any fights. Fingers crossed they let him back. If you don't mind me asking, Tom, how come you're here?'

'A good question,' said Elaine. She looked no happier to be here than Karina was. 'Tell them, sir.'

'I made the mistake of telling Major Incident Control that I was interested in suspicious deaths and that I was in the area, so they called me first. There aren't many DCIs without a regular case-load. As soon as I heard the details, I said I'd take command of the crime scene.'

'We,' said Elaine. 'You said *we'd* take command.'

'I get the message, thank you.' He paused then continued more briskly. 'Right, Elaine, tell them what we've got.'

She lifted a South Lancs Constabulary tablet computer (complete with snazzy branded case) and unlocked the screen. 'A member of the public was walking her dog through the woods when he went mad and started running in circles. When she went to see what the fuss was, she found a badly mutilated body and dialled 999. According to the witness, her dog didn't touch the body.'

Elaine looked up and a troubled look came over her. 'You'll see why that's important in a minute. First responding officers escalated the incident and set up a perimeter. We arrived shortly after the police surgeon, who pronounced life extinct at 12:07. The CS photographer finished about quarter of an hour ago, and the crime scene manager has had a first look at the body.' She looked at Karina. 'Has Conrad told you it isn't like it is on the telly.'

'Not much point,' I said. 'Karina's not a big watcher of TV drama, but I did tell her not to expect a forensic pathologist to turn up and solve the case.'

'I do watch TV sometimes,' said Karina defensively. 'So, why not?'

'Because they're very, very expensive,' said Morton, 'and they only work with dead bodies in mortuaries. We have much cheaper crime scene technicians who will bag and tag everything. I can tell you that the deceased wasn't carrying a wallet or any ID or a phone, but he did have a selection of condoms in his suit pocket.'

I raised my eyebrows. 'A selection, Tom?'

149

'Correct,' said Elaine with a straight face. 'Flavoured, thin feel with anaesthetic, ribbed and regular.'

'Well, well, well. When can we have a look?'

'As soon as you're suited and booted,' said Morton. 'The crime scene manager is over there. She'll sort you out and brief you. Don't worry, Conrad, she always has extra large suits in stock.'

The CS Manager was large enough around the middle to need at least XL herself, and was holding out Tall and Petite sets of coveralls before we even got there. Karina had been looking more and more panicked as we got closer, and the manager was giving her a boggle-eyed *who the F* are you?* Kind of look.

Aah. The robes. Not good with coveralls. I'd already seen that she had leggings on. Fingers crossed. 'Please tell me you have a top on under there, Karina.'

'I do,' she hissed, 'but it's a sports crop-top. I can't get changed here.'

I stepped forward and took the suits. 'Would you mind terribly turning around while my partner gets changed. I'm Conrad Clarke, by the way.'

'Tracey Kenyon.' A light came on behind her eyes. 'Haven't I heard of you? I normally work out of Cairndale.'

'Then you may have heard my name.'

'The Driscoll case! I processed the Coffin from Nowhere. It was so clean of trace evidence you'd think it wasn't made by human hand.'

'It wasn't, and don't ask me for details.'

'I won't. It would spoil the magic. Let's get on. Dave! Come here.'

Another technician came over with an iPad. All three of us turned away and made a barrier so that Karina could have a modicum of modesty. While she got changed, Dave entered our details into the crime scene record.

'We've got you on the system, sir, but not Lieutenant Kent. We'll need her prints and DNA for exclusion purposes, but we can sort that out later.'

'Not if I can help it,' I muttered under my breath. I moved the mask away from my mouth and said, 'Ready, Karina?'

She came round and presented herself for inspection. Tracey Kenyon gave her the once-over and said, 'Once you cross the tape, follow the green markers until you get to the metal plates. Walk on the plates and only the plates. We've swept two metres around the body, so you can do what you like there. I'll be around, so shout me if you want to touch the victim for any strange reason. And no pictures. If the SIO gives you authority, you can access all the reports and images on the HOLMES system. Any questions?'

'No, thank you, Tracey. Very clear.'

'Good. Knock yourselves out, guys. This is a bad one, I'm afraid.'

I ducked under the tape and held it up for Karina. It had been wrapped round a series of trees forming a rough circle about thirty metres in diameter. Five metres in, a series of square aluminium plates led to the centre. I walked slowly, taking in the surroundings and looking for inspiration. Nope. Nothing.

And then I got the smell, and I can now report that non-humans smell different when they're dead as well as when they're alive.

Karina was four steps behind me. I turned round and said, 'The victim is definitely a Calabrese.'

'That's not good, sir.'

'It's not. Is this your first time with a violent death?'

Under the suit and mask, I saw a tiny flinch. 'First time with any actual death. I didn't even see Ioan's body when Colwyn shot him.'

'Then you should think carefully before you follow me, Karina. Once you step off the metal brick road, there's no going back.'

'It's what I signed up for, sir.'

'Good.' I took five more steps and I was there, and what a mess. I was suddenly very glad we'd missed lunch, because something had definitely dined here today, and Gnome was on the menu.

The deceased was wearing a fine suit, leather soled shoes and was now lying on his back. I couldn't see his face because of the ski mask, which was a shame, because then I wouldn't have had to look at the rest of him.

'By the Goddess, in whose name has this been done?' said an appalled Karina. When the shock had worn off, she heaved twice and put her hand on my shoulder. Somehow, she kept it down and didn't vomit into her mask. I stepped off the last plate and squatted down. Tracey was right: this was a bad one.

Something with very sharp teeth had torn into the Gnome's shirt and then ripped open his abdomen to get at the tasty bits. There was bowel everywhere. You don't want to know. You really don't. They'd also eaten great chunks of his right thigh, stripping the meat down to the bone. I forced myself to check the whole body. Aah. There. 'What would you say was the cause of death, Karina? Specifically? I'll give you a clue: I know how he felt.'

She stepped off the plates and moved round to squat opposite me. 'Throat ripped out,' she said.

'Precisely. Exsanguination. Sadly, I think he knew a bit more about it at the time than I did.' I stood up. 'Tracey!'

She came down the metal path. 'Seen enough?'

'Not yet. Has anyone opened his shirt at the top to look for jewellery?'

'You what? That's for the post-mortem pre-processing. Is it important?'

'Very. If you can't open his shirt, could you at least feel round the chest and what's left of the neck for me? Or let me do it myself?'

She eyed me steadily over her mask, then shook her head. 'If you're so desperate to find out you're willing to get your hands on a corpse, it must be important. I'll do it. Stand back. No, don't. Stay there and give me a hand to hold on to.'

I stood next to the deceased Gnome while Tracey held my arm and knelt down to feel his chest. 'Pull me up. I really should join Slimming World again.' I heaved. 'Thanks. There's nothing, I'm afraid.'

'Thanks, Tracey. I think we're nearly done here. To save me asking, have you found anything else yet? This rain must have been good for footprints. Or paw prints.'

'We've found a lot of blood spatter, and the lie of the body says that he was definitely killed and dismembered here. Trouble is, this wood is so sparse that there's grass everywhere. The only paw-prints look like they're from the witness's dog.'

'Any idea of time of death? Has he been here all night, for example?'

'Some time this morning. Probably around eleven, but don't quote me on that.'

'Thanks.'

Tracey was about to go, and then Karina spoke up. 'See over there, sir, away from the path?'

'Yes?'

Karina steeled herself and made the effort to talk directly to Tracey. 'Erm, ma'am? Ms Kenyon? Has anyone checked down there?'

Tracey looked interested. 'Why?'

'Because that's the only place I can see brambles, and there's tears on his trousers and scratches on his leg. See?'

Without asking, Tracey grabbed my arm again and bent to look. 'How much are you on, love?'

Karina flinched back. 'I'm not on anything. I'm clean.'

Tracey laughed. 'I'm sure you are. I meant, how much money are you on?'

'I don't know. How much am I on, sir?'

'How can you not know that?' said Tracey.

Karina shrugged, embarrassed. Yet again, I stepped in, and said, 'Thirty-three thousand plus allowances.'

Tracey shook her head. 'Damn. No chance of poaching her then. My lot are on a lot less than that, and I'm not on much more. Close your ears.' She pulled her mask down and cupped her hands to her mouth. 'Gather round, everyone!' She lowered her hands. 'We'll get right on that. If he's run some distance, there could be secondary crime scenes a long way away.'

I removed my own mask. 'As a reward, can Karina tag along with you while I go and talk to the DCI? She really does know her stuff when it comes to evidence in woodlands, even if she wasn't expecting to be called into action today.'

'Yeah. Sure.'

'Thanks, I...' It was my turn to grab Tracey at that point, because all the squatting had sent my leg into spasm. Holding on to Tracey was like gripping a solid rock. At least I didn't hop into the body.

'Are you okay, sir?' said Karina.

'I'll be fine. Sorry, Tracey. It's an old wound that doesn't like bad weather.'

I flexed my leg until it behaved, then made my way slowly back to the perimeter. Dave logged me out and told me to put the suit in a secure rubbish bag. I put my coat back on and folded Karina's robes over my arm. I took the long route back to see Morton so that I could have a smoke. After seeing our deceased Gnome, I really needed one, I'm telling you, and the Sheriff didn't object when he saw me approaching.

'Bad news, I'm afraid, Tom. This was definitely one of the Calabrese.'

Morton lifted his right hand and moved it towards his left arm. Half way there, he realised what he was doing and changed it into a rub of his hair. 'How do you know?'

'Invisible tattoo. Or rather, it's visible, but only under certain light. What I can't say is whether that … man had anything to do with the Count of Canal Street's death. It could be absolutely unrelated.'

'And the manner of his death? Do I need to call the Special Forces wing of the RSPCA? What the hell did that to him?'

Have you ever had that feeling, when you have evidence of something but don't want to think about it? Like when you feel a lump in your body, or your child comes home from a night out with pupils like pinholes? Or when your partner starts taking telephone calls outside? I had that feeling right now.

One of the Lions of Carthage once bit my arm. I don't have a physical scar, but the mental one is still there. Everything about this crime scene said magick, and more than that, it said w*r*w*lf. I've used the asterisks because we don't use the word w*r* in the world of magick. What we say is *Dual Natured* in general and Mannwolf in particular. I'll explain what that means if it becomes an issue. However, I needed something less mind-boggling for Tom Morton's benefit.

'We've just found evidence that the victim was running away when he was attacked. I'm thinking that a pack of trained hunting dogs did this. If I had an obvious suspect, I'd be on the way to their kennels right now.'

Morton nodded carefully. 'You used to ride to hounds, didn't you?'

'I did once. Perhaps I will again now that I've got a horse. If Mina lets me.'

'I hope she bloody doesn't, or she'll go down in my estimation,' said Elaine.

'And mine,' said Morton. 'Regardless of that, you've seen foxhounds in action. Could they have done this?'

'No. Well, not a regular pack. They're trained from birth to follow the scent of a fox or a drag lure. Not a man. Someone, somewhere, has been playing a very dangerous game.'

'Could they be wild or escaped?' asked Elaine. 'People keep all sorts of weird things illegally. I was called to a house in Leicester once. Guy had a breeding pair of European lynx in his back garden. Could someone be keeping wolves or tigers or something, and they've got loose?'

'I've already checked,' said Morton. 'No unusual farm deaths have been reported. What you're saying is truly evil, Conrad. What would someone want with a pack of man-eating dogs?'

He was right, in one sense. It was truly evil. I forced myself not to think about it. Not yet. 'What do the rich want with superyachts or ten homes? These things are all status symbols. I may be wrong, of course. There may be a much more boring explanation.'

'I hope so,' he said. 'If you've got Karina's outfit, where is she?'

'With Tracey Kenyon, using her expertise. I had no more to offer at that point. I think I see her coming.'

I did. With her hood down and her overshoes and mask removed, Karina was jogging back to us round the outside of the inner perimeter. When she arrived, she was barely out of breath. 'We've found something,' she announced. 'A secondary crime scene where it looks like the victim was released.'

'Any trace evidence?' said Morton.

She shook her head. 'The ground had been blasted with something. We did find a bunch of roses tossed into the brambles. Recently bought, long-stem red roses, according to Tracey. She thought it was important.'

Elaine and Tom looked at each other and then at me. 'A hot date, then,' said Elaine.

'Looks like it,' I agreed. My phone rang and I checked the screen: Saskia. Eh? 'Excuse me.'

I took the call, and she said, 'Conrad, have you got a second?'

'A quick one.'

'I got back from Waitrose before lunch, and there was a motorcycle courier outside the lodge, getting soaked in the rain. He has a parcel for you and you only. He even has a picture of you in Indian dress to make sure. I've given him lunch and dried him out, but he won't leave until he's seen you. Are you going to be long, because he says he'll get a room at the White Horse if you are. He really is that dedicated.'

'I'm afraid I might be a while. Can I call you back in five minutes, please?'

'Of course.'

I disconnected and put the phone away. 'Important, but not urgent,' I said.

'So what's your take on this, Conrad?' said Morton with the air of the senior professional.

I pulled my lip for a moment to gather my thoughts. 'He was on his way to a date, hence the roses and condoms. He had no coat, so he wasn't ambushed in the woods. No one spends that much on a hand-tailored suit and then wanders coatless through the rain. He was intercepted somewhere else and brought here. His wallet and phone were taken and he was released. I didn't see any ligature marks on his wrists, so he was probably held at gunpoint. When they released him, a pack of animals was set to chase him. Anything to add, Karina?'

She didn't have any alternative explanations, but she did have a good question. 'What were the roses all about, sir?'

'A gesture of contempt, is what I'd say. The killers wanted to leave a clear message, but not too clear, that's why they took his ID away – to delay identification of the body.'

'That's pretty much my take on things,' said Tom. 'So, where do we go from here? I'm going to have a lot of explaining to do when they find out you've been all over a South Lancs crime scene. I can't be the SIO on this one unless someone pays my boss a lot of money, so a regular detective will take over as soon as they've dragged one out of the supermarket or off the golf course or wherever it is they spend their Saturdays.'

'Can you ask to be given a watching brief? I'll pursue enquiries from my end.'

'Will you now, Conrad? And will you tell us what you've found?'

He'd finally thrown down the gauntlet: was I just pissing them around, or was this a real partnership?

I'd been mulling this question over ever since I'd decided to call for his help. I respect him far too much not to give him a straight answer, and anyway, he's far too clever to fall for a simple lie or evasion.

'I can't promise to share everything, Tom. There are things I'm under strict orders not to divulge, and I happen to agree with those orders. What I can promise is not to undermine any police investigation and to share all admissible evidence. More than that, I will not be a party to a cover-up of any description, nor to a slap on the wrist for the rich and powerful.' I turned to Karina. 'What is the Boss's personal motto?'

She nodded her head, pleased to be given a question she knew the answer to. 'We can't be part of the solution if we're part of the problem.'

Morton didn't look happy. 'You talk a good game, Conrad, but you always did. I'll hold you to those promises.'

'No harder than I hold myself, Tom. No Clarke has broken his word since the Middle Ages, and I won't be the first. Did you come in separate cars?'

'We did. Are you after a lift somewhere?'

'I imagine you will have a hell of a lot of paperwork to do.'

'Tell me about it.'

'Then how about if Elaine takes Karina and me to Penwortham.'

'What for?' said Elaine.

'Partly to see if Kirk Liddington is still in one piece, and partly to see his face when I ask him some questions.'

'Sounds like a plan,' said Morton. 'Elaine?'

'It's a good job you're both not his size,' said Elaine to Karina. 'My back seats aren't that big.'

'Is there any chance we could stop at a big supermarket on the way?' I said. 'Not only am I starving, Karina could get herself a top to wear.'

'You're not the only hungry one,' said Elaine. 'My car's over there, away from the spectators. I'll see you in five, okay?'

'What should the force tell the media about this?' asked Tom, getting out his phone.

'That you're looking for a dangerous dog and its owner.'

'Fine. See you later.'

I walked towards her car, and Karina said, 'Thank you, sir. That's very thoughtful of you, asking to stop for clothes like that.'

'Not at all. I'm just going to make a call.' I connected with Saskia and asked her to put the courier on the line. As expected, he had a strong Black Country accent.

'Do you have to deliver at Middlebarrow?' I asked.

'No, mate. So long as it's in person it could be on the moon, but I'd need a bigger travel allowance to go there.'

'Good. Can you find Middleforth Green in Penwortham, Preston? I'll meet you there in about an hour. Get Saskia to give you my number.'

'No problem, chief. I'll see you later.'

'Who was that?' said Karina.

'Friend of a friend. I'm about to get a mysterious present from Clan Flint.'

'A present?'

'Yes, but don't get too excited. Now, if you'll excuse me…'

'Stand over there, sir, downwind by the trees.'

'Right. Will do.'

On the way to the trees, I got a text from Mina: *Call me when you can!* I called.

'I have gone outside,' she said quickly. 'Did you know what Karina was doing?'

'No is the short answer. In what way?'

'Ten minutes ago, there was a stir in the room and then Seth Holgate bursts out laughing. He comes over and says that I should congratulate you. When I asked why, he says that he is all over Twitter. I checked, and there are pictures of you two arriving at the woods. I presume it was you two, because the picture is one of Seth and Lois Reynolds holding hands.'

'Oh shit.'

'That's not the worst part. The Malchs have now linked you to the suspicious death. It's a good job I have no idea what's going on. Expect more calls soon. Seth loved it, but you are officially off Lois's Christmas card list. She did not find it in the least funny. If it wouldn't make her look like a killjoy, she'd be making an official complaint, I'm sure.'

Elaine had arrived at the car. 'I'd better go. Thanks, for the heads-up, love. Take care.'

'And you.'

17 — The Pointing Finger

Our star witness, Kirk Liddington aka Fae Klass, looked a lot better when he answered the door. You could tell that the terrible secret he'd been carrying was no longer eating away at him from the inside – his shoulders weren't as slumped and he made a valiant attempt at humour when he saw who'd come calling.

'Where's that nice Mr Morton?' he said. 'No offence, Conrad, but he's much better looking than you are.'

'It's a good job my fiancée disagrees with you,' I countered.

'Don't be too sure of that,' said Elaine. I think she was joking. I hope she was joking.

'And are you going to keep the ninja under lock and key?' said Kirk with an eyebrow raised in Karina's direction.

'That depends,' said Elaine, 'on whether or not you're a good boy and answer our questions.'

Kirk stood back and opened the door wide. 'Come in, come in, you're letting the heat out.'

We trooped into the house and immediately started shedding layers of clothing. It was boiling in there, and that's when I realised that Kirk was on the mend. He'd been out shopping, and the supermarket denims had been replaced by tight trousers and a tight tee-shirt, either from the women's or children's sections.

Elaine had followed Kirk into the kitchen to help make the tea, and was asking him the obvious questions (*Have you heard from the Fairy Gardens?* Etc.)

I leaned down to Karina and said, 'I know it's Shabbos, but the Boss needs to know about the dead Gnome. Why don't you do a quick report and send it to her. Just the headlines.'

'Now?'

'When the tea's made. He'll feel more comfortable if you're not there.'

She shifted from one foot to the other. 'I didn't like it when Elaine made a joke about me.'

'It is the time-honoured lot of the junior officer to be made fun of. My role is to make sure it doesn't amount to bullying, and your job is to deal with it.'

'Yes, sir.'

'Shall we go outside while the tea brews, big boy?' said Kirk. He grabbed a long puffer coat in black that was clearly his sister's and headed outside without waiting for me to reply.

I followed and gave him a cigarette. 'Is Amy on shift?'

He shook his head. 'She's gone out with the girls. I promised to clean the house while she was out. Try and give a little back. I don't know what would have happened if she hadn't taken me in. I did the bathroom and my room, then I had to lie down for a bit. I'm out of practice.'

His voice had settled down to what you'd expect: camp and still slightly higher pitched than normal. 'If I said that everything was okay, Kirk, that you didn't have to look over your shoulder any more, what would you do? It'll happen sooner or later.'

'I don't know. I really don't. Let's go back inside, I'm freezing out here.'

We took our tea into the living room, and this time I sat next to Elaine on the couch. 'Just a couple of questions,' I said. 'Did the Count, or Wayne, or the Management ever make threats?'

'What do you mean? If you're asking whether they coerced me or bullied me, they didn't. I'm a grown-up. I knew what I was doing.'

If only that were true. 'No, that's not what I meant. Did they ever say anything like, "We'll have to break his fingers"?'

Kirk scratched his scalp and winced. 'Wayne never threatened anyone with words. He just moved into their personal space. That made them shut up. Or if they didn't, he'd have their arm up their back and throw them out in seconds. The Count never threatened anyone, either. Not his style. The only one who needed to do that was JC.' For a second, he looked slightly uncomfortable. 'I'm not going to repeat them, but she used threats of a sexual nature. To men and women. "I'll sit on your face for a month," was one of the mildest.'

'It's not JC we're interested in,' I said.

'Thank God,' said Elaine.

Kirk started to shrug, and then remembered something. 'One night, the Count had a call from the Management. He'd been a very naughty boy, and she wasn't pleased. He came off the phone and said, "She's threatened to set the dogs on me."' He thought for a moment. 'No, he didn't. He said, "She's threatened to set the pack on me."' That was it. *Set the pack on me.* Is that what you wanted?'

I did want it and I didn't. Kirk had just filled in one of those asterisks, you know, in the w* word. Damnation. 'Thanks, Kirk. I'm going to repeat myself: that you should not get in touch with the Gardens or anyone from there. Not until I say so.'

'You're always welcome, but can you bring better news next time? And bring nice Mr Morton?'

'I'll tell him you're missing him,' I said. 'Let's go.'

Karina had slipped back into the house during our chat to Kirk, and we headed for the car park, all of us checking our phones. Mine told me that the courier was waiting for me and that Mina was on her way back to the Haven with Meredith Telford's daughter.

When Elaine had finished checking, she announced that she had to go to the Major Incident Centre in Bolton, and would we mind if she dropped us at

Lostock Station? 'There's loads of trains to Victoria from there.' She saw the courier watching us from a distance. 'Aye aye, who's that?'

'Delivery for me. Won't be a second.'

The motorcyclist took out his phone and checked the image on the screen against the reality of my person. Satisfied, he got a small package out of his top box and said, 'There you go. There's nothing to sign. Thanks for sorting me out, mate. Much obliged.'

I took the package and wished him a safe journey. He was gone before I'd walked back to Elaine's car.

'What on earth was that?' she said. 'Tom will go totally conspiracy theory when I tell him you're getting deliveries in a car park.'

I shook the box and tore at the grey plastic bag (which was completely plain – no name or address). Inside, I got a glimpse of a wooden box with runes etched into it. Better not show them that. 'I'll tell you exactly what it is,' I said. 'It's a burner phone set up for one of our contacts. I've been waiting for this so that I can try to get some answers. You'll understand if I don't use it until I get home.'

She nodded her head. 'Sounds about right.' She paused, with her hand on the car door. 'I hadn't started doing the CCTV trawl when the call came in this morning. I'm not sure I'll bother, now.'

'Oh? Why?'

'Tom messaged me the picture of you two arriving at the woods. I can't believe it. I seriously can't, but it's there in glorious HD colour.'

Karina looked panicked, as well she might. 'How did he get that?' she said.

'Because it's one of the few images about the case on Twitter. He's had to tell the media centre that you were witnesses who weren't required, and that's why their names aren't on the crime scene record. Right. Do you want a break, or can we please go straight away?'

'Let's go. It's been a long day.'

Elaine dropped us in the car park at Lostock Station and disappeared up the exit road. 'Go and get two tickets to Victoria and find out when the next train is,' I said. 'I'm going to open this package.'

'But…'

'I don't want to miss the train.'

I peeled off the packaging and looked at the box. As soon as I touched it, the runes dimmed and faded. They must have been keyed to me in some way, which was a surprise because Gnomish magick doesn't normally go in for that sort of thing. Perhaps it was because of my bond with their First Mine. No matter.

I didn't open it right away, because although I'm not paranoid, I am cautious: this box was the perfect size for a small bomb. I took it over to a wall, hid behind a car and used all my concentration to focus on blowing open the lid. I was still trying, and failing, when Karina said, 'What are you up to, sir? Would you like me to do it?'

'Thank you. That would be very good, Karina.'

She passed me the tickets. 'Next train in fifteen minutes. Do you really think there's something dangerous in there?'

'When you've med-evacced as many IED victims as I have, you try not to take chances.'

'Oh. Is that what happened to your leg? An IED?'

'No. That was a rocket grenade, and it was my own stupid fault. Now then, how are you going to approach this?'

'You were trying to use compressed air to lift the top off. The angles are all wrong with that. I'd like to smash it with a stone. Not hard enough to destroy it, just hard enough to set off a trigger.'

'Sounds good.'

She scouted around the rough stone car park and selected a flat piece of slate, perfect for skimming on water. She shied it at the box, reminding me of a baseball pitcher who was aiming for the batter's ankles. The stone hit the box just above the lid-line and stuck in the wood. Any magickal or mundane device would definitely have gone off with that.

She started moving and I grabbed her arm. 'Thanks, Karina. You stay back – that was addressed to me, not you. My risk.'

I used the toe of my boot to lift what was left of the lid off the box. As expected, there was a burner phone inside.

I waved Karina over and showed her what I'd got. 'What on earth prompted you to project an image of Seth Holgate and Lois Reynolds? Do you realise what a stink you've caused? Not only that, you've linked us directly to the suspicious death.'

'I am so sorry, Conrad. I really am. If I'd had a bit more warning, I'd have done better. They were the only people in my head from recently. I couldn't think of anyone else.'

'What was wrong with doing your father and someone like Erin?'

She looked appalled. 'I couldn't. That would have felt so wrong. And Erin doesn't like me anyway.'

'Then what about Tom and Elaine? That would have been easy for them to explain to their bosses, though perhaps not to Lucy and Rob.'

'I didn't think.'

'No, you didn't, and that's the real problem. If you were stuck for inspiration, you should have told me. As I keep saying, we're in this together, Karina. I'll message an apology from the train.'

She took a deep breath. 'Shouldn't it be me who apologises? It was my fault.'

'In this instance, the first apology has to come from me, otherwise it will look like I don't think you did anything wrong. You can message them yourself when we get back to the Haven. We'll move on, shall we?'

She nodded and looked even more miserable than normal. At least the train was on time, and we couldn't talk on the trip into Manchester. We couldn't sit down, either. Another bloody Pacer.

I stopped to get us coffee on the trip across town to Piccadilly Station, then found us a bench. 'What are your thoughts on the case?'

'Well, sir, I know we're meant to think it was the Fae. You do know that they like to keep packs of Dual Natured wolves, right?'

'Do they? Even in England?'

She nodded. 'The Prince of Arden doesn't, because he prefers to hunt on foot, but I know he's been invited to a couple of hunts where they run Mannwolves.'

'One of them wasn't in the North West, was it?'

'No. He doesn't have anything to do with the Queen of Alderley's line.'

'Damn and blast. That wasn't in any of the Merlyn's Tower reports. I wonder why not?'

She looked very uncomfortable. 'I couldn't say, sir. It's not something I'd talk about if we didn't have this problem.'

'Put it in a report. Something like that really should be on the system.'

'Do I have to? It's really not my place to say.'

'You're a Watch Officer, Karina. The fact that you grew up in Arden is just that — a fact. What about the new guy, Andy, who grew up in a city and who might need to know that?' She looked so upset that I took pity on her. 'Write the report for me, and I'll submit it under my name. How about that?' She nodded uncertainly. 'Good. Go on, you were saying?'

'We're meant to think it was the Fae. We're meant to think it was a revenge attack. I don't think it's a coincidence, though. Do you think the Gnome was from Clan Blackrod?'

'I have no idea. That's why I need to get in touch with Lloyd. Forget about the wolves. What does that leave us with?'

'The flowers. The ski mask.'

'Yes. Good. What about them?'

She risked a glance up at me. 'Gnomes don't go on a hot date with a ski mask, do they? You'd know more about that than me.'

'More about Gnomes, or more about hot dates? Don't answer that question. You're right, though. The mask was a mistake. They were trying too hard to make a point. There's one other thing: the actual presence of the body.'

'In what way?'

'It was meant to be found by the mundane police. Why? If it were Gnome-on-Gnome violence, that's not how they do things. I'm desperately hoping that a chance remark by Tara Doyle isn't as ominous as I think it is. She happened to mention that Big Wayne has a number of police officers on retainer.'

She pulled a face. 'Do you have to call him *Big Wayne*?'

'You're right. It's not an image I want to conjure too often. Are you ready for another Pacer experience?'

'No. They're horrible. And Manchester is even worse than Birmingham, and I hated that.'

I shook out my leg and started walking. 'How did you get on in London, then?'

'There's a hotel opposite the Tower. I stayed there.'

'Except for your trip to Norfolk. How did you get on with Cora?'

'She was very disciplined. She worked me really hard.'

'How was she?'

'Sad, I think. She didn't talk about herself a lot. She seemed a bit happier after she went out on Saturday night. She said she was going out for dinner and didn't come back until the next morning.'

Curiouser and curiouser. We entered the Piccadilly concourse and scanned the departure boards. 'Come on, Karina. There's one in on Platform 2.'

'Was she that bad?' said Mina when we finally curled up in the Deputy's suite at the Haven. Priority One when I'd got back was taking Scout for a walk, just to reassure him, and Mina had been helping Evie in the kitchen. When the dinner was in the oven, I'd made tea and carried it up to the very chintz but very comfortable sitting room in our little suite.

'It's hard to say. She did get quite animated when she was with the forensics officers, and she's definitely getting more used to talking to me. Unfortunately, she's still in fear of Elaine Fraser.'

'That is quite understandable. Having met Karina properly, I don't think she's autistic. Not that there's anything wrong with that. I do think she has a problem with social anxiety. Now tell me about this dead Gnome.'

When I'd finished, Mina looked very thoughtful. 'I think I might have something, Conrad. Bear with me. After you rushed off, Merry Telford put me with some of the younger Mages. Younger as in under forty. Every day with you I feel older. You are a bad influence.' She waved her hand around as if warding off premature ageing. 'They were all agog to hear about Princess Birkdale, aka Tara Doyle, but I had to give a little to get some back.'

'What do you mean?'

'They all know that she must have been visiting us for magickal reasons. I had to think on my feet, so I said that I'd seen Tara spend a long time talking to Cador Mowbray, and I dropped hints that she needed a top lawyer.'

'Clever. And Cador will neither confirm nor deny that.'

'That's what I thought. Once they thought they had some gossip, they were keen to top each other's stories about the Princess. One or two had been to the Sídhe, another had produced some special orchids for a party. That sort of thing. Our favourite Fae has a lot of property, it seems. Including a cottage in the Forest of Bowland. That sounds like a good place to hide a pack of werewolves.'

Mina is exempt from the prohibition on the w* word. She has faced down a Dual Natured cobra and won. She can call them what she likes.

'Any clues as to where it might be? That's a big area.'

'Someone said she bought it when she was the Count of Salford, also known as James Ash. I looked him up: he was a big player in the music hall business. I had to look that up, too. He once owned theatres all over Lancashire.'

I leaned over to give her a kiss. 'I knew there was a reason I'd proposed to you. Apart from your being gorgeous, of course.'

'Of course. I'm going to get out of this saree and have a bath before dinner. What about you?'

'I'm going undercover.'

She started pulling her hair up and walked towards the bedroom. 'Don't spend too long undercover, Conrad. I want you under the actual covers later.' She gave me a smile and disappeared.

I sent a short message to show that I'd got the phone and waited.

Back came this reply, almost immediately: Sandbach Services, Southbound, tomorrow, 11:00. Bring the Anvil.

I did groan a little. Did it have to be a motorway services? No matter. There's an outdoor seating area behind the Costa Coffee.

Karina was looking better at dinner, and couldn't wait to tell me that she'd apologised to the candidates.

'How did they take it?'

'Seth said he owes me one and that he's going to use the image in his campaign. Was he being serious?'

'No. Well, probably not. What did Lois say?'

'She accepted the apology on condition that I go to a masterclass in Glamours that she's running at the Alchemical Society. Should I go?'

'I think that's an excellent idea. And you can have tomorrow morning off. Sunday dinner's at two o'clock, unless there's an emergency.'

Karina turned to Evie, who was opening a bottle of wine. 'Do you think your mother would like some help with the cooking tomorrow?'

Evie paused. 'I think she'd like you to offer.'

Karina looked at me again. 'Are you and Mina going out in the morning?'

'I am. On business. Going to see a Gnome. Just me and Scout. Mina's going to do nothing, or so she says.'

'I am perfectly capable of doing nothing,' said Mina. 'You get a lot of practice doing that in prison.' She looked more closely at Karina and put her hand on her shoulder. Karina almost jumped out of her skin. Mina kept her hand where it was and said, 'You want to say something, don't you? Conrad will tell you that keeping quiet costs lives. I agree with him.' Only then did she take her hand away.

'I just wondered, sir, if you'll be all right on your own with the Gnome.'

'That's a good question, and if it were any other Gnome than Lloyd, I'd want you with me. Him, I trust. Sometimes in life you have to trust people.'

'But he's not people. He's a Gnome.'

'Even so, Karina, even so.'

Evie carried the casserole dish over and used her substantial hip to bash me further down the bench. 'You're on washing up, Conrad. I've got a date. Pass your plates.'

18 — Gnome Advantage

I hadn't lied to Karina. Nor had I told her the whole truth. Yes, the only Gnome I trusted was Lloyd, but how did I know that he was the one who'd summoned me to Sandbach? I'll tell you.

It was after eleven o'clock when I sauntered into the restaurant and made my way to the Costa Coffee concession at the back. There were a number of high, stand-up tables and I went to stand by the one with dirty crockery, putting my old cricket bag on the floor. One of the staff was going round clearing tables and came up to me. Her name badge said *Sammi*.

'The badge looks very authentic,' I said.

'It is, I'm an Artificer, remember darlin'?'

I winced at the exaggerated Essex-type accent. There was work to be done there, but otherwise Saffron had inhabited the persona of Sammi brilliantly. On a mission to Litchfield, we'd created a disguise that transformed her – wig, outfit and, how shall I put this, some silicone inserts to enhance her natural assets. I'd told her to work at it, and she had. The visuals were good, but the key was the magick. She'd messaged me from the car park to say that it was Lloyd and another Gnome, and that they hadn't rumbled her disguise.

All humans have Lux flowing through them, as does every living thing except bacteria. The key to going unnoticed if you're a Mage is to damp down emissions of Lux to the point where you look mundane. The downside is that you can't use magick to scope people out or sense trouble. It's very, very hard to pull off on someone's doorstep, but in a crowd…

'The younger one is getting restless. I went to clean outside five minutes ago and he was moaning to Lloyd about being cold. Shall I get you a cappuccino? Medium with an extra shot?'

'Thank you, Sammi. What do your new colleagues think of you?'

She grinned and flashed the perfect replica of a Midland Counties Police warrant card. 'I promoted myself to Detective Sergeant,' she said. 'I'm on undercover training. They think it's good fun, and they aren't going to say no to having an extra pair of hands, are they? One cappuccino, coming up. On the house. I'll get in position when it's ready.'

One of Saffron's new colleagues made the drink and put it on the counter by the fire door leading outside. When it was there, Saffron took a bucket of soapy water and went ahead. I counted to ten and followed her. Outside, the tang of metal wafted over from a table at the far end. The next time I go inside a First Mine, I may need to wear breathing apparatus.

Lloyd's companion was very young for a Gnome and looked barely past puberty. 'Morning, gentlemen. Sorry I'm late.'

Lloyd stood up and embraced me, then said, 'Conrad this is Albie – Albrecht Adams of the Second House of Clan Flint, to give him his full title.'

We shook hands and I made myself as comfortable as possible on the metal chair. Underneath their warm coats, both of the lads were sporting the old gold of Wolverhampton Wanderers. 'Is there a game today?'

'Yeah,' said Lloyd. 'But not until four o'clock. Plenty of time to get back to Molineux.' He leaned forward and looked around, making sure that the woman washing the tables couldn't overhear. 'Conrad, there's stuff going on. I don't think it's safe for you to be the Swordbearer any more. I think if you don't surrender it, someone's likely to challenge you.'

This had been on the cards since I'd accepted the sword in Niði's Hall. I only had one issue with what Lloyd had said. 'What about you? Surely this puts you at even more risk?'

'Don't worry about me, Conrad mate. It actually makes me safer. There's a new kid on the block, and it ain't Albie.'

'I ain't a kid,' said Albie. He kept looking at Saffron – or was he looking at Sammi?

'Yes you am,' said Lloyd. 'It's Saunders. He's decided to adopt an heir.'

When Lloyd's uncle was forced to step down as chief, the clan had chosen an irascible old Gnome called Saunders as the safe (if abrasive) pair of hands to lead them through the crisis. Saunders was childless, unmarried and the last of his house, and therefore had no incentive to get rid of Lloyd. This changed things.

'Surely you're in worse trouble now?' I said.

'It's a stand-off. He adopted a nine year old from the Seventh House. That will guarantee the future of Saunders' house and means that he'll need me to carry on as Clan Second. If you stay as Swordbearer, there's a good chance that someone would challenge you, and you'd have no support except me and Albie. This way, I can choose a new Swordbearer.'

'If you're sure…?'

'I am.'

'Then what do I do?'

'Pick up the sword, feel the pattern inside, then dip the tip in Mother Earth and let it drain away. Easy as that. You can do it now, and Albie will take it back to the First Mine. We could do it here, only we've got an audience. I'll put a Glamour on you, but that waitress is a bit too close. I think she might have a bit of latent talent.'

Saffron really had done a good job. Lloyd had danced with her (in a communal way) at the party two weeks ago and he still didn't recognise her. 'Go and ask her for directions to the Northbound footbridge,' I suggested. 'But ask her in Old High North Germanic and point inside.'

'Go on, kid,' said Lloyd. 'Show her your charms.'

Albie got out of his seat and strolled over to Saffron. He helpfully moved a chair for her and spoke something. Lloyd was looking at Saffron, and Saff glanced in our direction. I gave her a subtle nod to show that it was all good.

Albie pointed again, and I felt a tiny wash of Lux. Saffron smiled at him and picked up her bucket. She positively sashayed across the terrace to the door and disappeared inside with Albie.

'Right, quick,' said Lloyd. 'I'll put a Glamour on as soon as you open your bag.'

I took out the Anvil, drew it from the sheath and lifted it over my head, taking care not to look at it. I closed my eyes and felt the swirling pattern of Lux inside the blade. I've some idea what a human Imprint looks like, and the sword's essence is a bit like that, and two of the strands in the pattern glowed a pale blue. They were mine. In fact, they were part of me, created by energy being drawn from my arm. A lot of energy.

I reversed the grip and brought the tip down onto the stone flags, pushing at the pattern. Something inside the ground, a phantom wave of red-hot magick, like flowing lava, snatched at the pattern and whisked it all away, apart from the pale blue strands. I snatched my focus away from the sword and opened my eyes.

'Close,' said Lloyd. 'You nearly got a transfer burn there. I didn't expect our Mother to come in person. Well done, Conrad.'

I sheathed the sword before it could wake up again, and passed it to Lloyd. I was just about to light a cigarette when Albie emerged with a face like thunder. 'You set me up!' he said accusingly. To me. 'She's a Mage! What's going on?'

'Of course she's a Mage,' said Lloyd. 'Conrad wouldn't come here without backup. As soon as she washed that table for the second time, I clocked her. Do I know her?'

'It's Saffron.'

'No! Bloody hell, mate, tell her well done. I had no clue.' He frowned at his fellow Gnome. 'What tipped you off, Albie?'

'I went to touch her, and she gave me a burn on me arm! Look!'

He held up a meaty forearm with four red marks showing. Ouch. 'Let that be a lesson,' I said. 'In more ways than one.'

Lloyd laughed. 'Nice one. Here you go, Albie. Lay it in on the cairn of the First House and I'll see you at the match.' He passed over the sword and Albie stormed off in a real teenage strop.

As soon as he'd gone, Saffron came back out with two more coffees for Lloyd and me. 'I didn't hurt him, did I?'

'He'll heal,' said Lloyd. 'Well done, Saff, and I'm sorry about Albie.'

Saffron looked like she was going to say more, then shook her expensive wig and smiled. 'Anything else, Conrad? If not, I'll get changed and see you before you go. Unless you're off somewhere.'

'No. And thanks.'

We were alone, and Lloyd shook his head. 'There's more, Conrad. Stuff I can only tell you as a blood-brother, not as a Watch Captain. Can you do that?'

'And there's stuff I can't tell you as a clan second. Can you do that?'

'Unless it directly threatens our First Mine.'

'And unless it directly threatens the King's Peace.'

He extended his hand and we shook on it. 'You first,' I said.

He drank some coffee. 'I went to see Niði last week. He's doing well, by the way. There are four of them now, all plug-ugly and full of attitude. He really is a grumpy sod.'

Dwarves operate on a shared consciousness, of sorts, and they're not born: they emerge from the rock in their Hall. I've seen one growing, and it's the stuff of nightmares. I shuddered. 'I'm pleased he's doing well. The world of magick needs a counter-balance to Hledjolf.'

'That's the problem. Niði is convinced that Hledjolf is going to split himself and dig a new Hall. Up north. Sheffield. I'm just giving you a heads-up.'

'Thanks. You know that Sheffield is in the Danelaw? That's Jordan Fleming's Watch, and Hannah hasn't made me anyone's supervisor yet.'

'I know. It's still a long way from London. You might want to have a look around. Just in case. If I hear anything definite, I'll let you know. On the record.'

'Thanks. And I've got a real problem, Lloyd. I've got a dead Gnome killed by Mannwolves and a Fae Count assassinated by Gnomes, and for the life of me I can't see how they're connected.'

He looked at me as if I were mad. 'A Fae Count? Why is that your concern, and how did a load of overgrown dogs take down one of Mothers' children?'

'They had help. As for the Count, I've got a witness. I'll take you through it.'

I'd got as far as summarising Kirk Liddington's account of the murder when Lloyd stopped me.

'Is he sure there was eight of them?'

'Positive. 100%. That convinced me, given your race's special relationship with the number eight.'

He was very alarmed. 'You don't know, do you? On a special project there are *seven* of us. The eighth one is the spirit of the First House. Symbolic, like. You only get eight Gnomes acting together when it's an Octet.'

I scratched my head. 'Octet? Isn't that like saying there's eight of them? My mother would call it a tautology.'

'She might, but she'd be wrong. It's a translation of *frī-ahte*, which is the Old German for "Free Eight". It means there's eight Gnomes looking to dig themselves a new First Mine and form a new clan. It's what my brother was going to do. Until I chopped his head off. I never did find out which other clans were involved.'

I was reeling from that, and it took me a few seconds to realise what he'd said. 'What other clans?'

'You can't dig a new First Mine unless you come from at least three clans. I reckon that they've showed up on your patch. You know why we called them "Free"? It's because they ain't tied to a clan. No accountability, until they settle down. You could have your hands full with that lot.'

'Thanks. You're making me full of confidence, Lloyd. If you could start asking around, I'd be grateful. Any clues would be welcome.' Something struck me. 'What about clans from overseas?'

'Yeah. The Great Clan knows no borders. What makes you think that?'

'My witness heard two of the wives talking in modern German.'

He nodded. 'Good luck, Conrad. Sounds like you're gonna be busy.'

'You know me, Lloyd, never one for the quiet life. One last thing, Lloyd, I hope you have a word with young Albrecht. He was out of order.'

'I know. I won't let it go.'

'Thanks. I hope you enjoy the game this afternoon.'

'So do I. And there's one last thing from me, Conrad. I owe you a sword. I'll make it a good 'un. Take care.'

He jumped over the low fence and headed for the car park. After all that coffee, I needed to go to the Gents. Saffron was waiting by the Volvo and she already had Scout's lead on him. I didn't want him going mental when he smelled Gnome, so I'd left him in the car.

Sammi's wig, assets and scuffed clothes had gone and Saffron's white-blonde mane was back, as was the short dress and natural poise of the Mage aristocracy. 'Bloody Gnomes. He's lucky he didn't get a knee in the groin.'

'What did he do?'

'Released some of those enhanced pheromones, touched my arm and thought he was doing me a favour.'

'He's in trouble with Lloyd. Thanks for that, Saffron.'

'No problem. It was good fun and good practice.' She grimaced. 'Mostly. Being touched by a Gnome-child is not fun. Still good practice, though.'

'How's life at Elvenham?'

'Weird without you and Mina. I keep thinking I can smell cigarette smoke by the outhouse. I wouldn't leave it too long if I were you, or Myfanwy will get restless. She's already taken on two more pensioners' gardens to keep her busy.' She passed over Scout's lead. 'How's Karina shaping up?'

'As you'll no doubt remember, it's a steep learning curve.'

'Not half. Take care, Conrad.'

'And you, Saff.'

We leaned in for a hug, and she gave Scout a treat before heading for her car. If you're wondering how she got him out of the Volvo, as she said, she's an Artificer.

'Come on, boy, let's find something to sniff.'

'Arff.'

There is an old police control room at the Bolton Wanderers stadium, a relic from the days when not only were there a lot more police officers, there were a lot more Bolton fans, too. Tom was going through some paperwork in front of the many CCTV screen when the door opened and Elaine breezed in.

'Has Rob gone?' he asked.

'Yeah. Off to Scotland training camp for a week. Put me down for as much overtime as you want now.'

'You'll need it to pay for all the takeaways and meals in the Jade Palace. My offer of cooking lessons is still open.'

She slid into the chair next to him. 'I wouldn't deprive Lucy of your company. So, what's this all about?'

'At ten o'clock this morning, a woman walked into Sandbach services and presented a Midland Counties Police warrant card. She said she was doing undercover practice, and could she work at the coffee bar for nothing? The manager said yes, but something about her made him ring and check with Birmingham.'

'Oh yes? What was suspicious?'

'Her age. She claimed she was a DS and the manager thought she was ridiculously young for that. Midland Counties control room checked her out, and yes, it was a fake, but she used her real name, one Saffron Hawkins. That name raised a big red flag. She's MI7, and not only that, she's on a list that interested me. Do you remember me telling you about my old partner, Kris Hayes?'

'I do. It took you a while before you stopped comparing me to her unfavourably.'

'Ouch. Sorry. It was Kris who I got to check out Conrad Clarke's place in Clerkswell. Lieutenant Hawkins' little bit of deception was passed to Kris Hayes, because she was on duty, and she called up CCTV from the service station. Watch this.'

Tom activated one of the monitors and played a view of the car park. 'Does that Volvo at the edge look familiar?' he asked, indulging himself with a smug tone.

'Bugger me. That's Clarke's car.'

'It is. Here she comes.'

A young woman with huge white hair and wearing a floral dress, black tights and a denim jacket bounced across the car park. She fiddled with the Volvo and let out the familiar form of Clarke's dog, who seemed to know her. She put him on the lead and swept back her hair as the tall form of Clarke limped over. They spoke for a minute, embraced, and she left.

'If that was all there was,' said Tom, 'I wouldn't have dragged you in. It took me a while to find, but this bit is much more interesting.'

Another external camera covered part of the motorway and the back of the service building, where several tables were laid out for smokers. 'This is where I looked first,' said Tom. 'Those two guys have been there for twenty minutes, and neither of them smokes.'

'Bit cold for sitting around outside.'

'It is.' He fell silent, and a café employee came out with a bucket. Tom paused the image. 'Anything familiar?'

Elaine peered at the screen. 'Was one of those guys a suspect in that Liverpool case?'

'No. Have another look at the girl.'

'That's not Hawkins.'

'Oh yes, it is. Here comes Conrad.'

Clarke came out, put his coffee down and the older man got up to give him a hug, and Tom paused the image, the disparity in the men's height clearly visible.

'Calabrese,' said Elaine. 'Is it a genetic thing? Are they all short?'

'Who knows.'

They carried on watching as the younger man convinced Hawkins to go inside and then Clarke took a fishing rod out of his bag, practised a fly cast and handed it over. It was then removed by the younger man, who pointed to his arm first, in pain.

'I'm guessing that wasn't a fishing rod,' said Elaine.

'I doubt it. Clarke once told me he was into hunting and shooting, but not fishing.'

'Interesting,' said Elaine. 'He has to rendezvous with his contacts in public, and he gets an associate who's not Karina to watch his back. Proves he's on the case. Not that I doubted it.'

'It does more than that,' said Tom.

He had been seething all afternoon, and he was forcing himself not to take it out on Elaine. She didn't know Clarke like he did. Or Mina Desai. Clarke was so bloody plausible and Mina was so devious. That was the problem. He took a deep breath to calm himself. 'They're a rogue operation, Elaine, and I won't have it. I will not have men and women loosely attached to the Army walking around pretending to be police officers. I have no problem with the regular security services, but this is different.'

Elaine looked very uncomfortable, and Tom was aware that the bee in his bonnet was buzzing very loudly.

'Are you sure you want to go down that road, sir?'

'Don't worry, Elaine. I'm not going to sound off to the press or kick up a stink, I'm going to play them at their own game. I missed you yesterday afternoon, so how did you get on with Karina Kent?'

'I went into Auntie Elaine mode. While Conrad was lurking outside the superstore, I took her to the clothing section and held on to her stuff. Those robes are actually made of very fine material, much more comfortable than they look. Anyway, while she was in the changing room, I put the App on her phone.'

'How did you unlock it?'

'Tracey Kenyon came up trumps. While Karina was wearing gloves at the crime scene yesterday, she couldn't use fingerprint ID, so she typed in the passcode. Tracey collects useful bits of information like that. She knows both of ours, too. I've changed mine already.'

'And Karina won't know?'

'No. Payback time: it's the MI5 special, the one that replaces the standard mapping App seamlessly. All we have to do is activate it.'

'Then set it up for tomorrow.'

'Will do. How are the regular MIT team getting on?'

'Completely stumped. Absolutely no idea of the victim's identity, no witnesses, no traffic cameras. Nothing. The full post-mortem is tomorrow, so perhaps there will be trace evidence, like doggy DNA.'

'Or wolf. Those wounds are huge. Why the wait for the PM?'

'My last action as SIO was to order the top man, Michael Jepson. He was away for the weekend. Talking of which, let's go and enjoy what's left of ours. See you tomorrow.'

At four o'clock on Monday morning, a shiny black van pulled up to the hidden entrance of a hospital mortuary in Liverpool. The van was unmarked, except for a discreet sign on the back that said *Private Ambulance*.

Three figures got out of the front, two stocky men and one woman. The woman pressed the buzzer while the men unloaded a trolley from the back of the van. On top of the trolley was the unmistakable shape of a body bag.

'Fishers of Westmorland,' said the woman to the intercom. 'We've got an RTA victim from the M6 crash.'

The roller shutters next to the personnel door jerked into action with a clang and rattle. The woman went back to the cab of the van and took out a cardboard tray with four takeout coffees and a bag of pastries. When the shutters were fully up, the men pushed the trolley inside, and she followed them.

The two men left about fifteen minutes later, the woman ten minutes after that. When the men pushed the trolley out, it looked empty. A careful observer might have noticed that they took a lot of care and had to work very hard for an empty trolley, but there were no careful observers at that time of the morning.

Dr Jepson didn't order the unnamed victim to be brought up to the autopsy suite until ten o'clock, and that was when they discovered what had really happened. By then, Conrad Clarke had already gone into full emergency mode.

19 — Curried Worm Time

I stared at my phone as it sat, metaphorically steaming, on the breakfast table. 'How the hell did they find out?'

'Find out what?' said Evie while she buttered some toast. 'Whoever that was sounded very angry. I could hear them from over here.'

Mina raised an eyebrow in polite enquiry, and Karina looked worried. Every time there's bad news, she thinks it's her fault. I sincerely hoped it wasn't.

'That was Lachlan Mace of Clan Blackrod,' I said. 'The Gnomes of Lancashire know about their lost brother, and about the attack by the Dual Natured.'

'Alleged attack,' said Mina. Since the end of the cricket season, she's been growing her nails and she's still getting used to eating with her fingers. She held her slice of toast like it was a Leonardo sketch and peered at the butter level before adding Marmite.

'We've been summoned to see the clan chief at the First Mine in a couple of hours. He wants to know why the King's Watch didn't inform him.'

'Can you lie your way out of it?' said Mina.

'I'm going to have to try, but I doubt it'll buy me much time. More than anything, we need to track down Princess Birkdale's pack of wolves, and when I say *we*, I don't mean me or Karina. That version of *we* needs to report to the First Mine.'

'Can't I go hunting the wolves?' said Karina. 'That's my strong point, after all. Where are they?'

Really? She was asking that?

'I told you, Karina, we need to find their base first.'

'Can't we get someone to do that?'

'I could go to London tomorrow,' said Mina. 'After all, I am an expert on tracking down assets.'

'Do you want a hand?' said Evie. 'For the day rate, of course.'

'Me too,' said Karina.

'You just want to get out of meeting the clan,' I countered. 'You can't be in the Watch and not learn how to deal with Gnomes. Shit. I need to call the Boss.'

'Finish your breakfast,' said Mina. 'You'll regret it later if you don't.'

'Fine.'

I bolted down my food, poured a mug of coffee and headed out to the dog kennel. Scout had already had a long walk and breakfast, so he was flat out asleep. 'Alright for some. Here goes.'

'What?' said Hannah when I'd relayed the conversation. 'You've brought this on yourself, Conrad. You should never have involved DCI Morton. He's much smarter than you.'

'He is, ma'am, but I don't think he's been telling tales to the Gnomes. That body was left for me to discover, and without Morton, I wouldn't have found Kirk Liddington.'

'What the hell do you think is going on?'

'Honestly? I don't know. Since last night, I'm coming more round to the idea that it *was* Princess Birkdale who set her wolves on to the dead Gnome. I think she's trying to provoke them. It's the only lead I've got to go on.'

'This is such a mess,' she sighed. 'You do realise that if things get worse, I may have to take you off the case? It's not your fault, but if it's the only way to avoid a Fae/Gnome war, I'll do it.'

'If I can't sort this out, I may ask you to take over. I don't want to start a war, either.'

'So get on with it. And keep me updated, understand?'

'Ma'am.'

I disconnected and looked down. 'Don't get too comfortable, Scout. You're coming with me today.' I headed into the kitchen and put my mug in the dishwasher. 'Right, Karina, time to break out your uniform. This is official.'

'Do I have to?'

'Yes,' said Mina. 'For Conrad's sake. He finds it comforting.'

Charming. I wonder whether she's going to get worse when we're married. Probably. Still, if it gets Karina into gear without a strop, who am I to complain?

Despite the magickal sounding name, Clan Blackrod are called after the village of Blackrod, to the north west of Bolton, about ten miles from where the late Gnome was found. They are a big clan, with branches all over Lancashire and a fair bit of clout. I was not looking forward to this.

All Gnomes have a First Mine, where they worship Mother Earth, where they lay their dead to rest and where they keep their treasure. Sometimes the Mine is occupied permanently, sometimes it isn't. None of Lloyd's clan, for example, live in their Mine. Then again, the First Mine of Clan Flint is in the grounds of a sewerage works. You wouldn't live there, either. Clan Blackrod are different.

We collected our pilot from the SPAR grocery shop in Aspull, a young Gnome who had a wide eyed curiosity about his mission and strict orders not to say a word, not even when he was forced to sit in the back of the car with a dog who wanted to lick him all over. The one thing he did say was, 'Second left, then third right. You'll see the gates at the end of the lane.'

'Impressive,' I said when we drove through soot-blackened pillars and up a well-made drive to the house. 'Even more impressive. I do love a bit of Gothic.'

'It's creepy,' said Karina. At least she'd waited until we were out of the car and the young Gnome had gone. 'What are all the turrets and spires for? It's not a real house.'

'It sends a message. It says, "Powerful men live here." And also, "We have a lot of money." My ancestor did the same thing when he built Elvenham. On a smaller scale, of course.'

'No woman would build something like that. It's just unnecessary.'

'Vicky has the same opinion. She much prefers Georgian architecture. Are you ready?'

She nodded rather than risk an answer. I reached into the leg pocket of my combat uniform and fetched out a small packet. 'You haven't asked me much about my encounters with the Allfather, Karina.'

'Sir? No. That's private.'

'Do you know what the first piece of advice he gave me was?'

'No.'

I passed over the packet. 'Always take curried worms when you go underground. It saved my life.'

She stared at the turmeric-tinted, slimy invertebrates. 'Is that what you say to all junior officers? Is this a wind-up?'

'No. It most definitely is not. Keep them in a safe place. They're high in protein.'

'You eat them?'

'Just one. Just to see what they taste like. They are as disgusting as they look. Even Scout turns his nose up at them. Do you think it's safe to leave him in the grounds?'

'Those Wards are strong. He won't go near them.'

I slipped Scout off the lead and he headed for the nearest tree. 'Let's get this over with, then.'

When Karina said that it wasn't a real house, she was telling the truth. The impressive facade of Blackrod Mine does have rooms behind some of the windows, but mostly it's a big gateway to the big tunnel under the hill. A pair of Gnomes guarded the iron bound doors and held their long-handled, single bladed axes as if they were broomsticks.

'Who would approach the Mine of Blackrod?' said the one on the left.

'Conrad Clarke, Deputy to the Peculier Constable and Watch Captain of the Palatinate. I come in peace. This is Watch Officer Kent.'

The other Gnome used the butt of his axe to hammer on the doors. With a good creak and groan, one of the leaves swung inward. Now that *would* be creepy on a dark night. Inside the shallow building was a suitably OTT hallway with dark panelling and a lot of heraldic shields, mostly featuring braziers. If the outside doors were impressive, the ones at the back of the hall were jaw-dropping affairs of sheet steel and rivets, as if someone had cut a chunk out of the hull of an old battleship. They were plain to look at, but thrummed with magick. I resisted the temptation to use my Sight on them, and focused on Lachlan Mace, who stood at the bottom of a staircase.

'Thank you for coming,' he said. As if I'd had a choice. He did seem to have calmed down, though. 'We won't be entering the Mine today, as you're the Swordbearer for another clan.'

'Not any more. I surrendered the Anvil yesterday.'

He first looked surprised, then narrowed his eyes as he calculated what my news might mean. 'Thank you for telling me. I'm sure it will make a difference in the future. For today, if you could follow me.'

At the top of the stairs, a landing took us through open doors into the Chief's public receiving room. This was not a room designed to overawe (that would be the Hall underground), this was a room to make you know your place, and that place was outside the sacred confines. It was still impressive, though. Apart from the body bag on the floor. That was worrying.

The chief of Clan Blackrod sat behind a blackened oak desk that was raised a good eighteen inches above the rest of the room on a platform. His chair was also huge, and it was all designed to reinforce his status. And his stature, but we won't go there. In person, he was beefy, white haired and had a face that had seen a lot, with both pleasure and pain etched into the lines. Work hard, play hard. On a grand scale, like the house.

I bowed. 'Chief. You know who I am, and I come in peace.'

He remained seated. 'In peace, welcome.' He paused to show that even today, peace was a precious commodity that deserved respect. 'Why have I had to liberate one of my people from a mortuary, Mr Clarke?'

Please no. I looked North, towards Asgard and prayed. Allfather, please let this be one of your jokes. Please.

Lachlan unzipped the bag, and no one was laughing. There was the poor creature, still in his ski mask and silk suit. This was seriously bad news.

'Chief Stefan, you have crossed a line here.'

He slapped the desk with his hand. 'No! It is you have crossed the line! Your duty was to return our clansman and keep the mundane world away from us, but you neglected your duty. Any consequences are yours to deal with.'

'I...' I didn't know what to say. He was right. As soon as the late Gnome had appeared, I should have followed protocol and whisked him away for a 'special' autopsy. I'd burnt that bridge now, and Stefan was right: I had to deal with the consequences.

The chief waited until I'd zoned back in. 'This stinks of the Fairies. They are the only ones with pets who would do this. I am summoning the Clan. Our brother will be taken into the Mine and laid to rest. After that, we will want vengeance.'

'As is your right,' I said. 'I trust you choose your target carefully.'

'What are you saying, Clarke?'

'That my only aim is to keep the King's Peace, which is why I withheld the news of your brother's death. Do you know whose door to knock on?'

'We will find the door.' He sat back. 'As I said, vengeance can wait until Drake has been laid to rest. He was not just from my House, he was Clan Counsel.'

The penny finally dropped: he was giving me a window of opportunity. I had until the interment to jump through it and find the killers. 'His death is a terrible loss, Chief Stefan. Why would Drake have been targeted? Others in the clan would have been easier prey.'

'Lachlan will look into that with help from Drake's sons. He had dealings with many across the North West.'

'And may I ask if you or his sons knew what he was planning on Saturday morning?'

'He was playing golf,' said the chief.

Oh no he wasn't. I hoped that Karina had kept as straight a face as I'd tried to. As far as I could tell, neither Chief Stefan nor Lachlan had looked at her once.

'Which course?' I asked, when I'd got my surprise under control.

'Radcliffe. Up the valley from where he was found. I've sent clansmen to investigate. When we move, Mr Clarke, we will move swiftly, accurately and mercilessly. Good day.'

Lachlan zipped up the bag. 'I will show you out.' We followed him in silence until we got to the great doors. He placed his hand on a locking bar and paused. 'Why did you surrender the Anvil? Was it because your alliance with their clan second is over?'

'Oh no, Lachlan. I surrendered it to preserve my bond with Lloyd, not because it is any weaker.'

'I see.' He actually sounded as if he might.

The sound of that body bag being zipped came back when I heard a creak from the upstairs floorboards. 'You want to do it right, don't you?' I said.

'Of course.'

'Then do me one favour. Put Drake, as he is, into your cold store. Nothing else. Just that.'

He thought for a moment. 'We'll see.' He opened the door and stood back. 'Go well, Conrad.'

Gnomes have good hearing, so I strode away from the sentinels as quickly as I could. The sound of barking came from my right, and a raised voice. What the hell is he up to now? I pivoted and followed the noise.

'Ugh,' said Karina. 'What's that smell?'

'Gnome?'

'I haven't been blessed by Nimue, so I can't smell the Essence of Gnomes. All I can smell is their disgusting aftershave. It's not that, it's … oh.'

Scout had found the pigsty, and its ripe odour was just now getting through to me. A young lad (who should have been in school) was about to throw a stone at my dog, and that was not going to happen. I let out a loud whistle, and the boy looked up, hand raised. Scout also heard me and galloped over like he was at an agility class. On another day, I would have called out the boy and made sure he didn't try it again. Not today. I do not need another reason for Clan Blackrod to be annoyed with me.

Once Scout was back at heel, Karina turned away from the mine and pretended to trip. 'Oh dear,' she said. 'I nearly fell. Could that be because I didn't get his blessing? You are to go well, but not me. It's not just the house that's ugly and stinks, the whole place is a cesspit. It's vile. It's brutal and it's the enemy of everything good in the world. I don't know how you can stand them, let alone call one of them your friends.'

I stopped, somewhere in the middle of the grass that fronts the Mine, half way between the pigsties and the car. 'You don't have to like them, Karina, you just have to treat them equally. That's all. Give them the same rights as everyone else in the world of magick.' I made sure she'd got the message and turned to carry on walking. Both Scout and Karina rushed to keep up.

'But … But how can you, when they're like that?' she stammered.

I kept walking. 'Wrong question. The right question is, "How can *Karina* treat them equally when they disgust her?" You'd better find an answer.'

Yee Hah! Yee Hah!

Damn. We were back in mobile signal range. What did the Sheriff want now?

'Clarke. What the fuck is going on?'

It was the first time I'd heard Morton swear. I think. 'In what way?'

'In the way that there is no longer a dead gangster in the Liverpool mortuary. In that way that he's been replaced by a dead pig.'

I winced and screwed my eyes closed. This could not be happening to me. 'They put a dead pig in?'

There was a silence, and when he spoke again, Morton's fury had to turned to ice. 'You knew, didn't you? You were surprised about the pig, but not the missing body.'

'I've just heard. Literally while you were trying to ring me. I had no foreknowledge. None.'

'Where is it? Tell me who's got it.'

'I can't.'

He broke off for a second, then said, 'What?' to someone in the room with him. 'I'm putting you on hold, Clarke. Don't go away.'

I kept my phone pressed to my ear in case he came back on the line and said, 'Karina. Ring the Boss now and tell her to expect a shitstorm. Clan Blackrod didn't just take the body, I'm afraid. Quick, before the Angel of Death gets to her.'

'Who?'

'Now.'

'That's not all,' said Morton in my ear. 'There's been a straightforward break-in at the forensic laboratory. All the samples have gone.'

Now that was thorough. I tipped my hat to Clan Blackrod. I also cursed them for being bloody awkward. I was struggling for something to say to that, and before I could come up with a suitable platitude, Morton cut me off. 'I'm wanted in Warrington for a crisis meeting. I hope you're happy.'

He rang off just as Karina finished explaining the headlines to Hannah. I made a signal and she said, 'Would you like to speak to him, ma'am? ... Right.' She passed me the phone and I braced myself.

'Ma'am?'

'Give me something, Conrad. Give me anything I can use to stop our ship sinking in a sea of shit. I have never known such a mess in all my years of pain and torment. In Hashem's name, give me something.'

'I've just heard that the forensics lab has been turned over, too. All physical evidence is gone.'

For the first time ever, she raised her voice to me. 'I said give something good, not more bad news!' It was more than a shout, it was a cry of pain.

'That is the good news. It must have been an inside job. Tom Morton didn't tell me where the body was being taken and I have no idea who does their forensic science. It wasn't Morton who leaked it, because he's not in the pay of Clan Blackrod. Get on to John Lake. Tell him to get Morton's bosses, the Professional Standards people, to threaten an investigation. It will make the regular police drop the case like a hot potato.'

She was quiet for a second. 'Good point. That, I can work with.' She paused again. 'They'll want something in return. I can't leave you in charge, so I'm taking you off the case.'

'Am I suspended?'

She gave a hollow laugh. 'There was only one thing stopping me from giving you the Deputy's job, and it's this: I can't suspend you. Only the Duke of Albion can do that, and even then, you'd still be Priest of the Dyfrdwy

181

Altar and Guardian of the North. Only Nimue can take that off you, and she doesn't take my calls any more.'

I had a vision of her pinching the bridge of her nose and screwing up her eyes. 'And what's worse, Conrad, is that the only person who can take over is me. Or Iain Drummond. I shall come up on Wednesday.'

'What about Karina?'

'I shall have to decide when I get there.'

A tiny voice of hope spoke up in the back of my mind. 'On Wednesday, ma'am?'

'Yes. On Wednesday. In the evening. Now go away and let me fight the fire.'

I checked the screen and passed the phone back to Karina. 'Let's go.' When we got in the car, I held up my hand and said, 'I'm going to drive to Middlebrook. It's only five minutes and I need time to get my head together.'

The Middlebrook development was where we'd stopped to get Karina's top on Saturday. As well as the Bolton Wanderers stadium, it had a retail park with a huge Tesco and lots of places to stop for coffee. When Karina came out of the café with our re-usable mugs filled (I'd offered her the choice of buying the drinks or looking after Scout), I filled her in on the full horror of our situation. She chose to focus on the pig.

'That's disgusting. A deliberate insult to Boss Hannah. How can they get away with that.'

'You mean because Hannah's Jewish?'

'Of course.'

I shook my head. 'I doubt that Stefan Blackrod knows or cares about the Peculier Constable's faith. It was an exchange. Obviously it'll end up in an incinerator, but it will have been killed and processed to humane and food hygiene standards. In their eyes, if we choose to turn it down, that's our problem. According to Occult law, all non-human bodies are the domain of the race they come from.'

She wasn't happy. On all sorts of levels. Inside, she couldn't move on, so she said nothing.

'So, Karina, what do we do now?'

'What do you mean, sir?'

'Stefan Blackrod and Hannah have given us a tiny window. If Hannah didn't want us to carry on investigating, she'd be on the train now. If the chief of Clan Blackrod wanted a war, he wouldn't wait until after the burial. So, what should we do?'

'What can we do?'

'We've only got one lead – the Dual Natured wolves. We go after that.'

'Do you really think that Princess Birkdale would do something like that?'

'If she thought she could do it without her Queen finding out, she would. It's certainly stirred things up. I'll call Mina and see if they've made any progress.'

She picked up straight away and said, 'How was it? I didn't want to call because you might be busy.'

I brought her up to date and finished by saying, 'Please give me some good news.'

'Conrad. I'm so sorry. You have done everything for the best, and now this happens. And I have no good news about the wolf pack yet. We're waiting for a few people to call us back, and I'm afraid that I have something worse to tell you.'

'What could possibly make things worse?'

'Stacey has just called me. Guess who's coming into the Fairy Gardens tonight for a rehearsal?'

I groaned out loud. 'Not Fae Klass. Please tell me it's not her.'

'I wish I could. And they are expecting a replacement for the Count by the end of the week.'

I swore. Graphically and in German. The Princess now knew exactly what had happened to the Count. When she found out could be crucial.

Mina dropped her voice. 'Remember, Conrad, Ganesh does not close one door without opening another. You just have to look for it.'

'Are you anywhere near discovering anything?' I said, and I wasn't able to keep the pleading out of my voice.

'Perhaps a couple of hours.'

'I'm going to take a gamble. I'm going up the Ribble Valley so we're nearer.'

'Take care. I'll go as fast as I can, and so will Evie. I shall make her.'

She said the last bit quite loudly, and I guessed that Evie had heard most of the conversation. We said quieter goodbyes and I broke the news to Karina. She was happy that we were keeping going, and agreed to mind Scout while I went for a stroll.

Once I was out of sight, I called Kirk Liddington. 'You got me there, Kirk. Completely fooled me. When did they get in touch.'

'I don't know what you're talking about.'

'I'm in Bolton. Penwortham is about fifteen minutes away. I'll drop Karina off and let her question you, shall I? Just tell me the truth and I'll leave you alone.'

'You would, wouldn't you? You're not as nice as you look, Conrad, and I didn't think you looked very nice to start with. They came round the same day you did. Late on Thursday evening. Auntie Iris and Tara Doyle herself, completely incognito. She was absolutely lovely to me. Completely understood what I'd been through.'

'And she had some forest manna, didn't she?'

183

He drew in a sharp breath. 'How did you know that? Even I'm not supposed to know that's what they call it. The Count told me it's not illegal.'

'It isn't. Neither is smoking, but they're both bad for you. Anything else to add?'

'Will the trolley dollies or their boyfriends come after me? Tara said they wouldn't, but I think you know who they are.'

'I wish I did. No, they won't come after you.'

I got back to the car and said, 'I'm afraid that the Princess is firmly in the frame for Drake Blackrod's murder now. And if I ever speak to Tom Morton again, I will want strong words about what he put in his report. Someone accessed it before we'd got back to Middlebarrow. She had plenty of time to get her pets and plan the ambush.'

We got in the car and I started the engine. 'I'd say that this day couldn't get any worse, but that would be tempting fate.'

Tom found Elaine waiting outside, sheltering from a thin wind that promised rain sooner or later. Probably sooner. 'Don't tell me you've started smoking,' said Tom. 'You're lurking outside like That Man.'

'You mean Clarke, sir?'

'I do.'

'How did it go?'

He stared glumly at the car park, then turned to look at the building he'd just come out of. The headquarters of South Lancs Police was very similar to the people inside it: grey, low and undistinguished. No, that wasn't fair. The chief constable was popular and well known for standing up for his rank and file officers. It wasn't the Chief, it was Assistant Chief Constable Nick Schofield who really got up Tom's nose.

'Badly,' said Tom. 'Very badly.' He started walking towards his car, just as the rain made itself felt.

'How come?' said Elaine.

'Clarke must have been owed a lot of favours, and I dread to think how he accumulated them. I went in expecting to hear that this was going to be declared a major incident and that Serious Crimes were taking over. Ha. How wrong a man can be.'

He slumped in his seat, deflated and defeated. Even taking the keys out of his coat pocket seemed like too much effort.

'It can't have been that bad, Tom,' said Elaine.

'Don't you believe it.' He turned to face her. 'First, the hospital have had a Security Order slapped on them. As far as they're concerned, there never was a body in the first place.'

'And they've put up with that?'

'I doubt Michael Jepson will be happy, but he's like me: he doesn't have a choice. These gangsters, these Calabrese or whoever they really are, they've done us up like a kipper. Not only did the morgue fail to check the body that was dropped off with them, there is clearly a mole in South Lancs Police. How else did they know where to look? They even went straight to the right boxes in the evidence store.'

He thumped the steering wheel and hurt his hand. 'Ow. Blast. As a direct result, South Lancs are dropping the murder investigation. Not completely. Oh no, they're assigning it to the Ongoing Enquiry Team.'

Elaine looked suitably appalled. 'The Abandon Hope brigade?'

'The one and only.'

Elaine looked worried. 'But Tom, what about the gang war? If the body's been stolen, doesn't that make further retribution more likely?'

'It does. John Lake admitted as much. Clarke is off the case and will be investigated. Hannah Rothman is taking over on Wednesday.' He smiled. 'Funny that. John Lake referred to Hannah as *The Constable* as if it were a senior rank. Lake has also been on to Leonie, and we've been allocated the job of finding the mole. Again. I hate that.'

Tom often felt that he and Elaine were like a see-saw: whenever he was up, she was down, and right now she looked far more positive than she had a right to.

'That's good news,' she said. 'It means we can sort it out.'

'What on earth do you mean?'

'This Hannah Rothman person isn't coming up for two days. The service from Euston to Manchester is very good. She could be here in time for a late lunch if she wanted to. I think she's up to something, and if she is, you can bet that Clarke is, too.'

'Could be.'

'You know him better than me, sir. Do you think he had anything to do with the phantom pig?'

He thought about it, as he'd been thinking all morning. 'No, because he was really rattled when we spoke this morning. I've never seen him rattled before, not even flying a helicopter into a snowstorm.'

She nodded. 'This is what I think. I think that MI7 are losing control, and that they've told Clarke to sort it out. Under the radar, as it were. By Wednesday.'

'You could be right. We'll never know.'

'We will if we activate Karina Kent's tracker. He doesn't trust her to work alone, so wherever she is, he'll be there too. And so will we.'

'That could be very dangerous, Elaine.'

'What else are we going to do? Go through all the access records for HOLMES and do background checks on everyone who accessed the files? I vote we follow our noses. Or Clarke's nose, anyway.'

'You could have come up with a better image than that, Elaine. I don't think he has much of a sense of smell. On the other hand, I have absolutely nothing to offer that's any better. Go for it.'

She twisted around and grabbed her laptop from the back seat. Tom tried to keep in shape; Elaine made it look easy. She had once been a champion rock climber, and could twist into all sorts of shapes if she had a reason to get something.

'I'll nip back inside and get on the HQ Wi-Fi. Won't be a tick.'

Tom thought about following her and getting a coffee, but he didn't want to set foot over the threshold again. He fumbled for his keys and brought the car's electronics to life. When his phone had bonded, he called Lucy, just to hear her voice.

'I was going to call you,' she said. 'I've just had the weirdest conversation with Mina Desai.'

Tom sat upright. 'How long ago?'

'Just after nine o'clock, why?'

'I'll tell you later. Go on. What did she want?'

'It was weird. She started asking about recommendations for coffee shops and restaurants in central Manchester because she's doing some work there, then she somehow got round to Tara Doyle. I didn't even realise that she'd changed the subject until I found myself telling her who handles Tara's PR and which limousine company she uses. I only realised she might have an ulterior motive when she asked about lawyers.'

'Did she now?'

'Have I done something wrong? What's she up to?'

'It's him I worry about. Then again, they're as bad as each other. The original definition of thick as thieves. The only thing good about the Clarke / Desai alliance is that it saves two innocent people from being involved.'

'Tom! Mina seemed really nice. And she gave me a really good tip for a place to look at in Chester. I'm going to follow it up later. Have I dropped you in it?'

'Never, love. They're up to something, but I don't know what. There's been a lot going on. I'll tell you later. Elaine's coming.'

He disconnected and waited impatiently. Elaine dashed across the car park, holding her laptop under her coat against the rain. She chucked it in the back and climbed into the front. 'Buckle up, sir,' she said. 'We're off to the Ribble Valley.'

20 — *All You Can Eat*

'What makes you think this is the right place, sir?' said Karina as we left the tiny village of Newton and headed further into one of England's most underappreciated wildernesses, the Forest of Bowland.

'Because this piece of land is owned by the Vesta Tilley Trust.'

'I would have gone for the one near Pendle Hill. Why else would they call the business Sheep's Clothing?'

Mina had given me half a dozen likely spots in and around the Ribble Valley that might be associated with Tara Doyle in one of her many incarnations, and we were on our way to one now.

'I think you'll find that Sheep's Clothing is run by a shepherdess or a farmer's wife. It's a desperate business, hill farming. As soon as Mina told me who Vesta Tilley was, it had to be that one. She was a massive music hall star in her day, and a male impersonator, to boot.'

'Isn't that a bit obvious?'

'Only if you know that Tara Doyle is Princess Birkdale. These sort of things aren't meant to fool the magickal community. All I need now is for my contact at Lunar Hall to get back to me.'

'But they're an enclosed order. How will they know?'

I slowed down and risked a proper look at Karina. 'Because when you have little magick, survival depends on cultivating those that have a lot.' I looked back at the road. What little of it there was. I forced myself to slow down. 'Mother Julia used to be the magickal teacher at Stoneyhurst, the boarding school I pointed out on the way here. Five gets you ten that the resident Witch will be known to her. She may even have taught her.'

We lapsed into silence for a while, until I reckoned we were near enough to the target. I found a small gateway with enough room to get the Volvo off the road and pulled in. I checked for a mobile signal and turned the engine off. 'I'll take Scout for a walk for a bit. Coming?'

'We could be face to face with a pack of Mannwolves soon. If you don't mind, I'll set up my bow.'

Since she arrived at Middlebarrow, Karina has said that she's gone for archery practice on several occasions. Either that or communing at Nimue's spring. 'Of course. I should have thought.'

Because of the narrow road, I put Scout on the lead and strode out. The whole of the Forest of Bowland is quite hilly and full of sudden dips rather than the big valleys of the Pennines or Lakeland. We were towards the bottom of what poets might call a shady vale, with a low hill in the distance. Much beyond that, the view was obscured by the beginning of woods. I gave it half a mile, then turned back and crossed the road to give Scout a different set of smells. In that whole time, I'd seen not a single car, walker or any sign of life beyond sheep.

I was two hundred yards from the car when Mother Julia called. 'It's always good to hear from you, Conrad, but I'm not an informer. Why do you want to know this information?'

'Lives are at stake, Julia, or I wouldn't bother you. I'm trying to stop Clan Blackrod and the Fae tearing lumps out of each other.'

'So what are you doing up here?'

'That I can't tell you. Not yet, partly because I might be making an arse of myself. Again.'

'Very well. I think I might know someone who can help – she was one of my pupils a good fifteen years ago. She came from London and she went back there. I saw her a few years ago at a Stoneyhurst Mage reunion and she said she'd settled at a place on the Dunsop to Botton road.'

'Thank you, Julia. If there's anything I can do...'

'I know. Take care.'

Damn. I'd picked the wrong road – our target was on the other side of the hill. We'd have to take the long road round. Not a great tragedy in the scheme of things, but annoying.

Karina was testing the load on her compound bow. If you've never seen one of these things before, it's more like the engineering that holds up the power lines on a railway than Robin Hood's weapon of choice – all carbon fibre struts and wheels. I can't say it's my sort of thing, but my life might depend on her ability with that contraption, so I've paid attention when she's been waxing lyrical.

'All good?'

'Yes. I haven't got many Quicksilver arrows, though. Only five.'

'Hopefully, it won't come to that. Shall we?'

She placed the bow carefully on the back seat and stared at it. 'What smells does Scout not find interesting?'

'I can't say I've done any experiments, but he hates black pepper with a vengeance.'

She moved her hands in the gestures of traditional magick and lowered them over her bow. 'Don't want him licking it or biting it. If he chewed through the wrong part, it could snap.'

'Nasty. Good thinking.' I opened the tailgate and Scout jumped in. He went straight for the bow, of course, and backed off with a sneeze. When I see Mages doing something on an industrial scale, I don't feel in the least connected, but when I see them do something simple like lighting a fire or rendering items dog-proof, I really wish I could follow them.

'Is there any news from anywhere?'

She checked her phone. 'No. And my battery's nearly dead. It must be getting old, 'cos it usually lasts much longer.' She frowned. 'Didn't Mina have a charger in here?'

'She did, but she took it for her car.'

'I'll turn it off and save the battery. You've got news?'

'I have. It may be a wild goose chase, but I've got nothing better.'

'She's disappeared,' said Elaine. 'They've been at that spot for half an hour, and suddenly they've gone.'

'They're up to no good,' said Tom.

He didn't wait for Elaine to tell him that there might be a hundred innocent explanations. The last word he'd ever use to describe Conrad Clarke was *innocent*. He started the engine and headed for the country road where Clarke had last been seen.

Mother Julia had been vague about where this Witch might live, so we had no choice but to drive along the narrow lane and look for clues. At least the lack of traffic meant that I could take it slowly and give equal attention to driving and searching. I was getting ready to negotiate a bend when I saw the sign at the entrance to a rutted lane:

Gingerbread House
Small Boys and Girls Welcome!

'Bit of a giveaway, that,' I said. 'It doesn't look suspicious at all.'

'What?' said Karina.

'The sign.'

She frowned. 'The one that says No Access. Public footpath 100m further down the road ?'

'Have another look.'

'Oh.'

'Precisely. I must have seen through the perimeter Wards. Can you feel them now?'

'Yes. They're quite strong. You didn't even know they were there, did you, sir? You just saw through them.'

I shrugged. My magickal Sight comes and goes unpredictably, or so it seems to me. I told her as much and turned the Volvo into the track. We bumped up a hill that soon became very steep. Grass had grown in the middle of the lane, but someone had sprayed it during the summer and none of the potholes were actually life-threatening. By country standards, this private road was well cared for.

The track did a switchback to avoid a narrow wood on the crest of the hill and curved round to cross a cattle grid. I almost slammed on the brakes when I saw what was on the other side of the concrete yard.

'Bugger me.'

'It is a bit excessive,' said Karina. 'Takes a lot of Lux to keep up a Glamour like that. It's strong, too. I couldn't see through it without a lot of effort.'

Before us was the promised Gingerbread House.

Gingerbread walls supported a gingerbread shingle roof at a suitably Germanic steep pitch. The eaves were adorned with giant jelly tots and dolly mixtures; a stack of liquorice allsorts formed a chimney that was actually smoking invitingly. The windows were opaque purple glass and giant lollipops stood either side of the chocolate door. I was salivating just looking at it, and there was an added dimension to the illusion: smell.

I couldn't smell it of course, but in the back of the car, Scout was barking furiously and licking his doggy lips at the same time. His eyes bulged as he stared through the window.

'We'd better leave him inside,' I said. 'He'll only try to eat the walls and break his teeth. Assuming they're actually brick and not gingerbread.'

'Never mind him,' said Karina. 'I'm going to have a mint to take my mind off it.'

I undid my seatbelt , turned off the engine and activated my Ancile . 'You know what, Karina. The longer I spend in the world of magick, the madder it gets. Why, I ask you. Why have they done this?'

'Dunno. Let's see if she's in.'

Crossing the yard was like wading through treacle. The magickal push against me raised a sweat and my nose was twitching at the mixed caramel and fruit odours. The visual illusion didn't waver by one pixel, not even when I hammered on the door.

If the Witch was inside, she'd have known we were coming from the second I turned up the lane. When one Mage knocks at another's door, they always answer, even if the answer consists of a full-on assault. I rested my hand on the Hammer. Just in case.

The door opened with a Gothic creak the size of Notre Dame and a tiny face appeared at hip height. Tiny as in child-sized and attached to an equally child-sized body. It was a girl of about eight or nine with long straw-gold plaits that had to be clip-ons or extensions. No one with hair that blonde has eyes that brown.

The full-on fairy story ended with her outfit. Yes, she was wearing a peasant smock, but it was over pink leggings with unicorns and mermaids frolicking in some candy sea. And pink heelies. Last time I read the story, Gretel didn't skate.

'Who are you?' she said with a frown, as if I'd interrupted a summit of world leaders. 'And why are you dressed as soldiers?'

'Hello. My name's Conrad, and this is Karina. We're dressed as soldiers because she is a soldier and I'm in the Royal Air Force. See?' I pointed to the wings on my uniform.

When I became a squadron leader, the RAF sent me on a child protection course, in case I had anything to do with the cadets. We were taught never to assume that children had parents unless it was absolutely necessary.

I am still waiting to meet the child who has *never* had parents, even if they're no longer with us. Perhaps the world of magick will fix that. We were also taught not to ask children's names at the beginning of a conversation, so I'll carry on calling her Gretel, because what else would you call the girl in the Gingerbread House?

'Have you brought our tea?' said Gretel.

'I'm sorry, the RAF only delivers food during floods and blizzards. Are there any grown-ups that I could talk to?' I said.

Gretel was joined by her older brother who was probably on the cusp of being a teenager. He stood behind her and let her do the talking, and I immediately felt sympathy for him. Been there, done that.

She turned to face him. 'Does Auntie Rah-Rah count as a grown-up?'

He shook his head dolefully. 'No, she doesn't. Not at all.'

'What about the Professor?' said Gretel.

The boy nodded. 'Yeah. He's all grown up.'

She turned back to me. 'My brother will get him. I don't like Professor Moriarty. He scares me.'

The boy slipped away, and the girl, still clutching the door, made conversation. 'Do you like our house? Auntie Rah-Rah made it look like this for us as a treat.'

'She's done a very good job,' I answered. 'It even smells delicious.'

'It only smells outside,' she replied. 'Inside it's just smells of boring dust. Auntie Rah-Rah said that if any children come to the door, we can eat them because otherwise we won't have any tea.'

'It's a shame I didn't bring any,' I said. 'You could have cooked them for me.'

She looked alarmed. 'Not really. We don't really eat children.'

She heard a noise behind her and pushed the door further open to allow her brother to get by.

The lad was holding a large grey cat with luxurious fur and patient eyes. It must have been patient to allow the boy to carry him around.

191

'This is Professor Moriarty,' said the girl. 'Auntie Rah-Rah's Familiar.'

The cat took one look at us and squirmed until the boy dropped him. He shot back inside the house with a hiss.

'He can hear your dog,' said the boy. 'He doesn't like dogs. Is that your car? It's a bit battered, isn't it?'

'It's like me. It's had an interesting life.'

'You can come in. If the Professor doesn't like you, he screams, and he didn't scream.'

Karina and I looked at each other and shrugged.

'After you, sir,' she said. 'I'm not going in there first.'

In her shoes, I'd have said the same. I wiped my feet on the mat and followed Gretel inside.

She was right, the sweetshop smell dissipated in the dark hallway. I peered through the first door on the left, and the boy had already resumed playing a video game which involved both driving fast cars *and* shooting.

Gretel said, 'Follow me. If you can,' and scooted down the hall on her heelies, executing a perfect brake stop in the kitchen. If the resident Witch was indeed away, that would explain why we were greeted by a child and not an angry Mage.

From round the corner, I heard a harassed voice say, 'You'll get in trouble if your mum knows you've been skating in the house.'

'No I won't. You'll get in trouble for letting me. Here they are.'

'Here who are? Is?'

I knocked on the open door and peered round to the left, where a scene of utter chaos greeted me.

Somewhere under the pile of flour, cutting tools, books, craft paper, paint, glue, scissors, more books, chopping boards and rolling pins was a table, and seated side-on to the table was an evil witch. Well, it was a Witch in fancy dress. It looked a bit tight on her, to be honest, in fact it looked like she'd been raiding Gretel's dressing up box.

She had her nose in something; it was hard to tell what because of the sea of crepe paper. 'Is it the pack leader?'

'Oh no. It's a woman soldier with a knife and an RAF man with two guns.'

The evil witch jerked her head up and pushed the chair back, sending it flying very close to the grey cat, who shot out of the way and disappeared. Coward. She raised her hands defensively and I felt magick building. Now that she was standing up, I could see that she was short, even shorter than Mina. It was hard to tell what she looked like, because a black nylon wig covered half her face. It had white bits in it, probably food-related.

My Ancile was still in place, so I showed my empty palms. 'King's Watch. We need a word. Just a word.'

'Witchfinder! Witchfinder!' shouted Gretel, almost like a ritual, as if she'd heard of us but didn't believe we really existed. Just in case, she sheltered behind the evil witch's skirt.

'Shh,' said the woman. She looked around and felt her face, then stared at the wooden pillar next to me.

'Have you lost your glasses, ma'am?' I suggested.

'Who me? What? Yes. Are you really the King's Watch?'

I moved slowly across the kitchen, dodging a pile of dough that had landed on the floor. 'I am. Deputy Constable Clarke and Watch Officer Kent. I take it you're Auntie Rah-Rah?'

'Rachel. Yes. Would you believe that I'm child-minding?'

'We've had great fun,' said Gretel. 'We've made real gingerbread men, and pictures. Do you really hunt down Witches and chop them in half?'

'I have never chopped anyone in half.'

'But you do hunt Witches.'

'Only the bad ones. I'm sure there aren't any bad Witches here.'

I took a moment to scan the craft-related chaos on the table. 'If you'll excuse me.' I reached in and extracted a pair of large-framed glasses. 'Yours, I believe.' I waited until Rachel had restored her eyewear and had a good look at me. Her eyes, now restored to full function, lingered on my gun belt. 'We need to talk, Rachel. I think you know why we're here.'

She looked devastated. 'My sister will kill me, even if you don't.'

'Bad timing, I'm afraid. I think this is the moment when you tell your niece to go and beat her brother at a computer game.'

Pain flashed over Gretel's young face. She knew exactly what I meant. 'I'm not leaving. I won't let you hurt Auntie.'

Rachel made an effort to sound placatory. 'No one's going to be killing anyone, precious, but I do need to talk in private.'

'Are you sure?'

Rachel nodded, and Gretel walked past us with her head held high. Only the tremble in her lip gave away how scared she was. What did you do at work today, Conrad? Oh, I induced mortal terror in a nine-year old girl.

'How did you find them?' said Rachel.

I shook my head. That conversation was for another day. 'How many and where are they?'

'What are you going to do them?'

'Nothing. Being Dual Natured is not a crime in itself. I take it that the pack are under the protection of Princess Birkdale?' She nodded. 'Then there's no problem. Not for them. The Princess is another matter, and not your concern. How many and where?'

Karina gave a delicate cough, and I nodded for her to continue.

'Are they descended from pack Mackenzie?' she said.

Of course. I should have thought of that. If they were… Rachel nodded. Damn. That made the legal position more complicated. Mackenzie wolves are also Mages and should register as such. Also, that made them more dangerous. Obviously. I pulled my lip and waited.

'Three men, seven women and half a dozen cubs. I think. I've only met the pack leader once, and I've never been to the lodge. It's in the trees. You can drive out through the yard.'

'Thank you. You're not going to do anything stupid, are you, like contact them?' She shook her head. 'Then we'll be on our way.'

She pushed all the nylon hair out of her face and followed us down the hall. Moriarty appeared from his hiding place and hissed when I opened the door.

'When is your sister back?' I asked.

'Tomorrow night.'

'Just one last question,' I said. 'Why did your niece think that we'd brought food?'

'Because I didn't bring any shopping, and I can't believe this place. There's no Deliveroo and no UberEats. No one will deliver food here *at all*. I was going out, but now I'll have to wait until you're finished.'

'You should do what your neighbours do, Rachel. Hunt something down and eat that.'

21 — Queen Sacrifice

I drove the car to the edge of the yard, out of sight of the Gingerbread house and killed the engine. 'That was lucky. If her sister had been there, things could have gone very differently. Good question about Pack Mackenzie. We'll need to be doubly careful now.'

'How do you cope with it?'

'With what? I thought I was quite sensitive, given that there were children in there.'

'The insults. The hatred. Being called a Witchfinder.'

'Suck it up, Karina. Own it. Shame them with your professionalism.'

She didn't look convinced, but that wasn't all she had on her mind. 'Sir, I was looking it up last night. Don't all packs have exemption, with liability on their Protectors?'

All of Karina's confusion and uncertainty were in play on her face. She's been trying to come to terms with my world since she first met me at Henley in Arden, and the strong core that I know she has under the doubt was slowly bending. Right now, I didn't have time for that.

'And I'm sure that your reading also told you that the Occult Council in England never adopted the Mackenzie protocol. Then again, the Occult Council has clearly been turning a blind eye to the existence of Mannwolves south of the border. The lawyers are going to have a field day when my report goes in tonight. I don't think Rachel in there has any idea of just how serious this could be, even if this pack had nothing to do with the death of Drake Blackrod.'

'What about Rachel's sister, the resident Witch? Could she have run away because she's guilty.'

'Mothers don't leave their children behind.'

She went bright red and looked out of the window. Damn. I'd forgotten that her mother had done just that – in a way. When you're very small, even if your parent has been murdered, you still feel abandoned. And guilty. It was time to move on.

'We're going on reconnaissance, Karina. Our first priority is survival. We take no risks, and at the first sign of trouble, we get the hell out of there. Understood?'

'Yes, sir.'

'I want you to stay close to the car on the driver's side, ready to drive us out. Strap on your quiver and put your bow on the seat.'

'Yes, sir. I understand.'

'Good. Here we go.'

The track out of the yard was also well maintained, and that's because Mannwolves have just as much need to get around as everyone else, even if there aren't many who learn to drive. One of the resident Witch's jobs would be to drive the minibus that had been parked around the back of the gingerbread house.

I've been putting off telling you about the Dual Natured in detail because it's a complex subject and I've barely scratched the surface in my own understanding of it.

Mina knows more, because she had to deal with an Indian snake-woman, a Nāgin, called Pramiti. I did meet Pramiti, and I saw her change from woman to giant cobra and back again. Twice. The problems start when I tell you that 'change' is the wrong verb. It should be 'exchange', because the Dual Natured have one brain and two bodies that exist on different planes. What to us looks like a seamless change of physiology is our own brains trying to make sense of the phase transition.

I'm told, because I read about it, that Mannwolves are not rated highly in international circles. Pramiti is so old that she's ageless. She experienced the British empire in India at first hand, and her magickal power is immense. In that time, she's only had one clutch of eggs. If they take after their mother, that's probably a good thing. The lifespan of a Mannwolf is very different.

Until Pack Mackenzie became Mages in the eighteenth century, the typical lifespan of a Mannwolf was about twenty-five years, and it's now ten years longer. Thirty-five. Think about that: Mina would be into the menopause and I'd be dead. The original Mackenzie (yes, he was a person) summed up their attitude: A life is better lived quickly.

They even measure their lives differently: by moons. Their version of our three score years and ten would be a thousand moons, which sort of makes it sound better.

When Rachel talked about there being a number of cubs, she meant anything from a babe in arms to puberty. The difference between cubs and adults is that cubs cannot exchange forms at will; puberty and full growth both occur at around ten years old.

And one final thing: size. The human brain is eleven times the size of a wolf's; a proportionately larger wolf would be as big as a dairy cow. They're not, but they are much bigger than a grey wolf. And they have big, ugly heads. According to the pictures.

'Why do I feel funny?' I said as we neared the wood.

'Because we've just crossed the border into the Fae forest.'

I stopped the car again. 'There's one here?'

'Where else would they hunt?'

I waved my arm in a gesture of ignorance. 'In a regular wood?'

Her eyes widened. I get that a lot, though not so much from Karina. 'No, sir. They hunt the Phantom Stag, or the Royal Boar. Unicorns. That sort of thing. When they hunt mundane prey, that's just for their sport. And food, of course.'

'Right. There it is. The big low farmhouse. With outbuildings.' I couldn't put it off any longer, and drove quickly through a gate into a beautifully maintained property that reminded me of an Afghan village compound (minus the external walls), or one of those recreations of iron age homesteads. The large single-storey building was mostly an ancient great hall with a high roof. The more recent development curved in an arc of small family units, sheds, and the cold store.

The gardens in front were beautifully planted, both ornamental and vegetable, and all bedded down for the coming winter. There was even a cover ready to put over the substantial pond/pool. I stopped in the turning circle and said, 'Ready?' Karina took a deep breath and nodded.

In a smooth move, we got out and swapped places, standing by the car and trying to ignore the desperate barking and whining from Scout. He could smell them a long time before we saw them coming for us.

Mannwolves don't use (or like) the term *alpha male*. They call the pack leaders their king and queen, and that was who approached the car at a gentle jog.

They looked human. They looked about my age, and they looked a lot healthier. The King was Karina's height, his Queen about Mina's, and both had long hair pulled back. They were wearing what you'd expect country dwellers to wear on a cold Monday afternoon: warm but battered clothing in earth tones. And flip-flops. The small part of my brain that has never grown up immediately thought of the trolley dolly hen party going into action. This was nothing like that. I put my right hand on the Hammer and held up my left hand in a sign of peace.

They weren't too keen to get close to us and stopped about fifteen metres away. I could see the lines on the King's face from a life lived outdoors, and yes, they do have more prominent canine teeth. Just a bit.

'What do you want?' he said in a flat, northern English accent.

'King's Watch. Deputy Constable Clarke. All I want today is to ask you a few questions.'

'And tomorrow?' said his Queen. 'What comes then?' She was Scottish, with a musical, high pitched voice.

'Whose ground is this?' I asked.

'We are the Darkwood Pack. This is our ground and has been for generations.'

'But the land is Princess Birkdale's.'

He didn't look happy, which was understandable. I had just pointed out that they were being kept like a pack of foxhounds. 'Why are you here?'

'I...'

An ear-splitting howl broke the afternoon silence. All of us turned our heads to the right, away from the compound and over a wall into a field. Somewhere out there, a Mannwolf was in pain and trying to exchange. The

King and Queen forgot all about us and started running towards the cry, shedding clothes as they ran. What the hell?

'Grab your bow,' I said, and set off after them.

They vaulted the wall with the ease of athletes, and I vaulted it with the ease of someone a foot taller. When it came to running across the undulating meadow, there was no contest and they streaked ahead.

We'd crossed over the watershed now, and this land sloped down to where I'd parked the car when we were waiting for Mother Julia's phone call.

Behind me, I heard Karina shout something, then seconds later I heard barking. Stupid girl, she'd let Scout get out of the car. This was not good. At least the wall was too high for him. I picked up speed and tried to see what was going on.

Karina loped past me, bow in hand, built up a ten metre lead, then stopped at the top of a ridge and put her free hand to her mouth. I caught up with her and jolted back at the sight. My gun was in my hand before I'd fully taken it in.

Two of the pack's juniors were on their knees, hands behind their back, and one of them was doing the howling. Another, an adult, was curled up on the floor, moaning and holding her hands to her face. A fourth had been Tasered, and the one doing the Tasering was Elaine Fraser. Shit. Double damn shit and buggery. How had this happened?

'Take aim,' I said.

Elaine was trying to reload her Taser, and Tom Morton was trying to get his Airwave radio to work (it wouldn't. Not in a Fae forest). In his other hand, he had an extended baton, and in front of them something was about to change their world forever.

The King and Queen had stopped well short of the action, and with practised movements, they got the last of their clothes off. I'll never, ever forget the look on Elaine's face as it changed from baffled incredulity (why were these people getting naked in front of her?), then to simple incredulity and finally to abject horror.

The exchange took about five seconds. The pack royalty dropped to all fours and executed a perfect yoga downward dog as their bodies shrank, their naked skin changed to fur and bushy tails sprouted from their coccyges.

Morton and Elaine had obviously come the long way, over fields up from the road where we'd parked earlier, and they were at the bottom of the field, where they'd been intercepted by members of the Darkwood Pack. They must have climbed over that high, dry stone wall and now their backs were to it. The pack leaders were still at a good distance from them, part way up the slope, and we were at the top. I had held our position because if we'd gone any further, we'd have lost the line of sight.

I was breathing heavily from running across the field. At this range, even with a SIG based gun, it would be a difficult shot. I dropped down and took up a kneeling stance, left arm resting on my left knee.

While I watched the King and Queen exchange forms, I tried to see the scene from Morton and Elaine's viewpoint. They'd been attacked by four mad locals, and now two wolves were appearing. They would see me at the top and assume that I was in charge. Morton didn't trust me, and this would confirm it. They weren't going to lay down arms just because I asked them to.

'Take out the Queen,' I ordered.

Karina braced herself, took aim and shot Elaine Fraser in the leg.

What the fuck?

As Elaine was collapsing in agony, the black and white bullet of Scout shot into view. Perhaps if Elaine hadn't been so nice to him, things would have turned out differently. If Karina had obeyed my order, things would definitely have been different.

Scout saw Elaine as part of our gang, and he knew these wolves were the enemy. He vaulted over one of the fallen pack and took up a defensive position in front of Elaine, barking and letting those overgrown dogs know who was in charge.

Morton had already dropped his radio and took a step nearer to Elaine. Then he picked up her Taser, now reloaded. Mannwolves live sheltered lives. They don't watch a lot of TV. A Taser would have had no effect on their exchanged forms, because the electricity would have drained away on to a higher plane. They didn't know that. They just saw a gun. The King went to jump at Morton while his Queen stayed back, ready to join in. I shot the Queen because she was the stationary target.

To hit her, I took a deep breath and prayed that my dodgy, titanium left leg would hold still. And something happened when I focused on it, as if the metal rod had planted itself into the ground. I have never had such a stable knee to shoot from. I narrowed all my focus to the gunsight and my middle finger. More than one millimetre of shake between deciding to shoot and engaging the trigger would make me miss.

I hit her in the back leg. It was enough.

Morton had already saved his own life by dropping the Taser and bringing up the baton. It meant that the King knocked him over, but couldn't get a clear bite on his throat. When I fired, the King was going for Morton's arm and ignored the gunshot. He didn't ignore what happened next.

The Dwarven Work of Alchemy in my bullet unravelled the Queen's Imprint and sent her exchanged form back to the higher plane in a huge discharge of Lux that was like an SAS flash grenade: sound, blinding light and all of the Queen's pain projected magickally across the meadow.

The Mannwolves collapsed unconscious: they'd felt it in both their forms, doubling the agony. Except for the King. He staggered, but stayed on his feet.

I wobbled, struggled to breathe, then forced myself to stand up and advance in a shooting stance.

The King left Morton and went to his Queen, then looked up and charged at me. My arms were shaking so much that I couldn't risk a shot until he was a lot closer. I didn't need to in the end, because Karina shot him first.

I kept the Hammer raised and turned round, partly to see if Karina were aiming at me. She wasn't, she was walking backwards towards me, away from the rest of the Darkwood Pack who were now in a line on the ridge, all in human form and all naked.

I took my left hand off my gun and lowered the weapon to my side. 'Put down your bow,' I said to Karina. 'Now.' She followed my lead, and I raised my voice. 'Hold! Let there be peace here.'

An old woman, grey of hair and hunched of back, spoke for them. 'Who are you and what have you done?'

'King's Watch and two mundane police officers. They acted without my authority. This is a tragedy. Let it stop here.'

One of the younger adult males started to Exchange, and a voice from behind me shouted, 'Jack! No! Stand back!'

The old woman and a younger one grabbed the wolf's hairy coat as it emerged and pinned him down with force and magick. I watched and waited, holding my breath, until Jack had exchanged back to his human form. When no one else made a move to attack, I turned on my heel and looked around.

The King was human, too, and had an arrow sticking out of his hip joint. He was leaning up on his hands and breathing heavily. The Mannwolf who'd been Tasered was still flat out, and the woman clutching her face was now lying on the late Queen, whimpering with pain and grief. Morton and Scout were guarding Elaine, and Morton was trying not to drip blood on her from the tear in his arm. He was the one who spoke first. 'I'm not going to be infected, am I?'

Well, that was one way of dealing with what had happened.

'Sod that,' hissed Elaine.

I looked at the King. 'Do you still speak for the Darkwood Pack?'

He did his best to get further upright. 'Kneel before your King!' he shouted.

One by one, starting with the old woman, the pack bent their knee until all had submitted. At that point the King said, 'The hunt is over. I surrender.' Then he flopped down and grimaced.

I holstered my gun and said, 'Karina, release the cubs and triage Elaine.' When she moved, I spoke to the pack. 'Take your King and go home. Your sister needs lots of cold water in the eyes. Look up CS spray if you can. Leave the Queen where she is for now.'

I stood away to the side and put my back to the wall. The pack moved quickly and efficiently. In less than thirty seconds, they were gone over the ridge. 'Here boy,' I said to Scout. He was still shaking, and I bent down to hold him and reassure him. While no one could hear, I told him that he was a brave dog, and the best dog in the world. I got a tiny wag of the tail. 'How is she?' I said to Karina.

'The arrow missed the femoral artery, so there's no immediate risk. It should be left in and extracted in surgery. Sooner rather than later.'

'Too fucking right,' said Elaine. 'Much sooner, please. And you're wrong. The arrow didn't miss, you did. You did this to me. Whose fucking side are you on?'

Karina looked bereft, totally adrift of all anchors. 'I didn't want anyone to die,' she said.

Elaine dropped back on to the grass and carried on gritting her teeth. Tom waved his baton at the chaos. 'What is all this? What have I walked into?'

'You've walked into the world of magick, Tom. That's magick with a *k*. You can walk out, if you want, but you'll never solve the case.'

'Me? How can I solve this?'

'By joining me, before things truly get out of control.'

He looked around, then looked at my outstretched hand. He shook it. 'I'm in. What now?'

'Where's your car?'

He pointed over the wall. 'About half an hour's muddy walk that way.'

'Does it have sample kits?'

'What the hell for?'

'DNA. We need to take samples from this lot and get someone to compare them to swabs from Drake Blackrod. He was the one attacked in the woods.'

'You want to take DNA from werewolves?'

'Mannwolves. We don't use the w* word. We'll take this one step at a time, okay? It's too much to digest all at once.'

He looked at his arm, still dripping. 'Isn't it infectious?'

'Definitely not. It's hereditary, and this lot are all closely related.'

'Will they let you take samples?'

'If they're innocent, and I think they are, then they'll co-operate. But that's secondary. Elaine's the priority.'

'At last!' she said. 'But I'm not going with her.'

'No, you're not, don't worry. Just one question first: how did you find us?'

'Seriously?'

'Seriously. As Karina said, you're not going to die just yet.'

'I filched her phone in Tesco and loaded a tracking app, alright? Now can we go?'

Karina's unhappiness plunged to new depths when she realised her part in this fiasco. I had specifically told her to turn off Location Services, and because she hadn't, she'd led Elaine straight to us.

I took a deep breath. 'Karina, go and get Rachel. Tell her to bring the minibus up to the compound. Move!'

When Karina had run off, I knelt down and put my hand on Elaine's shoulder. 'There's a Witch in the lodge who can take you to Preston Royal. She's a good person, she'll make sure you're taken straight into A&E. She also needs to get a takeaway.'

'In the name of God, tell me you didn't just say that a Witch needs a takeaway,' said Elaine.

'Put out your arms,' I told her. 'I'll haul you up and take your weight. Tom can take the other shoulder. It's not far.'

We made it to the compound, and I started to explain the logistics of my plan, steering clear of the magickal elements. As we limped round to the turning circle, the minibus bumped into view. I scanned the compound, looking for an ambush. We were being watched from the main door, but nothing was lurking behind the walls, and I know that mostly because Scout would have told me if there were.

Rachel executed a twenty-seven point turn and we loaded Elaine on to a double seat. Gretel stood with her hand over her mouth, staring at the arrow shaft sticking out of Elaine's jeans, a little flow of blood welling up every time she moved.

Karina had one more thing to say before Rachel (no longer wearing the evil witch costume) drove off. 'Tell the hospital it's not barbed. It's a field arrow.'

'And I'm supposed to feel better?' said Elaine.

'You will,' I told her.

Morton gave her hand a squeeze and stepped out of the bus. He closed the door and banged on the panel. Rachel drove off, more carefully now, and I turned to face Karina, but she was on the move. She ran over the grass to the pool, and I was too exhausted to follow her at more than walking pace. Tom and Scout tagged along behind me. 'If you're really unlucky, Tom, you might get to meet a mad water Nymph in a second.'

Karina took out her Badge of Office, the dagger with Caledfwlch stamped in the hilt. She raised it and spoke. 'From the water to the water. From the water we came, and to it we return. I abjure this bond and return the mark.'

She plunged it into the pool, and there was another flash of light. I held my breath for a second, but Nimue didn't appear. Perhaps she doesn't do personal visits for Watch Officers. Karina pulled the dagger out of the water and stared at it; perhaps she was having regrets already, or perhaps she was wondering why the hell she'd volunteered in the first place.

'Does that mean she's resigned?' said Morton.

'From the King's Watch, yes.'

She was still sitting on the wall around the pool when we got close enough for her to hand over the dagger, now sheathed. I accepted it and said, 'Tell Tom what you did.'

'He saw what I did. I'm sorry it didn't save any lives, but I did it for the best.'

'Not that. Tell him you disobeyed a direct order. I ordered you to shoot the Queen.'

'Yeah, but that was wrong. She was trying to protect her children.'

There was nothing I could say to that. 'Hand over your Middlebarrow token. Saskia and Evie will get your stuff for you and bring your car out. Report to Merlyn's Tower on Thursday.'

'I've quit. I'm going.'

'You're still in the Army, Karina. You'll answer to the CO like any other officer. She might court martial you or she might just slam the door in your face. Be thankful it's not my decision.'

'And if I don't turn up?'

'Then you'll be AWOL. Token, please.'

She handed it over. 'What shall we do with her, Tom? Can you bear to have her in your car as far as Preston railway station?'

'Why not make her walk?'

'Because I want her to go to Birkdale and tell the princess what's happened and what I'm doing, and that if Princess Birkdale makes a move against Clan Blackrod, she will be making a very, very big mistake.'

'I'm still here,' said Karina. 'Why should I do what you want?'

'Because it'll make you feel better and it's the right thing.' She nodded reluctantly. 'Tom? Will you take her?'

'Will it save lives?'

'Probably.'

'Then I'll do it.'

'Good. Karina, take the Volvo and DCI Morton and get his car.'

'Shall I do first aid on his arm?'

'If he'll let you.'

'Will you be safe on your own?' said Morton.

'I won't be on my own. I've got Scout. And two spare clips of ammunition.'

'Right. Back shortly.'

When the Volvo had disappeared, I waved for someone to come out from the great hall. The pack elder, now dressed, made her way slowly down the path. 'You've lost your second,' she said. 'And you've sent the others away. I volunteered to come out in case you're going to start a cull. We don't read, much, but we all know the stories of the Pale Horsemen, of the Thunder. Why are you here?'

The Thunder? That was a new one on me. I filed it away for the future.

'Did your pack attack a Gnome in the Irwell Valley on Saturday morning?'

She shook her head. 'Is that what this is about? A dead Gnome?'

'Killed by a pack.'

'Not by us.'

'Then help me prove it.'

She nodded. 'Tell me what you need.'

When Tom got back, we took enough samples to cover the different familial strains. Of course, it meant that they had to exchange forms. Believe me when I tell you that taking a saliva swab from a wolf is not pleasant. I did two, then Tom joined in. When he took his first swab, I had a vision, a flash of memory, of a taller man having his hand bitten off by a huge wolf. I jerked my hand back and looked again. Tom was simply dropping the swab into a sample tube.

I had a mission for Karina while this was going on: go inside and supervise making of tea. I trusted the pack not to harm us, but why put temptation in their way? With the samples in my car, Tom and I leaned on the wall and looked over the land. The pack were going to bring their Queen back and we'd be leaving shortly.

'Did you talk to Karina before? When she was dressing your arm and going to get the car?' I asked.

'I did. You know my mother works for the Archdiocese of York, right?' I nodded. Due diligence and all that. 'Well, I asked Karina about her religion, and God. Or should that be gods? She told me some strange things, and she said that you've met at least two of these higher creatures.'

'I have. Listen, Tom, did you get in touch with Rob Fraser?'

'I did. He's on his way down from Scotland.'

'When you've been to the hospital, when Rob gets there, why don't you pick up Lucy and come down to Middlebarrow for dinner.'

'You're not dragging Lucy into this,' he said with some finality.

'I don't want to drag her into anything, but can you go home tonight and not tell her? Mina was still in prison when I was recruited by the Allfather. As soon as I'd survived my first mission, I had to tell her. Not just that, depending on how the next couple of hours go, we'll need to do some planning.'

He looked at me darkly. 'You're not doing the cooking, are you?'

'You must be joking. Think it over and text me from the hospital. I'd like to know how Elaine is, anyway.'

He finished his tea. 'I'll be in touch. What I did was stupid, Conrad. I may never forgive myself for getting Elaine shot and both of us nearly killed. You did tell me – several times – that your world was a deadly one. I should have believed you. If I'd left you alone, Elaine wouldn't have an arrow in her leg, the Queen of Darkwood Pack would still be alive and you'd still have a partner.'

We shook hands. 'You did me a favour, Tom. Your actions pushed Karina to the edge. Rather now than when even more lives are at stake. Until later.'

He waved and took his empty mug back to the pack elder. I think he was apologising to her, as well. She took the mug and nodded to him, then he got out his key fob and waved Karina over. I waited until he'd gone, and then got out the burner phone. Lloyd Flint answered on the third ring.

'Alright, Conrad. What's up?'

'Do you fancy a pint tonight? Got a proposition for you, Lloyd.'

'Tonight?'

'The White Horse at Great Barrow in Cheshire. Half past seven. Pack an overnight bag, and don't forget what you said you'd bring.'

'I've been working on it all day, mate. Private business, is it?'

'Yes.'

'Then I'll see you later.'

It was time for me to go. I didn't need to whistle for Scout because he'd barely strayed six feet from me. He looked very relieved when I told him to get into the car and he saw me getting in, too. 'Funny isn't it, lad,' I said. 'Mannwolves have no smell at all to me. Probably because they're all human or all wolf, so you're not redundant yet.'

I didn't ring Mina until I was in the car and well away from Darkwood. Next stop Blackrod.

22 — *On the Scent*

Lachlan Mace told me to meet him at Haigh Hall, the country park that sits on the hill above the First Mine of Clan Blackrod. They have a back exit from their property that goes through the park and makes it an ideal meeting place – busy and anonymous.

I had no idea what to expect when I pulled into the car park and took my ticket. He'd said to meet at the courtyard café, and I got ready to follow the signs when I noticed something about the clientele. Yes, there were a couple of runners getting ready to pound the footpaths, but most of the new arrivals were young women and a few grandparents getting buggies and prams out of cars, eager children bouncing up and down next to them, or running ahead in the case of the older ones. What on earth was the attraction?

I was so intent on following the children, like a reverse Pied Piper, that I passed the café without noticing. The object of their pilgrimage was a half-acre adventure playground, and all the steam they'd built up at school/nursery was being let off noisily and with total abandon. I was about to turn round and get back on track when one of the early arrivals, a girl of about six now taking a rest, gave me a funny look.

'Mum, that man's got *two* guns!'

What? How could she see them? I looked at the mother, an attractive but otherwise ordinary woman in her late thirties. She was looking back at me, at the Hammer, at my uniform. Of course. Where else would the women of Clan Blackrod bring their girls to play?

I bowed slightly. 'Ma'am.'

'Wrong way,' she said. 'Lachlan's over there.' She pointed to the conservatory building I'd passed.

'Thank you.'

I hastened away and scanned the café. Lachlan was there, stirring his coffee and giving me a puzzled look. 'You should have told me you wanted to meet my wife,' he said when I'd sat down.

'Sorry about that. I just wondered what the fuss was all about.'

'You don't have children, I take it.'

'Not yet. I'm sure Mina has a plan for that.'

He gave me a knowing grin. 'I'm sure she does. You've got until Lettie gets bored and hungry. What is it?'

'Did you do what I asked this morning?'

'Yes. Why? Don't even think about asking to take him away.'

'I wouldn't. I found Princess Birkdale's pack of Mannwolves today.'

'What! How did you do that? Half of the clan has been on the job since yesterday and we can't even get anyone to confirm it exists. Where is it?'

'They didn't do it, Lachlan. I'd stake my life on it'

His Gnomish eyes bored into me, and I felt a prickle of magick. He wasn't trying to perform a Work on me, he was just getting angry. It's one of those moments when you're reminded that Gnomes are not human.

'Your life is not worth much to us, I'm afraid. If it wasn't Tara Doyle's pack, then who else has one? And who's to say that she doesn't have *two* packs of hounds?'

I spread my hands. 'You're judging her by your standards, Lachlan. The Fae are tricky, but they're also lazy, remember? Have you come across a Fae who would keep two packs when they have one? She would be far more likely to use the first pack and butcher them afterwards. Only one of Mother's children would think to have a second pack.'

He grunted, partially appeased. Gnomes like it when you run down the Fae, though the reverse is not true: the Fae have such contempt for Gnomes that you sometimes have to build them up, to make them think they face a worthy opponent. Or so I've been told.

I opened my combat jacket and took out a bag with the lupine DNA samples. I placed them on the table and said, 'Swab Drake's wounds and send the samples to an animal DNA lab. There are some good ones near Newmarket. All the horse breeding.'

'That could take days. I'm not sure that Stefan will go for that, never mind Drake's house.'

'You agreed to meet me, Lachlan. That says a lot. That pack are innocent, and now that I know they exist, they get the same right to enjoy the King's Peace as everyone else. You know your clan. Do what you need to do. If this erupts, no one will be safe.' To hammer home the point, I turned to look at Lettie and her mother. 'No one. I'll be in touch.'

Tom and Lucy arrived at the White Horse well ahead of Lloyd Flint. The handshakes were rather formal, as you might expect, and Lucy looked like she'd dressed for a very formal business dinner. 'How's Elaine?' was my first question.

'Rob messaged while we were on our way here. The operation went well, the arrow hadn't hit any sub-arteries and she should make a full recovery. Eventually.'

'Who's driving?' I asked.

'Tom,' said Lucy. 'He said he couldn't cope with all this and a hangover. I told him I couldn't cope without several large gins. And I brought this.'

She fetched a plain bottle full of clear liquid out of a hessian bag. Naturally, she had one of her mother's creations as well. Not her di Sanuto Exclusive, but close. Mina would have handbag envy for days.

'It's Grandpa Berardi's home-made grappa,' she said. She put the bottle away. 'Have you left Mina cooking?'

'Sort-of. You're going to have to get used to some odd things, Lucy. One of them is that you can't get into the property without me to help you, which is why we're meeting here. I'd take you straight there, but one of the Calabrese is joining us, too, and we can drop the pretence now. Our victim on Saturday was one Drake Blackrod, of Clan Blackrod, Gnomes of Lancashire.'

'Gnomes,' said Lucy. 'Make that gin a double.'

'Coming up.'

We'd covered a lot of ground before Lloyd turned up (and Lucy had sent me back to the bar three times), and when I introduced Lloyd to Tom, I got the shock of my life.

'Good win on Sunday,' said Tom. 'You're from Earlsbury, so did you know Patrick Lynch, by any chance?'

'Everyone knew Pat.' He looked carefully at Tom. 'Remind me not to get on your wrong side, DCI Morton.'

Lloyd drove me to Middlebarrow, and pulled in by the Haven to allow Evie to get in Tom's car. Saskia had been rather annoyed when I told her one of the guests would be a Gnome. 'Text me when you're coming,' she'd said in a voice that didn't expect to be contradicted.

The rear lights of Tom's BMW disappeared down the drive, and Saskia emerged from the shadows, wearing a white cloak that I'd not seen before. It was totally out of kilter with her normal wardrobe. We got out of the car, and she gathered the cloak around her. I caught a glimpse of a blue symbol of some sort on the back, and she held out her right hand.

'This ground is pledged to Nimue,' she said. 'Children of the Iron Mother are welcome if they defer.'

'I'm glad I didn't get dressed up,' muttered Lloyd. He knelt down on the wet grass and took Saskia's hand, kissing a small ring on her middle finger.

'Follow me on foot,' said Saskia. 'Conrad will drive your car down.' With a swirl of the cloak, she turned to walk down the drive, and I got a better look at the symbol on her back: a blue triangle with wavy blue lines in it. I've never seen that before, and she'd disappeared into the kitchen by the time I'd parked Lloyd's car.

He was waiting for me and said, 'Got something for you, mate. Better do it now before we all have too much to drink.' He took a blanket from the back of the car and unwrapped a sheathed sword. 'I didn't make this. It takes months to craft something like this from scratch, but I have fettled it for you. It was made by Niði for a Watch Captain in the 1750s, I believe. It's got an Ancile and I've put a couple of extra edges on it.'

'Extra edges?'

'That's what we call little bits of magick in a sword. You won't notice them, but if you come up against one of us, it'll help protect you.'

'Thank you, Lloyd. You would not be popular if word of this got out. I do appreciate it.'

'Yeah, well, that's what this is all about, ain't it? You need help dealing with that Octet.'

'I certainly need help finding them. I wouldn't ask you to go against others of your people.'

'I know. Draw the blade and touch it to Mother.'

'Will that work in here?'

'Mother Earth is Mother Earth.'

I took the sword and drew it. It wasn't as big as the one I'd surrendered, which also meant it was lighter. The edge glinted in the outside lights, and the point was sharp. I felt the grip. It was big.

Lloyd saw what I was doing. 'That was one of the tweaks. You've got huge hands, Conrad, so I padded the grip a bit and widened the guard.'

I examined the intricate fretwork surrounding the basket guard. 'Exquisite.' I shifted my Sight into the sword and closed my eyes. He was right: compared to the sword of Clan Flint, this was simple and streamlined. And comprehensible: it had been made for humans. There was the Ancile, a pulsing eye of watchfulness, and there was the channel, from the grip to the point. I lowered the blade and touched it to the cobbles. A flare of heat shot up the channel, joining my arm to the Works embedded in the metal. It was now my sword.

'Thank you, Lloyd.'

'Can we go in, now? I'm starving and I can smell your Mina's cooking.'

Saskia stayed for the meal and one shot of Grandpa's grappa, which was potent and aromatic. Not my thing. The conversation was intense, as you'd imagine, and skirted the actual reason for the get-together.

When Saskia had gone, Mina picked up the bottle of grappa and said to Lucy and Evie, 'Come on, you two, I want to show you something.'

The rest of us adjourned to the study and sat down with Scout curled up in front of the fireplace. Tom had a question: 'You say that three quarters of Mages are female. So why are we three men?'

'Because Lloyd isn't a Mage, he's a Gnome, and you're not a Mage either, Tom. If Karina hadn't fallen at the last fence, it would be fifty-fifty, and as everyone will tell you, I'm not a real Mage anyway.' I pulled my lip and thought for a moment. 'If necessary, I'll call Elvenham and whistle up the Coven. I'd have to resign if I did, but I'm seeing this through.'

Tom lifted his glass of wine (he'd allowed himself one), and said, 'Tell Saffron her disguise skills are excellent. Nearly had me fooled.'

So, they'd spied on me. That's how Tom had known who Lloyd was. Fair's fair, I suppose.

'What do we know?' said Lloyd.

I brought him up to date.

'What was all that business with scaffolding poles really about?' said Tom.

'Cold-forged Iron,' said Lloyd. 'It's the only thing that really knackers Quicksilver magick. With that square in place, the Count was at their mercy. They used the spears to finish him off without getting close.'

We carried on until we'd exhausted the facts, which didn't take long, and moved on to what you could call interpretation. Or speculation. The first sensible suggestion came from Lloyd.

'I reckon that two of them are in Blackrod.'

'What makes you say that?' said Tom.

'How else would they have known how to target Drake Blackrod? Only one of his clan would know he was off seeing a woman and not playing golf. Even his sons didn't know what he was really doing, according to Conrad.'

I nodded agreement, and Tom said, 'Why?'

'He must have knowed something. Or they thought he did.'

'Does that help?'

'Only if we go to the clan with it, and that's not an option,' I said. 'What about the Count? Was he a random target, just to cause a stink?'

Lloyd shook his head. 'What they did was very risky. There has to be a very, very good reason for them to try a stunt like that. If he'd survived, they'd be dead.'

'So what did he have that they wanted?' said Tom.

'Entertainment. Sex. Property,' I said.

'Property,' said Lloyd. 'That's about the only thing that would make one of us deal with one of them.

Tom wasn't convinced. 'Have you heard about the Well of Desire, Lloyd? Couldn't there be a blackmail angle from that?'

Lloyd shook his head. 'I can see – just – that one member of Blackrod would get into something involving a place like that. What I can't see is a whole Octet assassinating this Count fella because of it. Just wouldn't happen.'

'So, what's their endgame?' said Tom. 'What is this Octet after?'

'They're digging a new First Mine. Once they've consecrated it, they'll be pretty much untouchable. Even Conrad here won't be able to do anything. They'll have to pay wergild, of course, but I doubt that Princess Birkdale or Clan Blackrod would attack a First Mine.'

'How can that be?' said Tom. 'They just pay a fine and walk away?'

It was up to me to answer. 'I call it the brutal reality of magick, Tom. One day I'll tell you how Ivan Rybakov paid his debt. Not tonight.'

'Hang on,' said Tom when his phone pinged. He stared at the screen and then turned it round to show a picture of Lucy, upstairs, wearing one of Mina's sarees and striking a pose she wouldn't have contemplated sober.

'It suits her,' I said. 'And I think you'd better spend the night here. I don't think Lucy is going to be fit to travel.'

'You're not joking. What can we do to track down the property side?'

'I could call Princess Birkdale,' I said. 'She knows about the Octet now, and it would be good to follow up Karina's version of events with mine.'

'What sort of property are we looking for?' said Tom. 'What makes a good choice for a First Mine?'

Lloyd rubbed his chin. 'It has to be private. Doesn't have to be in the middle of nowhere, but it has to be private. And it has to be somewhere you can actually dig. Obviously. That's why there's no Gnomes in East Anglia. All too soggy. And it has to be near a Ley line.'

'How near?'

'All Gnomes can create Ley lines, but we're not as good as the best human Mages. A few hundred yards at most. Say, a quarter of a mile.'

I nodded. There were maps of the local Ley lines in the Deputy's library behind my chair, but I wasn't in the mood to start looking just now. 'We could use more than your advice, Lloyd. How do you feel about this, now we're coming to the sharp end?'

His nostrils flared slightly. 'If I didn't think they was near consecrating a First Mine, I'd say it was definitely down to Clan Blackrod to deal with it. They've lost their Clan Counsel, so they've got a lot of skin in this game. Unfortunately, I'd also have to say that a whole clan will be very reluctant to start looking into their own when there's a perfectly good suspect over in Birkdale.' He stood up. 'I'm going back to Earlsbury first thing. Pick up some stuff. We might need it. I'll see you tomorrow. G'night.'

Tom and I stood, too, and I said that I needed to take Scout for a last walk; Tom asked if he could join me. 'I don't fancy breaking up the girls' night in just yet.'

'Wise man.'

I followed the path towards Nimue's spring and told Tom why I'd been in hospital at the beginning of the case. While Scout went for a good sniff around, I broke out the hip flask. Tom's capacity to absorb new ideas had been saturated, so we mostly talked about family, especially Mina's and Lucy's, and a little about our plans for the future.

'I need to get a proper job,' said Tom. 'Working for CIPPS means that I can be sent anywhere. I'm not saying I want to settle down, but neither Lucy nor I want to be nomads. Not really.'

I made light of it. 'Can you face putting down roots on this side of the Pennines? Wouldn't that be a betrayal of your Yorkshire heritage?'

He laughed. 'I've got a plan. Lucy's going to expand east, and when she gets to Burnley, I'm going to insist she hops over to Skipton. Then we can move back to York.'

I called Scout and headed back. 'Well I for one wouldn't bet against her taking over the whole of the North.'

Mina was waiting at the back door. 'Evie's putting Lucy to bed, Tom. I'll show you the way.'

211

Lucy inadvertently changed our plans next morning by being hungover. Lloyd was up and out very early, but because Lucy needed longer, we were still in the kitchen when Kirk Liddington rang me. I didn't recognise his voice at first.

Fae Klass was back, and a breathy contralto said, 'That man who was found murdered this morning. He was one of the Count's *special friends*. From the Well. Thought you should know. Bye, big boy.' He'd gone before I could open my mouth to say anything.

'Who was that?' said Mina.

'Tom, could you find out if there's been a homicide overnight?'

'That was Cinderella,' I said to Mina while Tom called the South Lancs control room. 'Trouble is, I don't know whose glass slipper she's wearing.'

Mina gave me a pitying look and pointed to Sheriff Morton. 'You have been spending too much time with him. Lucy says his metaphors are tied in more knots than … I don't know what. See? It's infectious. I'd better go and find Lucy something to wear. Do you think I'll be going back to London today?'

'I doubt it. Will Marcia get angry?'

Mina gave a very Indian head-shake of uncertainty and headed upstairs. 'Who knows?' she called over her shoulder.

Tom had missed that, of course, and had a grim expression on his face. 'A solicitor was found in his office this morning by the cleaner at a firm called Sadler & Robertson. They're a big noise in a big building, right in the middle of Manchester. I've told them not to disturb the crime scene until MI7 have paid a visit. It's a nasty one, I'm afraid, and that's not all: the deed store was opened and locked again afterwards.'

'How do they know?'

'Because Scene of Crime have already discovered microscopic blood droplets on the carpet leading from the victim's office to the deed store. The killers wore impervious boiler suits, which are great at stopping your trace evidence being left behind, but they shed everything you pick up everywhere, and there was a lot of blood.'

'We need Mina on this one. And we need to trample all over client confidentiality.'

He hesitated. 'Why Mina?'

'She found the pack, didn't she? If the Count has been hiding assets with this firm, away from the Princess, she'll find it. They may have taken the deeds and wiped the client records, but there will be evidence somewhere on their systems. In a cross-referenced file, an email, a Post-it note, a spreadsheet.'

'It doesn't need just her, this is my speciality, too. Sod it. I'll give her a hand.' He looked troubled. 'Is this what Noble Cause Corruption looks like,

Conrad? Using your authority to conduct a search I wouldn't otherwise have the authority to carry out?'

'Think of the Victorian police force, Tom. There was no professional standards or internal affairs departments, but was every bobby corrupt? No, not by a long way. The King's Watch is a bit like that, and Hannah is trying to bring us even more up to date.'

'I need to have a long conversation with the former DI Rothman after this.'

What on earth was going through this poor man's head? 'I think that's a given. She'll definitely want to speak to you. After she's vented her spleen in my direction.'

'Do you want to come?'

'Definitely not. Do you think Lucy would mind a visit to Tara Doyle's place? I can drop her at Southport first.'

'I think she'd jump at the chance.'

The girls appeared at that point, with Lucy now dressed in one of Mina's old kurtis, Mina's leggings and a pair of Evie's trainers worn with two pairs of socks because they were too big.

It was one of Mina's least favourite kurtis, a sort of washed-out salmon pink, and it did nothing for Lucy. I tried to keep a straight face. 'We're going to see Tara Doyle. She'll appreciate that you've made an effort.'

'Noooooo.......'

I could still hear the echo when I went to get my guns from the safe.

23 — *Dangerous Company*

It was only when Tom pulled onto the motorway that it became awkward. Having Mina Desai as a passenger while he drove to a murder scene was not something he'd ever thought would happen, bearing in mind that he'd first met her at the scene of two violent deaths, her husband's and the man who'd killed him. From the hints dropped by that weird Gnome character last night, Mina's capacity for inflicting grievous bodily harm had not been diminished by a spell in prison.

Of course, she looked a lot better than when he'd arrested her. When she'd lifted her head that day to look him in the eye, and he'd seen what had been done to her jaw, he'd nearly stumbled over the wording of the police caution.

And now here she was, sitting in his car (after moving the passenger seat to suit her tiny frame), and deeply embedded in this insane world of Gnomes, magick and fairies. *No, not fairies* he thought: *the Fae.* Despite the evidence of his own eyes, he was still waiting to be informed that it was all part of an elaborate conspiracy. Every time his rational, lawyer/policeman brain told him that it couldn't be true, two feelings reared up and slapped him in the face. First, it was the death of that werewolf creature. She hadn't just died, she'd *disintegrated.*

He'd seen the light go out in people's eyes when they passed on and felt a connection to their soul. This was different. It was like standing next to the hull of a spaceship during explosive decompression: all the creature's life blew out of her.

The second feeling had come when Evie Mason got in his car last night and touched her chest. A ripple of cold water had passed down his spine, and the impenetrable hedge around Clarke's bolthole became a gateway, and he'd been sucked into Clarke's world of madness. As the car had passed over the threshold, a little bit of him had been left outside, and he wasn't sure which part that was. Perhaps he never would be.

Lloyd Flint was another mystery. On the surface, he looked like a short, working class lad. Sounded like one, too. And then he had given Tom a small disk and told him to wear it all times. It was something called a *Persona,* apparently, and Lloyd had said, 'It will blur your Imprint from Sorcery and put you slightly out of phase. Makes you much harder to track, and don't worry if it doesn't feel magickal. It is.'

Tom hadn't understood one word of that, but when it came to magick he was happy to trust anyone that Clarke trusted.

'It was easier for me,' said Mina.

'Sorry, what?'

'You were miles away, Tom. I don't blame you at all. It was so much easier for me to accept the world of magick because I have felt Ganesh's presence, and because I was more worried about my relationship with Conrad than what he was getting up to. It wouldn't have made any difference if he told me that he was taking up professional morris dancing, I would still have been more worried about whether we were compatible.'

And that was another thing: their casual acceptance that there were many gods, and that some of them could text you. Every time he tried to wrap his brain around that problem, it slipped out from under him and he found himself thinking about how Lucy was coping.

Coping rather too well if last night were anything to go by. There was a bigger age gap between Clarke and Mina than there was between Tom and Lucy, but sometimes Lucy seemed to be from a different generation altogether.

Tom loved a pint of Guinness, and would have one every night if he had an excuse to go to the pub; Lucy could go for days without alcohol, and then let go completely, and when she let go last night, she seemed to have bonded with Mina in that easy way that women have. After the third bottle from the Deputy Constable's cellar, Lucy had even started calling Mina *Rani*. In an ironic way, of course, but still...

'You have two sisters, don't you?' said Mina, interrupting his reverie again.

'Fiona and Diana, yes. Fi's a GP round the corner from Lucy's place in Southport. Lucy's even helped out with childcare occasionally. She's a natural when it comes to children. Having so many younger half-siblings, I suppose.'

'You haven't met Conrad's family, have you?'

'No. I couldn't believe it when I found out what his mother had done for a living.'

He risked a glance at her, and he saw that quirky smile at the corner of her mouth, and the glint in her eye that made her so attractive, once you saw past her emotional reserve and the pointy nose that dominated her face now that her jaw was fixed. Did she even know how attractive she could be, he wondered?

'We have another forty minutes,' continued Mina. 'You tell me what it was like growing up in an ultra-respectable upper middle class English home, and I shall give you an insight into Conrad's life at Elvenham. It may help you understand him a little bit more.'

When they got to Manchester, Tom used his police badge to get as close as he could to the enormous Botham Tower, and he reflected that Mina had discovered an awful lot about his marriage to Caroline (now a distant memory), and all that he'd discovered about Mary Clarke was that she liked bridge. If Mina didn't have a criminal record, she would have made an excellent detective, which was probably why the shadowy Establishment of magick had snapped her up.

The only sign that the Tower had hosted a grim murder last night was the scrum of journalists being corralled by the in-house security team to a corner of the plaza in front of the entrance. For all but the seventh floor, it was business/life as usual. After all, over 5,000 people either lived or worked in the Tower, and this wasn't a terrorist incident.

Once through the revolving doors, things were more complicated. All visitors had to convince security that they had business inside, and Tom could see a police support officer by one of the lifts. He flashed his warrant card at the barrier and vouched for Mina. The guard greeted him respectfully. 'Lift six has been commandeered for the police, sir, and all the others have been programmed not to stop at the seventh floor.'

'Thank you.'

The PCSO saw him coming and brought up her clipboard. He showed his warrant card again.

'That's good,' she said cheerfully. 'You're on the list. The official perimeter is upstairs. I'm just the bell hop, so you don't need to be logged in.' She made a sweeping gesture towards the open lift. 'I'll take you up, sir, ma'am.'

The override key was in the control panel lock, and the PCSO pressed to close the doors, then thumbed the 7 button. 'Who's the SIO?' said Tom.

She named a detective whose name he'd only seen on paper, then said, 'Tracey Kenyon is the Crime Scene Manager. I think she muttered something obscene when she heard you were coming, sir.'

Tom knew that the PCSO hadn't seen the body, or she wouldn't be quite so light-hearted about things, and that was the last thought he registered before Mina shoved him in the ribs and pointed to the indicator. They were about to flash past the seventh floor.

'It's the Octet,' said Mina, reaching into her bag.

Tom went to grab his radio, and the PCSO just stared at the numbers 8 ... 9 ... 10 ...

Mina got her phone out and actually slapped his hand away from the radio. 'Won't work in here. Get by the doors and cover me when they open.' Her thumbs worked furiously for a second, then she spoke into the microphone. 'Conrad, we are being attacked. Botham Tower. Somewhere above the ... seventeenth floor.'

She pressed something else, then snapped the phone out of its rubber case and got down on all fours, like a sprinter in the blocks, and yanked off her sandals. The lift stopped at the twenty-first floor, and the PCSO got out her can of CS spray. She and Tom moved towards the doors, with Mina hidden behind their legs. As much as you can hide a woman in a lime green tunic.

He felt a weight press on his ears, and that running water trickling down his back again. He opened his mouth to ask about magick, and nothing came out. Not a sound. At that point, the doors opened.

It was like lineout in rugby. Both sides trying to jam themselves into the tiny space of the lift doors, and Tom felt like he'd jumped into a prop forward, a short unmovable mass of muscle wearing a gas mask. Like the slippery scrum half, Mina shot through a tiny gap. Tom was starting to feel giddy, and couldn't put up much resistance when the Gnome pinned his arms to his side and lifted him off the ground. By God, they were strong.

Behind the Gnome, Mina played dodge with a woman in camouflage sportswear, a branded parody of Clarke and Karina's combat uniforms. Mina didn't try to fight, but she did manage to slide her phone along the tiled floor like a curling stone. The phone skittered across the tiles and out of sight, Mina's attacker hesitated, torn between the phone and Mina. She opted for Mina, and grabbed her arm, twisting it up her back.

Tom was dragged out of the lift, as was the PCSO. In seconds, they were inside the hallway of a substantial apartment, and suddenly he could hear again. The Gnome span him round and slammed him into the wall. Before he could catch his breath, his hands were in restraints and light, female fingers were going through his pockets.

'This one's got magick,' said the Gnome with a strong Northern accent. 'Who the hell is he?'

'Another one of the Witchfinder's pawns,' said a woman he couldn't see. Her accent was as Irish as leprechauns. 'I think we'd better take him, too.'

Tom had been relieved of his phone, radio and warrant card. And then everything went black when a hood was jammed over his head. The unbreakable grip of a Gnomish arm propelled him out of the flat, along the corridor and into another lift. As soon as they got to the bottom, the magickal silence descended again. *Oh shit*, he thought.

'You're mean,' said Lucy. 'It would only take me two minutes to run in and get changed. *Two minutes*. That's all.'

'Sorry about that. Just try not to think of her as an Instagram star. Look on her as a … I don't know. As a villain from Doctor Who, or whatever it was that made you hide behind the sofa when you were a child.'

'Mamma and Dad arguing, mostly. And the nuns at the *scuola elementare*. They'd have made any child hide behind the sofa. I still don't get it. How can Tara Doyle be two hundred plus years old? I checked before, and her parents are in loads of her Youtubes. Did she make it all up? What about all the kids she went to school with? I even know a couple of them. Are they all…' she waved her hand. 'Are they all simulacra? Is that a real word?'

'It is, and they aren't. Tara Doyle is a changeling. I told you.'

'No you didn't.'

'Okay. Fair enough. I told you *last night*. Perhaps I should have told you before you opened the grappa.'

She pressed her hand to her head. 'Don't remind me. So, you mean that the fairies…'

'Do not use that word, Lucia!'

'Oy! You're not my dad. Only he gets to call me that. So, the *Fae* swapped a child for … but how can she be two hundred years old *and* be a baby? How does that work?'

I really did tell her all this last night, you know. Tom was paying attention; in fact I saw him reach for his copper's notebook at one point.

'The Fae have two choices in the mundane world: to live as adults, ghosting their way through it like the Count of Canal Street, or they can change places, usually with a sick child. Even by the standards of the magickal world, it is a bit gross. You don't want to know the details, not with a hangover, and especially not the details of how Tara Doyle got her ovaries.'

'Uerp. Oh, dear God, no.' She held her hand to her mouth for a second, trying to keep the bile down. 'But a child's body?'

'It's called Reversion, and it's supposed to be truly horrible. You walk into the Reversion chamber – which is made of cold-forged iron – as a thirteen stone man and you are carried out as a four stone girl, and the Hlæfdige clear up the mess.'

'What was that word again? I'm half Italian, remember, not half German.'

'Hlæfdige. Old English word from which we get *lady*. They are neuter Fae, a bit like worker bees. They look like women, but they're not. Auntie Iris was one, in Kirk Liddington's story.'

'And how should I behave?'

'How would you behave if you didn't know who she really was?'

'Like a total fan-girl. I might diss her on Twitter afterwards, but not to her face.'

'Then don't change a thing.'

'Right. And you're *sure* it's safe to accept hospitality. Don't the stories say that it's dangerous to accept fair… to accept Fae food?'

'It's dangerous to refuse. Would you walk into her house with your phone on Record and shove it in her face?'

'No!'

'Then take what you're offered. Literally. The one and only golden rule is to think *very* carefully about accepting a non-material favour.'

'Such as?'

'Oh, Lucy, would you like me to make that café owner in Cairndale sell to you at a knockdown price?'

'That was the worst Scouse accent I've ever heard. Try that in Caffè Milano and you'll get lynched.'

'Duly noted. Here we are.'

I pulled off the coast road opposite the beautiful stretch of golden sands north of Liverpool and leaned out of the window to press the intercom. The gates opened immediately, sliding back on well-oiled runners. 'Did you notice how quiet it was outside?'

'I did. No paps or stalkers.'

'That's Wards for you.' A few seconds later, I added, 'And that's what you get when you spend seven and a half million pounds on a new house.'

Lucy surveyed the Greco-Roman pile that squatted on the top of a slight rise, nearly a quarter of a mile down the drive.

'This Reversion thing,' she said, 'Does it boil away their taste, too?'

'The Fae language is so secret, we only know a handful of words, and one of them is *bling*. They more or less invented it. You saw Mina's new bracelet, I presume?'

'That was beautiful. This is just gross. I'm not a fan of footballer's architecture.'

'You and me both.'

We left Mina's Volvo in a car park that most country pubs would consider too large and followed the statues of nymphs holding flaming torches to the entrance portico. A heavy in leisurewear stood ready to open the way.

'Welcome,' he intoned with a bow.

'Thank you, Saerdam,' I responded.

'What?' said Lucy.

'He's a Fae Knight,' I whispered while the man heaved back the bronze door (with reliefs of football matches). '*Saerdam* is like *sir* and *ma'am* rolled into one.'

I said that country pubs would be jealous of the car park, well country house hotels would be jealous of the atrium beyond the doors. Small shopping malls would be jealous. I haven't seen so much pink marble since I went to St Peter's in Rome.

A circle of columns supported a dome, complete with fish pond under it and casual seating arranged artfully around. In front of the pool was the lady herself, flanked by a gum-chewing teenager full of attitude (who had to be a Knight) and an elegant woman in her thirties (who had to be a Hlæfdige). The Knight wore almost nothing (in October!); the Hlæfdige wore a business suit and Tara was dressed in her signature range of gym-wear. Literally her signature range – it said *Tara Doyle* up the leg and across the chest.

As far as I could see, all the mundane staff were elsewhere, so we got the full Fae welcome.

'Lord Guardian, you do honour to my home. In the name of peace, welcome.'

I bowed. 'I am the one honoured to be here. In peace, thank you.'

Before I could say more, Tara broke the spell by rushing over to Lucy. 'I can't believe that Paola Berardi's' daughter is here! How mad is that, eh?' She gave Lucy a hug, two kisses and an appraisal. She cast her eye over Lucy's outfit, then reached a perfectly manicured nail towards Lucy's bag. 'One of last autumn's Sorrento range, isn't it? And I'm guessing you didn't get dressed at home this morning? Have you been raiding Mina's wardrobe, eh?'

Lucy went bright red. 'Guilty.'

Tara put her arm round Lucy and crooked a finger towards the Knight. 'Take our guest to the studio. There's loads of stuff in there that'll fit her.'

The gum-chewing Knight gave Lucy a bewitching smile. 'You wouldn't believe the stuff we get sent, yeah?'

'And we'll have some coffee and Danish when I've finished with Conrad, won't we?' Tara addressed the last remark to her Hlæfdige, whose job appeared to include continuous monitoring of her mistress's phone. The Hlæfdige nodded and started typing.

A bewildered Lucy was propelled out of the atrium, and Tara pointed to a pair of couches next to the pool. We sat down and the Hlæfdige took up a position behind her, within earshot but not in Tara's personal space.

I decided to get my apology in first. 'My Lady, I deeply regret the action I took yesterday. I would not have taken the life of your Mannwolf queen if I could have avoided it.'

She waved it away, dismissing the Queen's life with a flick of her fingers. 'Your biggest loss was Karina. She was full of remorse for what she'd done. Wouldn't have any blame attached to you at all. I think she'd have cut her own throat if you'd have forgiven her. Never mind, eh? So what are you doing to track down these Gnomish lowlives?' She levelled a finger at me. 'And don't you dare say that *enquiries are proceeding*.'

I told her about the murdered lawyer. 'Have you heard of him?'

She frowned. 'No. Should I have?'

'He may have been killed because he was handling business for the Count. DCI Morton and Mina are looking into it now. And I've called up specialist reinforcements.'

'Who?' She was direct, and demanded an answer with all the force of her power. I had to keep her onside in the similar way to holding back the aggression of Clan Blackrod.

'I'm setting a thief to catch a thief. Lloyd Flint is on his way.'

'More like setting a ferret to catch a rat. Does he remind you of a ferret? He does me. Useful creatures, ferrets.'

The Hlæfdige behind her had become a statue while we were talking – the living model for a sculpture entitled *Woman with phone*. When she moved her head to look at me, I noticed straight away. Then she touched her finger to her earpiece and frowned. When she spoke, it was a complete shock. A total Pygmalion moment.

'My Lady, you've received a voice note from Mina Desai. I think it's for the Lord Guardian. Shall I play it? It seems rather urgent.'

'You what?' said Tara, bemused. 'Why would Mina message me?'

I was already half out of my seat. 'Because my phone doesn't do voice notes. Play it, please.'

The Hlæfdige put the phone on speaker, and Mina's voice burst into life.

Conrad, we are being attacked. Botham Tower. Somewhere above the ... seventeenth floor.

My heart stopped. It paused for a whole beat before starting again at turbo speed, pumping adrenaline around my system. I was about to dash off when I remembered that, to the Fae, nothing is more important than protocol. I sketched the smallest of bows. 'My lady, I regret that I must leave. Forgive me, and forgive my rudeness in postponing our hospitality.'

What a waste of words and time. On the other hand, had I not spoken, she might well have forced me to stay and keep eating for days. Seriously. It has been known. Instead, her eyes lit up and she gave me her best smile, the one with thirty-six teeth instead of thirty-two. You have to see it to know just how disconcerting it is.

'They've just signed their own death warrants, haven't they? No escape for them now. Go well, Lord Guardian. My table awaits your return.'

I looked at the Hlæfdige. 'Tell Lucy that I'm leaving in three minutes, with or without her.'

The Hlæfdige nodded and pressed her phone. I turned and left; the big bronze doors were already open by the time I'd crossed the atrium.

I got out my phone and lit a cigarette, to give me time to make the crucial decision: the attack was happening *now*. Who to call? I pictured the scene as best I could, and decided that the most important thing was the presence of the police. I scrolled through my contacts and pressed on Elaine Fraser.

'Hi Conrad,' she said in a low voice. 'I think the doctor's due soon to discharge me.'

'Tom and Mina have been attacked at Botham Tower. Somewhere above the seventeenth floor, and that's all I know. You can put a rocket up the police control room, and I can't. I'm on my way back from Birkdale. Call me when you know something.'

'How do you know?'

'Doesn't matter. It's not magick, if that's what you think.'

'Right. On it.'

I opened the front doors of the car and leaned on the roof. With one of her three minutes to spare, Lucy Berardi ran out of the palace, barefoot and clutching armfuls of clothing. 'What's going on?' she shouted.

'Get in and I'll tell you.'

I slid into the driver's seat and started the engine while she threw her haul in the back and joined me in the front.

'Put your belt on and check your phone. You may have the same message.'

She put her phone to her ear as I raced down the drive and shot through the security gate. I made a quick decision and turned east, towards the motorway. It was slightly longer, but would give me the option of going to Manchester if things changed.

Lucy's face drained of colour. 'What's going on? What is this?'

'I don't know. Elaine's on it. She'll call as soon as she knows something.'

'What can we do?'

'We're doing it now. We're heading for Middlebarrow and waiting for intelligence.'

'Why aren't we going to Manchester?'

'Because it's an hour away. By the time we get there, either it will be too late or they'll have been moved.'

'You think they're still alive?'

I have a bond to Mina that goes beyond being in love. I don't want to find out, but I think I really would know if she were dead. The Octet wouldn't just kill her for no reason, and this sounded like a kidnapping. Whether they'd take Tom, too, or kill him out of hand was an issue I didn't air in front of Lucy.

'Yes, they're alive,' I said, as if I knew for certain.

Lucy stared at her phone, and then started to look for live Tweets. I think. I focused on the series of roundabouts that would take me to the motorway.

Elaine took an agonising further five minutes before she called back. 'Conrad, they've been taken. Uniforms at Botham Tower have just found a PCSO tied up in a bedroom, along with their phones and Mina's sandals. They got out down the back way. The duty Assistant Constable has activated the protocol. I'm going to ring off and someone will call you. Give them anything you can that'll help them track them.'

I took a deep breath. 'Were there any signs of violence?'

'No blood found. And for God's sake, don't tell Lucy.'

'Too late,' said Lucy. 'You're on hands-free, Elaine.'

'I'm sorry. I … I'm sorry, OK? Bye.'

The line went dead, and Lucy said, 'Yeah, she's always sorry afterwards.'

My reply was cut off by an incoming call. A man identified himself as Gold Commander and did me the honour of assuming that I knew what he meant. I did.

'We're dealing with an organised, non-terrorist criminal organisation. Is that correct?'

'Yes.'

'Armed? Violent?'

'Yes to both.'

'A threat to the public?'

'Only bystanders.'

'Good. Now tell me who we're dealing with and how we can find them. All we've got so far is what looks like a Crime Scene van entering the service area. After that the CCTV stopped working.'

'A total of eight males and eight females, all IC1. Not all will be together. They will be using advanced technology to disrupt CCTV and number plate recognition, but they can't make a large van any smaller. The driver probably won't know the area intimately. They're cool customers, but they're on a deadline. I'd suggest roadblocks and random searches. It might prompt them to bail out leave the hostages behind.'

There was a silence at the other end: I'd been put on mute while the Gold Commander and his team digested what I'd said. We reached the motorway, and I put my foot down.

He came back on the line and said, 'Mina Desai is your fiancée, yes?'

'Yes.'

'We're going to implement a track-and-trace. The risk to the public is too high for further intervention in the city. I'll text you the address of the command centre. Could you come straight here so that we can get further information.'

I lifted my hand to make sure Lucy didn't say anything. 'Of course. I'm heading down from Bury right now.'

'And what vehicle are you in, so I can get the gate to open?'

I fixed my eye on the car I was about to overtake and described it to them, including the index.

'Thanks, Mr Clarke. We'll expect you shortly.'

I disconnected and Lucy gave me a look. 'No way am I going there,' I said. 'They'll never let me out, and if they're not going to stop the little shits in their tracks, someone has to.'

Lucy lifted her hands. 'What do they want? The Gnomes, I mean.'

'To scare me off. To buy themselves some time. To find out what we're up to. I think they went for the two-birds-with-one-stone option: they really did need to shut that lawyer up, and they took the chance to grab Mina at the same time.'

'What about Tom?'

I sighed. 'Wrong place, wrong time. They won't have known who he is until they found him with Mina.'

'So what now? Where *are* we going?'

'Middlebarrow. I need to think, I need my other car, and I need a rendezvous for the rest of the team.'

'What team?'

I passed her my phone. 'Dial Eseld Mowbray for me, would you?'

'Is that Petra Pan? Isn't she the one who likes dressing up and fancies you?'

Petra Pan? What on earth had Mina said when the girls went upstairs last night? That was a conversation for much later. 'She's a friend and an important ally and she's got two things we're going to need.'

The car speakers sprang to life with as the call connected, and I started calling in favours.

24 — *Whatever it Takes*

The magickal silence was lifted for a second, just after Tom had been hoisted up and dropped on something hard. Having no sight and no hearing was disorientating beyond words.

'We're going for a ride,' said the Irish woman's voice. 'I'm going to tuck you in next to your little friend and put my foot on you so you don't bounce around. Wouldn't want to damage the goods, now would we?'

The strong arms of a Gnome pushed him into something soft and human. Mina, presumably. As the sound disappeared again, he felt a foot pressed into his back.

He was glad of that foot. When you can't see what's coming, when you can't use your hands, every turn and stop of a vehicle comes as a shock. All he could do was focus on trying not to squash Mina. It was going to be a long drive.

His whole world shrank. First he couldn't think of what to do next, then he couldn't think of what Clarke might be doing, and finally all he could focus on was Lucy. Surviving for Lucy. Keeping Mina safe for Lucy. That was the most important thing.

The foot dug into his back with extra force, and the van rocked alarmingly: they were off the public road. It rocked again and again, and at last came to a stop. The foot came off his back and sound was restored.

'Just you two lie there for a wee while. You'll be on the move shortly.'

The van door didn't slam shut, nor did the blanket of silence descend again. He held his breath and listened for someone else's movement or breathing. Nothing. 'Mina? Are you okay?'

'Yes.'

He didn't say anything else, and neither did Mina. A minute later, the floor swayed as someone heavy got in. Another Irish voice spoke, deep and masculine. Irish Gnomes?

'Roll over, Inspector Morton. We're going to move you now.'

He did what was asked, and felt his arms nearly pulled out of their sockets when he was heaved to his knees and dragged to the edge of the van. Then he was lifted and lowered on to the ground and frogmarched, stumbling over the ground, until they stopped. The hand on his arms kept a strong and silent grip.

'Ow! Careful!' said Mina. He heard footsteps, boots crunching on rough concrete.

'Walk forwards. Both of you.' It was a different voice, male and Manchester. An echo told him that they had moved inside a large building.

Tom did as he was asked. 'Stop.' Hands gripped his arms again while the plastic restraints were cut off, then his arms were brought in front of him and something fastened round his wrists. 'Close your eyes or they'll hurt.' Again, he did what he was told, and more hands pulled off the hood. Light flooded through his eyelids, and he squeezed them more tightly until he could risk blinking. Footsteps receded. He still thought that they weren't alone, and when he blinked a little, the first thing he saw was two figures, arms folded, waiting for him and Mina to notice them.

During the abduction, he hadn't been able to focus on the Gnome's faces, so he didn't know if the male was one of them; the woman he recognised as the one who'd tackled Mina. He immediately gave them names, to try and give him some control over the situation. This was Gnome1 and Colleen, and they were standing at the end of a corridor made from bales of straw. Tom and Mina were at the end, and they both had handcuffs and long chains that were anchored to rings in the floor. Cement dust lying next to the rings showed that they'd only been drilled recently.

Mina was closer to their captors, Tom closer to the end of the corridor. They each had a bale of straw to sit on and a blanket. Placed on the floor by each of their straw bales was a bucket, a roll of toilet paper and a large bottle of water.

Mina grabbed handfuls of her long black hair and pulled it away from her face, smoothing out the mess that the hood had made. She was the first to speak. 'Something for my feet would be good. This floor is very cold.' Her voice was detached, impersonal, and Tom could hear the echo of generations of Desais commanding their servants.

Colleen looked at Gnome1, and he gave a curt nod. She walked off, and the Gnome spoke. 'If you're both lucky, your boyfriend won't try to find us, or he'll try and fail. Either way, you'll be home for breakfast tomorrow. If you're unlucky, he'll turn up and we'll have to kill you. Before killing him, of course.'

He didn't wait for an answer, turning and walking away to the left, towards the source of light, presumably the entrance to the barn, because that's where they were: a big metal barn on a farm. When quiet descended, Tom listened hard. There. The gentle lowing of cows kept indoors. They were on a dairy farm.

Colleen the captor appeared briefly at the end of the straw corridor and threw a pair of flip-flops to Mina. Colleen retreated, and someone shut the barn doors. Once the reverberation faded, they were alone. Mina pushed her feet into the man-sized flip-flops and shuffled to her bale of straw, the chain clinking as she moved.

'I am so sorry, Tom,' she said, looking him straight in the eye. 'If you had not been given that Persona, you would not be here, and your presence makes life a lot more complicated.'

What was she on about? Tom was under no illusions about how Clarke would see his involvement in this: Clarke would do everything he could for Tom, yes, but Tom had seen the way Clarke looked at Mina. Clarke would move heaven and earth to protect her. 'Conrad will put you first,' he said. 'I'm probably safer being nearer to you than on the outside.'

She shook her head sadly. 'I do not make offerings to Ganesh for this life alone. Conrad knows that when my life ends, I will be born again.'

Reincarnation? Was that a thing? Karina hadn't mentioned it in her little talk on *Gods 101* yesterday. Mina saw the confusion on his face and said, 'Tom, when Conrad proposed, I released him from his promise to always tell me the truth. A few days later, when he'd got used to the idea that we were actually going to be married, I made him promise never, ever to sacrifice himself for me, because Ganesh will open the door to my next life.'

It sounded like a piece of Eastern nonsense, and it was hard to take seriously. 'What about me?'

Again, the sad headshake. 'You have committed to no god, Tom. Who knows what will happen to your atman after you die.'

Oh. That was a stumper. His mind slid away from that thought and focused on something he knew better: the slippery nature of Conrad Clarke. 'What if Conrad breaks his promise?'

'Do you have a family motto, Tom? Your father is Lord Throckton, so there must be a coat of arms or something.'

There was. 'We don't talk about it.'

'Ooh! Tell me more, Tom. Look on this as a chance to get to know each other properly.' She spoke like she was flirting with him, and she even patted her knee while she said it. When she'd been under arrest last year, she'd barely given anything away, using her long hair as a curtain to shut out the world. Now she'd pulled back the curtain, and was it the original, pre-assault Mina Desai coming out, or had she become someone new entirely?

She was right about one thing, though. There wasn't a lot else to do. 'It's my Great Grandfather's fault. We call him The Original, because he was the first Thomas Morton. I should have been called Alex, but that's a story for later, when we get really bored. The Original married a very wealthy woman, so he took as his motto *Spurn not the Distaff.*'

'What does that even mean?'

'Don't ignore your women.'

'Aah. A wise man. Well, Conrad's motto is *A Clarke's Word is Binding.* He can't break his word. Completely and utterly.' She smiled. 'One of the side effects is that he rarely makes promises.'

'I see. So he might sacrifice his life for me but not you?'

She sighed. 'I'm afraid so, yes. Hopefully it won't come to that.'

Clarke had once risked his own life to do something that Tom couldn't do for himself; something that he shouldn't even have wanted, but Clarke had done it, and that sort-of obligation was one of the reasons he hadn't blocked Clarke's number and forgotten about him. The thought of Clarke dying for him, or worse still, of saving him, was one Tom couldn't bear, so he went back to families. 'Do they go in for mottoes in India?'

'We do. The literal translation is: *The Wise Tiger Fears the Shepherd.* That's what *Desai* means. Shepherd. Conrad modernised it for me: *No one pushes a Desai.* As the Octet will discover.'

Was it a movement of air? A noise he didn't register consciously? A newly discovered magickal sixth sense? Whatever the reason, Tom suddenly knew that they were being watched by someone on top of the bales of straw. Not *someone.* The watcher was a creature, because what farm has flip-flops lying around in October? A farm with a pack of werewolves living on it, that's what.

He turned his head to where the watcher was lurking but didn't look up. 'Hi there. I won't tell anyone you're in here. I promise. You can come down and say hello if you want.'

There was a rustle of straw and the sound of light feet dropping on to the floor behind the wall of bales. Tom and Mina listened for a few seconds. 'He or she will be back,' said Tom. He mouthed the word *Mannwolves.* Mina's eyebrows shot up, then she nodded.

'I'm glad you spotted him or her,' she said. 'And even gladder they've gone. I need to use my bucket.'

The message came through just before we got back to Middlebarrow Haven: We'll release them at dawn tomorrow provided you stay away. Don't try to find us or contact us. At the first sign of you or your friends coming near us, the hostages die and we vanish. You know we mean it.

That was pretty clear. I sighed and spent the last ten minutes of the journey explaining reincarnation to Lucy and what it meant for Mina. And the problem that Tom had just given me.

'Do you believe what they're saying?' she asked.

'I do. Supposing we look for them and fail: they'll release Mina because they've got what they wanted, and they'll know I wouldn't attack them. Not directly.'

'But that means they'll have got away with everything. Including at least two murders and two abductions.' She shook her head. 'No, Conrad. Tom wouldn't want you to do that.'

'How can you be sure you know what he wants?'

'Because someone he didn't like was once kidnapped. Tom followed them and put himself in harm's way. That's the standard he sets.'

A smile twitched its way on to my lips. 'Are you saying that I don't like Tom?'

She twisted some of her curly hair round her fingers and gave a very Italian shrug: stylish and asymmetrical. It was better than a Spanish shrug, but not quite as good as the French, and it was all the answer I was going to get.

'Have you got any hidden talents, Lucy?'

'Nope. Well, first aid, I suppose.'

'Don't knock it.'

'Let's hope it won't be necessary.'

I didn't disillusion her.

Lloyd was the first to check in, and did so by asking me to meet him at the White Horse. I told him I'd be ten minutes and that I'd see him outside. I took Scout and enjoyed stretching my legs. Real autumn was in the air, with sunshine and a lazy warmth that would turn into a cold night.

Lloyd wasn't alone at the table. I wasn't surprised to see young Albie, but I was very surprised to see Lloyd's uncle. When I'd first met the clan, Wesley Flint had been chief. He'd made some very bad decisions, and had also been duped *by a woman*. He was lucky to have survived the turmoil. What under the earth (as they say), was he doing here?

There was a pot of coffee in the middle of the table. Lloyd poured me a cup, using his left hand as naturally as I use mine, then jerked his head towards another table, further away. On the way over, he asked if there was news.

I told him about the message, and he nodded thoughtfully. 'And you'm going ahead with this?'

'I am.'

I left it there because he clearly had something to say before he signed up to the mission.

'If it was just me on this, I wouldn't hesitate,' he said, 'but we need more, and I can't ask Albie to join in to rescue Mina and a policeman, no matter how much I like Tom Morton.'

'I understand. What about Wesley?'

'I'll come to that. If we break the Octet before the consecration, I want the land.'

Of course. That's why Wesley was here. 'Can you take over another clan's First Mine like that?'

'No. Totally forbidden. Wouldn't work, either, but until the consecration, it isn't a First Mine, it's just a hole in the ground.'

'Where are your other five potential clansmen?'

'On their way. They won't be here until much too late.'

I offered my hand. 'As Deputy Constable and Guardian of the North, I offer you the spoils of war.'

He shook and said, 'So who else is in on this? Have you called up the girls from Clerkswell?'

We walked back to the other Flints. 'Too risky. They really would be in serious trouble if they joined in on this. I've gone outside the King's Watch.'

'Why? Who?'

'How would you find the target, Lloyd?'

He puffed out his cheeks. 'Dunno.'

'Let's go to the Haven, and I'll explain.'

Tom heard the rustling again in the middle of the afternoon, followed by a more serious sound of metal bending. It only lasted half a second, then one of those magickal silences descended. He could tell that partly because Mina looked at her left arm, where the scar was, just hidden by the sleeve of her kurti.

They were being watched from the top of the bales. A child. No, *a cub*. Like young humans everywhere, one of the cubs had found a way into the barn, and now the adults had followed, bending back the steel sheets to let their larger bodies through. The adults didn't climb on the bales, they walked round and stood at the end of the corridor.

There were two of them, and they looked very young, no more than sixteen or seventeen in human years. They were both wearing kilts and flip-flops below the waist, with a rugby shirt for the male and a white smock for the female. The tartan in the kilts, pale purple and light green, looked distinctive, and wasn't one of the obvious chain-store patterns. Mackenzie tartan, maybe? The boy was full-on ginger, cut to a tight fuzz, while the girl's jet black mane tumbled down her back. They stood and stared, as if what they were seeing were as incredible to them as the existence of Mannwolves was to Tom.

'Namaste,' said Mina, pressing her hands together. 'Please excuse the smell.'

'Who're yoo?' said the boy, his Highland Scottish accent like the wind whispering over the heather. 'And what're yee doing here?'

Mina bowed again. 'I am Mina Desai, the Peculier Auditor and also the betrothed of the Dragonslayer, Lord Guardian of the North.'

'No way,' said the boy to the girl. 'It cannae be.' He looked up. 'And who're yoo?'

Tom took his cue from Mina. She clearly thought that it was important to establish their identity, and he had a clue as to why that might be, given that the Mannwolves were sneaking into the barn and had no idea who they were. 'Detective Chief Inspector Morton, mundane police. Whom do I have the honour of addressing?' *Get me,* he thought, *I haven't spoken like that since I gave up being a lawyer.*

The girl snickered, and looked even younger; the boy's pale skin probably disguised his true age. He frowned, a deep frown that Tom knew well. It was the frown of a rookie police constable who found himself at the centre of a major incident. 'Wha's goon on? Why're you here?'

Tom lifted his chains and tried to remember the terminology. 'We are hostages. Your Protectors are breaking the King's Peace, and the King's Watch are coming. So are others, with Quicksilver weapons.'

The girl clutched his arm and whispered something in his ear, then spoke aloud. 'You know who we are?' Her accent was Irish, with a lilt that marked her as coming from a different place to Colleen.

'Yesterday we visited the Darkwood Pack,' said Tom.

'No, no, no,' said the girl. 'Mistress promised we'd be kept out of all their affairs. We need to go.'

'Go where? I'm not leaving without ma boy,' said the lad.

'They'll come for us next. We need to talk to Oma.'

She more or less dragged him away, and neither of them looked back. When they were behind the bales, the girl hissed, 'Fiona, get your arse down here now!'

Mina waited a beat, then finally lost patience with her hair. She attacked the hem of her kurti with her teeth until it ripped, then tore off a strip. She tied back her hair as best she could and looked up. 'Why did you go in heavy, Tom? You must have had a reason.'

'They didn't know we were here. The Darkwood Pack fought to protect their own, but they're like, I don't know, they're so used to being *kept.* Like a pack of dogs. Or slaves.'

She nodded thoughtfully. 'And the adults came to see for themselves, once the little girl had told them we were here.'

'Yes. Do you remember what Conrad said about their status in England? They've not been here long, I don't think. That girl, the Irish Mannwolf, she talked about *their affairs,* meaning the Gnomes. Conrad said that the Octet had help, and I think that a Fae noble has loaned them a small pack of Mannwolves.'

'Why would they do that?'

'You tell me, Mina. I've only been in the world of magick for twenty-four hours.'

231

She mulled it over. 'You're trying to make them think they're in danger.'

'Precisely. I want them to think of the King's Watch as a potential saviour, not a deadly enemy.'

'Because their so-called Protectors might not be anything of the kind.'

'That's it. Who's Oma?' he asked

'Grandmother. Those poor children must be the King and Queen, with Oma as the elder. Do you think they're holding the boy's cub as a hostage?'

'Sounds like it.'

Tom sat back down again, as did Mina. She also wrapped her blanket round herself and shivered. Tom looked at his handcuffs, specifically at the way they stopped him taking his coat off and offering it to her.

'Where were we?' said Mina.

'You were telling me what makes Gujarati cooking different.'

The third part of the plan descended from the sky in the middle of the afternoon and landed in a meadow behind the Haven.

'Who chose that colour?' said Lloyd. 'It's 'orrible.'

'It is rather striking,' said Lucy.

'And noisy,' added Evie.

'It's known as the Smurf,' I said. 'For obvious reasons.'

The Mowbray family helicopter was painted Mowbray blue, which is the sort of thing you do when you're the second biggest landowner in Cornwall (after the Prince of Wales). One of the passengers crouched *very* low when he got out, which is what you do when you're very tall, and when I say someone's very tall, most people call them giants.

Chris Kelly, Earthmaster of Salomon's House, had two bags with him, one full of magickal apparatus and the other full of dirty washing (I presume). The other passenger, his apprentice Kenver Mowbray, had three bags. When you're the apprentice, you always have to carry the extra bags.

We shook hands, and I made brief introductions, then said, 'Excuse me while I do a handover with the pilot.'

The chopper had flown up from Cornwall to Lincolnshire to collect Chris and Kenver, then over to Cheshire (with a brief refuelling stop). No wonder the charter pilot looked bug eyed. The Smurf was behaving himself, and all was good, so I took the keys and pointed at Lucy, now resplendent in Versace or whatever it was that she'd picked up. Shall we just say that although it was the right size, the dress had been designed for someone a lot taller and less curvy. At least her trainers fitted properly, even if they did clash. Or so I'm told. Lucy had forbidden photographs, so I couldn't get a second opinion.

'Lucy will give you a lift into Chester,' I said. 'And someone will pick you up in the morning.'

'Thanks. What's my accommodation allowance?'

'Whatever you want, within reason. Don't overdo the wine, though.'

He looked at my uniform and nodded. 'Understood. See you tomorrow.'

They left, and I asked Evie to take everyone through the Wards except Chris. This conversation needed to be private.

'What's going on, Conrad?'

Chris Kelly is now Britain's top Geomancer. The previous holder of that honour had been Kenver Mowbray's father, until he was murdered. Who knows, perhaps Kenver will be as good one day. My first question had nothing to do with Geomancy.

'How's Tammy and the girls?'

'The girls are fine. Growing by the day. Tammy is ... Well, I hear she's fine, too. We haven't spoken for a while. She doesn't believe I've forgiven her.'

I heard Saffron's salacious tone in my head *You've met the bodysnatcher!* Tamsin Kelly, going by physical body, had once been someone else, and Chris's then wife had taken over that body. It's a difficult story, made worse by the fact that Tammy lied about the circumstances, and it had been me who uncovered the truth. Families, eh?

'Sorry to hear that, Chris. Perhaps if we can rescue Mina, she might put in a good word.'

His eyes, always slightly prominent, bulged right out. '*Rescue* her? What's happened?'

I took him to Nimue's spring and told him the story while Scout chased after something. Rabbits, probably. Mad dog. I had to call him back twice.

At the end of my story, Chris got straight to the point. 'How in the name of Albion are you going to find them? They could be anywhere!'

'How good are you, Chris? How low would I have to fly for you to detect a new spur off one of the Ley lines?'

He looked at the silent form of the Smurf. 'How low can you fly?'

'With Kenver spotting for me up front, as low as you want. Once we find the spur, we'll gain height and follow it. Lloyd has a good idea what to look for.'

'Won't they hear us coming? Or sense the magick?'

'I haven't told you the tricky part yet. The Gnomes will lock themselves into the new mine at dusk. We'll have to do some of the flying at night.'

'Are you mad? No, don't answer that question. I've heard the stories.'

We walked back to the Haven while Chris mused on what I'd suggested. 'So let's get this straight,' he said. 'We have to identify the site of a new First

Mine, then carry out an assault on a group of desperate Gnomish wives who are holding hostages. And then we have to attack the mine.'

'That's right. I've got a plan for the mine, though.'

'That's so reassuring, Conrad.'

I ignored the sarcasm. 'Good. Lucy will be back from Chester in ten minutes, then it's time for tea.'

'Now I know you're joking. You're not going to stop for tea, are you?'

I felt the Wards of Middlebarrow Haven pressing against me. 'We need to eat, and I didn't think it would go down well if I called it a Last Supper. Got to keep morale up and all that.'

25 — *Armed Race*

Mina curled up in her blanket and went to sleep about four o'clock, and Tom gave thanks yet again that they hadn't taken his watch off him. When Mina was flat out, he tested the limit of his chains. She'd already told him about Gnomish metalwork and magick, and that not even Houdini could get out of these handcuffs.

If he stretched and twisted and extended his leg, he might, just might be able to touch toes with Mina if she were doing the same thing. So not a lot of use in other words. He had more joy getting to the straw bales, and pressed his foot against the stack. Useless. He couldn't topple that stack on someone the other side to save his life. Or Mina's.

The one thing he had some joy with was seeing round the end of the straw corridor. The door was closed, but all the interior lights were on, and he could make out the ends of some serious earthmoving kit. Inappropriate on a farm, but perfect for digging a mine. He heard a mechanical noise start up, and the cattle started making more noise. Who was milking the cows? Someone had clearly been doing it for a while.

After that, he sat on the floor so that he could have some back support. He was still watching Mina sleeping (it was the only interesting thing to look at) when the barn door slammed open. Tom struggled to his feet, and Mina uncurled like a snake.

Colleen and Gnome1 were back. Colleen had two McDonald's carriers which he barely noticed because he was totally focused on the axe. It came up to the Gnome's chest and had two blades of bright gleaming steel. Cold water ran down his back as little streams of light chased each other across the faces of the blades and down the hafts. If that axe could speak, it would have a vocabulary of three words: *submit or die*. His arm throbbed where the Mannwolf King had bitten him, and Tom's respect for Clarke went up several notches. If the man faced this sort of thing on a regular basis, then Tom had two questions: How are you not dead, Conrad, and how are you still sane? Perhaps he wasn't.

'I hope that is not a beef burger,' said Mina. Clearly giant axes weren't a novelty to her.

'Why the feck not?' said Colleen. 'They don't do Halal meat at MaccyDee's, so like it or lump it.'

Mina stabbed a finger at the camouflage clad woman. 'I am a Hindu, and you are ignorant.'

Gnome1 thought that was hilarious, and the hot flush which spread over Colleen's face said that the Gnome was laughing at her, not Mina. 'Can't do anything right, can you? First you let her use her phone, then you bring her beef,' he said. The woman looked at the floor, gripping the paper bags like they were stress balls.

The Gnome looked at Tom. 'Both of you, lie flat, face down with your arms out.'

Tom and Mina looked at each other and gave small nods, before taking their time lying down. Colleen's pink and white trainers came into view, and she placed the bags down quickly. When she'd finished, the Gnome told them to get up. 'Enjoy your meal,' he said. 'Goodnight.'

Tom examined his bag, and couldn't help himself. 'Mmmm. Coffee.' He grinned. 'I'm getting a lack of caffeine headache. Do you want my fries? Swap you for the burger?'

'That's very kind, Tom. I'll just pass the patties over and eat the bun.'

As they devoured the food, Mina held up a chip. 'If anything is going to happen, it will happen after sunset. We have another hour, I think.'

Tom grunted. 'I hope we have a lot more hours than that.'

Tricky little buggers, Gnomes. I had thought we had them bang to rights when we'd found a new, unauthorised spur off the Ley line. And then Chris had made me go a bit further. There were half a dozen of the bloody things, and a lot of them were very close to Manchester Airport's flight paths. The Controllers at Britain's second busiest airport were not happy about a helicopter flying in circles so close to the A300s and 737s queueing up to land.

I had tried telling them that I was a charter for Electricity North West and we were surveying power lines. No chance. Flying is an all-or-nothing business: no permission? Go away. Now. Before we scramble the RAF. I went.

'Sorry, folks,' I said over the intercom, 'We're going to have to do this the hard way. At least we have some starting points. We'll head back and look at the maps.'

I landed, and after I'd completed the shutdown checks, I limped back to the Haven and checked my phone. Damn. Five missed calls from the Boss and a message: *Call me now or you'll have no children.* Ouch.

'Ma'am?'

'Look up. Can you see the sun?'

Instinctively, I looked up. She has that effect on me. 'Yes, ma'am.'

'That's how deep you are in the shit, Conrad: as deep as the sun is high. Whose lives are you risking on this mad venture, because that's what you're doing, aren't you? You're going to try a rescue.'

'Only if we can find them. They're proving a little elusive.'

'That's probably a good thing. Who have you conscripted into your posse?'

'No conscripts, ma'am. All volunteers. The cream of Clan Flint will be with me. Chris Kelly and Kenver Mowbray are assisting but won't take part. Oh, and Lucy Berardi is our medic.'

'Chris Kelly! Kenver Mowbray! Are you insane? Yes, clearly you are. Kelly's a grown man, but if you don't return little Kenver to the bosom of his family, you will truly know pain. Are we clear?'

'Ma'am. I checked with Eseld first, you know. She thinks her little brother needs to have his eyes opened.'

I heard her draw breath. 'May Hashem guide you and keep you, Conrad, and may He bring you and Mina safely home and spare the others.'

I went to say *Thank you*, but my phone bleeped with the Call Ended signal. I stuffed it in my pocket and headed back to the Haven. Chris already had the maps out and Lucy was doing something with his laptop. 'I've had an idea,' he said. 'Lucy's getting the Livesat feeds. They're only twenty-four hours old, and any deflective Glamours will have been in place by then. We're going to look for anomalies along the line of the spurs.'

'That assumes the Octet won't have perfectly replicated the original topography.'

'Mines are big,' said Wesley. 'At least they are when you're digging. And our people aren't nearly as good at large scale Glamours as we sometimes like to think.'

There was a tense half-hour of ticking off the lists.

'Farmhouse.'

'Check.'

'Farmhouse.'

'Check.'

'Hamlet.'

'Ignore it.'

'Factory.'

'Let me see. No. Ignore it.'

And finally.

'Farmhouse and quarry.'

'Quarry?'

'Look.'

Chris peered at the screen. 'They've restored the image of the farmhouse, but that field, there, they've missed it. All the topsoil has been removed. That's got to be it. What do you think, Wes?'

'Arr. Reckon you're spot on there.'

I focused on the map and slapped my head. 'Of course. It's just north of Jodrell Bank. I didn't go anywhere near that, for obvious reasons. Air Traffic Control really don't like craft near our premier radio telescope.'

Chris looked pleased with himself. 'I know. That's why I posited a bridge between these lines.'

Posit? Never mind, I could look it up later.

'Are we all still on for this?' A series of grim nods answered my question. 'Lucy, Chris, Kenver, you're with me in the Battlebus. Lads, you take Mina's car. We'll rendezvous *here*.'

Lloyd looked at the map. 'All the humans together, eh?'

'I'm taking Scout. You know what he's like.'

A pained expression came on his face. Scout thinks that Gnomes are a treat. When he sees exposed flesh, he can't stop licking it. 'Fair enough. You do realise that there's two rivers and the West Coast Main Line between that rendezvous point and the target?'

'It'll be the least defended.'

I caught Lucy looking at her new trainers. 'Don't worry, if we pull this off, Tara Doyle will give you the run of her studio.'

'And if we don't?'

'I'll text her now and ask her to supply a pair to the undertaker.'

She went slightly green and swallowed hard. 'You're so thoughtful, Conrad. Now shut up and let's get going.'

Things got very interesting at half past six. Tom heard the rustle of Fiona climbing the wall of straw, and seconds later the Irish girl/Mannwolf came round the front of the corridor. She was holding a burner phone. 'Can you work this?' she said to Mina.

Mina's back stiffened when she saw the phone. 'If it's not locked.'

The girl shoved it at Mina. 'Try it, then give it here.'

Mina thumbed the phone. 'It's powering up … Searching for a network … found one.' She calmly offered it back. 'Yes, I can use it.'

Had they never seen phones before? The Darkwood Pack were aware of technology, even if they didn't have much use for it.

The girl weighed the phone in her hand. 'We'll help you if we get immunity.'

'What's your name?' said Mina quietly.

'Cara.'

'I cannot give you immunity, Cara. Only the Lord Guardian can do that.'

'Then send him a message. Quickly. And tell him not to call.'

Mina took the phone and started typing. 'It's a good job I know his number,' she muttered. 'There: *Pack will help in return for immunity. We are unharmed. Reply by message only.* Is that acceptable?'

'Do it.'

Then followed the agonising wait. Seconds dragged by. Cara's head whipped to face the door when she heard something. There was a *ting*. 'Yes,' said Mina. 'Immunity and relocation.'

'Tell him it's Brookford Farm and to follow the seventh star,' said Cara before she disappeared.

Mina worked frantically to type as the barn doors rolled back. She was still typing when they closed. In a blur of movement, she threw the phone into the air. A tiny, grubby, pale face reared up at the top of the bales and little fingers caught the phone. Tom's respect for cricket as a participant sport went up several notches.

Colleen stepped into the entrance with two folding chairs. She placed one facing them and one to the side. 'Good evening to you both. Won't be a tick.' She disappeared, and when she returned, she had a shotgun in one hand and a machete in the other. She placed the shotgun across the second chair and pointed the machete at Mina. 'If I hear any noises outside, you're for the chop, princess, and when I've finished slicing you up, your man here gets both barrels. Are we clear?'

The Ancile. Of course. By putting Mina at the front, the Gnomes had effectively given Tom a shield.

Mina bent slightly so that she could reach her hair and smooth it. With her back to him like this, her feet in the oversized flip-flops, she could be a teenager herself, like Cara. Her voice was anything but childish though. 'I understand you,' she said. 'But think carefully. If there *is* a noise, are you sure you know what it means? And if your fellow wives and the pack manage to repel attackers, would it be wise to kill us? So long as we are alive, you are not under a death sentence. As soon as you spill DCI Morton's blood, you have condemned yourself to death. As soon as you spill *my* blood, you have condemned yourself to a long and *slow* death. Let me tell you about the Blood Eagle. Conrad has sworn it on anyone who hurts me.'

'Shut your fecking mouth, you whore!'

'Make me. First, your back is carved open, then your ribs are cracked off...'

'Shut. Up.'

'Very well. When you sit in your comfy chair and you feel the support press into your back, that is where the incisions will be made.' With that, Mina turned round and sat down. Only Tom could see the big grin on her face.

'What's she on about? Seventh star?' said Lloyd. 'Are you sure it's her? Get down, you daft dog!'

I'd received Mina's text while we were working out how to climb the great fence that protected the main railway line, a line that seemed to have 225kph trains thundering down it every minute. And I wasn't the only one who received it: Lloyd and Lucy got it, too. Mina's always been good with numbers.

I pulled Scout away from trying to lick Lloyd and handed his lead to Lucy. 'Of course it's Mina. Brookford Farm is exactly where we're heading. I have no clue about the other part, though.' It was still dusk, and the stars of any description wouldn't be out for a while. 'What about this fence?'

It was eight foot tall, had no handholds and spikes on the top.

'We need to get a move on,' said Lloyd. 'Let me do it.'

I waved for him to go ahead, and he used his prosthetic hand and a considerable dose of magick to bend a gap that we could just about crawl through. 'I'll jog over and do the other side.'

If we were seen on the track by a train driver, British Transport Police would be all over us in minutes, so we had to wait until nothing at all was coming, and then we were over the track, through the other fence and only one field away from Brookford Farm.

The group was bearing up fairly well so far, considering what a motley crew we were. Chris Kelly is a long distance runner, and he could keep going all night and all tomorrow if no one stopped him. Gnomes are not built like that, but a light jog over a couple of fields was nothing to Lloyd and Albie. Kenver is young, and that left Wesley, Lucy and me. At least being the leader, I could set the pace, but Wesley is old in years and very well padded. He brought up the rear with Lucy who was discovering that designer gym gear is no substitute for actual exercise.

We gathered by a farm gate, and Chris said, 'I can feel something. Faintly.'

'Me too,' added Wesley.

I brought up the binoculars and studied the farm buildings, away across the next pasture. From here, all I could see was a substantial brick farmhouse to the left, and to the right, the back of a cowshed and milking parlour.

'We'll make for the far end of the cowshed, away from the road,' I said, and got six blank looks. 'The big building with the wooden sides and the gap at the top to let the smell out.'

'Right.'

'Gotcha.'

Lloyd pulled open the gate and we slipped through. I made for the cowshed at a fast jog. And kept going. And going. Until I got to a hedge.

'Fucking hell,' said Lloyd. 'It's getting further away. What the hell?'

'Wow,' said Chris. 'That's a multi-phase displacement. Only the Fae can do that.'

'Bastards,' said Albie reflexively, like a Roman Catholic crossing himself in a church.

'So how do we undo it?' said Lloyd.

'We don't,' said Chris simply. 'Unless you know the key, it's self-enfolding.'

'We do know the key,' I added. 'It's *Follow the Seventh Star*. Now what under the earth does that mean?'

'Any stars on the farm?' said Wesley hopefully, trying to use his Sight to scope it out.

'Excuse me,' said Lucy. 'Stop pulling, Scout! That plaque thingy in your study, Conrad. Doesn't it have seven stars on it?'

Of course. The Badge of my RAF unit, 7 Squadron, has Ursa Major on it – the Plough, the Big Dipper, call it what you want. Seven stars, and the seventh star, Dubhe, circles Polaris at about 30 degrees below due north. So where was it tonight?

I stared up. The stars were just becoming visible, but not yet the Plough. Not to worry. All I needed was good old Orion, which was there, so ...

'That way.'

'Are you mad? That's back towards the railway line,' said Lloyd.

'Look,' said Chris. 'A convoy on the lane. Three cars.'

Only he could see them, because only he could see over the hedge.

'Let's go,' I said, and struck out in what I hoped was the right direction.

We were half way across the field when I felt the Wards. Yes! 'Can anyone disable these?'

'I can,' said Kenver. 'Eseld showed me. They're not very sophisticated. Probably Gnomish.'

'Oy,' said Lloyd. 'We're above ground here, alright? We can Ward underground like you'd never get through.'

'Sorry,' said Kenver. He took a metal chain from his pocket and started whirling it round his head. Everything went dark for a second, and I started to sweat from the Lux being used. When the light came back, we weren't facing the railway line, we were ten metres from the corner of the cowshed, and something was going down in the farmyard.

'Brilliant, Kenver,' I hissed. 'Quiet everyone.'

I edged to the corner of the building and looked round. Oh shit.

I quickly made out a barn to the right and a pair of cottages to the left, forming an open ended square with the cowshed and the farmhouse. Two cars had driven in, and something had deflected one of them into the cottage wall. The other one had stopped at the edge of the yard. Black shapes were getting out, and a reception committee was waiting.

No, make that two reception committees.

A group of four women were in front of the farmhouse, armed with shotguns and spears. Facing them were a bunch of kids. A bunch of naked kids, to be precise. Two boys and four girls were shouting at the women and pointing at the cars, then they got a good look at the black shapes and started to exchange into wolves.

'What the hell are they?' I said, pointing to the black forms.

'*Nachtkrieger*,' said Lloyd. 'Night warriors. Fae Knights in psycho mode. Don't look at their eyes. This is bad.'

I'd heard of them, of course. Of all the things that lurk in the forest, waiting to drive you mad and drink your blood, the most terrible is the Nachtkrieger, and they'd come for the wolves.

The six Mannwolves spread out, each facing a Nachtkrieger. Or two. The wolves were outnumbered. At first, the Fae backed off, allowing the wolves to herd them towards the cottages, then they sprang their trap. Three of the black shapes turned on one wolf in a blur of shadows. I didn't see what they did, but when they broke out of the ring surrounding them, there was one dead wolf and three Nachtkrieger bearing down on the farmhouse.

Three of the women scattered at their approach and one held her ground, raising her spear to keep them away from the front door. And she kept it raised as one of them slashed her throat and two others hammered on the door.

'This is going to be a massacre,' said Lloyd. 'Eight against five, and they're after Mina. She must be in the farmhouse.'

I'd already reached that conclusion and had been working on a plan: keyword *herd*. I backed away from the scene and turned round.

'Who can get round the corner unseen? Not far, just along the cowshed.'

'Me,' said Wesley. 'I may be slow but I'm sneaky.'

'Good. On a count of twenty seconds, open the doors.'

'You what?'

'Go!'

He went.

'Lloyd, put a hole in this wall. As quietly and quickly as possible.'

He didn't argue, he just got on with it. Kenver had put himself next to Lucy so that he could create a floor-level Silence. Scout was not a happy dog. I raised a Silence of my own and took Scout's lead from Lucy.

Lloyd had also used Silence, and his prosthetic arm, to simply break the wooden slats, and there was now a hole in the cowshed. My internal count had got to thirteen and I waved the others forward, through the hole and into the byre.

There must have been a much, much bigger herd recently, judging by the space available. Around thirty Friesians were moving quickly away from us, and were already distressed by the screaming and smell of wolf coming through the walls. Once they saw the Merlyn's Tower Irregulars, they set up a huge bellowing. I dropped the silence and gave my order.

'Follow the cows and take out the Fae.'

Right on cue, Wesley drew back the roller door. The cows weren't interested in going out there, so I slipped Scout off the lead. 'Come by, lad, come by.'

Lloyd cottoned on first and started pushing the herd towards the opening. With a nip on the ankles from Scout, one of the girls pushed two more, and then they were streaming outside, rushing to get through the mayhem as quickly as possible.

It was like being hit by a tsunami. Wolves and Nachtkrieger scattered, allowing Lloyd and Albie to target one of the Fae. Another Nachtkrieger tried to use magick to stop an onrushing cow in defiance of all the laws of momentum. The cow swerved, but the Fae had stopped moving to perform its Work. As the cow charged past, the smallest of the wolves sprang into the air and sank her fangs into its neck.

I took all this in as I raced to the farmhouse. The three Nachtkrieger had been distracted by the stampede, and still hadn't got inside the house. I got to the wall, raised a Silence, raised the Hammer and fired.

The last time I'd shot a Fae, she'd absorbed the bullet. This one didn't: its Imprint blew apart, and I switched to the next target. Its eyes met mine. Her eyes met mine. It was the Lady of the Night, and I knew that there was no point shooting, because you can't shoot the Night. I lowered my weapon and she came towards me.

Her face was beautiful, as beautiful as the Northern Lights flashing over Midwinter in Norway. And those nails, so long, so elegant and so sharp. I prepared to give my whole self to the Night.

Ooof. A lilac missile hit my side and knocked me over, making me drop the Hammer. Lucy.

We landed in a heap and she rolled off as quickly as she could, but not quickly enough to stop the Nachtkrieger picking up my gun.

I backed off, staring at the creature's clawed feet. Ugh. I was also drawing my new sword and activating the Ancile inside it. To my intense relief, I heard Lucy scrambling away, back towards the cowshed.

I focused on the lower half of the Nachtkrieger. They didn't have weapons, or none that I'd seen. Perhaps maintaining that shape was too big a drain on their resources. I moved forward a step, then another, then I slashed at the creature's outstretched arm.

And cut through empty air, just as the real creature raked her four inch talons at my face. I jerked my head away and saved my eye, but the nails sliced from my temple to my jaw. Ow. Fuck.

I pivoted away and heard the farmhouse door start to splinter. Shit. What now?

Lloyd knew I was after the Fae. Long-term. He wouldn't have stinted on that, so I risked letting my Sight flow into the sword. Gnome, human, Gnome, Gnome, ???, Gnome ... Fae. Right at the end of the blade was a sliver of ice-in-iron, a cold-forged steel tip.

'Come and get me, Lady,' I said, locking eyes with her and raising the sword to point it at her throat. She started forward as soon as she felt my eyes lock, then flinched back when she felt the magick in the sword. One step. Two steps. Three steps and her back was to the wall. Four steps, five steps and I pushed the sword into her neck. I flicked my wrist, cut her carotid artery and dashed for the door.

Inside was a farmhouse kitchen and a half. Very modern and very chic, with a conservatory to the right rear. A conservatory with bars. A pen. And inside the pen was a small child, a little boy so scared that he couldn't even scream. Outside the pen, at the end of a long chain, now slack and pooled on the floor, was an old woman. She was about to give her life to stop the Nachtkrieger getting at the child, just as soon as the Fae had dealt with the human standing in her way.

It was a tall, powerful woman, and she knew what she was doing. She didn't look her enemy in the eye, she jabbed a kitchen knife at the Nachtkrieger, and of course, she missed. The creature grabbed her wrist and flung her across the room to smash into the granite-topped kitchen island. That just left the Mannwolf Elder.

They were too far away for me to reach them. I shouted. I roared defiance and raised my sword. The Nachtkrieger turned around for a second and hissed at me. The old woman took the chance to use magick, pushing the creature with a blast of air and knocking it back a metre. I started to run, and the creature turned back on the old woman, now collapsed with exhaustion. I wasn't going to make it. But Scout did.

He shot past me and skittered across the tiles, crashing into the Nachtkrieger and wrapping his jaws around its leg. The Fae slashed down, I slashed up, and my sword bit into its arm, snapping the bone. Withdraw. Reverse. Lunge. Dead.

I looked around the room. 'Where are they? Where are the hostages? Upstairs?'

'In the barn.'

Shit. Double shit and buggery. I tore out of the house and across the yard, pausing only to pick up my gun.

It started with racing car engines, screeching tyres and the thump of a vehicle hitting a solid object. Everyone stood up and looked towards the door, even if Colleen was the only one who could see it.

Mina started to whisper a prayer, and Tom moved as close as he could get to her. Colleen hefted the machete and flicked her head between Mina and the (closed) door. Then the howling started, and every hair on Tom's body rose away from his skin. Every sinew inside him wanted to run away, and he pulled on the chains in frustration. Another noise drowned out the wolves: frightened cattle. What the hell? Cows bellowed, wolves howled, wild creatures shrieked, a lone dog barked, and then Tom knew what was happening: Scout was here, and where there was Scout, there was Clarke. To prove the point, a gunshot echoed round the farmyard.

Colleen looked terrified as she suddenly realised that she was as trapped in here as they were. Something inside her snapped and she raised the machete to attack Mina, swinging it down in a great arc.

Mina dropped to her knees to give her the maximum chain length and brought it up between her fists. Because she was so short, she got enough height with the chain to intercept the blade, locking her arms at the elbow. Human steel met Gnomish chain, and the Gnomes won. The machete bounced off the chain, and Colleen had put so much force into the blow that she dropped her weapon. It bounced off the floor to one side, and she reached for it.

'Noo!' shouted a little voice. A blur of red landed on the ground and snatched the weapon away. Fiona, a tiny child in a red smock and white leggings scuttled away from Colleen and round the corner. Colleen chased her and swore when the little girl got through the gap in the wall.

That would have been Tom's moment to be the hero, if he could have pushed those bales over. He pushed his foot against them and roared in frustration, even louder than the cows outside.

'Well, I'll just have to do it the old fashioned way.' Colleen was standing at the entrance to the corridor, legs apart, hands on hips. 'Right, you little whore, let's see how strong you are.'

Colleen danced forwards and aimed a punch at Mina, who dodged it and got a kick to the knee for her pains. Colleen jumped on to Mina and grabbed her chains. Mina fought back, elbow to the face, and got a second's grace. She knuckle-punched Colleen in the temple, but missed, hitting her ear. It was painful, but it didn't stop Colleen forcing Mina down and wrapping the chains around her throat. Mina was going to die, and there was nothing that Tom could do about it.

Mina tried to bring a knee up, and missed. With her last breath, she flailed an arm in the air. Tom was going to close his eyes, until he realised that watching Mina die was the only thing he could do for Conrad.

'Aauurgh. Urrggh. Feck.'

Not Mina. It was Colleen who was dying. An arrow stuck out of her back. She reared up and the bloody thing had gone all the way through. The great barbed head was sticking out of her left breast. She staggered to her feet on pure adrenaline and looked into the dark. Without a sound, not even a *thunk*, another arrow sprouted from her gut. This one didn't go through – it stuck in her spine, and she collapsed in a heap, still gasping to make her shattered lung work.

Still wearing her Army uniform and 2nd Lieutenant's pip, Karina Kent appeared round the corner.

Mina was coughing and retching, so Tom spoke. 'Thank you.'

'No problem,' said Karina. 'Let's just hope the good guys outside win.'

'What's happening?'

'I don't know. I was late to the party, and I only came in here because I saw the little girl run out.'

'Ghaaah,' said Mina. 'Ganesh opened that door for you.' She bowed. 'Thank you, Karina.'

There was a slap of footsteps and little Fiona reappeared, dragging an older sister by the hand. 'Here they are,' she said. 'Oh. The nasty lady's dead.'

There was an almighty clang and screech of tortured metal as the door blew off, and a roar of, 'Mina!' from Conrad Clarke.

'Here!'

He limped into view, sword in one hand and gun in the other, and blood streaming down the right side of his face. It had already obliterated the name over his breast pocket. He sniffed the air, for a half-second looking like his bloody dog. Well, they do say pets resemble their owners, and vice versa.

'Lieutenant Kent,' he said. 'Your handiwork, I presume?'

'Sir. But I couldn't have done it without help from the little girl.' She pointed to Fiona, now swinging her pigtails and stuffing her left fist into her mouth.

'She saved my life. They both did,' added Mina.

'And mine,' said Tom quietly.

'Well done!' said Clarke in an exaggerated, children's entertainer voice. Then he bent down and shot Fiona in the head from point blank range.

26 — *Keep your Friends Close*

How did I know which little girl to shoot? As soon as I saw that Mina was safe, my new Nimue nose told me that there was a Fae in the room. I had a good look round, and the only anomaly in everything was the smaller girl. She was supposed to have saved everyone's life, and there she was acting like a two-year-old in a beauty pageant instead of a Mannwolf cub. That's why I leaned down to get a good sniff, and that's why I shot her: in a second, she could have used the *real* Fiona as a shield.

When her head exploded with Lux, the Glamour on the real Fiona dissolved, and she jumped back, away from the body. 'Did you really save Mina's life?' I said in a normal voice. 'If you did, you were very brave.'

Fiona nodded and pointed to a woman in camo leggings and top, currently busy dying. 'She was mean. She was going to hurt the princess.' She looked at Mina. 'You're a real princess, aren't you?'

Mina bowed as low as she could. 'Yes, I am. How did you know?'

'You're brown. I've never seen a brown person before.'

'Not all brown people are princesses, but I am, and you will get a special sash to wear now that you've saved me.'

'Good. Is Oma still alive?'

'Let's have a look, shall we.'

I was going to saunter outside, until the scream of a car engine made me break into a run, and the *crump* of an explosion made me hit the deck.

The car that had crashed into the wall had exploded, and the other one had reversed out and was now racing down the lane to the public road. Damn.

It was pretty clear what had happened: whichever Fae had loaned the pack to the Octet had decided to rub out the evidence. One of the many peculiarities of Fae biology is that their DNA unravels once it leaves their living body (except for sperm; let's not go there), so all the corpses were useless for identifying which line they belonged to. Never mind.

Everyone moved like a well-oiled team, which was quite gratifying to see. None of my party was injured (except me), and no more wolves had perished. In seconds, I had five naked teenagers running around. One rushed to scoop up Fiona, another went inside the farmhouse (with Wesley and Lucy), and two more helped to round up what was left of the Gnomish wives, another of whom had been crushed by the stampede of cows.

The Mannwolf who'd helped Fiona looked up. 'The farmer! He's locked in the cottage. The fire could spread.'

Lloyd and Albie took charge of finding the yard cleaning hose, and soon, with magick and water, the fire was under control. Wesley emerged from the farmhouse with the Pack Elder and a red-headed lad who cradled the little boy/cub in his arms.

'Where's Lucy?' I shouted.

'First aid,' boomed Wesley. 'Looks like a broken arm. Is your fiancée safe?'

'Chained up in the barn with Tom Morton.'

'I'll get them out.' He waggled something shiny. 'I knew these lock picks would come in handy.'

There was more sorting out and moving round, and then Mina and Tom emerged from the barn, followed by Karina and Wesley. Tom jogged past me with a nod, heading for the farmhouse, and Mina ran up to me.

'Your face,' she said. 'Does it hurt?' Her voice croaked, and in the fading light, I could see marks around her neck.

'Yes it bloody well does, love, but we're alive. We're all alive.'

She gave me her special smile. 'Do you mind if I don't kiss you just yet? Where's the first aid kit?'

'That's Lucy's job, but it'll have to wait.'

'Are you going after the Gnomes now?'

'No. The cows.'

'The cows?'

'Yes. Don't want them escaping on to the road, do we?' I whistled, and Scout came running. 'Lloyd!'

'Yeah?'

'You're in charge for a bit. I need the cowshed fixed first, and then you know what the priority is, don't you?'

'Put the kettle on.'

'Good man.'

Karina came to help me with the cows. Good job, too, because they were pretty spooked. 'That Irish Gnome's wife?' she said, 'She died in the barn before Lucy could get to her. Not that there was much she could have done. How can I help?'

When we were done, Karina drifted off leaving the farmer and I to settle the herd. He was younger than I expected, early forties, perhaps, and under the enormous stress, much better groomed than your average dairy farmer.

'What happened?' I said. 'How did you get into this mess?'

He moved some straw with his Wellington boot. 'Someone invited me to the Well of Desire.'

'How long ago?'

'A couple of years. I didn't notice what was happening until too late. By then, I'd swapped the farm for a lifetime's membership and a bit of cash. I used the cash to refurbish the farmhouse.'

My mind boggled. 'The whole farm?'

'It was mortgaged to the hilt.' He shrugged. 'I've been making more money as a tenant than I ever did before. Then he sold it to that lot.' His gesture encompassed the farm, but it finished out beyond the yard, over the barn and up a slight rise. That's where the mine was, and where Chris and Kenver were surveying.

'What did they do?'

'Moved in, for one thing. Kicked me out of the farmhouse and made me sack the workers. The wives have been taking it in turns to help with milking. I haven't left the farm in six months. Not since they started digging. What the hell is going on, Wing Commander?'

I shook my head. 'Someone will tell you once dawn comes. Until then, this is an active operation. You're going back to your cottage, and you're going to stay there.'

'Has anyone fed the pigs?'

'What pigs?'

'As well as digging that bloody hole, they built a flaming pigsty round the back of the barn. Totally unlicensed and unregistered. I had the devil's job trying to hide the fact it's here. You're bleeding again.'

I patted him on the shoulder and commandeered the other cottage. It was a bit musty, but didn't have any bodies or chains in it. Lucy has a real knack for first aid, and soon patched me up. 'If you don't see a doctor soon, it'll scar,' she concluded.

'Not top of my priorities, but thanks.'

'It's a good job you didn't agree to marry him for his looks,' said Lucy to Mina.

'Mmm,' she replied. Traitor.

Mina, Tom, Lucy and I sat at the kitchen table, bringing each other up to date and holding hands (as appropriate). When we'd finished, I started with Karina.

'You've had your uniform tailored,' said Mina accusingly.

'Let me guess,' I added. 'Princess Birkdale. She's signed you up, hasn't she?' Karina nodded, deeply embarrassed now that the action was over. 'How did you find us, and why?'

'I followed you from Birkdale to Middlebarrow. I thought I had no chance when the helicopter arrived. I heard you and the Earthmaster talking.'

'Aah. That explains why Scout was acting up. He could smell you.'

She gave a real smile. 'He wanted to play. I was going to give up, and then you came back and drove off. I just followed you, but it took me ages to work out how to get through the displacement. I arrived when you released the cows, so I ducked into the barn.' She shrugged. 'That's it.'

'Why get involved?'

'I left location services enabled on my phone. I wanted to help put it right.'

I poured myself a third mug of tea. 'Which leaves you serving two mistresses: Hannah and Tara Doyle. I won't stop you walking away, Karina.'

She looked down. 'I'll still see the Boss and take my punishment.'

'Good.' I looked round the table. 'Let's see. Lucy saved my life, and you saved Tom and Mina's. With joint accounts, I reckon that in the end, I owe you twice over, unless you want to collect from the others.'

Karina nodded. 'No offence, Mina, but I don't pay any taxes or play cricket, so I'd rather collect from you, sir.' She gripped her hands into fists. 'Can you get the file on my mother's murder from Merlyn's Tower? Boss Hannah wouldn't let me see it. And if I come back, will you help me deal with her killer?'

'I should be able to get the file. Hannah would have let you have it eventually anyway. As for the second part, I'll help you as Watch Captain. Remember the golden rule.'

She didn't look happy, but she nodded. 'Yeah. Part of the solution, not part of the problem.'

'Good. Are you staying for part two?'

The glint was back in her eye. 'Yes. And I give you my word that I'll follow all orders.' Before I could stop her, she whipped out a knife and cut herself. 'In blood, it is written.' She took some blood on the tip of her knife and made an X on the table. 'In blood it will be honoured. I'll go.'

Mina and Lucy wouldn't let her leave without a hug, and there were tears in her eyes when she dashed out of the cottage. Poor kid.

While the girls were hugging, Tom leaned over. 'Is there a lot of that? The blood stuff.'

'Not so much. Depends on your affiliations.'

The Mannwolves were next. Tom had told me about them, that the girl was Cara, and the boy introduced himself as Alex. They brought the Elder with them, though she sat on the sofa, cradling Alex's little boy. Cara placed a pile of clothes on the table in front of Mina. 'For you.'

Mina shook back her hair and bowed. 'Excuse me.'

In seconds, the torn, blood-stained kurti was in the bin and she showed off her new look: a red smock, a Mackenzie tartan kilt over leggings and flip-flops that fitted. Even the Mannwolves winced when they saw her swastika tattoo.

We quickly established some ground rules: I wasn't allowed to ask where they'd come from, or who their Fae Protector had been. Apart from that, they were very keen to talk.

There is a real issue with in-breeding within packs. The Fae (and it's nearly all Fae) who act as Protectors like to move them around, and this pack was assembled a couple of years ago with individuals from Scotland, Ireland and the south of England. The original King, Queen and two Elders had died when the pack was set to hunt and kill Drake Blackrod.

'He went down fighting, then,' I said.

'Aye,' said Alex. 'With magick and his bare hands. One of the Elders was mother of my boy. Before then, it was all so easy. We just had to stay out of sight on the farm. They used to take us to different places at the Full.'

That's the one part of old w*r*w*lf lore that's true: they do have to exchange forms at least once when the moon is full.

'Are you viable?' I asked. It was blunt, but necessary. Without enough bloodlines, the pack wouldn't be viable, long term.

'Sure we are,' said Cara. Dressed, she looked fourteen going on forty, and was actually nine. That is, she was born nine years ago. 'There's bloodlines from four surviving packs amongst us.' She turned to Alex. 'He's going to be busy.'

Now that was hard to stomach. Lucy's eyes bulged, and Mina looked down.

'There's something we'd like to ask youse,' continued Cara. 'We want you to be our Protector. Please, Lord Guardian.'

'You're all equal in my eyes,' I said. 'Be your own Protectors.'

The pack Elder spoke up from the sofa, with a strange old-sounding half German accent. 'I told you he'd say that. He's not of the Fae.' She looked at me. 'If you let us loose, we'll be caught and enslaved in weeks, and yes, I know what real slavery is. We are not human. Let us be who we are, and be our Protector.'

Mina kept still: this was my decision. I looked at Tom. 'What do you think?'

'Do you really want to know?'

Mina patted his arm. 'He always means it when he says that.'

'Then take them on. It's not just the Fae, think about Clan Blackrod. From what you've told me, they need a reason *not* to hunt the pack down. Give them one.'

'Good point. In that case, I offer my Protection.'

Alex and Cara got up and stood back. They lay face down on the floor, and Cara pulled the hair away from her white neck.

The Elder shifted the boy in her arms. 'Tell them our new pack name and say, "My arm is your shield." Unless you want to kiss one of their necks.'

'Why on earth would I want to do that?'

The Elder's smile was grim. 'You can take Alex or Cara for the rest of the night. Or both if that's your inclination.'

That went straight into my Top Ten Most Alarming Magickal Moments list. Top three, probably.

'You are the Elvenham House Pack, and my arm is your shield. Now please get up before Mina says something rude.'

The King and Queen of the newly minted Elvenham House Pack got up and offered me their hands to shake. Far more civilised. 'Your arm is our shield, and Great Fang our blade, Sire.'

'Great Fang? You're not talking about Scout, are you?'

Cara burst out laughing. 'Go away wid you. He's sweet an all, but he's only a dog. Your sword. I heard the crunch when you took out that Nightmare, and I swear it was possessed by Great Fang, our first and last king.'

I do wish everyone could agree on terminology. I called them Nachtkrieger, they called them Nightmares. Doesn't help. And now my new sword was haunted by the ghost of the mythical First Wolf. Allegedly.

'Thank you,' I said. 'I will take great care of Great Fang.'

Alex and Cara helped the Elder to her feet, and she had something else to add before she left.

'The Gnomes are divided. We heard more than they thought, and not all of them were happy with the attack on Drake Blackrod, and there was nearly a rebellion when Fergus said he wanted to kidnap the Rani. You should bring Ilse up here on her own.'

As they walked out, Alex looked over his shoulder. 'How're you going tae get into the mine?'

'Briefing in here at Eight o'clock. One hour.'

'Aah ken how to tell the time, Sire.'

'And no jokes, yee great Saxon!' added Cara.

Lucy's hair seems to rise a centimetre when she's genuinely confused. 'What jokes?'

'You were in Italy, *cara mia*,' said Tom. 'British children still play a game called *What's the time, Mr Wolf*.'

'You could have asked me first before you rejected their offer,' said Mina when they'd disappeared into the night. 'Alex might have had something we could learn from.'

Tom went bright red.

'How do you keep a straight face?' said Lucy.

'It's because I'm so twisted inside,' said Mina. 'I shall go and get Ilse. Which one is she?'

'The one with her arm in a sling,' said Lucy. 'The one who tried to save the Elder. The taller of the German girls.'

'And bring Lloyd,' I added. 'This is his business as well.'

Lloyd appeared first, with a carrier bag full of bits, including Mina's bag, their phones and their ID. He also had a pile of car keys. I put them to one side.

Ilse's arm was probably broken, but not badly, and she had a cracked rib or two. With the help of the Internet, Lucy had fashioned a sling that pinned her right arm to her left shoulder. Ilse was the tallest and strongest of the wives, if you're measuring muscle mass, and her English was as good as you'd expect from an educated German. So far, so predictable. When she came in, Lloyd casually mentioned that she was a Witch.

'I thought that didn't happen,' I said, blurting out more than I'd meant to.

'Most Witches have more sense,' said Ilse, 'because your daughters will not be Witches unless your husband's mother was a Witch, too. Hans' mother was a Witch. I am not a very good Witch.' Her sentences were delivered in short bursts of small breaths. If it weren't for the painkillers, she'd be lying down in a lot of pain.

'Interesting.'

She shrugged, and immediately regretted it. 'Acch. Zo. What is your plan? All must die?'

'No one must die,' I said. 'If they surrender and submit to the Cloister Court. Simple as that.'

She thought about it. 'What will be the charges?'

I pulled my lip. This was going to be a difficult situation. I was theoretically off the case, and charging decisions weren't mine to make. I started with the obvious. 'All thirteen of you, the survivors, were involved in the assassination of the Count of Canal Street.'

Ilse snorted. 'He was extorting us. He wanted to be our "Protector", as if we were like those wolves. We gave him a chance to back out.'

'Nevertheless…'

She raised her hands. 'Ja. I understand. Princess Birkdale must see us all punished or she will lose face.'

'There's also the attempted murder of Kirk Liddington,' added Tom.

'Who?'

'Also known as Fae Klass.'

'Oh, her. We wouldn't kill a human. Only kidnap for a few weeks. Gregor was adamant that human murder would bring the King's Watch down on our heads.' She laughed bitterly. 'When he heard you were on the case anyway, that's when the problems started.' She tapped the table with her left hand, her voice full of pleading intensity. 'Gregor is of Blackrod, and his brother also, but his brother does what Gregor says. Gregor will be chief.'

'Is he the one with the axe?' said Tom.

'Ja. When he becomes chief, he make Fergus second and give him the axe. Gregor insisted that Drake Blackrod must die. He said that Drake was on to them, but I don't think so. I think it is because Drake wants to marry Gregor's daughter.'

'Who was the Irish woman in the barn?' said Tom.

Ilse looked disgusted. 'She is the wife of the other Irish brother, Colm. I cannot pronounce her name, so I call her Gudrunna. She thought she was going to be First Wife.'

How was that possible? Best not to ask.

Tom coughed and pointed his pen at Ilse. 'I've investigated some big gangs.' Did he look my way when he said that? Whatever. He continued, 'The biggest problem is the cut-throat defence, when everyone blames everyone else. What evidence can you give us? How do we know you're telling the truth?'

Did you notice? He said *we*. For now, anyway, I felt a lot better.

Ilse had a counter-problem. 'How are you going to get them out of the mine without collapsing it?'

'Trick them.'

'Then you need help from some of us,' said Ilse with finality. 'It will never work without us. And I want to be there to tell Hans to surrender. You are good, Dragonslayer, but you do not have enough to take on the Octet if they all fight back.'

'She's right,' said Lloyd. 'We need them cut off from the mine, and we need some of them to surrender.'

She was right, and this was going to be a big risk, but I didn't see an option. 'I agree,' I told her. 'Let's hear it.'

27 — *And your Enemies Closer*

Before the operational briefing, I took Tom back to the barn. It was a huge thing, specially built to house and hide the construction equipment for the mine, most of which had now gone. In the empty space at the back, well beyond his temporary prison, was a fleet of cars. If six vehicles count as a fleet: two white vans, one of which he'd been transported in, three 4x4s and a brand new BMW 5 Series estate, with all-wheel drive, leather interior and all sorts of goodies. I pointed to it and said, 'It's about time I replaced the Battlebus. What do you reckon?'

He struggled to cope with the concept. 'How? What?'

I encompassed the fleet. 'This is all plunder. By right of law, I get to keep the lot.'

'But … there must be over a quarter of a million pounds worth.'

'Yes. I'm expected to distribute it. Lloyd has first dibs on the vans, Karina wants the Evoque, so you can choose between the two Mercedes.'

'I can't do that.'

'It's the law, Tom. If you can't cope with one for yourself, take one for Elaine. She deserves it. Let her choose whether to keep it or sell it and give the money to charity. You've got to drive off in one tonight, anyway.'

'Why?'

'It's time for you and Lucy to go. And Mina. Mina's going to wait at Knutsford services and would love you to join her.'

'Right. There really is no point in me staying, is there?'

'None. You're witnesses to what's happened so far. I'd like to keep that testimony safe.'

He took the keys to a Mercedes and stuck out his hand.

'I've been wondering what to say, Conrad, after what you did, and after what's happened over the last week. I can't think of anything better than *good luck*, so that's it. Good luck.'

'Thanks. See you back here later.'

He walked towards his new car, and I went to open the doors.

The Octet were sealed up underground. After a fashion. The entire King's Watch and half of Salomon's House would be needed to breach the outer defences of the Blackrod First Mine, if you were mad enough to try. Brookford was a different matter.

As Lloyd said, it wasn't a First Mine yet: just a big hole in the ground with fancy steel doors. There was fertiliser in the barn and a diesel tank; I could make explosives and blow the entrance to kingdom come. Wesley had the skill to turn that same fertiliser into nerve agents, and I could waft it down the ventilation shafts to kill the lot of them, and those were just the obvious approaches. None of them were acceptable. The Octet had to have the chance to surrender.

So how to get them out?

The consecration of a First Mine needs a huge amount of Lux, and the Octet were drawing that from the Ley line spur that ran across the farm. I'd asked myself what would draw them out of their bunker, and the only thing I could think of was to interfere with the supply of Lux. Not to stop it (I could do that myself), but to restrict it and set up a dangerous fluctuation in frequency. For that, you need the Earthmaster and his apprentice. This was their show, and the operation began as soon as they were ready.

The Octet had made use of the topography behind the new barn, where there was a natural hummock on the rise of the land. They'd dug down and into that, levelling the ground in front of it to give extra depth and a more cliff-like front, and that was what we'd seen from the satellite images. Alex, the Mannwolf king, had taken me on reconnaissance and shown me the vents, further away and in three batches.

The biggest cluster was exhaust, with heat and smoke pouring from it. Not a huge amount of smoke, because they were using Lux rather than coking coal, but enough to be noticeable and pungent. The other vents were fresh air intakes; when the mine was fully developed, all of these would be replaced and hidden.

They'd also used the spoil to bank it up even further behind the doors, and that was my post, above the doors. I had Lloyd and Albie to my right, with Karina to my left. There was so much magick surrounding the doors that being close to them was the best way of concealing ourselves. I made one last check of the Irregulars and flashed my torch: dash-dash-dot dash-dash-dash. *GO.* And nothing happened. Nothing I could feel, anyway. I lay down and braced myself in the firing position.

Chris and Kenver were invisible in the darkness. With starlight and my ever-improving night vision (a side effect of magick), I could see a fair bit, but not as far as their position. Wesley was guarding and shielding them, because if the Octet came out they must not have any idea that the supply was being manipulated deliberately.

Wesley flashed his torch: dot-dash-dash-dash-dash. *1.* The first part was working. I flashed *2* at the rest of Irregulars, arrayed in front of the mine, and put my torch down. All we could do now was wait.

And wait. And wait.

'They're coming,' whispered Lloyd. How the hell did he know? Must be a Gnome thing.

'I hear them,' said Karina.

There was no signal for this. Everyone should know what to do straight away.

I felt the heat from the doors as the magick changed, then I heard the great slabs of steel start to move. Light spilt out from inside the mine as the left hand door heaved open and two figures emerged. We'd been shown pictures of the Octet, and I reckoned this was Colm and one of the pair from London.

Colm carried an axe and the other Gnome had a brass thingy that was a bigger version of the brass thingy Chris Kelly had been using to choke back the Ley line. I know, I'm supposed to be a Geomancer, too, but I am only a beginner: to me it was a thingy.

When they emerged, they headed left, towards the Ley line, and they saw their loving wives gathered around a wood fire, holding a vigil for them. At least that's what I hoped they saw. In reality, three of the wives were dead (including Colm's; awkward), and three were tied up in the barn, so only two of the wives were there in person: Ilse and Kathe from Germany. The other five apparent wives were really the Elvenham House Pack using Glamours.

'Where's herself, then?' shouted Colm, deviating slightly towards the group. He must not get too close. He must not…

'Gudrunna is guarding the prisoners,' said Ilse, improvising. 'Is there a problem? You can't be finished already.'

'Nothing we can't fix. It's going great guns,' declared Colm. He was now well lit by the fire and still well within range. My range. 'Now,' I hissed to Karina.

She stood up and put her hands to her mouth. She took a deep breath and poured magick out to amplify her voice. 'In the name of the King, surrender!' I let Lux flow through my hand into the Hammer, activating my Badge and announcing my authority.

Colm looked around him, in panic. My worst nightmare was him plunging ahead and attacking Chris, but Wesley did his bit, and the Gnome didn't see them. The Glamours were gone, the Pack were exchanging forms, and Colm did what we hoped: he grabbed the other Gnome and ran towards the mine, right into my sights. I stilled my heart and fired.

And the bullet bounced off him. Shit.

It had to happen sooner or later: someone would create an upgraded Ancile specifically to deal with my bullets. The old arms race. Time for plan B.

'Down!' screamed Karina.

She and Lloyd were a careful three metres away from me, putting them outside the blast radius of my one remaining MK3A2 concussion grenade. Pulling the pin on an old, abused grenade was scary, and I closed my eyes. Why? Primal instinct. I released the lever and cringed.

Ooof. Still alive. And-one-and … Drop. Right at the leading edge of the open door. Head down.

Dirt, rock and bits of steel flew in all directions. I peered over the edge and saw that the blast had twisted the door on its hinges as well as punching a bite out of the bottom corner. They wouldn't be closing that in a while.

If Colm had wanted to live, he should have run in the opposite direction. He didn't. He picked himself up and saw that the Gnome with him was kneeling with his arms in the air, surrendering. Colm lifted his axe, ready to decapitate his prospective clansman.

There was a snarl and a howl, and suddenly the surrendering Gnome was protected by the pack. Colm swore and ran as fast as he could towards the doors.

Karina, Lloyd and Albie were scrambling down the bank, and I joined them. Colm saw us and brought the pommel of his axe down with a burst of magick. Shock waves spread out, turning the loose rock underneath us to gravel. We all lost control of our descent, and instead of four on one, Colm had a free pass to attack or run. He ran. Into the mine.

'All OK?' I shouted. We were. I drew Great Fang and followed Lloyd through the doors.

The tunnel was short, steep and held up by a rough concrete roof and floored with packed dirt. Not dirt. Something red. It was wide enough and high enough to get machinery down, and the only sign of magick was a chain of Lightsticks. As we began to descend, the temperature rose dramatically and a whiff of sulphur hit my nostrils.

Lloyd moved slowly, scanning for Wards and traps. 'They're arguing,' whispered Karina, presuming that I couldn't hear it. She was right.

I moved to Lloyd's side as we approached the end of the tunnel and put my arm on his shoulder. He stopped, and I lay down to get a better angle – the downward slope meant I couldn't see very far into the chamber beyond. When I saw no one waiting, I stood up and pointed down. We charged.

A big round space. Twin scaffolding towers reaching up to the domed roof. Two archways leading off with concrete lintels. More red rock packed down for the floor. All as expected. The Octet – now Septet – were grouped at the foot of the right hand scaffold tower.

Gregor had his axe lifted on to his shoulder, listening. His brother, Andriss, was at his side, and Colm had joined Fergus opposite them. That left Hans and two others trapped in the middle.

We spread out in the same formation as on the roof and stood well back. 'In the name of the King, surrender!' I shouted.

'We're leaving,' said Gregor. 'You can get out of the way or you can die.'

A skitter of claws on stone, and five wolves weaved their way into the chamber, staying behind our Anciles for protection and ready to cover the gaps.

Gregor lifted the axe off his shoulder as if it were a broom handle and pointed it at Lloyd. 'Why do you stand next to the Witchfinder. What is this wet one to you?'

'He is my brother in blood.'

Gregor nodded slowly. 'And here he is, threatening the children of Mother Earth. Will you follow him in that?' He lowered the axe and switched to Old High North Germanic. This was the moment of truth.

'What are they saying?' hissed Karina.

'Search me.'

Lloyd replied with a smile on his face. I think I caught a word with *wîb* in it. *Woman*. He turned to me and said, 'Old prune face over there says he won't attack you if you don't attack him, and that means I'm not obliged to support you. He's got a point. Not only that, he said he'd gift me the mine and farm if I stand aside. I said yes. Sorry, Conrad.'

It was my turn to nod slowly. 'I understand, Lloyd. You helped me before because Mina was kidnapped. I'd rather keep our bond intact than risk it over this lot.'

'What!' said Karina. 'You can't let them get away, sir. Not now. Not after what they've done. You can't.'

She was furious. Incandescent. It would not go well for her if she returned to Princess Birkdale having let the Count's Killers live.

'Stand down, Lieutenant,' I said. 'Remember your blood oath.'

'No.'

'Stand down!'

She lowered her bow, pain and anger twisting her face.

'There's just one small problem,' said Lloyd

'Oh?'

'They want their wives back. The ones that are left.'

'What have you done to them?' snapped Colm. In English.

'Arrested most of them and tied them up.' I pointed to Colm. 'Your wife tried to kill my fiancée and one of my team. Lieutenant Kent here shot her. Twice. A small part of me hopes she died in pain. The others are in custody. My custody.'

All the heads bar mine turned to the tunnel behind us. I must get my hearing checked out. Ilse appeared, and tried to rush through our cordon until Cara the wolf growled and made to snap at her ankles.

'Ilse!' shouted Hans. He spoke in modern German, so I understood what they said next. 'Are you okay?'

'Yes, and so is Kathe. In the name of the Mother, surrender Hans. I have. Kathe has. You are not one of them.'

'Silence,' roared Gregor. 'We leave them behind. We have a deal with Lloyd. You heard the Witchfinder.'

'Sorry,' I interrupted. 'I haven't finished yet. You can walk out with what you're carrying now, and you can take a van. You've got until dawn, and then I make my pronouncement.'

Fergus had remained silent so far. His weapon was a sword, and he drew it casually, as if he were putting up an umbrella. 'Since when do Watch Captains make pronouncements?'

'Classic fail,' I said. 'Your intelligence is out of date. I'm Deputy Constable of the Watch, now. Also Lord Guardian of the North. When dawn breaks, I will pronounce each one of you an Outlaw, beyond the protection of the Watch. Lieutenant Kent will WhatsApp your details to Princess Birkdale, and Lloyd will do the same to Clan Blackrod. Unless you surrender.'

I turned to Karina. 'Do you think the Nachtkrieger are watching the farm?'

'Bound to be, sir.'

'Tough luck, that,' I said, more loudly. A disinterested observer might have noticed that the wolves changed their circling pattern. None of the Gnomes did.

'What Nachtkrieger?' said Hans.

'They came for the pack,' said Ilse. 'It was the Witchfinders and their friends who fought them off. And the pack. I'm sorry, Fergus, but she didn't make it. Caught in the crossfire. Two Nachtkrieger escaped. They are out there.' She added, in German, '*I swear it.*'

All Gnomes learn to fight, and all Gnomes have weapons, much like human men did before the nineteenth century, but like them, not all Gnomes are warriors. Hans bent his knees and launched himself into Colm, barrelling him into Fergus. Then he ran towards us, diving through the red grit like an American baseball player and shouted, 'I surrender.'

The two other Gnomes in the middle tried to follow him, yelling their submission. Kathe's husband just made it; the other was not so lucky: Fergus shoved his sword into the Gnome's back, killing him instantly.

In a heartbeat, the pack surrounded the prostrate Gnomes, howling and baring their fangs.

It was now a Quartet ranged against us, and they paused for half a second, staring at what had happened.

'Fergus, that man had just surrendered, so you're under arrest for attacking my prisoner,' I said. 'Karina, at the ready.'

We'd passed the point of no return, now, and Fergus charged, making straight for me. The rest of the Quartet joined in: Colm moved to take out Karina, his wife's killer, while the Blackrod brothers joined together and attacked Lloyd.

Karina fired an arrow into the dirt in front of Colm, well ahead of his Ancile. It exploded, sending smoke and red dirt flying everywhere. Some hit my lip, and I knew what it was: rock salt. Of course – the Cheshire salt mines.

Colm's Ancile protected him from the direct blast, but it didn't stop the grit and particles hitting him, nor the second blast, to his right, nor the third. Even Fergus swerved to avoid it, and he came at me from an angle, sword raised to hack me open. I had no option but to go two-handed and meet his blade, forcing it down into the dirt. He backed up before I could recover and thrust at him.

'Good one,' he said. 'They said you could use a blade. Let's see who's better, shall we?'

'You can still surrender,' I offered.

I glanced left and right. Karina had swapped her bow for a short dagger and dived into the cloud of dust and smoke surrounding Colm. After that, she was lost to view. On my right, things were not going well. Gregor and Andriss really did know what they were doing: they'd lured Albie into attacking their flank while Lloyd was engaging both of them.

Gregor took a big swing of the axe, Andriss covered him and Lloyd stepped back. Albie thrust at Andriss, who dropped to the ground. Gregor continued his swing and buried his axe in Albie's leg.

Fergus's sword was longer and heavier than mine. His arm was stronger, too. And also shorter. He feinted, I thrust, he parried, knocking Great Fang to one side and coming at me with the reverse. I dodged. That was too close. If you're wondering why a wolf didn't jump on his back, that's because I'd ordered them to protect anyone who surrendered at all costs.

Fergus's strategy was clear and simple: keep beating me back until there was nowhere to go, which would be in about six feet. I'd also felt him trying to use some of the magick in his blade, and Lloyd had done me proud: the resistive Works in Great Fang pulsed and pulsed again as they stopped Fergus trying to bend or break my blade.

Andriss was not so lucky. It was his sword and Gregor's two-bladed axe against Lloyd's single blade, and Gregor had got carried away, impeding Andriss and allowing Lloyd to swing up, into Andriss's chest.

That was all I could risk looking at, because Fergus had pushed me back two more steps, right into the wall. 'Look at your death, wet one,' he said, taking a step back and working out his approach now that I couldn't retreat any further.

'*En garde*, shortarse,' I countered. 'It's time for you to show me whether that's a sword or a fishing rod. Do you want to know how Juliet died, Gnomeo?'

Gnome jokes. Below the belt, but seriously justified. To add insult to injury, I placed my left hand on my hip and struck an old-fashioned fencing pose.

'I'm going to enjoy this,' said Fergus. 'And then I'm going to hunt down your whore and enjoy her.'

I focused everything I had on his eyes, drawing him in. 'Your woman was trampled to death by a herd of cows. She was running away. Don't worry, little man, we've already dealt with her body.'

He came at me, and I let him lock swords, pushing me back and sliding the blades down towards the guards, when I would be at the mercy of his enormous strength and power.

And he would be in my personal space, Anciles voided. That hand on the left hip, it had drawn my mundane SIG from its occluded holster. Three shots rang around the cave. I stepped over his body and went to look for Karina.

She was lying on top of Colm, clutching her right knee and trying not to stare at the bone sticking out of her shin. Her dagger was buried in Colm's neck. I pivoted, and turned to Lloyd.

He was tiring, stepping back and back away from Gregor's swinging axe, unable to break his rhythm. I circled round, aiming to approach Gregor's right.

'I got this,' said Lloyd. 'You'll see.'

Unlike Fergus, Gregor had nothing to say. He swung the axe again and again. Sometimes Lloyd parried, sometimes he dodged. What the hell was he doing?

Working an angle, that's what. He was leading Gregor to the scaffolding tower, and when it came up on Gregor's right, Gregor switched his swing. Lloyd dropped his own axe, went on one knee and lifted his left arm. In a blur of magick and steel, he caught the blade of the axe with his prosthetic hand and wrenched it out of Gregor's grip, pitching the other dwarf onto his face. Lloyd jumped on his back and broke his neck.

The *crack* echoed around the chamber as more than just sound, it was a ripple in the magickal fabric as something half-done was undone. In the silence, our ragged breathing, the panting of the wolves and Karina's moans were twice as loud.

28 — *Leader of the Pack*

'Someone go up and get the others,' I told the wolves. 'And tell the Earthmaster what happened so that he can call Mina.'

Cara detached herself from the pack, loping up the tunnel, and I dashed back to Karina.

'Why does my knee hurt more than my leg?' she said.

'Hands on your head, Karina. It's good that you're lying on your enemy, but enough's enough. I'm going to drag you off him. Try to roll onto your left side a little.'

She gave no more than a low groan through gritted teeth when I dragged her to the wall and propped her up.

'That was awful, but yeah, better.'

I squatted down and put my hand on her shoulder. 'Did he land on you?' She nodded. 'I think you've ruptured a ligament. That's why it hurts more. Well done, by the way. Apart from your obvious mistake.'

'You mean getting rolled on by a Gnome?'

I took a packet of curried worms out of my uniform pocket and showed them to her. 'You forgot these. I'll leave these with you for next time.' I gently unfastened her breast pocket and dropped them in. 'There you go. They really do make a difference.'

'No they don't, but I appreciate the thought.' She ran her hand down her leg again. 'This is bad.' She breathed out slowly and closed her eyes. 'You set it all up, didn't you? You and Lloyd?'

'We did. And Ilse. Couldn't have done it without her.'

She looked upset. 'Why didn't you tell me?'

This was no time for sugar-coating things. 'Do you remember Piccadilly Gardens, outside the station?'

'Yeah. What's that got to do with it?'

'The Mayor of Manchester has been trying to reduce the number of homeless for years. The ones left are all addicts, and that's their favourite spot. Addicts will do anything, and I mean *anything* to keep their supply going. I wanted to see whether Princess Birkdale had reeled you in.'

She looked down at her leg again. 'I suppose I deserved that.'

I stood up. 'There was another reason. You're a terrible liar, Karina. Like Vicky. I needed an honest reaction from you to convince the Octet. We'll get you to a hospital as soon as we can. I've got to go now.'

'Thanks, sir. Thanks for giving me a chance.'

Lloyd had put a tourniquet on Albie's leg. 'He needs to get out right away,' he said. 'And he can't join us for the Consecration.' He looked up. 'Here come the others.'

I could get used to having a pack of Mannwolves at my service. What I couldn't get used to was the presence of naked teenage girls. Still, that was my problem, not Cara's. She had a whole pile of flip-flops in one hand and she was followed by Wesley, Kenver and Kathe, who rushed straight to her husband. Wesley headed for Lloyd, and Kenver came to me.

'The Earthmaster's on the phone to Mina,' he said.

'Good. I've got a boring but really important job for you, Kenver: gate duty. There's going to be a lot of comings and goings over the next few hours, and someone has to let them in and out. Did you sort out those access tokens?'

He nodded.

'Good.'

I surveyed the scene and who needed what. I arrested the two Gnomes, Hans and Max, then put them to work making a stretcher, under the supervision of the Pack. They were both dazed and stumbled off to do their duty, and that included clearing the dead, once the living had been evacuated. Ilse and Kathe didn't need instructions – they were already heading for the cottage kitchen.

I took one last look around the chamber and climbed the tunnel to the surface. That night air felt good, so naturally I lit a cigarette. Chris Kelly had just finished on the phone and gave me a smile. 'Mina says she's got a surprise for you. They're on their way, and Tom Morton is organising an ambulance with police escort.' He stared at the twisted door to the mine. 'It's been an eye-opener, Conrad, that's for certain.'

'Thanks for everything, Chris. We had the bare minimum tonight. I couldn't have done it without any of you, and that's the scariest part.'

Yee Hah!

'What the hell?' said Chris.

'Excuse me. That's Tom Morton.' I walked away and took the call.

'Ambulances are on their way from Macclesfield, Conrad. I've got the control room on hold. Anything to say to them?'

'Yes. Albie needs to get to the nearest trauma centre asap. For Karina, can you pull rank and order them to Queen Elizabeth's in Birmingham? I wouldn't want her anywhere else. I know it's a long way, but they did miracles on my leg, and what little social support she has is in Warwickshire.'

'Right. Anything else I can do?'

'Yes. We're going to need your specialist skills tonight.'

He could hear something in my voice. 'As what?'

'A lawyer. There's a conveyance to transact.'

'You know what, Conrad? That's the most outlandish thing I've heard today. Right, I'm going. See you soon.'

He arrived at the farm entrance shortly after, and the Gnomes ferried the wounded down to meet the paramedics under my guidance.

Mina arrived just behind the ambulances, with Lucy, Scout and another passenger: Hannah. Crap. What was the Boss doing here?

I ignored that issue because Mina was here, and that took priority over everything. As I swept Mina up into my arms, I saw that the Boss had got into Karina's ambulance. Whatever.

'Do you want the good news or the bad news?' whispered Mina. 'The bad news is that it doesn't get any easier waiting for you to live or die. The good news is that it hasn't got any harder.'

We kissed again, enough for now, then separated.

'Walk back with me,' said Hannah.

'Do you mind if Scout joins us?'

She reached down to scratch him. 'He's not quite 100% dog, is he?'

'I think he's about five per cent Pale Horseman. Why else would he think Gnomes are tasty? It's quite embarrassing in a small space.'

She stood up and we started walking. After two steps, I had to catch her when she stumbled. 'Are you alright?'

'Yes. It's bloody dark is all.'

'Oh. About that. I think I'm becoming part Gnome – I've developed some night vision. Take my arm?'

'So long as that's the only Gnomish trait you've acquired. Go on.' We linked arms and continued.

'If you're wondering how I got here,' she said, 'it's down to Saskia. I called her and told her to keep me in the loop. As soon as I heard about Mina and DCI Morton, I got a taxi to Euston Station. Vicky kept me up to speed as well.'

'Of course.'

There's a lot I haven't told you about tonight – we kept the Clerkswell Coven up to date, for example, but only when it was too late for them to get here.

'Saskia drove me to Knutsford Services,' she continued, 'and I had an interesting chat to DCI Morton. Tom. The only thing that worried me, Conrad, was that you'd Entangled him deliberately. You didn't, so you met the challenge.'

I shivered, and hoped she thought it was the night air. 'Challenge?'

'These sorts of things happen often enough. We don't write it up when the Fae and the Gnomes tear strips out of each other. The Fae Queens, out of courtesy, always ask me if we're interested in getting involved, and I've always said no. Until now. I wanted to see how you handled it, and I'm very, very sorry that Mina got dragged into it.' She squeezed my arm. 'Can you forgive me?'

'You've forgiven me often enough, Hannah.'

'I've needed to. Your chutzpah gets bigger by the day, Conrad. Only you could walk out unscathed *and* with your own pack of Dual Natured wolves.'

I thought about mentioning the claw marks on my face, and then I thought of her head. I passed.

'I've been thinking. About Tom Morton,' she continued. 'You were right: we need more police support than Ruth can give us. I've offered Tom the job of MI7 Liaison, and he said yes.'

'Good. He and I seem to have reached an unspoken understanding, and besides, Lucy has hired Mina as her financial consultant.'

She laughed. 'And so would I, if they paid me enough to need one. Tom said that his first job tomorrow is looking into that burnt out car. We're used to Mages driving round with fake index plates, but they don't generally change the VIN. Could be interesting.'

'There's something else, ma'am. I can't be Deputy Constable like this. I want the King's Watch to lease the Smurf from the Mowbrays. They'll give us a good rate.'

She stopped and pulled her arm away. 'Tell me you're joking.'

'No. I'm using it tomorrow to transport the pack to new ground. I won't use it frivolously. Promise you'll think about it.'

She put her arm back and said, 'If I must. And besides, I've already got my revenge in advance.'

Hannah doesn't have an *I'm joking!* tone of voice; instead, she has an *I might be joking* tone, and that was the one she'd just used to tell me about getting her revenge in first.

'Go on,' I said. 'Tell me the worst.'

'It's like this. When I called the President of the Occult Council to tell him about Princess Birkdale's pack, and that they'd been officially discovered, he whimpered. He said, "Why me?" And now you have your own pack, he may faint. There's going to be a Council committee of enquiry, and you're going to chair it.'

'Tell me you're joking, ma'am. Please.'

'Now you're management, you have to get used to it.'

'Fine. There's a good train service to Manchester. I'll hire a committee room in the Alchemical Institute.'

'You'll hold it London.'

'If you want it in London, Hannah, chair it yourbloodyself.'

She snorted. Demurely, but a snort nonetheless. 'So be it. And you'll be wanting a new partner.'

'Needing, more like.'

'Stay out of trouble for a week while I think about it, okay?'

We passed Kenver at the edge of the Wards, and the Boss made doubly sure that he hadn't been in any real danger.

We were nearly at the farm when I asked, 'What about Karina?'

'I thought long and hard about her, and I've given her a mention in dispatches. She deserves that. She also deserves three days in the Undercroft for disobeying orders. If she reports to the Bailiff when she's left hospital, I'll wipe her record and transfer her to the Reserves.'

That's why I love my Boss. Firm but fair.

'What now?' she asked. 'Do you want me to ring Princess Birkdale and the Blackrods?'

'Blackrod will be here shortly. We have business with them that you might not want to watch. A conversation with Tara Doyle would be a very good idea. There are things she needs to hear about her beloved Count.'

'Fine. I presume there's tea on the go?'

'Always. Let me introduce you to Alex and Cara first.'

We gathered in front of the mine, light spilling out from twisted doors and supplemented by a couple of magickal lanterns. The bodies of Fergus and Colm had already been disposed of, and that left three laid out on tarpaulins in front of the doors: Gregor, Andriss and the poor Gnome who'd surrendered and still been stabbed in the back. He would be returned to his clan in due course.

Behind the bodies, pushed down on to their knees were the surviving prisoners: Hans, Max and Ricky. They'd been as good as their word after I'd arrested them, doing what they were told and helping out, but now was the time of reckoning, and I'd put them in restraints. The wives, all five of them, were locked into the spare cottage. This wasn't about them.

Tom Morton stood to the left: for one night only, he was acting as Counsel to Lloyd and Wesley. Mina stood to the right, now almost swamped by a padded jacket and almost hidden by shadows. Her job was to act as witness for the Cloister Court. I stood at the front, because the first part, at least, was my show.

Clan Blackrod arrived in a Bentley Flying Spur that whispered over the gravel as if it were on a dancefloor and pulled up just beyond the circle of light. The driver got out and opened the rear doors.

First Chief Stefan, then Lachlan, and finally two younger Gnomes emerged. The younger ones would be Drake's sons. Stefan took his time looking around and scoping out the magick before coming round and shaking hands.

'Lord Guardian. You've had a busy night.'

'We have, Chief. The four who killed Drake are dead. Two of them were of your clan, and both died at the hand of Lloyd Flint.'

'Only four?'

'Only four.'

'And what of the Mannwolves?'

'At the time, they were under the Protection of an unknown Fae. They are now with me.'

He nodded. 'Was it that whore from Birkdale?'

'It was not. When we find out, and we will, then I will see justice done.'

'So be it.'

'I offer the bodies of the two who turned against their own clan to you.'

He bowed. 'Thank you. Boys? Take them away.'

I stepped aside, next to Mina. The two sons of Drake Blackrod quickly wrapped Gregor and Andriss in their tarpaulins and loaded them into the boot of the Bentley. When they'd finished, they remained by the car, watching and listening.

'We're not done here, are we?' said Stefan.

'No, Chief,' said Lloyd. 'This night we Consecrate a new First Mine. Here.'

'We?' said Stefan mildly, as if it were of no interest to him. No one was fooled.

Lloyd spoke up. 'Myself and Wesley, with others who are on their way. Two from Clan Trent and two from London. There's a lot trying to leave Octavius at the moment.'

'So I hear,' said Stefan. 'That makes six. And the other two?'

'Hans and Max here, Clan Palatinate.'

'You would consecrate a mine on my doorstep with two of those who killed Drake?' Stefan's voice was icy now.

Lloyd stepped forward and pushed the two Gnomes from Germany face down. He pushed gently, but when your hands are tied behind your back, it's hard to fall flat on your face with any dignity. Their necks were now exposed, and Lloyd picked up the blood-stained axe that Gregor had wielded. He stepped into the open space and offered the hilt to Stefan. 'Take this offering. If you have a quarrel with Hans and Max, show it.'

I'd warned Tom that this might happen, and that the prisoners wouldn't actually be beheaded in front of him.

Stefan took the axe and weighed it in his hands. 'A fit offering to our Mother.' He turned to me. 'These two will face your judgement.'

'They will.'

'Then I have no quarrel with them, nor with the other one.'

Lloyd lifted the two prostrate Gnomes back to their knees, then helped all three to their feet.

It was Stefan's call, now. 'There's been enough blood this year. Rivalry is always a good thing. From a tribute clan, of course.'

Lloyd spread his hands. 'We could pay tribute to Blackrod while we set up. For a limited time.'

'By eight by eight,' said Stefan. 'You'll be a slow-growing bunch.'

What he meant was 8x8x8 – five hundred and twelve years. 'We thought once,' countered Lloyd. 'Eight years is enough.'

I'll spare you the haggling. They agreed on sixty-four years in the end, with further offerings thrown in. At the end, it was Tom Morton and Lachlan Mace who shook hands on the deal, Counsel to Counsel.

'What name will you take?' said Stefan as he prepared to go.

'Clan Salz,' said Lloyd. *Salz* being their word for *salt*.

'Fitting. It does stink of salt here. What will you specialise in?'

'Watch this space, Chief.'

Stefan grunted and got back in his car. Once the Bentley had gone, Lloyd rubbed his hands. 'Right, we ay half got a lot to do.' His first job was to cut the restraints and embrace his new clansmen-to-be. He sent the others down the mine and started to examine the doors, with a view to repairing them.

I released Ricky and told him to help out down at the farm. Wesley came up to me and said, 'It's time to say goodbye, Lord Guardian. I never thought, when you walked into Flint House that it would end here. Never in my wildest dreams.'

When Wesley went through the doors, he wouldn't be coming out. Eight would enter the mine and only seven return: Wesley was giving himself to Mother Earth. His sacrifice would be the Consecration that turned the salty hole in the ground into a First Mine.

'Thank you for tonight,' I replied. I couldn't thank him for much else, because we both knew that his rule of Clan Flint had been pretty disastrous.

'It was an honour to stand with you,' he said. 'Here. Take this. It's a little something I've been working on.' He offered me a brass tube, sealed with a screw cap at one end. 'There are four poles in there. As in North Pole. A portable Limbo Chamber. You might find it useful.'

'Thank you. And may the Mother receive you.'

We shook hands and he turned to go. I watched his silhouette pass through the doors and disappear into the light.

I turned to Tom. 'You've got more work to do, haven't you?'

'Thank God for the Internet. I don't think I've ever done a conveyance like this. Tell me, Conrad, why did Chief Stefan take the two bodies? I thought he'd have wanted nothing to do with them.'

'About that,' I replied. 'I'm afraid there's no way to shield you from this, Tom. Not that I want to. Gnomes are very particular about their dead. Most are laid to rest in the First Mine of their clan.' I pointed to the remaining body. 'This guy will be laid outdoors, exposed to the air, for as long as he would have spent in prison. What's left after that will go underground.' I sighed. 'Gregor and Andriss were traitors. They'll be cut up and fed to the pigs.'

'Tell me this is a joke.'

'I wish. Lloyd did it to his own brother. Fergus and Colm have already been chopped up because they have no clan: it ceased to exist last year when the mine was destroyed. By the Fae.'

Tom looked a little green about the gills, and if I hadn't seen Lloyd spit on his own brother's body, I'd feel the same. 'Can't this Occult Council control that sort of thing?' he asked.

I shook my head. 'Humans can change quickly. Gnomes can't. Dwarves can't. The Fae can't. None of them can. Their essential nature is different to ours. Some of the Creatures of Light are changing. Slowly. One day, perhaps.'

'And Hans and Max are going to this Undercroft prison?'

I laughed. 'No point. They'd just reach down to Mother Earth and dig their way out. The prison for Gnomes – and their wives – is a boggy island in the Wash. There is no metal on the island *at all*. Not even a nail, and they can't dig more than two feet down before they hit water. As soon as the Mine is Consecrated, they'll be taken into custody.'

He put his hands in the pockets of his Crombie overcoat, which had survived today's ordeal without so much as a stain. How does he do that? 'Tom, can you do me a favour?'

He gave me a dark look. 'Depends. I've learnt a lot about you and your favours.'

'This one has the Boss's approval, even if it is a little personal. Do you remember what I told you about Piers Wetherill?'

'That he dropped you in it with this Nymph? Yes.'

I held out a piece of paper. 'Piers was a member of the Lib Dems, for some reason. To do that he needed to be on the electoral roll, and to do *that* he needed an alternative identity. He registered himself at Saskia and Evie's rental property. They had no clue. Could you see if you can find him?'

Tom's hands stayed in his pockets. 'With a view to what, exactly?'

'With a view to having a quiet word. That's all. Part of the solution, Tom, part of the solution.'

He took the paper and shoved it into his pocket. 'Right. I'd better go underground and finish this conveyance.'

'Thanks, Tom. And remember, if they offer you refreshment, accept it. Trust me, the beer is excellent. See you later.'

I took Mina in my arms when we were alone and pulled down her hood. 'How do you feel now?'

'Happy. Relieved. I've already told Marcia that I'm taking the rest of the week off to recover. Shall we give the Coven a call now that we've got a minute?'

'Good idea. Let's walk up to the top of the mine. Don't want to be interrupted.'

I took a lantern and found a safe path to the top of the mound over the mine. Mina passed me her phone and we soon had a conference call going with Vicky, Myfanwy, Saffron and Erin on the other end. They knew the headlines already, so we filled them in on the details and plans. At the end,

Myfanwy coughed and said, 'I know you've been through a lot, you two, but I can't put it off any longer.'

'You mean you're about to burst,' said Vicky.

'Shut up, you. Right. Here's the thing. I'm expecting. It happened the night of the party, would you believe.'

'Wow! Congratulations,' said Mina. And being Mina, she added, 'You'll be eight months gone at my wedding, won't you?'

'I know. I can still manage a toast, cwch.'

'That means she's out of the running for chief bridesmaid,' said Vicky.

'She was anyway,' said Mina. 'Not being able to leave the village meant she couldn't join the hen party.' She paused and changed tone, 'I am so thrilled for you Myfanwy. I really am.'

'And me,' I added.

I drifted away while there was much baby-related talk. When Mina joined me, I had turned the lantern off and I was staring at the Plough.

'You know something,' she said. 'When I first fell in love with you, I looked up 7 Squadron. And the badge.' She pointed up. 'In India, the Plough is called the Saptarishi. The Seven Rishi, or wise men. And the seventh is Kratu. He was the one who led you here to rescue me, because as soon as the Nachtkrieger arrived, I was a dead woman. Ganesh opened the door for you, and Kratu gave you the wisdom to enter. I will make puja very soon.'

I kissed the top of her head and held her close.

'Kratu and his wife had 60,000 children, you know. Each one the size of a thumb. I don't think I want that many. Imagine trying to remember their names. And it's an average of 165 birthday parties *every* day. I worked it out at the service station while I was trying not to think about what was happening to you.'

She pulled me closer and buried her face in the part of my uniform that wasn't covered by blood. 'There was something else I thought about,' she murmured. 'What if you could only become pack Protector after having sex with the Queen?'

'Thankfully the question is hypothetical and I'm not a paedophile,' I replied. Where on earth was she going with this?

'But what if it wasn't hypothetical? Did you lie with Nimue when she drank your blood?'

'It was offered. Of course, I declined.'

'One day soon, one of these non-human creatures may demand something of you. If it means saving lives, do it. I mean that.'

'Do you?'

'You can't leave the word of magick, and I can't leave you. If it is the only way to get through a door that Ganesh has opened, you have my blessing. And don't tell me. I'll know, but don't tell me. Promise?'

She was deadly serious. I bit back on the jokes and said, 'I promise.'

She had one more thing to say. 'In her world, Cara is a woman. She and Alex are already hard at work on securing the future of the pack. Shall we go?'

I released her from my arm and re-lit the lantern. 'Yes, love.'

29 — *Air Lift*

There was a lot to do overnight. Calls were made, Gnomes arrived, prisoners left and the farm rang to the sound of the mine doors being hammered back into shape. At two o'clock in the morning, I'd insisted that they place a Silence on their activities so that I could get some bloody sleep, thank you very much.

I surfaced and took my coffee into the yard at seven o'clock, just as the farmer was heading back from milking. My breath steamed in the pre-dawn light, and I could see a hoar frost glistening on the pasture.

'Is it really all over?' he asked. 'No one was around when I got up. Seems impossible.'

We looked at the cows having a good munch as they wandered around on the clean straw in their byre. 'First day of a new era,' I said. 'You can stay and re-build the herd or get out. Up to you. Either way, you can actually go shopping if you want, and you can move back into the farmhouse soon. I'd steer clear of the Well of Desire for a bit, though.'

He grunted and went into his cottage for breakfast. Just before we all gathered at the mine, I caught sight of Hannah sneaking out of the farmhouse. Actually sneaking. And carrying a black bin liner stuffed full of something. I intercepted her on the way to Karina's new Evoque, which she'd volunteered to drive down to Birmingham. 'Morning, ma'am,' I said. 'A little plunder of our own, perhaps?'

She jumped and dropped the bin liner. 'Oy vey, Conrad, what are you doing up?' She scrabbled to pick the bag up again, and the plastic slipped in her fingers, revealing bright red fabric inside. Of course: the Trolley Dolly uniforms.

'You wouldn't by any chance be saving those for the hen do, would you?'

She gave me her evil grin. 'Only to scare them. And then I'll produce something even worse.'

'Your secret is safe with me.' She stuffed the bag in the car as more of the gang appeared.

After a quick breakfast, everyone made their way to the doors of the mine: the pack, including the cubs; Ilse and Kathe; Lloyd's wife, Anna, and their three girls; three other wives and children of the new clan; Tom and Lucy; Chris Kelly and Kenver Mowbray; Hannah, Mina, Scout and me.

'Is it auto-suggestion, or does it really feel different up here?' said Tom.

'It doesn't just feel different, it smells different,' I said. 'The whole area reeks of Gnome.'

At seven thirty, the first rays of a clear day hit the doors, and they swung open. This was no longer a hole in the ground, it was the First Mine of Clan Salz. The new chief came out first.

Lloyd was carrying a very different axe to any I'd seen before: a white head of high-tech ceramic sat on top of a carbon fibre haft. Clan Salz was going to specialise in new materials, and it would be a wake-up call for a lot of the clans. He was followed by the other six, including Hans and Max.

He didn't make a great speech, he just lifted the axe and said, 'I am no longer Lloyd Flint. I am Lloyd Salz, chief of Clan Salz, first member of the seventh house of Clan Salz. This is the sacred ground of Clan Salz, and you are all welcome here. Witness that I name Edmund as the Clan Second.'

He passed the axe to one of the Gnomes from Nottingham, and accepted a sword from Hans. 'I chose the Seventh House to honour the Lord Guardian, and I name him Honorary Clan Swordbearer. As a tributary clan, we will have to wait for the right to name a bearer of our own. Until then, he will guarantee the agreement between us and Clan Blackrod.'

I accepted the sword. It was simple and could only perform one act of magick: it would allow me to open the doors of the Mine.

I was going to say something, but I heard a noise in the west. Everyone else heard it, too, and sooner, but only I knew it was the twin turbos of the Smurf. 'I am honoured, chief, but the pack's new home awaits. Incoming chopper.'

'Then go in peace and go well,' said Lloyd.

I picked up my rucksack, gave Scout a scratch and gave Mina a kiss. They wouldn't be coming on this journey. 'Let's go,' I said to the pack.

They followed me to a flattish meadow outside the area of displacement, and I chucked a flare downwind of the LZ.

'In the name of Great Fang, we cannae go in that!' said Alex when he saw the Smurf descending for a pinpoint landing.

'Yes you can. It'll be like nothing you've ever experienced.'

'Tha's wha' worries me.'

The charter pilot cut the engines and went through the shutdown procedure. We waited patiently until he emerged, and I led the pack over the grass.

'What the fucking hell happened to you?' he said when he saw my uniform, the blood and the bandage. 'And what's with the school outing?'

'Thanks for getting up so early and being here on time. Much appreciated. DCI Morton will pick you up and take you to the nearest mainline station. There's been a change of plan.'

'Oh?'

'The Smurf is being relocated to Chester.'

'Oh. Right. Fair enough. Where shall I wait?'

'Over by the road. He'll be along as soon as we're gone.'

We shook hands, and he gave me the tablet computer and keys. I opened the cargo bay and the pack slung their meagre possessions inside, then I supervised getting five adults, one Elder and four cubs into the back, belted up and put on the intercom.

Just before I started the engines, I turned the intercom off. There was going to be screaming. I just knew it.

We made good time on the 200 mile flight north, into the proper North of Northumberland, land of wild forests and home to the Northumbrian Shield Wall, a Circle of Mages dedicated to the Allfather. They know exactly who I am, and of my relationship with Odin, and they keep pestering me to visit them. I'd have to go soon, but not today.

Vicky had been on the phone much of the night, and when I found the tiny cottage at the edge of the Northumberland National Park, there was a black figure waiting for us. Vicky had been introduced to the world of magick by a Goth, she'd told me, and said Goth had agreed to be the Pack Witch until we could find a permanent solution.

'Brace yourselves,' I told Alex. 'Down in two.'

The cubs ran out under the slowing rotors like you'd expect a bunch of kids to run, eager to let off steam and explore their new home.

The Witch spoke to the pack first. 'I'm Dawn, and welcome to Loki's Run. It's a bit basic at the minute, like, but we'll soon sort that out. I'm sure you'll be happy here.'

Alex turned to me with a great big grin on his face. 'Here? Really? It's a paradise. I cannae believe it after what we've been through, and we cannae thank you enough, Sire.'

'Cup of tea?' said Dawn. 'I'd offer you something stronger, Lord Guardian, but you've got to fly home. I suppose.'

'Thank you.'

'I'll go and get the gas stove working. I think you've got a visitor.'

She was right. Loki's Run was right at the head of a dale, and I'd landed the Smurf on a flat section of heather moorland, just off the property. Dawn made her way towards the cottage, and the pack had mostly scattered down the slope, through the trees and towards the burn (stream) that had carved out the valley. Guarding the entrance to the estate were a pair of yew trees, and under one of them stood the cloaked figure of the Allfather. I crossed over and bowed. 'My Lord.'

'I had not expected to see you again so soon,' he replied. He lowered his hood and showed me today's face. He'd opted for the Classic look, all long white hair and grey beard. The only modern note was his eye patch: a purple number with the outline of an eye stitched on it in gold thread. Yes, it was very creepy.

'You know Zeno's Paradox?' he said.

'I do. It once passed some very slow hours in Afghanistan.'

'We have a different version, called Loki's Puzzle, and yes, it passed many an hour in Asgard. It reminds me of you.'

'That was not reassuring, My Lord.'

'Nor was it meant to be. I think you are around half way to finding the *Codex Defanatus*. The next half of the next half will be just as hard, as will the half of the half after that.'

'You don't know who has it, do you, My Lord?' I made it a question, not a statement, but it was still fairly rude by divine standards.

'Only the universe is omniscient, and we are part of the universe, so none of us can know everything.' His lips peeled back in the scariest smile of any creature I have ever encountered. 'Nimue once bore me a son, you know. I wonder if you're descended from him, Lord Guardian? It's a title that suits you, by the way.' He lifted his hood back up. 'You've no doubt heard the saying: *Winter is Coming?*'

'It has become rather popular in the mundane world.'

'That's not the original version. The original version is: *Winter is always Coming*. Go well, Lord Guardian.'

A rustle in the branches made me look up, and when I looked down, he had gone, and I was alone. Or so I thought.

'Was that the Sigföðr?' said Cara. She'd crept up behind me, quiet as the wolf. I tried not to jump out of my skin.

'I don't know. I've not heard that name before.'

'The Father of War, I think it means. Being Irish, I'm not so good on your German.'

'Father of War. Yes, that was him. Does he feature in your stories?'

'Oh yes, Sire, he does indeed. When you come back, for a proper feast, I'll get Oma to tell you some of them. Proper scary they are.'

'I look forward to it.'

'Good. I've a message for you from Dawn: tea's ready.'

'And I'm ready for tea. Thank you, Cara. I'll be there in a minute.'

She ran across the grass, barefoot, shorn of all care for a while. She jumped over a fallen branch and her hair streamed behind her. Her body said exactly what I felt:

Life can be good. If you let it.

Conrad, Mina and the whole gang's story continues in:
Six Furlongs–
the Eighth Book of the King's Watch, now available from Paw Press.
You can also find out how Conrad and Vicky finally settle the score
with Adaryn ap Owain in:

French Leave– A King's Watch Story

The Fourth King's Watch eBook novella is now available to pre-order
from Paw Press on Amazon.

There were six Druids in the Dragon Brotherhood.
Three are dead.
Two are doing time.
One has been on the run for months...
But there are no cold cases in the King's Watch.

**Conrad last saw Adaryn ap Owain on a wet Welsh hillside, and
she'd just stopped Vicky's heart. Now he has a lead on her, a lead
that will take him to Brittany. Foreign soil. Who on earth can he
rely on to help him when he's a stranger in a strange land?**

Find out who joins Team Conrad in *French Leave*.

The Next Chapter

Six Furlongs
The Eighth Book of the King's Watch
by
Mark Hayden
Saddle up for the ride of your life...

Swinging from a tree on the Furness Peninsula is the body of a Mage.
A renegade Mage.
His brother finds him, and his brother calls in the only person he
knows who can help - the new Lord Guardian of the North.
The only problem is that Conrad has no real jurisdiction in the
Lakeland Particular, and no one is keen for this death to be
investigated.
If that wasn't enough, he also has to deal with the election of the new
Warden of Salomon's House.

Now Available from Paw Press.

And why not join Conrad's elite group of supporters:

The Merlyn's Tower Irregulars

Visit the Paw Press website and sign up for the Irregulars to receive
news of new books, or visit the Facebook page for Mark Hayden
Author and Like it.

Author's Note

Thank you for reading this book; I hope you enjoyed it. If you did, please leave a review on Amazon. It doesn't have to be long. Reviews make a huge difference to Indie authors, and an honest review from a genuine customer is worth a great deal. If you've read all the books of the King's Watch, please review them, too – even if you're in a hurry to read the next one.

Shakespeare said that A good wine deserves a good bush. In other words, a good book deserves a good cover. I'll never be able to prove it, but I strongly believe that The King's Watch would not have been the same without the beautiful covers designed by the Awesome **Rachel Lawston.**

It therefore gave me great pleasure to not only dedicate this book to her, but to include her as a character. Those who know her better can decide whether the portrayal is an accurate one.

The King's Watch books are a radical departure from my previous five novels, all of which are crime or thrillers, though very much set in the same universe, including the Operation Jigsaw Trilogy. Conrad himself refers to it as being part of his history.

You might like to go back the Jigsaw trilogy and discover how he came to the Allfather's attention. As I was writing those books, I knew that one day Conrad would have special adventures of his own, and that's why the Phantom makes a couple of guest appearances.

Other than that, it only remains to be said that all the characters in this book are fictional, as are some of the places, but Merlyn's Tower, Middlebarrow and Brookford Farm are, of course, all real places, it's just that you can only see them if you have the Gift…

This book could it have been written without love, support, encouragement and sacrifices from my wife, Anne. It just goes to show how much she loves me that she let me write the first Conrad book even though she hates fantasy novels. She says she now likes them. And, as ever, Chris Tyler's friendship is a big part of my continued desire to write.

Thanks,
Mark Hayden.

Dramatis Personae

Clerkswell

Conrad Clarke	Me.
Mina Desai	My fiancée.
Rachael Clarke	My younger sister, now resident in Mayfair and a big cheese in wealth management.
Sofía Clarke (Torres)	My half-sister. A student at the Invisible College.
Scout	Formerly my Familiar Spirit. A Border Collie.
Myfanwy Lewis	Our resident Druid/Housekeeper. Currently serving a sentence for her involvement in Dragon rearing. A Herbalist and excellent bat for Clerkswell Ladies Cricket Team.
Ben Thewlis	Myfanwy's fiancé. A cereal agronomist and captain of the men's cricket team.
Carole Thewlis	Ben's sister. Works in the oil industry. Very good friend of Rachael's.
Erin Slater	An Enscriber who rents one of my stables. A good friend to Myfanwy. Member of the Arden Foresters Circle of Mages.
Miss Parkes	Former headmistress of the village school. A Formidable Person.
Lloyd Flint	A Gnome. Clan Second to Clan Flint. My magickal blood brother.
Anna Flint	Lloyd's wife.
Wesley Flint	Lloyd's uncle. Former chief of Clan Flint
Albrecht "Albie" Adams	A young Gnome of Clan Flint
Stephen & Juliet Bloxham	Owners of Clerkswell Manor, the Big House. Stephen: developer and chairman of the cricket club. Juliet: housewife and captain of the ladies' team. Hereditary enemies of the Clarkes. Up to a point.
Ross Miller	Young fast bowler.
Emily Ventress	Ditto.

London

All of these people feature in the following story, even if only in passing. I've grouped them by association.

The King's Watch

Hannah Rothman	The Peculier Constable, head of the King's Watch. Referred to as the Boss.
Victoria "Vicky" Robson	My former work partner and good friend of all at Clerkswell. A Geordie and proud of it.
Saffron Hawkins	My current work partner. One of the "Oxfordshire Hawkins" and well connected in the world of magick. Second cousin to Heidi Marston.
Rick James	Senior Watch Captain. Also responsible for the Watch of Wessex. Ex-husband of Cordelia (see Glastonbury)
Xavier Metcalfe	Vicky's current work partner.
Li Cheng	The Royal Occulter. Once hid the Great Pyramid for a bet. He's good.
Tennille Haynes	Hannah's PA. Mother to Desirée Haynes
Iain Drummond	Deputy Constable. Has responsibility for prosecutions in the Cloister Court
Annelise van Kampen	A Watch Officer and assistant lawyer to Iain Drummond. Originally from Holland.

The Invisible College / Salomon's House

Cora Hardisty	Dean of the Invisible College (who wants to be Warden). A consummate politician and an ally rather than a friend.
Dr Francesca Somerton	Keeper of the Queen's Esoteric Library. A wise woman who has not hung up her dancing shoes.
Selena Bannister	Mistress of Illusions. Cora Hardisty's best friend.
Chris Kelly	The Earth Master of Salomon's House – a Geomancer and expert in Ley lines. Almost a friend.
Tamsin Kelly	Chris Kelly's wife. Apprenticed to the Fae Prince of Richmond as a Plane Shifter.
Eseld Mowbray	A tutor of Wards. Also an heiress to part of the Mowbray fortune. A good horsewoman.
Kenver Mowbray	Youngest of the Mowbray clan, heir to the main part of the Pellacombe fortune and a gifted Geomancer. Apprenticed to Chris Kelly.

Cador Mowbray	Not a Mage at all, but I've put him with his siblings. A barrister who takes cases in the Cloister Court.
Heidi Marston	Custodian of the Great Work and Master Artificer. A larger than life character in all senses of the word. Saffron's cousin and a member of the Hawkins clan.
Oighrig Ahearn	The Oracle – senior Sorcerer at Salomon's House. Cora Hardisty's protégé.
Desirée Haynes	A postgraduate student at the College. Vicky Robson's best friend.

The Cloister Court

The Honourable Mrs Justice Bracewell	Senior judge in the Cloister Court. May or may not be known as Marcia to her husband.
Stephanie Morgan	Deputy Bailiff to the Cloister Court. Wields a mean axe and bakes very nice cakes.
Augusta Faulkner	Legendary barrister in the Court. Mostly famous for her work as a defence lawyer. Mother to Keira Faulkner.

Everyone Else

Alain Dupont	A Frenchman from a small village in Bordeaux. Founder member of the Merlyn's Tower Irregulars. All his Christmases came at once when he got a job as a paid intern with my sister Rachael at her wealth management firm.
(Mr Joshi)	A part-time Hindu priest and retired civil servant. For further details see Ring of Troth

The North

Taking the Deputy's job meant getting to know a new landscape. I've included a column here to show how I came across these people/creatures.

Saskia Mason	Middlebarrow	Warden of Middlebarrow Haven and guardian of Nimue's spring.
Evie Mason	Middlebarrow	Housekeeper of Middlebarrow Haven. Also a creative writing student.
Piers Wetherill	Middlebarrow	Watch Captain of the Marches who has been covering the Palatinate Watch while there was no deputy.
The Kirkham Family	Ribblegate Farm.	Joseph, his son Joe, Joe's wife Kelly. Owners of a dairy farm. Old friends and allies of mine.
Stacey	Blackpool	A former prison colleague of Mina's. Has unfortunate taste in boyfriends.
The Queen of Alderley	The Fae	A Fae Queen who lives near Alderley Edge.
Princess Birkdale	The Fae	A Fae Princess in the line of the Queen of Alderley. Home in Birkdale.
Tara Doyle	The Fae	The human face of Princess Birkdale. A footballer's wife, model and Instagram superstar. Winner of Strictly Come Dancing.
Count of Canal Street	The Fae	A Fae Count in the service of Princess Birkdale.
Wayne	The Fae	A Fae Knight in the service of the Count of Canal Street. Also his head of security.
Fae Klass	The Fae	A human entertainer who lives with the Count of Canal Street.
JC	The Fae	A human entertainer who works for the Count.
Stefan Blackrod	Clan Blackrod	Gnome chief of Clan Blackrod.
Lachlan Mace	Clan Blackrod	His Counsel and friend to Seth Holgate.
Seth Holgate	Manchester Alchemical Society	An Artificer. Current President of the Society and would-be candidate for Warden of Salomon's House.
Meredith Telford	Manchester Alchemical Society	Former President of the Society.
Lois Reynolds	Manchester Alchemical Society	A Sorcerer of some power from Yorkshire and would-be candidate for Warden of Salomon's House.

Made in the USA
Las Vegas, NV
29 December 2021

39754862R00166